In the Walled Gardens

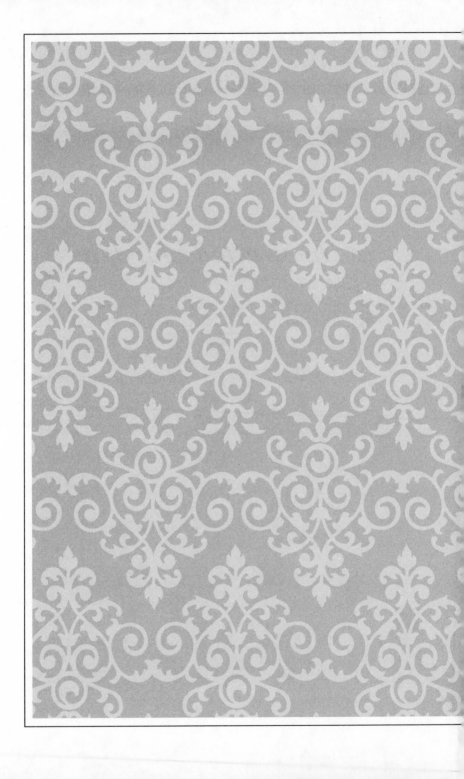

In the Walled Gardens

a novel

ANAHITA FIROUZ

LB 1837

LITTLE, BROWN AND COMPANY

Boston New York London

FIRST EDITION

ISBN 0-316-60854-8 (hc)/0-316-09105-7 (int'l. ed.)
LCCN 2002102891

10 9 8 7 6 5 4 3 2 1

Q-MART

Designed by Cassandra J. Pappas

Printed in the United States of America

For my daughter and my son,

Anousha & Amir-Hussein

The dust of many crumbled cities
settles over us like a forgetful doze,
but we are older than those cities.
. . . .
and always we have forgotten our former states. . . .

MAULANA JALALEDDIN RUMI

I would like to thank the Library of Congress, especially for making available the microfiches I requested from the *Iranian Oral History Project* (Center for Middle Eastern Studies, Harvard). Of all my research, these unpublished interviews with a number of political dissidents active before the 1979 revolution were invaluable primary sources. I would also like to acknowledge the Carnegie Library in Pittsburgh.

This story and all its characters are entirely fictional, belonging to a vanished world.

A special thanks to Dan Green and Simon Green, and Judy Clain at Little, Brown.

Principal Characters

THE MOSHARRAF FAMILY

Mahastee, *married to* Houshang Behroudi,
with two young sons: Ehsan *and* Kamran

Nasrollah, *her father*

Najibeh, *her mother*

Kavoos, Ardeshir, *and* Bahram, *the three older brothers*

Tourandokht, *the old nanny*

THE NIRVANI FAMILY

Reza, *the son, a Marxist revolutionary*

Hajji Alimardan, *his father, deceased, once overseer of the Mosharraf family estates*

Shaukat ol-Zamon, *his mother*

Zarrindokht (Zari), *the daughter,*
married to Morteza Behjat, *with three children*

JALAL HOJJATI, *a radical revolutionary, a friend of Reza's*

THE BASHIRIAN FAMILY

Kamal, *the father, a civil servant and a colleague of Mahastee's*
Peyman, *his son, a university student*

In the Walled Gardens

Prologue

THE WHITE JASMINE WAS in bloom. Blossoms were gathered in silver bowls throughout the rooms, and the scent had taken possession of the house. That night, Mother said, summer would be celebrated with a dinner party on the back veranda. They'd strung up the paper lanterns, their orbs swaying in the evening breeze. From my bedroom window upstairs I watched the garden, the curve of flower beds, the gardeners spraying the lawns, fans of water arcing out at sunset.

Dinner would be late. My brothers were having their friends, and I was having mine. At quarter to eight, Father, immaculately dressed, came out in the upstairs hall and settled down to read yet another version of the rise and fall of our history. Mother was fretting downstairs, orchestrating our life as usual. She called out to my brothers to bring the stereo system out into the garden.

My three brothers, not married yet, went out often with a lot of girls and brought many of them home. That summer of my sixteenth year, I watched them go out into the world and I watched them return. Always triumphant. I couldn't decide if it was their freedom that made them that way, or the privilege and certainties of home. I believed in never letting on how much I knew, preserving power. And secretly I longed to see my life ravaged so I could see it rise up again from its own ashes — a riveting thought.

I went out into the hall dressed in ivory muslin and pearls for dinner. A manservant ran halfway up the stairs to make a hurried announcement.

"Sir, madame says it's Hajji Alimardan! He's here with his son! They're waiting in the living room."

Father, breaking into a smile, said, "What a splendid surprise." My pulse raced. Reza was back for the first time. I hadn't seen him in two years.

We descended, Father telling me as usual how much he missed Hajj-Alimardan, how he'd never understand why Hajj-Ali had suddenly left his services, the properties and gardens he once oversaw now in decline. How he had been not just an overseer but a confidant, a friend.

They were in the living room with their backs to us when we entered.

"Hajj-Ali!" Father said, and they turned.

Our fathers shook hands with long-seated affection. Reza, even taller than when I'd last seen him, looked me over, then nodded. His father still had that strange mixture of rectitude and kindness but looked pale and surprisingly aged. His eyes were misty, like my father's as he embraced Reza.

"How are you, my son? Look at you, a man now! How old are you?"

I knew. He was sixteen; he and I had also known each other a lifetime.

Hajj-Ali had come on a private matter. I suggested to Reza a walk in the gardens, and we left, passing through the back doors to the veranda. We stepped out, the evening revealing itself in a hush.

He saw the tables set with white tablecloths and turned, pride darkening his wide-set eyes, the angles of his clean-shaven face shifting with the light. We went left up the gravel path toward the arbors, my ivory dress whiter at dusk, like a bride's. He didn't say a word. When we got to the trees, he turned.

"You haven't changed much," he said.

I smiled. "You thought I'd got bigheaded? That's why you never visit?"

"Tonight Father insisted."

I wanted to ask him why they'd left that summer so suddenly, but looking at him now, I knew he wouldn't tell. I knew he was stubborn, reticent, unwavering, that he kept secrets with tenacity and vision.

"You look nearly old enough to be married," he said.

"This autumn I'm going away to study in England," I said defiantly.

"Of course, England. Isn't it good enough staying here?"

"It's what we've all done."

Suddenly he smiled. "Then what?"

"Then I'll come back, of course."

Behind the wall of cypress, we turned into the greenhouse. Passing through the potted orange and lemon trees, he stopped.

"I think Father is gravely ill," he said.

I flinched. I thought of Hajj-Ali as blessed and immortal. He said his father was at the doctor's constantly for his heart. We wended our way out and to the far side of the rose garden. I asked about his school. He named a public school. It was a rough place and had gangs. "We're into politics," he said, his jaw setting suddenly with this. Voices rose from the veranda, laughter, then someone put on a record. A slow, dreamy summer love song.

He stared at the trees. "You have guests. You should go back."

"Remember when I taught you to dance?"

"That was another life."

He said it with a quiet anger, then stared at me, the anger plucked away, his eyes searching my face. The hum of cicadas rose to a throbbing around us, the leaves above shivering with a breeze that ruffled my dress and hair. He hovered in the shadows for a moment, then stepped in close. He bent down and, gripping me, pressed his lips to my mouth with a quiet urgency, then a crushing force, and I felt shaken as if given desire and elation and life forever.

Emerging through the trees to the sweep of lawns, we saw in the distance the house rising, the veranda draped in flowering wisteria, the spectacle of guests under lanterns. We hovered like phantoms at this distant border, and I thought, That's what we are, he and I, a separate world.

"Look! Safely back where you belong," he said.

We came up along the side of the house. Mother, presiding over her guests, saw us and followed us with her gaze, watching to see if I would give anything away. She pointed over to my friends. The boys eyed Reza with that who's-he, he's-not-one-of-us look. The girls smiled and made eyes at him. He slipped past them and whispered to me that he had to leave, his father was waiting.

We found him in the library alone.

"Hajj-Ali, you must stay for dinner!" I said.

"It's getting late. I get tired quickly," he said. "We must go."

Father reappeared and gave Hajj-Ali a large and thick sealed envelope, and we accompanied them to the door. I rushed back to the veranda.

Mother came up and whispered to me, "You look ashen. As if you've seen a ghost. The climate in England will do you good."

The moon was up, and when the music rose and I was asked to dance, I turned, looking down the lawns at the immense shadow of trees.

ONE

I SAW HER for the first time after twenty years, at an afternoon concert of classical Persian music in the gardens of Bagh Ferdaus. It was an outdoor concert in early autumn. Summer still lingered, the leaves of the plane trees and walnuts brown and withering at the edges. The sky was overcast, threatening rain, the afternoon unusually muggy. She wore yellow, the color of a narcissus from Shiraz. I knew it was her in a split second even after all those years.

The bus had taken forever all the way from downtown. As we crawled north, the mountains loomed closer and closer. The traffic on Pahlavi Avenue was terrible, even worse when we reached Tajreesh. Two friends who work at the National Television were waiting outside the gate with tickets. Abbas gave me one and we rushed in. He's grown a beard recently to go with his political leanings.

"Classy affair, isn't it?" he said, pointing.

"It's going to rain."

"Lucky you didn't have to park," said Abbas.

We walked past the pavilion — a Qajar summer palace — and down the lawns to the concert, which had already started. There was a crowd and all the chairs were taken, so we stood. Two television cameramen with headsets were recording the event, black cables snaking by their feet. I watched the old trees at the periphery of the garden and listened to the music. The *santour, kamancheh, nay,* the *tonbak.* My friends wandered and talked. They hadn't come for the music. When the concert was over, they introduced me to colleagues who were making a film on old monuments. We strolled back up to the pavilion and stood under the porch, looking out to the gardens. That's when I saw her coming up the lawns, the yellow of her suit conspicuous in the crowd, her face unmistakable. She was talking to friends, and a sudden gust of wind ruffled their clothes. When they left her, I saw an opportunity and was happy that she'd come alone. Then two dapper men stopped her to talk, and the three of them drew together as if conferring. From that distance it looked serious.

"Coming?" Abbas asked me.

"I'll see you by the entrance."

"Who's the woman?"

I shrugged and they left to get the car. I whipped around and saw her standing by a sapling, and she seemed distracted, suddenly distressed. A light rain began to fall and she looked up, squinting, her hair falling back, slithering, let loose, still a deep brown like chestnuts. Nothing had really changed her in twenty years.

I wanted to go forward and say, Remember me? Reza Nirvani. Son of Hajji Alimardan, overseer of your father's estates. I knew she would.

The sky thundered, an eerie color; then suddenly there was hail. The garden turned gray and menacing, shrouded by hailstones the size of bullets. She came running in under the roofed porch, her hair and face wet, now just a few feet away from me.

Her eyes, hazel, familiar, were scanning a limited horizon, but she didn't see me. The crowd pressed in, keeping us apart. She dropped her program, shook her hair, leaned against the white wall, and took off her shoes, legs still slightly tanned from the long summer, toenails vivid red. The television crew jostled past us with bulky equipment. People made a dash for the gate, scrambling into cars. I waited, though I knew I'd lost the moment. Now just a handful of people remained under the porch, the hail pounding into the lawns.

I stood by a column, at right angles to her. She looked out with an expression of alarm, even dread, as if gripped by something terrible. Knowledge, premonition?

"What an afternoon!" the caretaker said next to her.

"Inauspicious," she said, barely audible.

Then she picked up her shoes and headed for the gate. I followed her, her feet weaving past puddles until she put on her shoes by the gate. She crossed by the grocery store, got into a car in the side street, lit a cigarette behind the wheel, and just sat there smoking. Her windows fogged up. I'd heard she had a wealthy husband and two children. I stood waiting for my friends, the last to leave.

Evening fell with the streets washed down, the pavement glistening like coal. Summer was finally over.

TWO

I GOT IN BEHIND the wheel and threw my heels in the back and lit a cigarette. I could have sworn a man was watching me from the other side of the street. Now I was getting paranoid. Whoever it was got into the backseat of a navy blue Peykan that swerved down Pahlavi. I rolled down the window, dragged on the cigarette, fretted with the gold lighter Houshang had given me. My husband always gives me expensive presents when he gets back from abroad. He thinks I suspect nothing as long as I enact the role he's deemed suitable for me and let him conduct life as he pleases. I count his failings like darts on a board.

Bagh Ferdaus. What a name, Garden of Paradise. Grandeur and peace. Perfect for an afternoon concert. The green lawns freshly cut, fragrant, with folding chairs in a semicircle. The event televised and well attended. Music rising to gray skies, the afternoon warm, oppressive. It was too late in the summer really for wearing yellow; I should have worn something else. Yellow looked jarring under gray skies and hail. Yellow was definitely out of place.

I shook hands with them after the concert. They were so matter-of-fact that anyone watching would have thought we were discussing music instead of dismal information. I had mentioned the private matter to them at a luncheon two weeks before, telling neither Houshang nor Father. Father hasn't much influence left and Houshang only uses his for business. He doesn't like to get involved in matters of conscience. So there we were, the three of us on the lawns, cordial and diffident. What a place for a conversation about the secret police, in the Garden of Paradise. But bad taste reigns these days. They're always cordial at first because of Father. "And how's Mr. Mosharraf? Please give him my very best." Why don't they do it in person? Father isn't fashionable to call on anymore; he's one of the has-beens they've shelved. How did they put it after that? Succinctly. "That's all they'll say. Don't ask more questions." Why not? A country without questions is a land of indifference. They don't even hear the questions.

I rolled down the window for more air. What could I tell Mr. Bashirian? Your son's in Komiteh Prison. They reserve the right to keep the boy, the right to detain him without a defense lawyer, a trial. The right to imprison him, burying him in a cell. His mother died years ago when he was a child. His father wants to leap to the ends of the earth to get him. He wept when he told me, put his face in his hands and wept. To my shame, I sat watching him woodenly. He's just a student. What do they think he'll do? Blow up the army base at Doshan Tappeh, gun down a general? They're paranoid, shrouded in secrecy and hunting shadows. It's their own shadow they should be afraid of.

Dusk at the foot of mountains. I felt them pressing in, looming. We were invited to an embassy dinner and I'd be late. I sat in the car, watching people going in and out of the grocer's. Pedestrians buying provisions for dinner, children dragged along by flustered parents into backstreets. I thought of my two sons, sheltered. . . . I stayed in the car, waiting. The streetlights came on and I felt the ground being swept away from under me. Music, grandeur, assurance, composure, all gone. There was nothing to hold on to.

The hailstorm, like an omen, beating down suddenly. Standing there under the pavilion, I felt the premonition. Looking up at the sky, I saw it huddled, livid, and knew we'd all have to pay.

GUESTS CIRCULATED THROUGH enormous rooms. Hors d'oeuvres were being passed around, but by the looks of it there weren't many left. Dinner would be announced at any moment. Houshang loved to make an entrance, his pretty face suffused with a sudden flush for being invited, for being permitted to keep such company. They love him, he's charming and sociable, he's good for business. But he was very annoyed with me for being late.

They had rounded up the usual bunch, and the powerful were holding court. Mrs. Sahafchi, the wife of the wealthiest man in the capital, and her pampered daughter reigned in Saint Laurent like most every other woman in the room. Tiny waistcoats and ballooning sleeves and bright skirts in taffeta with cummerbunds. Tribal costumes at the embassy? The West sells back Eastern ideas to us at one thousand times the price. It's not our ideas we like so much as their labels. Wives exhaust their husbands' bank accounts around their necks and ears and wrists and fingers. I felt the twinge, not of envy, but of regret. We've turned into the handmaidens of opulence.

Embassy parties are dull. We're on the B-plus list, though Houshang wants to make the A list the fastest way possible. He knows how. I think these parties are held so foreigners can gather information. They're really here for oil and gas and coal and minerals and strategic points. To secure border stations to eavesdrop on the Soviet Union. To sell arms and fighter jets and bring in the giant tentacles of their conglomerates. They need to boost their sagging economies, all the while gathering statistics. That way they get to lecture us.

Thierry Dalembert, a French banker, threw his arms out before me. *"Ma-has-tee!"* he exclaimed with admiration, embracing me. He wanted gossip about Mrs. Sahafchi's daughter, whispering about how long it would take him to seduce her. I told him he didn't stand a chance. They were keeping her on ice.

His blue eyes glistened. "Who's the lucky man?"

"He's being perfected by God!"

He laughed, exhilarated, quite certain he was nearly perfect himself.

"You look bored," he said craftily.

He seized the last two glasses of champagne from a passing silver tray and offered me one. The embassy, known for stinginess, was splurging. They were drumming up business. These were intoxicating times.

"What's new?" Thierry said.

"I could ask you the same."

"Houshang wants this port like nothing I've ever seen before."

Thierry wanted gossip about the Bandar Kangan project on the Gulf. He hadn't managed to talk to Houshang yet. There are major projects worth billions of dollars coming up along the Persian Gulf. The commercial port on the island of Gheshm, the naval port at Chah-Bahar, the expansion of Bandar Abbas. But recently we've had sudden government cutbacks in expenditures, with grand projects like my husband's new port teetering in the balance. Houshang's company, in a joint venture with a British firm, is the general contractor for Bandar Kangan, an expensive port by the old coastal town of Kangan, with its dusty palms and fishing boats and distinctive architecture, three hundred miles from the port of Bushehr. But will it ever get finished? Houshang dismisses such questions.

Kangan is a dream project. "The navy wants it!" he keeps saying. Like Houshang, the military always gets what it wants.

Thierry was courting us. We were his designated couple from the in crowd, always invited to his elegant dinner parties at his home in Sa'adabad. He wants us to meet his big boss from Paris, due to arrive in Tehran a little before the official state visit of the president of France. I've heard Thierry and Houshang chuckling about Paris. Maybe he wants to wine and dine my husband there, taking him to the best nightclubs so he can whisper about business in Iran, lucrative contracts, insider favors, kickbacks to an account in Zurich. He could even foot the bill for the most exclusive call girls of Europe. Not that my husband needs help there. Everyone watches a man for his weaknesses.

Thierry offered me a cigarette. He'd turned sullen. He dislikes women who don't talk, who don't shed words like clothing, and leave him in the dark. I smiled when I realized how he could prove useful to me.

Houshang was deep in conversation with the ambassador and two ponderous men. Things were going swimmingly, I could tell. We'd make the A list any day now; Houshang can't think of anything better.

We were called in to dinner.

I took Thierry's arm and whispered, "Be patient."

He beamed, thinking his charisma had overcome yet another obstacle. He would boast to his compatriots about seducing the exotic locals. Exotic was everything distant that they didn't understand, nor ever really planned to. But he possessed worldly charms and wit and a magnificent education. They'd sent us their very best. I like him.

The problem with most foreign men is that they're too blond and too rapacious. They think they can rule the world. Dollars and francs and pounds and marks bobbing in their eyes instead of pupils.

In the Walled Gardens

THE ROADS WERE DARK and quiet all the way to Darrous. Houshang drove fast, not completely sober.

We'd stopped off at the Key Club after the embassy with the group from London. "It's important to impress them," Houshang whispered to me after dinner. "They're already impressed!" I said. "Especially by all the money they stand to make." But Houshang wasn't listening.

He cosseted them at the club, plying them with drinks and flamboyant attention. He danced and talked to their wives as if they were promising starlets and he the great director. And the wives giggled, fugitives from the confines of their dull European lives and the doldrums of marriage. Houshang introduced them to his good buddies, squished together at adjacent tables, who more than obliged, laughing the night away with them, all hung up about foreign blond women. Their husbands — anchored to their Greco-Latin pedestals — pulling loose their ties in dark corners, ogled Eastern women ten times more alluring than their wives, dreaming of how to satisfy their whims in exotic places and run back to Europe.

It's so nice to have a country everyone loves coming to. You'd think we're adored! You'd think we're the center of the world.

The house was dark, only a light on in the hall upstairs. I looked in on the children. Rumpled hair, fluttered breaths, pudgy cheeks on pillows. My sons, sovereign in my heart. In our bedroom we went about undressing without conversation. These days we feel more compelled to talk to others. We don't even regret it. I wanted to read and Houshang wanted to sleep. After thirteen years, if nothing else, we have our habits.

"We were late for the embassy," he said irritably.

"How's the port coming along?"

"I'm proud of my efforts. They've finally paid off."

"Your port is going to destroy the town of Kangan."

"It's going to drag that sleepy old place into the twentieth century!"

"Thierry didn't get a chance to talk to you tonight."

"The leech wants introductions! Let him learn to suck up properly."

I was tempted to tell Houshang about Mr. Bashirian's son, stashed away in some dark cell at Komiteh Prison. I wanted him to suck up to a rear admiral or one of his influential contacts and ask them to look into the matter. But he wasn't going to make waves, now or ever.

"Mahastee," he said in bed, before turning over, "I want to tell you something."

I thought he meant about intimacy, affection, our life together. How we'd grown apart that year. We hadn't been close in months; I wouldn't let him touch me. I began to consider how much to forgive him.

His head hit the pillow. "Forget all that intellectual bullshit you go in for. This is no time for anything to go wrong for me. Understand?"

Houshang can be uncannily prescient.

I walked down the hallway to the upstairs study, pulled up a book, but never turned on the light. I left the book on my lap and lit a cigarette and smoked in the dark. The prospect of boredom together was lifting. Houshang and I were developing an appetite for war. He'd turned out like the rest of them, taking the smallest unexpected idea as an absolute attack on all conventions. The dictates of his ambition clouded his vision, requiring you to agree with him wholesale. Otherwise you were intellectual, which meant you'd succumbed, subscribing to and awash in some suspicious ideology. A dissident, according to such irrational rules, before you even knew it yourself.

THREE

I WOKE UP at five-thirty as usual. The sun wasn't up yet, but the birds were singing under the roof. At that hour I'm especially thankful I'm a bachelor and live alone and I have peace and quiet. I closed the window, the one facing the back alley, then washed and shaved and set my bedroll against the wall.

I made tea, not on the samovar but on the kettle crowned by the teapot with pink roses Mother gave me. We bought it in Lalehzar, with all my dishes and cups and saucers. I said, "Mother, why get me a teapot with roses?" She said, "That's all they sell and this is the country of the rose and nightingale." Father adored her until the day he died. I think he still adores her beyond the grave. She knows it — I see it in her eyes.

I had hot tea and rolled up pieces of bread with feta cheese for breakfast. I listened to the radio, reread between mouthfuls the revised statement of purpose for our underground group at the end of the month. I edited and scrawled in the margins, expounding on our main themes — the right of self-expression, the dignity of democratic freedoms, political pluralism. I inserted sentences here and there to underscore our purpose — how we intellectuals of the Left want to liberate the present from the past once and for all. We want to see the collapse of this dictatorship, a world of endless decrees, obsolete political patterns, and paternalistic interventions. We want a constitutional democracy with independent political institutions. And a parliament and political parties elected and willed by the people and representing them, instead of authoritarian royal directives and rigged elections. We want to stir up the masses by giving them a political education and objective. We believe that imperialism — the age-old adversary and economic exploiter of the Third World — is wheedling and coercing this regime, its willing servant, to keep us beholden and dependent. And that capitalism, with its cunning distortions and ferocious bravado, is working its ways to repress the inevitable — class warfare. We want to show how this regime's power is primarily bluster. Its show of strength, vast resources, machinery of state, pitted against our determination and our tenaciousness.

I poured another glass of tea. There were only three cubes of sugar left. Habib *agha*'s grocery store downstairs supplies me with most things. I will tell him that the cheese he got from Tabriz this month is particularly good. He's a decent man but barely makes ends meet with all those children.

At seven I hit the pavement. Mashdi Ahmad, the local sweeper, swept the sidewalk. He's so thin his shabby cotton trousers are several sizes too large for him, and he's bowlegged, with a funny way of sidestepping when he sweeps. If it weren't for his olive skin and sunken eyes and bony cheeks, he'd be Charlie Chaplin. Mashd-Ahmad, the Charlie Chaplin of Iran! His mother is very ill and I dared not ask this morning.

I greeted him and said, "It's a fine day."

"Whatever you say," he said, and kept on sweeping.

I have under an hour to walk to work. I go through Lalehzar, past the fruit and fish markets of Estanbul Street, and on past cinemas and cafés and barber shops and photography studios and dance studios and bookstores and stationery shops and tailors and jewelers and curious tiny stores going sideways. I like to chat with the street vendors and shopkeepers. Afternoons they call me in for a glass of tea, especially the money changers and rug dealers on Ferdausi. By day I work as a civil servant. The Department of Educational Affairs for the Provinces is affiliated with the Ministry of Education. Our section was moved up recently from Ekbatan Avenue to a new high-rise of concrete and glass in midtown with a guard at the door and steel desks and several new divisions. I take home twenty-two hundred tomans a month. Evenings I teach night school in Moniriyeh, and late nights I'm part of a Marxist underground organization.

Mother longs for me to find a wife, but I don't want to be accountable to a woman. Mine is an uncertain life. Years of clandestine activity have hardened me. Sooner or later my politics will land me in jail. All political parties have been banned for years and now there's only one party, decreed by the state.

Mother lives with my sister. Zari has three small children and a stingy and insufferable boor who calls himself her husband. He's loud and reeks of vodka on the rare occasion he comes to see me. He's a lowly functionary in the Ministry of Post and Telegraph, not that he'd ever admit it. Now that he's got a car, he's got a nasty habit of swerving down the road as he drives and laughing like a lunatic. I know he sees whores. One day I will get him. We should never have given Zari away to such pretentious people and instead should have sent them packing — the Behjat family — the day they came to ask for her hand in marriage. She was only nineteen and thought he somehow fit into the love poetry she leafed through in her bedroom. His whole family came for tea. Morteza, the apple of their eye, came hosed down with cologne, hair swept back, with a garish tie and a lecherous smile. He couldn't wait to get his hands on my sister. He left his polished shoes by the door, eyeing them as if he were afraid we'd steal them. Zari was so nervous she noticed nothing. His mother and sisters sat to one side primly, nibbling on Mother's homemade almond rolls and baklava and walnut cookies and sweet fritters as if they were sprinkled with poison, surveying our rooms and silver and rugs and samovar and dishes, taking inventory. As if Mother didn't notice. Father was the very picture of discretion as usual. He'd never believed in accumulating worldly goods and instead contemplated the interior life, prayed on an old, faded rug, and read far into the night. Ferdausi, Attar, Maulana, the Constitutional Revolution, agricultural tracts, the precepts of the first disciple — the Perfect Man — Ali. My father was a lion in the wilderness of a desert; Ali, the Lion of God.

For years I taught mathematics in a public high school for boys. Every day was a battle, but I enjoyed their humor and directness. I valued their disrespect gathering steam beneath that eternal veneer of obedience, their insolent tauntings and undiluted politics. These were the minds that would dare think instead of doing as they were told. This was the force necessary to build the future. I got them all before they could become sellouts. Before their inevitable concessions would soften them up, make them jowly conservatives, neutered by government handouts and scholarships and promotions and international conferences. I believed in them, understood them, before they got smothered by the state or the hallowed fears sown and harvested in their souls by religion. Some we tracked, eventually recruited and trained, and then sent out to recruit others their own age. Only the young make revolution.

Then I shifted to a private high school and for two years I watched the lambkins of the privileged and their parents. It will take more than rich fathers to make men out of these boys. They're given the hollow arrogance and false assurances of their social class and believe in nothing but themselves, all soft and pampered.

It only confirmed what we already suspected. If they are the future of the Right, then we on the Left can defeat them. Paper tigers, they will go up in smoke one day.

When I applied for an opening in the Ministry of Education, I got this job. The department is in charge of all the educational needs of the provinces: policy, budgets, curriculum and textbooks, recruiting teachers, leasing buildings. Now I can evaluate civil servants. We have meetings with other divisions and we're sent for official visits to the provinces. I talk to colleagues and listen to their disaffection and unremitting cynicism about the higher-ups who run the country. Their most virulent ridicule these days is directed at our new single party — Rastakhiz. One thing they know is how to undercut everything. They whisper that the regime is losing its bearings. It has lost touch. They talk about their dreams of getting rich and moving to Los Angeles. Of their friends who are doing so well in business. Meanwhile they keep their government salary and benefits and pension and free milk and education for their children, then cut work and slink away to private jobs in the early afternoon, making fast money in a pumped-up economy. The state is breeding vipers in its own bosom.

I walked up Ferdausi, past the circle, double-decker red buses breaking at the bus stop. Around the corner, airline offices sell tickets to places around the world. But I haven't gone abroad yet and may never go.

The first month of autumn is a mutable month, with chilly mornings graying at the temples and leaves gone dry and brittle like Mashd-Ahmad. Branches shrivel and the wind smells of smoldering fires.

FROM THE OFFICE I called my friend Abbas, who works for the National Television. The janitor passed through with the first tray of tea for the morning. There would be more to come, linking up like compartments on a train steaming through the day. Abbas said he had news and told me where to meet him next day.

It's this business about Jalal. He's disappeared without a trace. Long ago he broke with his family, and he's been on his own since high school. I met him one spring years ago when I was tutoring my two younger cousins — boys of eighteen — to help them with finals and prepare them for the entrance examinations to university. They brought around Jalal, also in his last year of high school, talented, angry, revolt in his blood. I was the first man to give him a political education. Then years ago we parted ideologically, and he moved into the murky depths of the radical Left, but he always kept up with me. He's a rabid revolutionary.

Three months ago he warned our group of a SAVAK raid. If it hadn't been for Jalal, that night eight of us would have landed in jail. In a flash we cleared out of the basement we rented, taking typewriters and the mimeograph machine and political literature and our lists and personal papers and archives. They hit within hours. We thought we had a SAVAK collaborator, a snitch. The following week, in late-night sessions charged with hostile recriminations — exposing years of hidden rivalries and old wounds and dirty laundry — we tore through our entire organization, insulting and accusing until the animosity and ill will threatened to destroy us. That was how the group of three took control and held inquisitions and purges. They were young hotheads — emotional and dogmatic and vain without knowing enough about anything — who had run leftist cells in the provinces and now thought they'd take over in Tehran. They started on me. How had I known the secret police would hit that night? What was I hiding? Maybe I'd set the whole thing up to pit us against one another? Maybe I was the snitch? Until the last night, when I shot out of my seat and told them they could go to hell! We called ourselves progressive intellectuals? Freedom fighters? We were a bunch of sick, suspicious bastards. No wonder the country never got anywhere. I walked out.

It was shortly after that Jalal and I got drunk one night, unduly cynical about the world, unduly cynical about the loyalties of our respective comrades and the ever-present prospect of getting stabbed in the back by one of them. We made a pact that had nothing to do with politics. It was a personal pledge. We would watch each other's back.

I'm sure he was taken Wednesday night. He told me to meet him that night at nine-thirty at a café near Tehran University. He had something important to tell me. I waited for an hour, but he never showed up. He never made it home that night, his landlady told me. He never reappeared. I went by his coffee shop, but it was shuttered and padlocked. Jalal never closed shop, and if he couldn't be there himself — which happened frequently — he had young loafers looking for odd jobs to fill in. Familiar faces, student types, manning the store while he was away.

I went by his apartment on Jami and rang the doorbell, but there was no answer. I checked again with his landlady, who said he'd never come home that night. She was sure it was Wednesday night. She'd been unwell and had seen him go out at seven and called out to him, trying to collect her overdue rent, but he'd rushed off. She had decided to nab him when he got back. She'd left the radio on and barely touched her dinner and stayed up late waiting for him. She was fed up. Jalal had been avoiding her for weeks. She'd even left the front door of her ground-floor apartment ajar in case he snuck by. "He's a clever one!" she said. But he never showed up. At the crack of dawn — she could hear the *azahn* from the mosque down the street, the call for prayer — she had knocked on his door again, but no answer. She'd tried again all day, that night, the next morning. On the street the shopkeepers said rumor was Jalal had been arrested for being a profiteer. That's a cheap lie. A coffee seller is small-fry in the scheme of things. Still, the devastations of the antiprofiteering campaign by the government blaze through the city, inciting rabid disaffection, punishing small merchants and retailers and shopkeepers in the bazaar for high prices, but leaving the big fat ones at the top out of the fire.

Jalal wasn't taken for profiteering. They would have made a spectacle of that. I'm sure he was taken in the dark by the secret police to some dark cell in this city.

Shirin called around midafternoon about dinner at her house. Jalal introduced us last year, telling me how she was a convenient woman. I take her type to late dinners at the College Inn, then back to their apartments, where they conveniently live alone. I've tried going out with teachers and upwardly mobile secretaries and civil servants, but I always leave them — these women forever looking for promises I will not keep. Shirin is divorced, without children, and an executive secretary to a big industrialist. Hourglass figure, spiked heels, dyed hair. She's easy and never asks what I do and where I go and what I think or tells me why I shouldn't. She splurges in the expensive boutiques and primps herself in bourgeois clothes and likes to be seen at the Copacabana cabaret, and at Cuchini and Chattanooga for dinner — the haunts of the bourgeoisie. Every year she treats herself to a new country. This summer she took off for Rome and Naples and Capri on Jahan Tours and brought back gifts and pictures of herself, the petit bourgeois tourist, in sunglasses and tight dresses, plastered against Italian monuments, dark boys salivating around her like dogs.

At nine-thirty that night in her apartment, she was purring sweet nothings to me and feeding me dinner. She brought out creamy desserts, droning on about leaving for New York together, where we could be free. "Free!" she repeated upstairs, releasing her black garter. She murmured another heartrending love song by Haideh in her dusky bedroom, where she did everything to please me. "I like you too much," she whispered at midnight. "You're like a drug."

But I was thinking of Mahastee. The peculiar sensation of seeing her. An hour in a garden, and the past had erupted before me like a geyser.

THE NEXT AFTERNOON I got a haircut at the barbershop on Manuchehri, then met my friend who works at the National Television. He was waiting at the corner drugstore on Takhte Jamshid across from the National Oil Company. He'd hitched a ride down from work. I'd told him about Jalal after the concert because I knew he knew someone in the Department of Police. At first he resisted, but I argued it was time to test his contact.

We walked past Shahreza and Rudaki Hall and the old mud-brick walls of the Soviet embassy compound, black crows rising from the towering trees, cawing.

"Once we were the servant of the Russians and British," Abbas said. "Now the Americans. In the ass-licking department — that's progress!"

I needed to buy shoes on Naderi, and he wanted to buy music.

"He's in Komiteh Prison," Abbas said.

So they had Jalal. An ominous feeling swept over me. "You're sure?"

"He hasn't been interrogated yet. Let this go, Reza. I don't like what I hear."

We stopped at the traffic light, backed-up cars honking furiously at each other in another afternoon of gridlock and exhaust fumes and rotten tempers. Pedestrians jaywalked through the traffic, cab drivers swearing at the lot of them.

We crossed past Starlight, the lingerie shop of the Armenian sisters, with garters and flimsy nightgowns and their own brand of stockings in the windows. We picked the Melli shoe store on Naderi, and I tried several styles and settled for a black leather pair; then three doors down Abbas selected cassettes. We parted at the bus stop.

I walked on, jostled by pedestrians at dusk. Komiteh was a prison where they tortured answers out of prisoners. Things they did were told in whispers. Jalal's coffee beans and poetry and literary jargon were a thin veneer. They would break him into pieces, disassemble him, body and soul.

AT THE FRUIT MARKET on Estanbul Street, I stopped to buy two bags of bloodred pomegranates. A movie marquee loomed high above, advertising an Indian film with a doe-eyed girl, finger to the chin. In the Indian subcontinent they have to twirl around trees to declare their love. Hassan *agha*, the fruit seller, said he preferred any movie starring our very own sex bomb, Forouzan.

"Mr. Nirvani!" he said. "One day you'll be minister of education! When you are, don't forget me, your humble servant!"

His reverence for lofty posts and habit of self-abasement really annoys me. A ready recipe for breeding impetuous resentments.

"I don't want to be minister of education," I said.

He looked incredulous. "Why not? It's a terrific thing to be!"

I caught the bus near Baharestan Square to see Mother.

Baharestan always reminds me of Father. He loved the square, the white-columned building of the parliament and its rose gardens and the mosque of Sepahsalar. This was the heart of the city for him.

The bus was crowded, and by the time I got off half an hour later it was dusk. When I rang my sister's doorbell, she opened the front door as if she'd crouched behind it, her three children tugging at her skirt. They yelled, "Uncle!" and jumped into my arms like monkeys. I set my shoes by the door and gave my little nephew, Ali, a bag of pomegranates, and he grabbed it and ran off, his two little sisters chasing after him. Zari said she'd bring tea. She's forever changing her hairstyle and hair color these days and wears too much jewelry and cheap perfume to console herself for her washout of a husband. Mother came in from chatting with the neighbors, and I rose to greet her.

"You've lost weight," she said.

She always says that when she feels I'm trying to hide something from her. We sat on the rug and sipped tea while Zari's children hopped about.

"You should get married," Mother said.

"He's waiting for the perfect woman!" said Zari.

"Let him wait," said Mother. "In the meantime, there's Mrs. Amanat's daughter. I think you should consider her seriously."

"Reza wants a modern woman," Zari said.

They stared.

Zari went to get more tea, and Mother picked up her sewing.

"Jalal's been arrested," I said.

She looked up, startled. "I think you're mixed up in something yourself. I worry."

She resumed sewing, her needle and thread looping deftly to complete a seam. She bent over, cut the thread with scissors.

"I'm going to see Nasrollah *mirza,*" I said. "To help Jalal."

"After all these years?" she said. "Go, in your father's memory."

We sat quietly. Outside, a roving vendor's singsong cry floated in the dusk. I remembered my father long ago buying a dark suit one day in the street.

"Won't you stay for dinner?" Mother asked.

"I must be going."

"Your brother-in-law never comes home," she said.

Zari brought tea and date cakes and insisted I stay for dinner. She's got wrinkles by her mouth and callused hands, and her eyes are vacant and her eyebrows so waxed there's nothing left of them.

The children wanted a ride on my back, so I took them around the room, and they laughed and screamed and kicked and fell over giggling.

It was pitch-dark when I left. I kissed Mother and Zari and the children. The streetlights were on; a dog barked in the distance. The new moon was out.

FOUR

THE SCHOOL BUS CAME in the morning to take the boys, who both had coughs and colds. I hugged them by the garden gate and they scrambled past me, the clinging mother, and rushed off, coats flailing.

Houshang barely ate breakfast, paging through the local English morning papers, griping about the perpetual shortage of skilled labor and cement. We had an argument as he tossed off the paper. I'd failed to perform, to look interested, the night before at the club. He thinks I do it on purpose.

"Why can't you be more attentive?" he said. "Why can't you be more — more wifely?"

The chauffeur drove him downtown. I like to drive myself, to come and go as I please, and I dislike the chauffeur, who's snoopy and whose only loyalty is to himself. My husband treats him like a personal adjutant, but I think he can't wait to hack off the hand that feeds him. He'd betray the lot of us in a moment.

I had decided Thierry could help Mr. Bashirian's son and just needed to be persuaded. He's a well-respected banker, a man who commands attention in Paris. One call to a noted journalist there, and they'd come after the story. Young innocent snatched off to prison versus oppressive regime with oil money louder than rights. That's how they'd write it. The story would sell itself, turning up the pressure here. There's no such thing as an objective journalist. They have their own axes to grind, blinded by their own civilizations. And I don't trust the motives of newspapers. They run on abridged perceptions. They see us as a stinking oil-rich country lecturing them back, and they can't wait to burst our bubble.

Thierry would of course resist at first. He'd resist any sort of meddling that could mean serious trouble. He does big business in this country and wants to keep it that way for as long as possible. The story would have to get out without being traced back to him.

I didn't want to call him but suspected he'd show up at the French Club for lunch. I'd arrange to bump into him. It was short notice, but I first called my two best friends, then several others, until I found one who could make lunch at one-thirty.

As a manager in the division of the High Economic Council in charge of publications, I went from meeting to meeting all morning. We commission and publish research papers, analyze government statistics, produce a monthly bulletin and a quarterly journal. I was hoping to avoid Mr. Bashirian. I hadn't a shred of consolation, only bad news. I would tell him soon enough.

The French Club serves the best lunch in town. At one-thirty, heads turned as Pouran and I were seated by the window. I was disappointed; I couldn't see what I had come for. The garden was strangely nondescript, with towering and anemic fir trees, the light bright and hard.

Pouran had dyed her hair another nasty shade of blond. Her face was gray at midday, despite the makeup. She asked if I liked the new color.

"Wonderful."

"I prefer yours. Iraj likes me blond," she complained.

She likes to complain because it makes her feel important. We ordered. Friends of my parents' stopped by our table on their way to bridge upstairs. When I turned to flag the waiter, I saw Thierry come in with three men. They passed by us to the main dining room, Thierry deep in conversation.

"He's ravishing," Pouran whispered.

Pouran has been fidgety for months. A cruise in the Greek islands in early September had only piled gold on her, but provided no solutions. We lit cigarettes with coffee. Pouran ran through her standard list: our beautiful women; who had a superb figure or skin and hair; whose husband was richer and threw bigger parties; and who was on which diet and lover and had plastic surgery and bought which clothes from which designer and stayed in which European hotel. I had to get to work but needed Thierry. Pouran needed him more than I did. He had all the right markings to leap to the top of her guest list.

"He looks good enough to eat!" she said, biting her lip.

Her coarse sexuality can be quite beguiling. She sauntered over and Thierry rose and they kissed, and he introduced her to his colleagues. He wears dark suits like no other man, ramrod-straight. Steel blue eyes like silvery mirrors. I stayed at our table calculating the tip. When I looked up, he waved and I walked over. He said Pouran was having a party Thursday.

"It would be the greatest honor of my life to have you there," she said to Thierry.

Her exaggerations sweep the world, evacuating truth and meaning and finer distinctions in their wake.

"And bring your friends!" She smiled at the others.

My appeal for Peyman Bashirian had to wait for Thursday.

LATE IN THE AFTERNOON Mr. Bashirian sat before me. He'd closed the door to my office as if I held new hope.

"Your son's in Komiteh Prison. There's nothing you can do. They'll be calling you." I'd repeated the message a dozen times, repeated it in different ways, though the message wouldn't change, no matter how I tried. He stared expectantly, as if I were holding back or better news was at the end of some sentence not yet uttered. I told him there was nothing more. He asked again, then stared blankly at the wall. He looked like he hadn't slept for days. He said he was on Valium.

"Tea?" I asked.

He shook his head and just sat there, the silence awful, his appearance alarming, anemic. He sagged. I suggested he go home early. He said he couldn't stand home without Peyman, so I offered to give him a ride. As we left, the secretary in the outer office stared after us.

He lived near Dampezeshki and gave directions and thanked me for driving him home more times than was decent for a man of his standing.

I asked if he was eating properly. Expounding on the benefits of nutrition, my tone clipped like a nurse's, to steel him.

Dusk. The sun deserting. The tail end of the day shortened and dark. People in coats called out their destinations to orange taxis.

Mr. Bashirian pointed to a small house and invited me in. Who could refuse a grieving father? He had several rooms and a narrow kitchen and tiny backyard with a grape arbor. Dark rooms with speckled gray tile flooring and feeble overhead lights. They were the rooms of a father and son. There wasn't the slightest vestige of a woman.

He made tea. I walked about the small living room. The heavy-handed oil paintings on the walls were his. He'd been taking lessons for years. I saw his small and modest signature, slanted like two birds flying south: *Kamal.* Nostalgic renderings. A virginal maiden with clasped hands and soulful eyes. Wispy willows bent over a stony river. Silvery moonlight over desolate hills. He came in, pointed to the steel bookcase holding his son's collection of photographs, tucked away into albums, from his travels around the country.

"They haven't gone through his stuff. They haven't come yet."

He was waiting for the secret police. He expected them, like a sort of death.

We sat at the table in the hallway and laid out the last batch of pictures Peyman had taken. Mr. Bashirian handled the photographs the way I imagined he would have handled his son — discreetly. They were pictures from Peyman's last journey to the eastern border of the Kavir in Khorassan Province, towns ringing the Salt Desert.

"From Kashmar to Gonabad, then Ferdaus, Boshruyeh, Tabas, and Robaat-Kur down to Robaat-Posht-Badaam," said the father.

Places in the dust. He'd come to see them through the eyes of his son. He spread out the photographs with quiet hands, leaning over them, peering.

"He understands these places," said Mr. Bashirian. "The way the sun breaks on their backs. Their strange and deserted silence, the light in the eyes of their inhabitants."

Together we stared at the photographs.

"He loved the desert," he said. "You can't imagine how he spoke of it. It was a mystical thing. He told me it was there he could find God. Alone in that desolate place where man is stripped of his earthly masks and material wealth, where nothing can be faked."

His voice broke. He wanted to ask for the hundredth time why they had taken Peyman. The question hung between us, unspoken. He went to bring tea.

He was so resigned. Why wasn't he angry? Anger was a way out of grief.

When I left, he waved from the doorway, already sinking into the marshes of desolation. The light was to his back, his body silhouetted in the doorway. He smiled and I smiled back, walking away from him.

His grace had allowed me to leave with impunity. He blamed no one except himself.

FRIDAY I WOKE UP late with a headache. I called in my sons, Ehsan and Kamran, who were playing soccer in the garden. We had breakfast in the upstairs study, going through photos of our summer at the Caspian. They climbed over each other to see first or better, pointing to our friends, the villa, the local caretaker and his family, the mimosas, the old hotel, the lush green mountains of Ramsar sliding to the shore. They laughed, ended up on the floor slugging each other. Ehsan, a photocopy of his father, is already more handsome, nearly regal in bearing, calculating. Kamran looks like Mother, with light hair and a broad face and my hazel eyes and our penchant for sarcasm.

I sent them off to get dressed. Houshang had a squash game at the club.

I was going to tell Father about Peyman Bashirian's arrest. I planned on telling him after the family lunch. He's been moody for weeks, growing old, assailed by a host of invisible afflictions.

Last night Houshang and I had an argument before going to Pouran and Iraj's party. We're out nearly every night. We had an argument after we got back. That's how we keep up with each other.

When we got up to our bedroom, I said we'd be at my parents' for lunch the next day instead of his. That blew his top. He started about my flirtations with Thierry.

"You were whispering in a corner," he said.

"The music was loud."

"Then why not dance?" he said, laughing like a hyena.

He does that to keep cool in a rage; I'm allergic to the sound it makes. He thinks he's guileful and indirect. But I know he whores around with foreign and expensive imports, a tradition he maintains accompanied by loyal friends. Their tribal ritual. They trade stories about procuring pleasure behind closed doors. They snigger, invent. They should learn to make love instead of buying it — to give of themselves, if that were even possible.

Houshang believes it my duty to turn a blind eye. He bears gifts. I'm the kind who looks a gift horse in the mouth. Three years ago I realized he had a mistress. Unlike the generation of my parents, who had arranged marriages, I couldn't shrug it off. I hadn't been educated for this. My generation flatters itself that we determine our fate; we are liberated, individualistic, self-reliant. Our marriages require absolute compatibility and possession, a form of predestination and myth we can't escape. I confronted Houshang, but he denied everything, remarkably well rehearsed for the occasion. I was the one ill prepared, stunned at the limits of emancipation like a fish out of water. I warned him then and there. Later, I realized it was a rut I would be in forever. To preserve my dignity, I feigned nonchalance but kept an eye on him, looking for signposts and slipups. A steely warden in an institution, that's what I've become. Distant, hard-hearted — for which I blame him and dislike him even more.

He went up to bed with pills and a bottle of water and bloodshot eyes. I stayed downstairs, shuffling through pages of a report at two in the morning.

Thierry had come to the party flanked by his banker friends.

They met haughty courtiers and enthralled diplomats and feverish MBAs and businessmen and jaded loafers and professional free-loaders and part-time intellectuals and full-time charlatans and brats. His friends looked impressed. "Especially by the women!" they kept repeating. Not too original, still, they spoke from habit. Who knows what the truth is abroad.

Iraj and Pouran Mazaher are the perfect embodiment of the new elite of the capital. They're social arbiters, beholden to no one and nothing, their home a consummation of the boom mentality, slightly chilling with its grip on grandeur.

There was throbbing disco music, important bouquets from Rose Noir in all the rooms. The grand salon was set with the requisite faux gold knockoff Louis XIV furniture, set under knockoff tableaux of bucolic scenes with maidens in bonnets among cows and sheep. A friend had told me Iraj liked his call girls dressed up that way — as shepherdesses. The other rooms were set with gargantuan modern Italian furniture and bogus modern art. There was opium and grass in the private den, where the door remained shut. A mound of pearl gray caviar in a silver bowl on crushed ice surrounded by toast and fresh limes was carried around by a sullen manservant in white jacket and white gloves. Guests were already planning to go on to La Cheminée, or La Bohème for the Dark Eyes Band, though La Bohème wasn't as fashionable anymore. Dinner was served too late as usual, the succulent foods piled and steaming around the dining table, overlit by a fearsome chandelier. Fish and partridge and roast lambs and stews and silver trays heaped with rice. The host was on the prowl, roaming rooms gratifyingly decorated to his tastes. Shirt tight, hands wandering. My husband and Iraj are two peas in a pod, chewing the end of their Cuban cigars in well-orchestrated candlelight. Pouran kept pinching her breasts together, busy laughing in all the rooms, whispering to choice guests it was the greatest honor of her life to have them there.

Halfway through the night, Thierry heard my case about Peyman Bashirian in a corner. False arrest, the rights of prisoners, an appeal to human rights organizations. "I know the boy's father," I said. At first he looked amused. That nearly did me in I felt so insulted. Then he began to flirt, by reflex, like a dog salivating. I countered, going on about torture, electric prods, mutilated genitals. He cooled off astonishingly well, nodding with the aplomb befitting a very distant heir to the Enlightenment, more pantomime than compassion. I pressed on and he listened in earnest, suddenly turning chilly — this wasn't his idea of fun at Iraj and Pouran's. He said he'd commit to nothing except thinking about it and calling me later. "When?" I insisted. "Later," he repeated. Pulling in closer, he asked me to dance, his eyes glassy, the song blaring from the towering speakers. He was about to take advantage, and I refused too quickly. Bad move, I thought, walking away. If you ask the favor, you dance. But I'd seen Houshang watching from across the room and had no need for a showdown, which came anyway once we got home.

Around midmorning I called Mother to ask if she needed anything for Friday lunch.

"The marzipan cream cake from Danish Pastry."

"The green dome?"

"The green one," she said, and hung up.

We both hate small talk.

Pouran called five minutes later. Thierry had made a pass at her, she gushed, tripping over her words. "See," she said, "he's in love with me! Of course, I adore my husband!" Cocky from the merest whiff of success, she gossiped about her guests. She collects people so she can watch them up close, then trash them, drawing satisfaction from denigrating them for a host of imperfections. She complained that her servants were turning sullen.

"The ingrates!" she said, yawning. "I've applied for Bangladeshis to rid me of these local asses sulking and glaring at us so disapprovingly."

Pouran and Iraj would rather import a whole country to avoid contact with our masses. They throw a bash a week, and every night they're either out or have guests. He's my husband's best friend; she's neurotic. An unlikely mixture of savvy, naïveté, hard glamour, and shaky self-respect. Her impetuous generosities and revelry are offset by flashes of vulgarity and malice.

She hung up, saying I looked on edge.

AT A QUARTER TO ONE we were speeding up Saltanatabad, the green marzipan cream cake on my lap. The children had been picked up earlier by their uncle. We were behind a brown car with a dented fender. Within seconds Houshang was trying to overtake it. The driver weaved left, then right. Four men were in the car. Houshang honked and the car accelerated. He shifted gears, swearing under his breath.

"The cake," I said.

Houshang floored the gas pedal, but the brown car cut in left again. Houshang swung back abruptly. As I swayed toward the window, I caught sight of one, then two gendarmerie jeeps in my side-view mirror. The jeeps honked. We were within a mile of the army barracks. Houshang, provoked and indignant, wouldn't let them overtake us.

The jeeps turned on their sirens, and Houshang slowed down. The jeeps pulled out, speeding past us, two army vehicles now visible behind them. Then something peculiar happened in front. The jeeps jackknifed into the brown car suddenly, forcing it off the road. Houshang slammed his foot on the brakes. I lurched forward with the cake. The two armored vehicles tailing the jeeps overtook us, barricading the brown car within seconds. Uniformed men poured out, shouting and pointing guns at the four men in the car. Suddenly there were gendarmes and soldiers and guns and men barking orders everywhere.

An agitated gendarme ran out and jumped in front of our car. He screamed at us, motioning frantically for Houshang to drive on. The armored vehicles were blocking our way. We had to back up.

I turned for a quick look at the men. Two were being dragged out by force, their arms covering their heads. Two were already up against the car, legs spread, arms high. I saw them in profile; they looked so young — black hair, jeans and sweaters and sneakers. Student types, but impassive, unafraid.

The gendarme slammed his fist on our hood. "Go!" he shouted, pointing.

Houshang backed up quickly, then shot up the road. Every month they ambush armed guerrillas in the streets in shoot-outs. We get lists and mug shots in the papers, but these boys hadn't been armed. Houshang said SAVAK was infiltrating underground organizations, uncovering nasty plots of insurrection against the monarchy like clockwork. Someone had to do the dirty work.

"Better count your blessings," he said.

"Which blessing?" I said. "Killing boys like them? Living in a bubble?"

"What, you want pandemonium? Don't be irrational! We're kept from raving maniacs and ruthless Marxists and bloodthirsty ideologues."

"Don't exaggerate."

"You're *such* an idealist!"

I looked into the side-view mirror until the men were distant specks.

By the foothills past the palace, we turned left into Niavaran and to the narrow side streets beyond. Friday is quiet, especially deep in the side streets, quiet if you only hear what you want. There have been more than twelve political assassinations carried out by the Left this year. Last month armed Marxist rebels gunned down three American military advisers to the Shah at midday downtown. This month in three separate incidents armed guerrillas have been gunned down by the security forces in the streets. Their names were in the evening papers: Aladpoush, Ahangar, Davari, Olfat. I read them out for my brother on the back veranda facing the garden, but he shrugged it off. I read them out for Father after lunch, but he dozed off. Repeated the names in the bathroom mirror all week. Who were they? These young men, prepared to die for a cause. Prepared to die like heroes in an epic. SAVAK — ruthless itself — decries the ruthlessness of guerrilla groups who purge their own, kill each other off, then burn the bodies and dump them in the city and blame SAVAK. Houshang — supposed realist — dismisses all such incidents as minor blips on an unclouded horizon.

We turned in at the gates of the old garden on the foothills of Shemiran. Once there were open fields here.

Mashdi Hossein, the gardener, waved from the small porch of his quarters by the old grape arbor. On the other side of the driveway, his youngest son crossed the lawn ploddingly with a rake. The children congregated by the pool were pointing and shouting. They parted as Mashd-Hossein's son stepped up to the perimeter. He lowered the rake, nudging the soccer ball floating in the middle of the pool among the leaves.

I counted cars all the way up the driveway. My parents had all their children with their spouses and grandchildren, which came to fifteen, and several aunts and uncles, who brought nieces and nephews. Thirty for Friday lunch was usual, not counting friends who dropped in. Houshang was sulking because they were all my relatives instead of his, but he was charming the lot of them within minutes. He worked the living room and I headed for the kitchen.

Mother was tucking lamb into hot, fluffy rice. Mashdi Ghanbar, our cook for more than thirty years — reciter of epic poems, and repository of Napoleonic longings — was quibbling ostentatiously about the whereabouts of four canisters of cooking oil. The new maid, a girl of eighteen from the village, came in the back door carrying fresh, long loaves of *sangak* bread. Mashd-Ghanbar gave her his most menacing look. She'd come to learn that meant she might as well take poison.

I opened the cake box.

"It's dented." Mother pointed to the green dome.

"We were in an ambush!"

She nodded, heaping more baby lima bean rice onto her china platter as if the outside world didn't really count.

FIVE

I CALLED MR. MOSHARRAF, who was delighted to hear from me. "It's been so long!" he said. The last time I'd seen him, Father had forced me to go when he was suffering from a failing heart and I was a student discovering politics.

The gardens of Shemiran sprawl for miles. In the summer, past the forbidding walls and iron gates flung open, you can see their winding driveways covered with the finest pebbles, the freshly cut lawns bordered with ribbons of snapdragons and petunias and marigolds. Vast gardens, with tennis courts and swimming pools. Well past the shrubbery and rose arbors and cypress, the houses are covered with honeysuckle, morning glory, and wisteria. It's serene here, the world at its best, not congested and crude and hectic like downtown. If you stand up here long enough, you think nothing will ever go wrong.

Nothing could be further from the truth. The history of families residing in these gardens has been as fickle as fate. Their fortunes have cringed and surged at the whim of politics.

Nasrollah *mirza* Mosharraf is from an old aristocratic landowning family, with one branch in Azarbaijan. His wife is from a clan of landowners in Tabriz; blue-eyed, blond, obdurate, from a family with a flair for commerce. A formidable woman, Nasrollah *mirza* liked to tell Father. He congratulated himself often for winning her hand, disobeying his imperious mother to marry her. Just like his own willful father a century before — a member of that large tribe that had ruled then as the Qajar dynasty — who had disobeyed his pious yet calculating mother and refused to marry a relative, a Qajar princess. Instead Fathollah *mirza* — named after the spiritual and eminent sheikh and writer buried in Najaf — had headed north for Rasht and taken the boat from Enzeli across the Caspian to Baku and boarded a train from czarist Russia across Europe. He had sown his wild oats all over Saint Petersburg, then Vienna and France, and graduated from the Sorbonne. Then he'd come home to marry the haughty and impossible daughter of the eccentric and ferocious Ebrahim *khan* Sardar Bahador, who commanded his own army and whose ancestors had come from the steppes of central Asia near the river Amu Darya. He'd brought her Russian crystal chandeliers, Viennese vases, silk brocades, and a magnificent dinner set for eighty-four, hand-painted in Saint Petersburg. She had been raised as few women in her time, fluent in French and Russian and Turkish, riding bareback and hunting and presiding over her villages and crops and lands herself, settling disputes and meting out justice like a man.

Their forefathers had fought in the wars against the Ottomans and Russians. For centuries they had worked the land and owned villages and orchards and pastures in Azarbaijan. But the newly wed couple chose to live in Tehran in a large house designed by a famous Russian architect, with porches and columns, and there threw the most unusual parties for the most unusual mixture of guests the capital had ever seen — with poetry and music and theater and women mixing with men — until the court expressed displeasure with Fathollah *mirza* and sent him into exile, charging him with political intrigue. He had laughed it off and buckled down on a diet of yogurt with mountain herbs and bread and fruit to write a travelogue, a history of eastern Azarbaijan, a classic study of the *qanat* underground water-channel system of Iran, three primers on fruit trees, a book on herbal medicine, and his memoirs, lost to future generations through neglect. He had entertained there — intellectuals and poets and governors and freethinkers and French, British, and Russian delegates coming through Azarbaijan. They had enjoyed his hospitality and conversation so much he'd been recalled to the capital, returning to favor in his elegant Russian coach guarded by his riflemen and followed by his entire household and retinue of servants, and the formidable Delpasand, his old black nanny from Madagascar. Officer, governor, and minister, Fathollah *mirza* — awarded the title Mosharrafsaltaneh — was also a constitutionalist. He had had five daughters and a son. Their firstborn, a daughter, had died within the year, in the cholera epidemic of Tehran. In her grief his young wife had left for Tabriz and there called for my grandfather, who knew her family well and was a respected religious man and Sufi, a gentle soul who had come to console her. She had stayed on, and in time he had taught her the mystical texts and then brought his whole family and his son, Alimardan, my father, then a young boy. She had grown so attached to this son that when returning to Tehran she had insisted Alimardan return with her and enter into her household, and she had prevailed.

Ten months later, on a snowy night, her second-born, a son, Nasrollah, had been delivered by a Georgian doctor from Tbilisi. "A big, fat, healthy son!" she'd said, grateful year after year, telling everyone it was my father who had brought with him from Tabriz her good fortune. And so he had remained in Tehran with the family and held a special place in her heart. And the year she'd taken her pilgrimage to Mecca and become a *hajjieh,* he had become a *hajji,* because she'd taken him along with her other attendants. They always spoke Turkish together, Mahbanou *khanom* and Father, and she'd had him tutor her son and daughters at home so they would learn their mother's first language. And so in time when Father was appointed overseer of Nasrollah *mirza*'s estates, the two spoke Turkish together, for them a language about peasants and farmers and weather and land deals and crop yields and local elections and their various troubles and private political convictions. When Father taught me Turkish as a child, it was the language of his own father and mother and of another life abandoned early in Tabriz; and the stories of that childhood, and speaking his mother tongue far away, drew him back there and to that time, and drew me. In that language too he whispered to Mother a lifetime — though she spoke it little, she understood it — his private thoughts at the end of the day, and his sudden endearments to her, which were so rare and true they made her blush and bite her lip and look away.

When Nasrollah *mirza*'s mother died, Father gave a eulogy for her outside Tabriz on one of her estates, and the entire audience of peasants and family attendants and villagers from far and wide, standing before him and pouring out the doors and into the gardens, had wept. Father said he'd seen nothing like her, her skin pale like the Russian pearl necklace she always wore, her eyes hazel and arresting — I saw her in her old age, and her eyes were still arresting — perhaps an impossible woman, Father said, because of the high standards she kept, her insight unequaled. For her son, she had brought tutors to the house in the turbulent times of Mohammad Ali Shah, then sent him abroad to Vienna and the Sorbonne. To Father she had given one of her estates, named after him, Mardanabad, which years later provoked a nasty land dispute and was finally appropriated by one of her nephews.

Nasrollah *mirza* had returned from abroad, feisty and charismatic, and served his country — well but erratically, Father used to say — now and then allying himself with the wrong side, and at such times retreating to one of his gardens. Father, who had known him since childhood, thought he actually preferred these retreats to all else. He said Nasrollah *mirza* possessed, of course, a sense of general superiority — understandable and appropriate, considering his breeding — but suffered from a crankiness that often landed him in trouble and engendered bouts of solitude and gloom. In time the family's large estates shriveled with the years and the proclamation of the Land Reform Law, which, striking like an earthquake, abruptly shattered a system entrenched for centuries. Father had overseen them all. He said the Mosharrafs talked about soil and orchards and homestead and heritage the way the devout talk about God.

He'd known them all so long, he said they had become his family. And when he finally married, he asked and was given a distant relative of theirs as his bride. Her father was a small-land owner who owned vineyards, and she brought with her a modest dowry. Mother, reserved and devout, spoke seldom of her affection for them, perhaps because she was a poor cousin and knew them little and felt far removed from them except through blood.

THE GARDENER GREETED ME at the gates of their garden. He didn't recognize me, and I had to tell him who I was.

"Good to have you back!" said Mashdi Hossein.

We shook hands and he held on to mine, all the while asking after Mother and praising Father's memory. He'd grown bonier and slightly stooped. He told me with pride, beaming, how his older sons now attended university.

The old house was exactly like before. I couldn't even count the times I'd come and gone during my entire childhood and early adolescence. I felt a surge, a strange fulfillment. Even the position of the flower pots hadn't changed on the stone steps going up both sides of the white-columned porch — pots of geraniums and fragrant white jasmine — the balconies on the upper floor overlooking the gardens trailing wisteria. A garden unaffected by the world outside its walls. Friezes of lapis blue and turquoise and yellow tile with foliations graced the pale brick along the entire front of the house. The stained glass glowed red and blue and green above the front doors, backlit by the Russian crystal chandelier in the hallway. Father had brought me for years, his felt hat on his head, then in his hand as we passed through the doors.

I climbed the steps, hesitated on the stone porch. I had come back a changed man, not in the mold of my father. I was about to see Mahastee. When I'd seen her at the concert in Bagh Ferdaus, she'd triggered emotions I'd long forgotten. Any moment now we'd come face-to-face. This was her home, a house set long ago into my flesh and bones.

I STOOD IN THE DARK vestibule; the foyer just beyond was the axis of the house. Two magnificent oil paintings of the epic battles of the *Shahnameh* still faced each other on the walls. Corridors with numerous doors stretched to the sides and back, their tiled floors covered in fine old rugs. The central corridor had double doors at the end with stained glass, mirroring the entrance, giving on to a large garden of cypress and walnut and fig and mulberry.

Coming down the center hallway, the old nanny of the household, Tourandokht, stalked a toddler with a bowl and spoonful of food. Swaying and clucking like a hen, she was in slow and painful pursuit of the child until she saw me. The child escaped.

"Reza!" she cried in surprise, heaping endearments on hugs and noisy kisses. "Let me get a good look at you."

She said I resembled Father more and more. She insisted I take lunch. I told her Nasrollah *mirza* was expecting me, and she understood and waddled away to tell him. Children I didn't recognize ran down one corridor and up behind Tourandokht, mimicking her waddle and giggling.

The elaborate chandelier with crystal prisms was dusty. The walls needed a fresh coat of paint. The old grandfather clock was still in the dark corner — the word *Tehran* set large and gleaming gold above six o'clock, the placid pendulums stately in the etched-glass case. I could hear it ticking. It was running eleven minutes late. I heard doors slamming and children laughing upstairs and the adults' indistinguishable voices in the drawing room and, to my left, the clunk and clatter in the kitchen every time its doors swung open. Lunch was over.

Nasrollah *mirza* never keeps one waiting. Tourandokht emerged from the far room, waving impatiently.

"Come on!" she said, summoning me before the group.

I went, the moment strangely mesmerizing but distant, like nostalgia.

"My dear boy!" cried Nasrollah *mirza* Mosharraf at the threshold, embracing me. He called to his wife and all his sons, Kavoos and Ardeshir and Bahram, smiling all the while as if the years gone between us didn't matter.

The drawing room was crowded, and the women assembled at one end looked me over with polite society smiles as the men, snug in tailored suits and old-world etiquette, scrutinized me. Behind them, the walls were adorned with friezes of plasterwork set above Qajar court paintings; potted palms stood in the corners; and the scent of tobacco and cigars mingled with sweetmeats and perfumes as a manservant took around a silver tray of tea, children threading their way past him, dodging mothers who were telling them they had to go upstairs to take a nap. I saw them all in one sweep, but I was looking for Mahastee.

SIX

MY HUSBAND WAS EMBELLISHING the gendarmerie attack in the dining room before my entire family.

"They're gunning them down these days in the streets!" Houshang said.

He spoke well, judging by his audience. He has presence and impeccable timing, and his ambition is to enthrall, for which I admit an ambivalent admiration. But he's omnivorous. Sometimes he gets on his high horse and stays there all during lunch. I get dagger looks from Mother, snide remarks from my brothers, who put him in his place from time to time, but not nearly enough. He's irrepressible.

He stood at the far end of the dining table, directing the children to turn down the two o'clock news on the radio. Father didn't object. He preferred the news, hovering by the old radio with his bowl of *asheh-reshteh*. He savors his traditional Friday soup while listening to news. But he does like acknowledging his one and only son-in-law, and Houshang takes advantage. Mother, stately and scented with Shalimar, kept her guests around the dining table. Mr. Mostaufi, old-world politician and ex-ambassador, and his wife, a Qajar aristocrat and wistful poet. Mrs. Vahaab and the colonel. Mr. Malekshah, poet and scholar. Dr. Atabak, with impeccable bearing, Father's old friend and family physician, called away to the phone as usual. Pushing back heavy strands of blond hair, Mother rearranged the greens and radishes, introducing her favorite stews as if they were members of the family. She encouraged more forays on the food, impeccably arranged on the rose-medallion china, interrupting Houshang as often as she could.

"More lamb? Try it with walnut pickle. Please take more *fesenjoon.*"

Houshang criticized the recent reshuffle of ministers in the cabinet, especially the four who had been dismissed. My youngest brother cut in about the mayor, reelected the week before. He adores criticizing the political oligarchy, though his burning ambition is to join it as soon as possible. Father complained the yogurt was too watery again. Wasn't it from the bazaar in Tajreesh? Dr. Atabak came back from his phone call and protested Mother had heaped too much food on his plate. The colonel had heaped enough on his to feed an army, his mustache bobbing up and down as he ate. He looked even less intelligent when chewing. Mother said the cook was now taking an inordinate amount of time to pray. It was so inconvenient! The colonel said religion was our failure. A modern army and modern economy and modern factories were the only answer.

"Modern progress is marvelous!" he said.

Mother said the new maid, aiming to be modern, was making eyes at the oldest son of the gardener. A grumpy son, and surely a leftist. "All leftists are grumpy!" said Mrs. Vahaab, stuffing the perfect O of her mouth with a morsel of bread loaded with feta cheese and spring onions and baby radishes.

Of Father's four sisters, the three there were having an argument about religion. The youngest was an armchair socialist and once-marching suffragette. The other two, pious aunts, spinsters who lived together, were devoted to French novels and religious vows and paid preachers who retold holy tragedies, and had taken the pilgrimage to Mecca and once taken me to Qom. Mr. Mostaufi tried arbitrating between these impossible women, mustering the skills of an old-world diplomat but to no avail. Mother's youngest brother was complaining to Dr. Atabak about his brutal migraines. His wife, with theatrically penciled eyebrows, tittered all over the room, eyeing Mother — her formidable opponent — furtively. And eyeing the Qajar glass lusters dripping with cut-glass prisms — family heirlooms — their tall tulip-shaped globes bearing gold-leaf portraits of Nassereddin Shah. My oldest brother, Kavoos, sat watching quietly. The way his wife — Miss Universe, as we call her behind her back — fritters away his money would turn anyone mute. She sat across from him gossiping, blond and pale and groomed and combed and cosseted into vacant perfection. He looked like he'd just stepped out of bed, maddeningly disheveled. He was once thrown out of a cabinet minister's outer office, he looked so slovenly. In a society where style means absolutely everything, they'd mistaken him for a loiterer. Mother says he does it on purpose. The more ostentation he sees in the capital — and his wife — the more rumpled he gets. Kavoos has Mother's blue eyes, and such aptitude for business that he gets Houshang's undivided attention. When dessert arrived, they were off talking tariffs.

The servants brought in fruits and halva and cakes and custards and sweetmeats and tea and the dented green dome of the marzipan cream cake.

"Look at the dent!" the colonel called to Houshang.

They exchanged dirty jokes, Houshang recasting the ambush as entertainment, yet another detail under control. Mr. Malekshah interrupted him. He was sullen because everyone had kept interrupting him at lunch and hadn't given him the chance to exult in his high-minded scholarship. Mother was fond of putting him in his place, like a lion tamer standing over a squirrel. Mr. Malekshah picked up the old argument he had going with the colonel about the state of our poetry since the Samanids, one thousand years before.

"What's it got to do with Marxists?" Houshang said.

"It's more important, that's what!" retorted Mr. Malekshah.

Houshang doesn't really care about the Samanids, nor any of their poets, nor anyone since who hasn't done really big business. He thinks of Father's old friends as fuddy-duddies of a bygone age. Irrelevant but tenacious, doomed to extinction.

Father had been saying he expected a guest at three-thirty, repeating it four times, but nobody had taken notice. He finally told me.

"Who is it?"

"Hajj-Alimardan's son."

I could hardly believe my ears when Tourandokht came in to announce Reza.

HE STOOD IN the doorway. I flinched. He was a man now, strapping, solid. Face ordered around cheekbones, composed.

The last time I'd seen him, he was an adolescent with an Adam's apple. He'd just started shaving, in that rite of passage to becoming a man. Though already then he'd had that perfect virtue, being manly. Watching him across the room now, it seemed as if he were returning only an hour later, so disconcerting was his presence and that face I knew well, its expressions and entire set of motions fixed permanently in my mind. Clean-shaven, steely, sedate. I'd watched him up close for years. As children we'd never hidden our feelings from others — that populated world of adults and relatives and strangers — climbing plum trees, bickering with my brothers and ganging up against them, riding in the open fields of Morshedabad. Reza rode better than the rest of us but never took notice of such things. We'd taught the village boys volleyball and organized teams, but Reza tutored them all year and helped them do homework. He'd taught them how to swim, lined them up like soldiers by the lower pool, overgrown with moss, and taught them to dive in. "What patience!" my brothers said. Then that last year he started to defy his father and look away from his mother, and everything shifted, the way he and I looked at each other, looked at others. From that weekend that last spring, when I brought records my parents had bought in Europe and threw a party for cousins and friends. Reza didn't show up, and I left the chitchat and laughter to go find him and persuade him to join us. He came out under the grove behind the house and stood. Defiant, glowering. I went up and insisted he join us, then unexpectedly raised my hand, rubbed my palm across his face, and laughed and teased how he was going to be prickly forever. He grabbed my wrist and pulled, and suddenly we were two inches away from each other, staring, alone under the trees, our breaths close, our irises dark moons in the sea of our eyes. Then someone called out my name and we pulled away. After that night and for that last vacation there with him, everything was different, as if he and I had made a promise to each other and intended to keep it. We'd hidden it well from others, what we felt for each other. And then they had left suddenly. And when he'd come back that one summer night when we were sixteen and had kissed me in the garden, its fiery pleasure had stayed with me, that night and long after, its sheer force relenting, shifting, but remaining sheltered in my imagination through whatever came later — wisdom, experience — like a source remembered by the river.

It all came to me in a rush, disorienting, but intact and unequivocal like revelation. I kept back. I wanted to watch him before he could watch me. That inscrutable face, slightly scowling but even-tempered, eyes like his mother's, quick and quiet. His father, we had adored. He'd always had a singular awareness, nearly eerie, able to read what I was feeling. No man could do that anymore.

He didn't see me, what with Father calling to Mother and all my brothers gathering by the door to greet him. Funny how Father forgot to call me, introducing him all the while to others. I stood back, taking it in. I couldn't run up and throw my arms around him like the others. We'd shake hands, smile, act cordial. Father turned and saw me.

"Mahastee, it's Reza!" he said, beaming.

Father beams so seldom. I nodded, setting down my glass of tea.

Reza was staring, ever the straight shooter, and I went over and shook hands. We smiled, cordial, neither of us much good at small talk. My youngest brother took over, firing questions. "So where have you been?" "You're married?" "Which ministry?" "How's . . ."

I listened for a bit, then turned back to where I'd been sitting to pick up my glass of tea, catching my reflection on the way in the painted Qajar mirror. I was smiling. That's when I saw Houshang's reflection watching from behind me, the light catching his glossy black hair, which he so prizes and fingers. His high forehead, well-proportioned features, the spoiled-brat mouth unaffected by age. It was his eyes that betrayed a peculiar expression, as if he'd seen the next move on a chessboard he disdained.

My eyes swept back to my reflection. I looked older than my husband. Something steadfast, abstinent, about my features. What had my face betrayed to him? Lost pleasures. The past can't be wrenched away from you. Only the future. It's the future we can't possess. Walking through the door, Reza had brought the two colliding. I sat down, the crowded room falling away, a strange feeling resounding through me as if the past had come to subvert the future.

SEVEN

NASROLLAH *mirza* SAT IN the armchair of his study, surrounded by his books, his white hair capping his head like snow on Mount Damavand, his puffy eyes behind glasses, capped by lush eyebrows. He still possessed that augustly discreet presence and the unassuming charm. His ancestors were up on the walls, with holster and gun and horse and homestead. They held poses under cypresses, erect on bentwood chairs, clenching walking sticks, in Qajar fezzes and karakul hats and Pahlavi caps. Never smiling — it wasn't fashionable to smile in pictures in those days. Revealing anything to posterity was unbecoming, even revealing anything to oneself.

A manservant brought a tray of tea and sliced cake with a green frosting and left it on the desk. My eyes flitted over the vast collection of books — the entire far wall foreign books — registering works by Shadman, Isa Sadeq, Natel Khanlari, Foroughi's classic three-volume *History of Western Philosophy,* a bound copy of Moayyer al-Mamalek's *The Notables of Nassereddin Shah's Era,* and

Mohammad Massoud's antiquated novels, *Nocturnal Pleasures* and *Life's Springtime*. On the small side table by my elbow lay an old and slender rare book — Mohtasham al-Saltaneh Esfandiari's *Causes of Our Misery and Its Cure*. I remembered Father telling me about it.

"How's your mother, Shaukat *khanom?*" Nasrollah *mirza* asked.

We reminisced. I said Mother was as well as could be expected, her grandchildren the light of her eyes. He told me how much he missed Father. "My troubleshooter, my old friend . . . ," he called him, his voice tapering off. He said Morshedabad was now a neglected estate, their lands in Azarbaijan gone, his peasants now strangers to him and beholden to the government, the regime holding families like his at arm's length and with suspicion, even though their holdings had shrunk and an entirely new generation now prospered. "'Those reactionary landlords,' that's what they called us!" he said. "They hated us strong, they patronize us weak." He recalled his father and mother buried next to each other in the family mausoleum in Reyy. He remembered the houses of his parents, the legion of attendants attached to them, the nannies of his childhood squatting at the edge of the pool, scrubbing clothes and gossiping. He smiled, growing younger at this. He said once he had shared a life with them and the tenants and peasants on his lands in Azarbaijan. He stared into space. Then he came around by recounting a hunting trip he and Father had taken together at the invitation of the chiefs of the Bakhtiari tribe; the year a hot wind had burned eight hundred pear trees and shriveled them; the house in the garden of Morshedabad he'd overseen being built brick by brick.

The old days. Nasrollah *mirza* said they had been good.

"At my age, saying anything less would be admitting defeat. Futility," he said. "I'm left to mull over the past. Whatever the mistakes, it's too late now."

He leaned forward, offering me a glass of tea.

"I don't understand what's going on anymore," he said. "It's become a — such a circus. We're under the illusion we've leaped forward body and soul. It's no good leaping by decree. If anything, our underpinnings should be secure, permanent. I'm not so sure if — well, we'll see —"

He paused. We drank tea and he insisted I try the cake.

"We'll see," he repeated absently.

I started telling him about my friend Jalaleddin Hojjati. He listened, veined hands covered with liver spots and fingers interlocked. A flicker constricted his eyes when he heard the words *SAVAK, Komiteh.* Disappointment. It was inevitable; no one liked stories about the secret police. I'd ruined his Friday, perhaps even stirring the languid profundity of his obscure disillusionments. Then ever so quickly he resumed an air of gracious concern.

As long as I'd known Nasrollah *mirza* he'd possessed tact and poise, he had emanated goodness, but that goodness was now muted and irrelevant.

He didn't say a word until I had said more than was necessary. He understood about trouble, abuses of power, dead ends, but spared me the exposition.

"I saw his mother and sister in the street," I said finally. "The mother looked haunted."

"Yes," Nasrollah *mirza* said vaguely. He reached for a gold Parker pen, asked for Jalal's full name, and wrote carefully, promising to make calls and consult Kavoos. "My son's the one with contacts in high places. I wonder about this country when I hear about his contacts. They're such — such pretentious people."

He accompanied me to the hall with his customary tact, murmuring it was time for him to slip away upstairs for his nap.

I wanted to make my exit then and there, since I had no business back in the living room. The Mosharraf brothers I'd once been friends with when we were children and had been thrown together ignorant of the world and friendship had been easy, but that seemed long ago. Their father had evidently retreated discreetly into a shell, into ever-constricting circles in order to safeguard and cultivate his integrity, typical of his class. Mahastee I'd seen all of three minutes. Perhaps another time, I told myself just as she came out into the hall. As she walked toward us, I felt a surge of indignation at how much I wanted to see her, this sudden weakness I felt. In my anger I decided to leave quickly, before she had the chance to talk to me, but still I waited as she covered the distance.

She was ten feet away when I remembered suddenly how one summer they had arrived for the holidays in Morshedabad and she had jumped out of the car and run over to me and thrown her arms around me and cried, "Reza! It's summer! I'm so happy to see you!" I had felt my cheeks flush while she had danced around the trees. I was impatient for every vacation, always asking Father when they'd arrive and how long they'd stay. With each year my exasperation increased every time she left. She emitted radiance, changed the garden and meaning of life when she was there. She brought me books from Tehran and odd things like colored globes and flashlights and card decks and pens, and then once a Meccano set from abroad, which I later discovered she'd bribed one of her brothers to give to me. She was uncanny in her deceptions. "But I prefer your house to mine!" she'd say. All because she knew it was easier for her to visit mine and stay until all hours since Mother didn't like it when I stayed over too long at theirs. The only gift I ever gave her was a blue-glazed octagonal tile with a chip in the corner. "It's from the shrine in the village," I said. "I found it in the rubble. It's for good luck." "I didn't think you were superstitious," she said. "I'm not, but you are," I said.

That day she threw her arms around me, I had that sudden intake of breath, a strange quivering ripped through me. When I turned, I saw Father staring at me as if he'd become stone; then he turned and walked away. My heart sank, knowing that he understood more than I wanted him to, more than anyone else, and I had to resort to concealment. I disliked the change — the heaviness of his gaze, the obscure signs of his displeasure, the implication that she and I were not equal, for she thought I was her equal and behaved that way and that was enough, though I couldn't see her father or mine doing the same. From that moment until they left, Father started giving me chores constantly to keep me away. She'd run through the trees calling to me — "Reza, I'm bored! What's keeping you away?" — and I'd wait and watch until Father was off somewhere to go join them. The next summer when they arrived, he must have thought I was cured he was so indifferent. He went off to Azarbaijan to oversee their estates, and we spent entire weeks in the garden together, and running through the trees after dinner, I knew we were free and loved this freedom fiercely, all the more because I sensed it wasn't ours and could be taken. I knew, long before she did. That last spring, in my fourteenth year, my sense of freedom suddenly evaporated as I went lurching between feeling angry and frustrated and solitary. I kept arguing with Father that I wanted to leave for Tehran and attend school in the capital. Gripped often by maddening flashes of rage at the limits of freedom and Mahastee's appearances and disappearances, which were determined by her world and always beyond my control, I knew nothing could assuage my feelings. I turned to books more and more. Then I read in a novel how those who love fiercely so young see that love destroyed as adults. I knew it was a lie. I thought then nothing could destroy what I felt.

As I watched her now, a woman self-possessed, it seemed impossible that nearly nothing had once stood between us. Then two feet away I saw straight into her eyes. She was still utterly herself; I knew her well. The moment was hypnotic because I knew the fullness of desire — desire and regret — can never be understood nor fully exist until you leave. As I had long ago.

EIGHT

FATHER SPENT HALF AN HOUR in the study with Reza, the door closed.

My sisters-in-law set up a table for bridge while exchanging gossip about dinner parties inaugurating the season. "When is yours?" they asked me.

Dr. Atabak was praising the latest medical breakthroughs in France when Mr. Malekshah, always the pedant, interrupted him to define the complete benefits of parsley and carrot juice. Then just as he was getting started on the marvels of Swedish calisthenics, they were asked to play bridge. My two pious aunts retired upstairs to take their afternoon nap. The marching suffragette went up to read Toynbee, but not before hearing the ladies hold forth on the fabulous new pearls of our favorite jeweler, who always fawned on them and was always willing to make exchanges with tact and discretion.

Before Reza's sudden arrival, Father and his lifelong friend Mr. Mostaufi, abandoning the damask-covered chairs of the dining room for the corner armchairs under the imperious portrait of Grandfather garnished with medals, had been indulging in one of their favorite pastimes: proceeding through the vast and interconnected family trees of the aristocracy, branch to branch. This was always triggered by some news of an impending wedding or funeral or someone indisposed — as they called the sick — and they were off, going from parents to grandparents to aunts and uncles and progeny and intermarriages, fanning out into ever-rippling circles, all the while approving of each other's memory and knowledge and dedication in this field by saying, "Yes, yes, and of course you know . . ." Now Mr. Mostaufi was dozing peacefully, alone in the corner. We all knew his wife would wake him up to lecture him any moment.

Houshang looked around and announced he wanted to go home immediately. He'd charmed everyone long enough and the show was over. I wanted to talk to Father about Peyman Bashirian, so I told him to go ahead. He hung back and said we'd all leave together, taking up backgammon with my brother Kavoos and the colonel. Houshang is so predictable, staying only to see what I was up to.

We had more tea with dates and dried mulberries, choosing from a succession of sweets arranged in perfect pyramids on footed silver dishes around the drawing room. The dice rolled while the men played, cards shuffled at the bridge table. The afternoon sun was sinking behind the heavy drapes.

I waited. Suddenly I wasn't waiting to talk to Father but to see Reza. With my husband watching from across the room, I thought of him, what he and I possessed together. A childhood, coming of age, families entwined for generations. What we had escaped was the fate — the compulsion — of being together.

I listened for footsteps in the hall, beyond the curtained French doors, eyeing my watch. Mother eyed me, talking about the potted plants and Seville orange trees in her hothouse to her good friends

Mrs. Mostaufi and Mrs. Vahaab. Mrs. Mostaufi slipped away to awaken her dozing husband. Mrs. Vahaab took up much of the sofa, her ample body dipping into a green velvet dress and resurfacing at very puffy ankles. The penciled mole by her penciled lips shuddered as she spoke, her inflection epic, like her proportions. She's known for her voice. Her husband, the retired colonel, lives at her feet. When she croons old favorites, he dabs his eyes with a starched handkerchief, overcome. Today she was talking about her bunions. The colonel said with military panache that it was time to leave. The Mostaufis returned arguing about the appropriateness of napping and, overhearing the colonel, agreed it was time to leave.

Mother accompanied them outside.

I flipped through magazines, mostly cut-and-paste rehashes of foreign periodicals. True confessions, crimes of passion, the art scene, cooking, pop singers like Aref and Googoosh, trendy movie stars, nostalgic tributes to dead artists like Mahvash. Mother subscribed to them all, embracing the grand and trivial with the contemplative enthusiasm of a philosopher. A door opened and closed, and I went out into the hall. Father and Reza were shaking hands by the grandfather clock between vistas of epic battles. I walked toward them and they smiled at me guardedly. They couldn't have only been reminiscing. Reza made to leave and thanked Father, very official, and Father made him promise to visit more often.

Then he turned, and his eyes fixed on me for an instant with the measureless look of someone about to leave on an interminable voyage. And the moment came back with full force — how he'd left through that door when I'd been sixteen. With agonizing recognition I felt that old panic, taking fate with a blow, then turning away down the long tunnel of years.

I didn't want him to leave again. I asked how it was that he worked in an office.

"Don't you like teaching anymore?"

He smiled. "Of course I do."

"My sons need a tutor," I said.

He forgot to say anything. My first thought was I'd insulted him, now that he worked for a government department. Father interceded by saying I couldn't find a more gifted and dedicated teacher than Reza. Unless he was too busy? Reza said, "No, no." We made arrangements by the front door.

I wanted to walk him out, but when he opened the door we saw Mrs. Vahaab gesticulating to Mother by the driveway. She could never stop talking.

At the wheel of his great big American car, the colonel raised his voice, entreating. "Get in, madame, for God's sake, get in."

Reza left, and I remained in the entrance, an adult in possession of my life realizing we could never be in full possession of our emotions, their great force like a wind.

I looked up. The Russian chandelier was dirty. I told Father, who said dusting in a city with desert winds was an exercise in futility.

He made his way back into his study at my request, a little peeved, but mostly abstracted. I speculated on what Reza had told him. Housing trouble, an illness in the family, an unsecured debt? Father sat, withdrawn. I told him Peyman Bashirian's story all in one go. Father took it, impassive, the pout in his face deepening.

"What do you think?" I said, sitting by the sepia picture of Grandfather with a handlebar mustache and stern eyes. He had studied at the polytechnic under Prussian and Austrian instructors before going abroad.

"What's the world coming to?" said Father wearily. "Reza was here about his friend who's a political prisoner. But these things don't concern us."

I felt dismayed at Father's reticence, though I knew it was his exacting tact that made him so impassive. And also the insularity of a supremely refined man who had been cut off from the daily life of his own country.

"What's the point of rebellion?" Father said. "It's unseemly — it's vulgar. Why don't these young people use the proper channels?"

Pitting the words *proper* and *unseemly* and *rebellion* against one another in one sweep, Father had given expression to the disposition of an entire culture.

I asked again how we could help Mr. Bashirian get his son out of prison.

"Surely he has someone to turn to," Father said.

"Of course he doesn't."

"You're certain this isn't some mistake?"

"Father, his son's in there. What can we do?"

"My dear," Father said discreetly, "tell him to be patient."

"That's easy for us to say."

Father sighed. "Let's see what I can do, if anything."

I find what I said to him after that inexcusable. I looked him straight in the eyes and said, "Father, what's wrong? Can't you see what's going on around you? What have we got to lose? They've already turned their backs on you. You're the one who always lectured us on principles and integrity. As if they're the cure-all and be-all! Now you say, 'Let's see'? 'Let's see' is the worst kind of excuse. But to say 'if anything'! That's giving up hope."

AT NIGHT I STARED at the photograph of Grandmother that I kept on my desk.

She sat under poplars shimmering silvery in quiet splendor. Father's mother. Austere with the widow's peak and square face, the look in her eyes sweetened with old age, still wearing the pearl necklace. It gratified her to be feared. She said it scared off bores and hypocrites. She adored the pageantry of small moments. She adored rituals — early morning inspections of her rose garden, tea at five for the oddest assortment of people, whom she contradicted and provoked unfailingly, though they always came back, the *iftar* evening meal during the month of fasting, exacting interrogations of her household over accounts and alms for the needy and the doings of each and every member of her unwieldy retinue in Tehran and on her estates in Azarbaijan. Father had given me her necklace on my sixteenth birthday. I'd worn it for the first time the summer night Reza had come back and I'd taken him through the garden. Grandmother's pearls, brought back in the winter of 1911 from Saint Petersburg, where Grandfather had been told of political agitations by radicals and anarchists, and one night, returning in a carriage from a formal dinner there in honor of two Romanov princes, he'd seen students thrashed, then arrested three blocks away, and his friends had reassured him, "Think nothing of it." Instead his host, the grand duke, had taken him the next morning to buy the pearl necklace and an exquisite enamel frame by Fabergé, crowned with diamonds. Everyone said I looked like her, Grandmother, and Reza's father had said the same watching me grow up year after year. "May God never take her from us!" he said. "She knows our heart. Because she sees with the inner eye and her intuitions are spiritual." After her death he had indulged me with stories about her and that vanished world, stories that consoled us both and that he told better than anyone else, even her own children.

I HAD BROUGHT office work to finish at home. I pulled out the report we'd just completed for publication, plopped down on the couch, read far into the night. Here was a whole country made up of statistics and graphs and charts. Apparitions on paper. But where was meaning?

I'd confronted Father as if he were the progenitor of all deeds and words, accountable for the doings of a nation. I should have brought him tea at his age and asked about the old days. We would have strolled out into the back garden between the trees. And he could point to where he'd pruned and planted, where he cultivated seedlings, and he would say: My father planted those and I planted . . . that mulberry, to bear fruit, like the quince and crab apple. The walnut to please your mother, the mighty oak to celebrate a firstborn son, the almonds for a white spring. The weeping willow by the stream of mountain water, and the pomegranate for its exquisite fruit. The Judas tree and lilac for their color and fragrance. He'd take my hand. He likes to walk that way. Never depending on his cane nor on what Dr. Atabak prescribes for him. He likes his garden more than people, more than governments, adornments, and even ambition finally.

He knows, he knows. He thinks it's futile. And anything he says is dust in desert winds.

NINE

I GOT BACK AFTER NINE from teaching my classes at the Rahnema High School. I changed and wolfed down dinner while reviewing the new agenda for our underground group — the compelling points of our new bulletins, the importance of our *Night Letter* and its distribution to students and workers and teachers, the long list of translations for Dr. Hadi.

Early summer brought us hysteria and paranoia after the SAVAK raid. For years we had been carefully evading the secret police. That day, Jalal knocked at my door at six in the morning and said he'd been tipped off. He wouldn't tell me how he knew. "They're going to hit before midnight!" he said. "How much do they know?" I asked. "Not much, not much," he said impatiently, "just your location." I ran around all day to find the others, then got all tied up renting a van to move our mimeograph machine, and then we got stuck in traffic and got there late. We left a watchman at the corner, then couldn't find parking. We backed the van into the narrow side street, double-parked, and went in. Panicky that they would hit any minute, we frantically swept through our two-room basement to salvage our files, dragging out the mimeograph machine, rushing up and down the stairs, ignoring one of the neighbors, who came out on his landing to ask questions. One of our guys finally threatened him, and they started to quarrel and I had to pull them apart. "You're crazy!" I hissed, dragging him away. "They'll get here any minute!" We first packed the van, which was obstructing the street, repeating our escape plan as we did, then we shoved everything else in the car and took off, narrowly escaping.

One week later we met at a brand-new location in Pamenar. As soon as we got in, the clique of three stood up and went on a diatribe about betrayal and blood and revenge. "They're so full of shit it's unbelievable!" I whispered to Dr. Hadi. They were the graduate students from the cities of Tabriz and Mashhad, always shrill and dogmatic and belligerent. They continued all night, keeping the upper hand as the hours progressed with veiled threats, pretending they had special information about how we'd been betrayed. They started interrogating us one by one like a military tribunal, bragging all the while about their greater commitment and purity of purpose. "We brought you new blood!" they cried. Then they turned to me. They had disliked me most since that winter when I'd come up against one of them for the editorship of our paper and won out.

That night they took their revenge and started grilling me like a criminal, disassembling my life, denouncing my background and family and loyalties. I was bourgeois, I wasn't committed, I was impure, I was an equivocator. I didn't follow the code of behavior and reasoning they upheld. "Where is your burning dedication to absolute revolution?" they yelled. I was always equivocating. I was an agitator, a revisionist, a renegade. I said, "The only absolute I feel is a revulsion for you. You reason exactly like the regime you condemn!" At this they got so outraged they resorted to hysterics. They threatened to search my home, confiscate my papers, denounce me to the Left as a traitor. "Wait and see what they'll do to you then!" one of them shouted. "They'll shoot you in the street!" "The hell with you," I said. "You've turned into SAVAK yourself! Learned well from the very power we detest. It's our own methods that have become detestable." I went home, I didn't care what they did. We had forsaken all democratic principles and turned ugly and demagogic and dictatorial. Years of painstaking work, and we were about to crash and burn! We were our own worst enemy.

I stayed away. The others sent me private messages, which I ignored. I was already planning another group, making a list. After a month, one night several of them came knocking at my door. They said we'd had a crisis, bad blood, but it was over. The clique from the provinces had splintered off and the rift was complete. They made promises. We had a history together, shared a vision, we couldn't throw it away. One week later we hammered things out. The upheaval had forced us to reassess everything and finally change the way we did business. We split into four sections of nine, redid our chain of command, the arrangement of our cells. Any key member could start another cell of nine, but only the few at the top knew the arrangement of our network and key contacts. I was asked to head our youth group, reorganize, and find a place for its headquarters.

That night I could finally report at our ten o'clock meeting that I'd found a safe house downtown for our youth group. My new recruit, Hossein Farahani, had already proved himself unusually valuable. I had a perfectly located site, and well disguised — the back of the auto repair garage off Fauziyeh Square, where Hossein worked. I'd also been charged with finding a property outside Tehran, and I'd located a garden in Karaj to house the printing press for our organization — this through an old contact of mine, Majid M., a fellow student from my school days.

Majid and I had come of age during the politically charged days of Mossadeq. We'd sold papers then for all political parties without really understanding their differences — Pan-Iranist, Third Force, Iran Party — in Lalehzar and Estanbul. We lived in the same neighborhood and attended the same school. Late nights we snuck out of our rooms and ran through the streets scribbling nationalist slogans on walls with bits of charcoal, distributing leaflets we pulled out of our socks in the dead of night, running ahead of patrols that were sweeping through Tehran to arrest us. Father caught me several times sneaking out late at night and threatened to confiscate my bicycle. Always repeating, "A boy shouldn't be involved in politics." But it never stopped me. Then he threatened seriously, the night I admitted I was there with Majid at the Saadi Theater for the opening of *Lady Windermere's Fan.* That night the Left had sent a young recruit to take a famous journalist and anarchist to the theater to avert a plot by the regime's thugs to assassinate him in the offices of his newspaper *Shouresh.* Majid and I were fascinated by the anarchist and knew the recruit — a high-school student who greatly impressed us — and we'd tagged along. Father was furious. He said I was playing with fire, I would be arrested, he didn't approve of the leftist friends I kept. I would burn in their hell! He was going to send me back to the provinces. I didn't see Majid again, but we kept in touch even after he left for university in England. He returned once from Manchester years later when our group was reunited and took part in large demonstrations that threatened the stability of the regime and once again failed. Two months ago he returned from abroad, sent in across the Kurdestan border to take charge at home. He's teaching English at the Simin Institute. At night he teaches revolution, spewing political idioms in English, which intimidates the guys in the Left at home. He's our connection to the antiregime Confederation of Iranian Students in Europe.

I looked at my watch. Before leaving for the meeting, I had to scrounge around among my books and files and papers. I had an obligation to Jalal since his disappearance. First I had to find his parents, but I'd lost the address.

Hojjati. There it was, the scrap of paper, in a tin can on the shelf by the tea and sugar. Backstreets near the train station with a telephone number. The father was a devout mason from the provinces. He'd thrived in the capital jerry-building in Eshratabad. Once, in faraway Semnan, he'd tended sheep around desolate villages, married a first cousin, then apprenticed in town with a local mason who beat him. But he'd learned to lay bricks like lightening. One year he'd taken his wife and hitched a ride on a truckload of pistachios to Tehran, first living in a hovel south of the city, a hole in the ground covered with sheets of plastic. Then he'd moved up, bought a house close to the train station. Khaniabad, off Masjed-e-Qanari, that was where I'd find them.

Jalal never discussed family. They didn't exist for him.

His younger sister told me bits and pieces on a crosstown bus. I'd seen her once at Jalal's shop when I'd come in and overheard them arguing in the back. I heard him say, "It's none of your business." "You're a no-good son!" she countered. That's all I heard, and she'd brushed past me, flushed with anger.

A month later we were waiting at the same bus stop by Najmieh Hospital, where she worked as a nurse. We boarded the same bus, and she talked. Her name was Soghra. I felt her motive for opening up to me was to chastise Jalal. She had lighter skin and a frail but cunning disposition, and eventually she started to flirt. She smiled at me; she had a gold tooth and looked like a washerwoman. She gave me her address on a lark and said she lived with her parents. "When you call," she whispered, "say it's from the hospital. Say you're a doctor." She couldn't have callers but had dreams of snagging a doctor. I took the paper, registering her nerve, considering her pious background. When she got off the bus, I saw her take out a light blue scarf and cover her head quickly.

I GOT OFF THE BUS the next night near the train station. The man at the greengrocer's told me to turn left at the intersection beyond the public bath. He knew the Hojjati family. But I didn't stop to chat.

Dinner hour, with throngs at the traffic lights in the noise and smog and hustle. A vendor in a threadbare jacket dished out steaming ruby-red beets from an old rickety cart. Laborers carried home freshly baked loaves wrapped in newspaper, the backstreets smelling of fried oil and kerosene and coal.

We knew doctrines and dialectics, but not yet how to reach the masses. We had no roots here.

I dipped into narrow back alleys right and left and rang a doorbell. I'd come late to catch them at home. His father opened the door. He had dark skin stretched over high cheekbones, a taut and ferocious face. Turkoman blood. I introduced myself as his son's close friend before he let me into a half-lit passage. He called to his wife. A small woman came up and peered at me, chalky pale, birdlike and shriveled, her dark chador wrapped at her waist and slung over her head. I recognized her from the time in the street.

The father grilled me. He'd retained the provincial accent.

"He gave you our address?"

I equivocated, said I'd come for news of Jalal. "Have you heard anything? Has anyone called about him?"

He shook his head. "My daughter told us. She saw the shop shuttered and asked on the street. She checked hospitals and police stations. Even the morgue."

"When did you last see him?"

"He didn't want us," he said gruffly. "He's an ungrateful son."

"Maybe he's been arrested —"

The mother started to weep. The father stepped in front of her; I could see he was frightened.

"What d'you know?" he demanded.

"Nothing," I said. "I'm here to see if you do."

The mother flinched as if she'd been struck, letting out a small wail. "He's disappeared. Just like that. Melted into the ground! O God, pity him and help us! He's our one and only. The light of our eyes."

Grabbing her chador, she wept, beating her chest lightly with her fist. Her husband ordered her to calm down.

I asked the father if he'd checked Jalal's apartment. He didn't even know where Jalal lived.

"Can't you help my son?" the mother implored me.

"What're you talking about, woman?" the father snapped.

She started weeping again. They made a pitiful twosome. I asked if Jalal's sister could get into his apartment.

The father squinted, cheekbones rising to engulf wary eyes. "How d'you know her?"

I said I didn't. He said she was on night shift at the hospital. I suggested someone search the apartment to remove damaging evidence. Not that there was any, I added.

"Just in case," I said. Surely SAVAK had already taken what it needed.

The father didn't object. I was about to give him his son's address.

"You do it," he said. "My daughter's always at the hospital. She wouldn't know what to look for. I don't have much education. Do us this favor."

I said I knew Jalal's landlady and could get into the flat with her latchkey.

In the alley he took me aside to tell me he'd appealed to a *hajji* in the bazaar to find Jalal. "He's devout and principled. I trust him. He says nothing is sacred for this government. They're out to ruin the bazaar merchants. There's a conspiracy to tear down the bazaar. What for, to build a four-lane highway? To build more casinos? They have no shame." He shook his head angrily. "I'm at the Jazayeri Mosque there every chance I get. I hear what's going on. The *hajji* belongs to an influential group. It's through them I send my dues to our ayatollah in Najaf. Our beacon in darkness. God willing, may he come home one day. God willing."

On the main street a boy cried, *"Kayhan . . . Ettela'at. . . ."* I bought an evening paper under the streetlight. The front page had an item at the bottom about an ambush against terrorists. They'd arrested four men in north Tehran, armed to the teeth and dangerous. They were routing them out. The article vituperated against the Red Reaction, the Black Reaction, lauding the glories of the White Revolution. There they went again, pontificating with colors. Eternal barren rhetoric.

I SHUT THE DOOR on Jalal's flat at a quarter past nine the next evening, turning off the lights before leaving. I returned the key to the elderly landlady, Esmat *khanom,* who detained me to groan about her bad heart and crippling arthritis. The light showed up her beaked nose and yellowish skin and hair. Jalal said she was a vicious gossip. Much as I tried, she kept me outside her front door with digressions that threatened to go on forever, her dentures clicking. I looked at my watch.

"Nine-thirty!" I said.

The building was on a dead end, an enclave for Assyrians, who were exemplary boarders according to Esmat *khanom.* "They are clean!" she said, in the fastidious way one discusses those of foreign origin.

Then she got in her digs. "Though I would never touch tea from their glass nor food from their plate. And they drink so, dear Mr. Nirvani. And their young, well, they've got such an indecent lifestyle. They're promiscuous, these Christians. Without a thought of burning in hell!"

She said the city had become a vile and shameless place full of lechers and sinners and she was waiting for the Absent One — the Twelfth Imam — coming at the end of time to deliver us of all evil. Absentees are her favorite subject. I said good night before she could get on to her absentee husband of fifteen years, who had left home one night, never to return. She was still waiting, as if he'd stepped out for fresh air and was due home any moment. Jalal said the man had taken a mistress and lived blissfully in the provinces, in Behbahan. The building was all Esmat *khanom* had in the world, thanks to her departed father, an enterprising tailor and dry cleaner.

For a woman so morbidly fond of absentees, she hadn't started up about Jalal again. When I'd rung her doorbell and asked for the key, I'd lied by telling her I was running an errand for him. "He's in Bandar Bushehr," I explained. "And last week you came here all worried!" she said, reminding me to tell him she wanted her rent. This she now repeated before I took off.

"Tell him," she called after me, "or I'll throw his stuff out!"

I turned into Jami, a tree-lined residential street. Immediately at the corner I noticed a dark car with two men inside. They were watching me. I continued without missing a beat; they had no way of knowing who I was. When I'd gone far enough, I stopped and looked back. Neither of them had left the car. I leaned against a tree away from the streetlight and waited. Five minutes. The two men got out, dark suits carrying one box. I followed at a distance and saw them enter the building. I waited outside and watched for lights on the fourth floor. They came on at the count of fifty-seven. They hadn't stopped to interrogate Esmat *khanom,* but they would on their way out. The only way she wouldn't squeal about me would be in my presence, so I slipped back into the building. Checking up the stairwell, I rang the doorbell to her ground-floor apartment. She wasn't overly surprised to see me.

"May I come in?"

I stepped in, closing the door behind me, which alarmed her. I said I'd forgotten something important and she thought I wanted the key again. As she shuffled away to fetch it, I remembered *Crime and Punishment,* when Raskolnikov comes in to kill the old woman.

"Why the peculiar look?" she demanded, back with the key.

The two men were upstairs going through Jalal's life. Downstairs I temporized with Dostoyevsky, waiting for them. I wasn't about to let Esmat *khanom* betray me. Taking the key from her, I held forth with a fairly comprehensive summary of the novel. She listened, lighting up at the pathetic sufferings of the Marmeladov family, bewildered at Raskolnikov's confession. When I heard footsteps in the stairwell, I quickly asked to use her bathroom. Slightly dismayed, she pointed to the back. The doorbell rang and our eyes locked as I went past her into the next room. I kept behind the door there, listening, eyeing the window through which I could escape.

The two men at the door said they wanted information on her fourth-floor tenant.

"Hojjati, Jalal," barked out one of them.

They inquired about his comings and goings. Friends, habits, visitors. She obliged, effusive from terror, her inflection shallow, revealing Jalal to be a quiet tenant minding his own business. No one ever visited him.

They asked how long he'd been a lodger. Two years. Who had a key? No one except the lodger, as far as she knew. Had anyone come by these past days? Anything peculiar? Be honest. She denied it.

"We've been watching the building," they said.

"I wouldn't notice."

"Anyone tonight?" they repeated.

She said no, a shade too quickly. "Why, what's he done?"

They left her midsentence, the clatter of their regulation shoes hollow. She shut the door with a loud thud, eyeing me nervously as I came in from the back room. I handed back the key.

"Where's Jalal?" she demanded.

"They have him."

"I want my rent."

"You'll have to wait," I said.

"I don't want trouble. I'm a lonely, miserable old woman. Look how everyone treats me, like dirt!"

I checked at the window. The car was gone, so I could leave.

"Why did he confess?"

Jalal hadn't. She meant Raskolnikov. "It's a long story —"

THEY HAD LIED about watching the building, or at least about how long they had been there that night. I'd spent about forty minutes in Jalal's flat, and if they were already parked at the corner, they would have seen the lights going on and off. They hadn't. They'd arrived after nine, making it sound like they were there night and day, watching.

Jalal's two rooms were modest. The place didn't look like it had been touched in weeks, a fine layer of dust on everything. An unmade bed, several melamine dishes in the cupboard, the table in the kitchenette with a half-empty bottle of Ettehadieh vodka and two rickety chairs, dirty dishes in the sink, and on one of the two electric burners, a small pot of desiccated Turkish coffee. There was one picture, of Forough, plastered inside the door of his closet. A dead woman, killed long ago in an accident. "Our first sensual rebel since Eve!" Jalal said. He admired how her famous poems had gone against everything, her intimate torments, daring confessions, her dramatic death. Dark hair, penciled eyes, hair piled up. You'd think she was actually his lover.

Jalal was in his prime, proud of his razor-sharp insight, his analytical powers. He had a keen and fiery intelligence and an unfailing knowledge of people, nearly eerie. In the early days when we'd first met, after watching him for a while I had finally invited him to join our restricted circle. We had started as politically active students in the electrifying days of Mossadeq and the National Front and nationalization of oil, terminated by the CIA-engineered coup against Mossadeq. We were indelibly marked by those events.

We were Jalal's first stop along the Left. I was his mentor then, and he was an eager and restless novice. In those days I wrote about liberation movements like the Algerian War of Independence and submitted to certain magazines until I got censored. Jalal would bring his writings, ask for advice, then get all worked up when I edited them. He detested being criticized. A feverish writer, he was attending Tehran University for a degree in sociology, always arguing with his professors. And forever casting around, shopping for doctrines and ideologies that could measure up to his appetite. Then he disappeared.

Later when he called Mother and Zari and left a message for me, he'd already completed his military service and owned the coffee shop. He kept a picture of Che in the cash register under all the bills with the imperial picture. Che this, Che that, he kept saying. Che! The Perfect Man. He needed money and started borrowing from me but always paid me back. All the while he kept up the front, talking about being enrolled in a graduate program — he was out of the shop so often — though he was vague about this to everyone. I knew it was a lie. Militant, atheist, he was sophisticated for the son of a shepherd and bricklayer. Very disdainful of his lower-class family and peasant heritage, which went against what he preached.

We had arguments. Jalal hated how I accused the new generation — his — of being rootless. Of not knowing anything about its political history. Of being shut out, cut off. He much preferred arguing that great big engine of history — class struggle. Or lecturing about the struggling masses, though his concern seemed aloof and perfunctory. He knew our group had connections with Marxists in Europe from the Confederation of Iranian Students there and in the progressive National Front. But we had avoided the old mold of a Leninist party structure. We kept small — a political association, recruiting and training. We maintained a shrewd and disciplined group, secular intellectuals intent on proving our ideological independence. Unlike the pro-Moscow Stalinist Tudeh Communists, whom we distrusted. They always use the same old bankrupt tactics — forever clobbering the regime but also clobbering every other ideological and liberation movement in sight. Jalal tried them and every notch along the Left. Then he started touting Safai Farahani's book on the necessity of an armed uprising instead of studying Hegel and Marx, growing ever more militant, insisting on the relevance of Maoist radicalism in the Middle East. He preached armed insurrection. I said he would crash and burn. He said revolution was blood! No bureaucracy, but straight from the gut. He was typical of the Radical Left, reckless and half-baked, furiously outdoing himself to be more revolutionary than anyone else.

I surveyed his room. If they had wanted his stuff so badly, they would have come and taken it as evidence. I poked under the mattress and threadbare rug, in the closet, where he had a few items of clothing, and in the space behind the adjoining metal bookcases. I found a black plastic comb there. I went over the place inch by inch, but there were no personal scraps, no family pictures, just an antiseptic life. I sat in the kitchenette and stared.

That's when I saw the newspapers, a stack of old papers in the corner. Jalal never read *Kayhan* or *Ettela'at*. "I'll never pay to boost the circulation of mouthpieces for the regime!" he said. Both of us ran and circulated underground papers. I bent down and moved the stack, peering at the tiles. The caulking around several of the tiles had worn away. I took a knife from a drawer, tapped the tiles, then pried one up. The floor had been slightly hollowed out underneath, but there was nothing there. I sat down again, thought back. He liked looking out his kitchen window to the back alley — a man standing above the world surveying it from his perch. One thing was clear — he burned to change the world. One time I got up to the fourth floor and found his door slightly ajar — it mustn't have been closed properly and had blown open — so I walked in. He was standing by the open window and whipped around suddenly. I'd caught him off guard. He detested being caught off guard.

I got up from the kitchen table and went over to the window and looked out as I had so many times before. There wasn't much to see except rows of small windows set into the dark brick wall of the building facing his and the one at the end. All the windows had drawn curtains, electrical lights filtering through here and there. The occupants didn't like facing a drab and narrow back alley. I opened the window, stuck my head out, saw sky and walls of brick. I looked down at the back alley. What had Jalal been doing at his window that day? I pushed down on the ledge and leaned out farther to try to see what he'd seen. Then just as I was pulling back in from the window, I noticed the corner of what looked like a metal box right under the ledge. I leaned over to see it better. It was the size of a satchel, with a protruding lid, like a mailbox. Easy to miss, the way it was placed just under the ledge with only a corner sticking out, nailed into brick. Some sort of utility box, maybe for electrical wires, except it had a lid and no wires leading into it and was in an impractical and inaccessible place. It couldn't have much of a purpose, all the way up on the fourth floor where you couldn't even reach it with a ladder from the alley. I felt around, lifted the lid, and stuck my hand in, half expecting to touch electrical wires. I felt plastic and tugged a little. A plastic bag. I squeezed what seemed like a wad of papers, then pulled and grabbed the bag with both hands to make sure it wouldn't slip down into the alley. A taped plastic pouch full of papers. I ripped off the tapes, dumped the contents on the kitchen table, and a mishmash of typed and handwritten pages fell out. An ingenious way to hide documents, suspending them outside in an innocuous metal container resembling a utility box that no one could reach.

I closed the window, went through the stack. Handwritten papers, typewritten pamphlets. Revolutionary titles — treatises on how to topple the regime. Manuals, instructions, insurrectionist theses. I leafed through. Here, the inner workings of an ultraradical organization. *Procedures for an Armed Struggle. Epic of Resistance. What Must Be Done Now? A Revolutionary's Execution. Today All Heroes Are on the Left.* The texts were underlined in red here and there, annotated with Jalal's very own handwriting in the margins. He had edited and inserted, using some of my very arguments to attack other groups like ours on the Left. The stapled sheets of lined loose-leaf were covered with longer commentaries by him. Still a lousy writer, overblown, intellectually sloppy, but animated. Here was evidence SAVAK killed to find. Marxist-Leninist edicts capping directions on how to make explosives, a report on assembling eight hundred grenades in a garden outside Tehran in Karaj and how they were distributed by motorcycle, the rigors and advantages of Cuba's guerrilla tactics versus Maoist China's theoretical courses, how to attack and disarm policemen in the street, how to blow up banks and government offices and military installations. Invaluable underground documents. They would use them against Jalal, both the Right and Left. Jalal had said the Tudeh Communists, another underground party, rather than the state, were the ones spreading the most vicious lies and rumors against his group. I shredded everything to pieces, burned them on the bathroom floor, and flushed the ashes down the toilet.

TEN

I WAS RUSHING to make the lecture at the Institute for Social Studies and Research and then get home in time to catch the children before their bedtime. To my surprise Mr. Bashirian was waiting by my car in the parking lot. Brown raincoat, tweed beret, hovering. His face was suspended with sorrow, aging.

Smiling feebly, I endured guilt and remorse. He had started clinging to me. Of course I couldn't blame him. He couldn't let go. I was beginning to dread our unexpected meetings. Nothing positive came of them for his son except the bond Mr. Bashirian and I were forming.

He apologized in that most considerate manner of his for delaying me after work, but he had news. They'd come to the house the night before. They'd turned it upside down. Of all Peyman's books they had taken his copy of *A Guide to Khorassan* by Shariati. But it was just a guidebook! Then they'd taken away Peyman's collection of photos.

"The travel albums?"

He nodded, wringing his hands, wondering what they wanted with endless pictures of tiled domes and villagers and caravansaries in deserts.

"They're looking for something specific," he said. "I'm sure, I'm sure."

People from work were going by. We were attracting attention, so we decided to walk. Up by the light, we headed north, the street thick with traffic. I didn't tell him I'd talked to Father. What was there to report except promises? So I repeated what I'd said before.

"Don't worry," I said. "He'll be home in no time."

"First I consoled myself by saying it was a mistake. But he's still not home. That can only mean bad news."

He tormented himself like this each day. From what he'd gathered, they'd taken Peyman in a day of rioting at Aryamehr. A crowd of students had gone on a rampage, breaking windows and furniture on the pretext the cafeteria food was contaminated and inedible. Everyone knew it was an excuse. They wanted the right to form associations for debate and politics and sports, prohibited by law. A special unit of the army had been called around midday. They'd driven up Eisenhower Avenue, turning in at the gates. Soldiers had poured out, rounding up students and forcing them into trucks in the front courtyard. The professors had retreated to their offices as usual and locked their doors.

"Last night, did they say anything?"

"They kept me in my bedroom," he said.

For a moment I felt his pain catch my throat, as if he'd passed it to me, beyond words, beyond the smallest gesture. His eyes fastened to hope like a man drowning. His son had become a phantom, burning brightly at the extremity of his vision.

"I don't understand," he murmured, shaking his head.

He thought back, told me about the time Peyman had traveled into the mountains of Kurdestan with a friend from the Literacy

Corps. About his trip to northern Azarbaijan, then Gilan, and through the rice plantations of the Caspian. A week in Yazd one winter. Khorassan was the last journey — I'd seen those pictures at his house. And the summer he'd traveled south to the Gulf to visit a friend in Ahvaz. In that searing heat, they'd traveled the coast from Bandar Bushehr to Bandar Abbas — they were young, after all.

"What does he like?"

"Mountain ranges and desert, out-of-the-way places. He likes children."

"He has a girl?"

"He only studies."

They'd taken what they thought of as evidence. So they were building a case, a verdict, we reassured ourselves. They'd contact him any day now, permitting him to see Peyman finally after all this time.

"I can't thank you enough," he said again in the street. "You're the light in a dark room."

I cringed at such gratitude, even before I came to know the fate that was to befall his son.

THIERRY CALLED the office several days later and said we should talk. Where better than his house up in Sa'adabad, say around six-thirty? I equivocated when he said "house," suggesting a public place. But he said he was having drinks at home for some French businessmen staying at the Hilton before taking them to dinner. If I didn't mind. . . . I decided to make the best of it.

The maid opened the door.

"Mrs. Behroudi," she said, her tight-lipped smile implying disapproval.

I was a married woman who'd come alone to the home of a foreign bachelor.

To my surprise I found I'd arrived before the other guests. Thierry had said they were coming at six-thirty. He breezed into the living room with goodwill and vitality, wearing an open shirt, chinos, and loafers — no attire for business guests and dinner. He kissed me on the cheeks, took my hand, brushing his lips over it, lingering. I pretended not to notice.

"And your guests?" I demanded.

"We're meeting at Chez Maurice later. My secretary got things muddled. Hope you don't mind. What will you have?"

I asked for tea by the sliding glass doors facing his pool and garden, trying to overlook the compelling possibility he'd never planned on having anyone else there but me. He spoke about his house, the luxury of living abroad, pouring himself a Scotch over ice. Wandering, I admired his collection of carved Buddhas and jade figurines from the Far East, though I'd seen them before when Houshang and I had been invited to his dinners. Thierry flopped on the large sofa, arms splayed, features poised with effrontery and luster. An introduction to trouble, if I'd ever seen one.

"Seen Pouran lately?" I asked.

"Only when you're around!"

I stayed by the window, pulled out a cigarette, lit it before he could get over.

"You're fast," he marveled.

I smiled. "Efficient."

The maid brought tea, then turned to him.

"Moosio Dalembert, r-reean doploo?" she asked in a funny accent, smiling at Thierry coquettishly despite her apparent prudery and advanced age.

He'd inherited her from his predecessor. In broken Persian he said, in the most elaborate way, that he was dining out and dismissed her. They'd crossed languages, displaying skills for my sake. It was a bit of theater. We heard the front door slam as she left.

I could see why she had greeted me that way. He'd never told her to expect nor prepare for any other guests.

I took the armchair by the window, as far away from Thierry as possible.

"Tehran's an ugly city," he said. "But — it has timeless charms."

"Spoken like a colonialist!"

He laughed, excited at the possibility of being outwitted. It prolonged the seduction.

"Thierry, look —"

"Efficient again?"

He sauntered over to my armchair, stood over me. He was being impossible. Looking straight in my eyes, he said just above a whisper, "Come on, you know how I feel. Stop fighting it."

I dragged on my cigarette, asked if he'd made a decision about Peyman Bashirian. He walked away.

"Your record on human rights is atrocious," he declared.

"It isn't mine!"

"See! There's no upper class less committed to the very regime it depends on. It's — disgraceful."

Now that there was to be no seduction, he was making his points, one by one.

"At the slightest rumble they'll all desert ship," he said, eyes glinting. "Like rats."

He wanted to get even. But I'd come for a favor, not to argue fine and arguable points. The regime didn't rule with or through us, nor any particular social class.

He poured himself another drink, saying his boss was coming in from Paris. He said he had an offer: he'd help me if I'd help get Houshang to use his influence in favor of Thierry's bank. I paused, then accepted, pausing for his sake, not mine. The French admire reflection.

He told me to write up what I knew about Peyman Bashirian's

case there and then. He'd contact a newspaper and a human rights organization in Paris as I'd requested. He went into the next room and took a white sheet and pen from the desk by the window. I said I preferred dictating; he could take notes.

"Really!" he said. "Who'd recognize your handwriting? I won't tell."

I shrugged. I had obligations. Still, I'd just avoided even committing the account of my friend's son to paper. My inbred discretion was craven. A telling milestone, I thought with resentment and contempt. I grabbed the pen and paper and wrote.

"Either way, you're playing with fire!" he assured me.

His culture, like mine, thrives on heightened emotion and theatrics.

By the door he tried to kiss me on the lips, but I turned my cheek.

"I want you," he whispered.

In the street I laughed at his ambitions.

I TOLD HOUSHANG ABOUT the banker's reception in the car. The invitation had been hand-delivered that day. He shrugged it off, exasperated at something else. We were on our way home from a reception for yet another visiting trade delegation, this one from the Far East. I longed to be home with the children. I never managed to spend enough time with them. With bumper-to-bumper traffic, the drive uptown was taking forever.

Houshang kept honking at cars cutting in left and right, griping about letting off the chauffeur earlier than usual, and about how a deputy minister had snubbed him at the reception. "The idiot has an inferiority complex!" he said. He was exasperated with the new snags each and every day at the Ports and Shipping Organization.

"The project's going to be canceled?" I asked.

"Not with our kind of clout!"

My husband thrives on clout.

He shrugged. "I'm not worried."

I was surprised Bandar Kangan was going full-force ahead, unlike other major projects recently aborted. Houshang didn't want to speculate, so I told him Reza Nirvani would be coming to the house to tutor. His reaction was irrational.

"I don't see why we need him in the house!"

We argued on until I finally lied and said Father had arranged it. Houshang dared not dispute nor ridicule Father's judgments so readily.

"You mean there isn't another tutor in the world?" he demanded. "I need to be consulted when it concerns my sons."

"What do you have against Reza?"

Houshang lit a cigarette, dragging on the filter with derision. "Don't tell me he's a friend of your brothers'. That's ridiculous! What does he want?"

"He doesn't want anything. He's a friend of the family's."

"He's a peasant."

"No he isn't!"

"So he's the son of a sharecropper."

"It so happens his father was a distinguished man, and his mother is a distant relative of Father's."

"We're all also distantly related to apes! I didn't ask for his genealogy. Why are we arguing about this chap anyway?"

And so it was I came to inform my husband that the matter was already settled.

ELEVEN

THE MAID OPENED THE DOOR and introduced herself as Goli, Tourandokht's great-granddaughter. She said her mistress had already told her I was the new tutor. She kept house for Mrs. Behroudi, her husband cooked, and they had three children. I said I'd seen her great-grandmother the week before, a woman who had brought up several generations in the Mosharraf household and who didn't have a birth certificate but claimed she was born during the Tobacco Boycott against the British. Goli giggled and said she had forgotten the story. Frivolous and insubstantial compared to Tourandokht.

We heard Mahastee upstairs reproaching her children.

Goli directed me to the living room and left. I stood at one end before the old glazed pottery propped up on glass shelves. Farther along the same wall were two groupings of old miniatures with gold leaf. Leyli and Majnoun in robes of purple, recumbent in a pavilion; Sufi dervishes by an indigo river; Rostam the hero battling Afrasiyab; Yusuf and Zuleikha under stylized clouds, attended by stylized courtiers in turquoise and saffron. On a side table was a collection of Qajar pen boxes, painted and lacquered, with hunting scenes, nightingales among roses, bearded noblemen, and oval medallions with portraits of Europeans. I picked up a *qalamdan,* pulled out one end.

"Looking for a pen?"

I turned to face Mahastee, expecting her to be robed in gold and flowing magenta. I'd seen her in yellow in a garden under hail.

She smiled and we shook hands. I told her I was there to help out for a few weeks. Besides the department I was also teaching night school. I had asked around to find her a suitable and permanent tutor.

She smiled. "You're doing me a big favor."

She wore dark slacks and a white shirt, stylish and sedate. And still true to herself, instinctively unpretentious. I complimented her pen boxes.

"You still do calligraphy?" she asked.

"My father was adept. He had deep faith guiding his ink and pen."

"You don't?"

"I had his until he passed away."

So many years gone by, and we could feel them buckle under us, our smiles slightly strained at the realization, and at being alone together. She explained that her sons would appear shortly. Aged ten and twelve, they were lazy, unfocused students and needed discipline, the rewards of hard work.

She went through milky curtains, unlocking a French window, the curtains billowing as she flung open the casements. She turned, her face opaque behind the drapes, her eyes restive; then she stepped outside and I followed. She pointed to her bed of roses and we started walking. Gusts blew the dried leaves of plane trees, scattering them over the lawns. In the midst of cooler days, we'd hit upon a mild afternoon. As she spoke, her eyes flitted back and forth, the light hazel of their irises darkly outlined, her elongated eyebrows ornamental, her skin pale, flawless. She told me about the years since she had left for England and returned, a succession of events proceeding like clockwork, her tone meandering, then efficient, as if their passage had been mechanical. I talked about university and teaching and my job at the department, outlining without essence. "And you're not married?" She smiled. "No, not yet," I said. Explaining had distanced us from each other with time and place, making sudden strangers of us instead of bringing us closer to the emotions we felt at seeing each other again. The lawns sloped down to a pool, and she descended, limber, and we circled down, drifting to the side of a gardening shed by the farthest wall. For a moment she stood, uncertain, as if about to disclose something, then changed her mind.

Standing there at the far end of the garden, I found her exactly as I'd known her twenty years before. All she had related about what she'd done and who she'd been with were irrelevant. I found that astonishing, this phantom truth crossing twenty years — this elemental connection between us, though everything else in our lives had changed.

We climbed back up the slope, and her sons came running out the open French window of the living room, and her expression changed, slackened, though her body grew taut. She waved, drifting toward them like a ship berthing. They ran round us in circles, chasing each other and shouting, the large white house towering as we gathered to go back inside.

I TOLD THE TAXI to drop me off in Dokhaniyat, and although I'd got off only three blocks away, still I was running late.

There was a nip in the air. I was hungry, but there was no time for dinner. I had been given the code and a succession of knocks to get into the house for our meeting. Seven of us were there. Our host — a chemical engineer and the son of a cleric in Mashhad — had first read Hegel in Arabic and joined an Islamic student association there until discovering the secular Left at the polytechnic in Tehran. The others were a lecturer at Tehran University on modern history; a young filmmaker, still editing his documentary on village life; Dr. Hadi, a radiologist who had studied in Paris and was also a translator; a newspaper columnist who resented his state-sanctioned prose and dug out scandals on corruption; and our playwright and literary critic, a chain-smoker and pedant who emulated the prominent dramatist Sa'edi. We sat in the small room around an Arj steel table and chairs, flimsy curtains drawn. Our host brought in a jug of water and tea after turning down the radio a tad in the other room.

We had a watchman in the street, a boy sitting under a streetlamp. Poor bastards, all they ever got to do was watch and wait.

We passed out the study questions given to all four of our sections: What kind of revolution today? Who will make it — the people, the party, the revolutionaries? Can there be revolution without a political party? In what form can the historic vanguard appear? What kind of party do we make? What kind of rapport with the masses? Then we moved on to the main topic for the night — the continuing problems for the Left at Tehran University. It had started with a poisonous article by Mo'meni, a leftist hero to students — a Fedayee guerrilla — now dead, arrested and executed along with other leaders. But when he was alive, his diatribe against the faculty had thundered on campus, accusing, naming names — professors of economics and sociology, especially those who taught anything about Marxism. "Far from dedicated intellectuals, they're corrupters, informers, collaborators of the regime!" he'd warned students. "Trust no one!" In class they'd pointed at teachers and said, "You must be in with SAVAK." We were incensed. Just when we'd gained momentum and the students were more involved than ever — resisting, participating, committed — this blow had been delivered to the Left by the Left. The Left was still paranoid, and it continued to demand mind control and enforce censorship.

The journalist was taking the minutes. Dr. Hadi unlatched the window to air the room — four of us were smoking. Someone asked, as always, if Mo'meni had actually written the article and if it wasn't another SAVAK conspiracy.

"He wrote it, that Stalinist despot!" said our host.

"Of course students are entranced with guerrillas!" said the playwright. "They're armed. They're epic. They're in the vanguard."

We discussed how the Left was splintered and all over the place, deathly afraid to criticize and rectify itself. Meanwhile the tide had turned antisecular, with Shariati the rage and students finding religion, calling Islam our legitimate roots and heritage. Even society philosophy professors and men of letters — those coddled by the regime — were siding with Islam to retaliate against the Left by saying nothing worthwhile came from the West, and not just trash like Marx. They lectured on how Western civilization itself was a sewer of corruption, whereas the East had Islam, Sufism, and didn't have the need to rebel. They were even bringing back writers like Al-Ahmad, a censored author until recently banned and maligned himself, to counter Marxism —these jet-set thinkers educated abroad.

"The girls want a separate cafeteria!" the lecturer said. "They don't want to eat with the boys. They don't want to take exams with the boys."

"The Black Reaction!" said the journalist.

"What's rational about fanning religious babble?" said our host.

"A hundred Fedayee with dead leaders versus tens of thousands of clerics. Who wins?"

"The regime," I said.

PAST MIDNIGHT in my room I took out paper and the inkwell and the pen box of reed pens. Father had left me his set. His father too had been a skilled calligrapher, and a mystic, a cleric who had left his village and old garden — a place of mystical legend, a garden of unusual light and spiritual inspiration — for Tabriz, to teach jurisprudence and theosophy. They had said about him that he possessed Sufic chivalry, healing gifts, exceptional powers.

I pulled over the low table before me, laying out my implements, trying my hand after years. I sat cross-legged, dipping the pen in black ink, drawing the tip against paper. An old *ghazal,* a throwback to timeless verses for her. For that time some twenty years ago when I had loved only her.

Autumn. Father long dead and this another season. His picture before me on the wall as I slid his reed pen against paper for this woman he'd known as a child. Had he known then how I loved her? Known and disapproved and in his wisdom kept quiet, while I measured his faith in me and the insurmountable obstacles he saw in the world. He knew their world well, had known it living in the household of her grandmother, Mahbanou *khanom,* year after year. He had received their benevolence — especially hers, as long as she lived — their infinite loyalty and grace and sense of extended family, but also witnessed their imperious treatment of others, their intrigues and family feuds, their secret political machinations. He lived between several worlds, his entire life made up of negotiating the infinite demands between them: the Mosharrafs, the many cultivators of their lands who held inheritable tenant rights, the peasants with their wily logic but also ignorance and superstition, the village elders and gendarmes and government tax collectors, the turbaned clerics surrounding his father in Tabriz. I thought Father infinitely judicious and resourceful in his ways.

Except as Mahastee grew older, when she arrived in Morshedabad and I went out to see her, he'd turn steely with apprehension. He loved her. But she was the daughter of the man he served, and that distinction would remain for him forever. To Father distinctions were there to be upheld. I thought his manner especially austere when she was there, perhaps to steel me against her and the world. To say, Things are never how you think. Prepare, prepare for what will come. He'd known then he wouldn't succeed with me — known perhaps what could come — and had bided time for the intervention of fate.

Now, long after, I wrote the words of an old master. The room was quiet except for the rasping of a blunt instrument; the letters, long and drawn like cypresses. Black, night arcs. Tipped. Hooked. Latched. Round and capacious like empty basins.

THE NEXT MORNING I called Jalal's parents from the office. I left a message with the mother, who kept referring to her husband as *hajj-agha.* He called at midday. I recognized him from that first "Allo!" spoken crudely like a peasant and barked into the phone, his sentences all pitched higher at the end as if everything stated were an impertinent question. He wanted to see me immediately. Had I done the job? He coughed, a loud hacking noise.

"Tonight," he said. "Something happened."

I was at his doorstep at nine, this time addressing him as *hajj-agha.* He took me along the half-lit passageway, at the end of which there was an interior courtyard with a blue-tiled pond of stagnant water. We took off our shoes and he opened a door, and we stepped up into a small white room with a brand-new Kashan carpet touching the walls. There were bolstered cushions opposite the door. We sat cross-legged under framed portraits of the Prophet — faceless and robed, with a golden halo and angels above him — and of the first disciple, Ali, bearing the sword of Zulfaqar. He took out a rosary from his pocket, fingering the pale green beads. They clicked in the room like the ticking of a clock. His feet smelled terribly.

The door opened and his wife entered in a white chador, bearing a brass tray of tea. I raised myself in greeting. She left the tray on the carpet and sat away from us on her knees, looking like an aged twelve-year-old.

"That *hajji* from the bazaar came late last night," the father said. "The rug merchant. The one who said he'd help. I was groggy with sleep. He brought bad news. He said, 'They've got your son in Komiteh Prison. They say he's a Marxist guerrilla.'"

He stared at the floor, shaking his head, ran the palm of one hand over the stubble of his beard.

"He was raised a good Muslim," he protested. "The only battle worth fighting is in the path to God! Like Imam Hossein, who was martyred in Karbala."

His wife wiped tears from her face. "I know my son. He's a good boy! His heart is pure. He wouldn't harm a soul."

The father scowled. "What d'you know about a son you never saw? This city corrupted him. Like it does everyone else."

She hung her head, and he looked away in silence. The mother rocked to and fro, whispering lamentations, the father's gaze fixed on the carpet, running fingers over his rosary. In this city, even after so many years, he was still in exile.

"About the apartment —" I began. Vaguely I mentioned the pamphlets — without saying they were on armed insurrection — that I'd ripped up and flushed away. I didn't want to frighten the mother. I said it appeared nothing had been touched there before me. I didn't mention the two SAVAK agents in the street but said Jalal owed the landlady rent.

"How much rent?" the father demanded suspiciously.

"Your tea's gone cold," the mother said, staring at the tray. She seemed nervous. "Let me get you a fresh one."

"Don't trouble yourself," I insisted.

I grabbed a glass and saucer, the dark and tepid brew bitter even through the sugar cube melting on my tongue. The father started on me, demanding to know if I'd found anything really important. Incriminating evidence? Drugs, a stash of money, arms? I shook my head.

"What money?" I said. "He owed rent."

"The *hajji* told me they found evidence," the father said. "In my son's apartment." He stared at me. "You promised to destroy evidence."

"I told you I did."

"You're educated. You know a lot. You said you were there first!"

I stared at him.

"They said they found evidence. Why did you go, for the money? To take something? Plant something?"

I saw how the mother looked embarrassed. He believed I'd lied to them, suspecting I'd had other motives all along. He didn't trust anyone.

"Who are you?" he demanded. "Someone like Jalal? Or tell me, are you an informer?"

I said I was his son's friend.

He couldn't be sure of anything except the bitter certainty of all the betrayals he'd already seen and anticipated. He'd migrated to the city with so many others and seen gray for so many years that the more he saw the more he was disgusted.

"The only truth today is spoken in the mosque," he declared.

His wife was beseeching God and the Twelve Imams under her breath. The father said the way he saw it his sole duty in life was donating funds to the clergy for his religious obligations. Now he would be doubling the funds, even tripling them. He said he had no other allegiance.

"They're the only source of moral authority," he said.

I said I was sorry about his son.

"We must all fight the battle of Karbala!" he said, rising.

I thanked the old woman for the tea.

"I should've stayed in my village," the father said. "Why did I leave?"

I left, relieved to get away. Twisting in the darkened alleys past the mud-brick walls, I thought how so many of the people who lived here harbored regrets and how many of their children had deserted them to move up and away from them in this city.

TWELVE

MR. BASHIRIAN CAME IN with a wad of folders. His trousers were too long, like the sleeves on his shabby tweed jacket. He was shrinking.

"Really!" I said. "You're disappearing."

He left the folders on the table, sank into a chair. He visited me daily. I walked around the desk and stood leaning against it.

"You must eat!"

"I can't," he said.

At first, years ago, he'd annoyed me. The ceremonious demeanor, the persnickety work habits, that austere guise like that of a maiden aunt, finicky, brooding. Then one day I saw him in Bamdaad eating ice cream and cream cakes with his son, and as I watched them it changed my opinion of him forever. He was such a tender father. They ate custard tartlets covered with fruit, they ate éclairs, they ate creamy roulette. They ate and ate, laughing together. Peyman was nine at the time, with big cheeks and a crew cut and eyes the size of saucers. They were so engrossed with each other that they didn't see me. Later when we were better acquainted Mr. Bashirian told me about his wife — how she'd died in a car accident in the mountain passes of Gachsar. After her there could be no other woman, he said. He had his son, his work. At night he listened to Shajarian and Banon on the radio, and to old records of Badi'zadeh and Ghamar, and weekends he painted. He had taken classes from the famous Katouzian. One time he brought in a small oil painting wrapped in brown paper, a gift for me. A tranquil sea with bloodstained sunset and red clouds and floating gulls. Maudlin, pretty awful actually, but touching. When I took it home, Houshang laughed.

"Are you painting?" I asked him.

He shook his head. "I pray."

He'd always been rational and solid, a man devoted to secular liberalism, measuring the progress of this nation inch by painful inch. I couldn't imagine him fatalistic, submissive.

"I've made a vow," he said, "to Imam Reza."

Kavoos had told me to put him in touch with a certain lawyer. I put this to Mr. Bashirian. Here was something solid. I felt in this way I would wash my hands of the whole affair.

He wrote the name and phone number in a small blue calendar he took from the inside pocket of his jacket.

"You need time off," I said. "Take a week. Why don't you arrange —"

He refused immediately. "Never! I need to work. More work. Anything to keep from agonizing."

I argued for a bit. He could be insufferably stubborn. I asked if he had any relatives in Tehran, but he said his sister lived up north, in Sari.

"Any nieces and nephews?"

"They live up north. Why?"

For his own sake I said, "Say you have an ailing niece. She's deathly ill. People are asking questions. They think something's wrong. Don't you see? Please, let's give them some sort of answer. For now."

He agreed, reluctant, pushing his folders like a proud man fiddling with defeat.

THE DIRECTOR QUESTIONED my judgment the next day. He's hugely distracted and under enormous pressure, rushing to meetings and official events all week, arranging for conferences and endless foreign visitors. Recently the buoyant effect of all that has receded, leaving him looking oddly vacuous. He seemed deflated when he called me into his office. First we went over new papers for our journal and publications. "Statism and the Dangers of Economically Interventionist States Engaging in Monological Speech." He said nobody read this stuff anyway, especially way at the top! He flipped through the article "The Rentier Economy and Rentier Mentality in Iran," then skimmed through the first two pages of "Our One-Product Economy — Oil — and Patron-Client Relationship with Foreign Powers," poking at it with his pen.

He said, "As always it comes down to the obvious need for scientific study versus the obvious need for censorship."

Then he complained how he wasn't pleased at all with Mr. Bashirian.

"What's going on? I hear he's a poor manager. He's hostile and curt with colleagues and impossible in meetings. I hear he's sneaking home papers and photocopying documents."

"He would do no such thing."

"Then what's the problem? His colleagues are complaining."

"He's an invaluable employee."

"That's not what I hear anymore. Ask Mr. Makhmalchi."

Mr. Makhmalchi was a snoop, a clever and overbearing toady promoted instead of Mr. Bashirian, whose competence and very principles were now in question.

"Mr. Bashirian's a hard worker and an honorable man. He hasn't changed."

"Of course, you wanted him promoted. You're biased. I'll give him two weeks."

There was a message that Thierry had called when I got back to my desk. I called, but he was in a meeting. He called back in the afternoon.

"About your friend," he said. "Someone's in town who'll meet with him."

We weren't to discuss Peyman Bashirian's case openly on the phone.

He said, "Here's the opportunity to talk to a French journalist."

"I'm not so sure my friend will agree."

"I don't understand."

"Try," I said, fiddling with the pencils on my desk.

"I'll really never understand things here," he said before I hung up.

I called in the secretary, a most efficient woman and world-class gossipmonger. I couldn't trust Mr. Bashirian to play the game nor deal effectively with rumors about his recent sullen disposition.

I explained how I wanted several things typed, then offered her a cigarette, complimenting her outfit.

"You're always so well dressed," I said.

She launched into a shopping guide, from the cheaper department stores like Kourosh to the exorbitant boutiques on Shah Abbas, which got her into the bizarre story of the general's wife. Everyone was speculating about it all over Tehran.

"Haven't you heard?" the secretary said. "The general's wife was attacked by masked gunmen inside a boutique while fingering cashmere sweaters and high heels from Rome and Paris. Her enormous diamond ring and other jewelry were snatched. The men got away within minutes. The police were called and arrived in full force, sirens wailing. She made phone calls to higher places, screaming and cussing into the phone. She threatened the trembling boutique owner, saying she'd have him shot for complicity. She threatened the police and Special Forces when they arrived. Screaming at the top of her lungs, 'Don't you fucking know who I am? Can't you fucking assholes do your jobs properly?' Imagine, the woman's a bitch and her jewels are financing a group of terrorists. Whoever they are, they're armed and dangerous! The original plot was to kidnap her for ransom. They came in two cars, seven of them with face masks to hijack her and the bodyguard, but he fought them off alone and heroically, until he got shot. First they said he was dead. But he isn't! Actually he's alive. They say first the general gave him the beating of his life, and now SAVAK's torturing him to get information. Of course, he must've been in on the plot. How else would the attackers have known exactly where and at what time she'd be shopping? To think urban guerrillas are stalking public officials and their families. The diamond ring isn't even fully paid for. Imagine the nerve to call it yours! Imagine being so loaded with jewelry on a morning shopping spree! Imagine having her kind of nerve and clout and mouth to threaten the armed forces! She slapped an officer before leaving in an official car. She screamed, 'You better mobilize all your fucking forces *immediately* to find my jewels!' That diamond ring's a slap in the face of the nation. A slap in the face of decent and hardworking people. Too bad they didn't kidnap her! To think the general's job is protecting and defending the honor of our country. The diamond's being paid off with the general's fat kickbacks from the millions of dollars dealt in American armaments. That's how America keeps its foreign cronies on top! Bribing its puppets and fattening them up. We're always selling out. It's disgraceful." The secretary leaned in. "They say it's the biggest diamond in Tehran! An eyesore even for the royal family. The general's in *big* trouble —"

I cut in. "You know about Mr. Bashirian?"

"No, why? Except he's been weird lately. Everyone's wondering why."

This, after the lawyer, was to be my last good deed for him.

So I said, "One of his close relatives is sick, very sick. He's heartbroken."

"What relative?" she asked. "Not the son? His son's adorable. I saw him once on the street. A real looker! I mean — Mr. Bashirian's ugly. A bit like a hippo — wouldn't you say?"

Poor Bashirian. Hostile, sullen, and now a hippo.

"He's so jumpy these days," she said. "No one can talk to him anymore!"

"Well, it's the niece. His favorite niece. She's in the hospital. Tragic for such a young girl to be struck with a fatal disease."

"What is it?"

I whispered. She shook her head. Worse, I said the girl was about to be married, she had the white dress, the veil, the . . . Tears welled up in the secretary's eyes. Still, she craved the more horrible details. She was easy to please. I told her to treat Mr. Bashirian with kid gloves and not to spread this around the office. She couldn't wait to leave.

THAT NIGHT HOUSHANG and I met downstairs in the front hall, all dressed up for another event. He'd come in late and showered and changed in fifteen minutes, and I'd been sitting with Ehsan and Kamran in the pantry while they ate dinner and I grilled them about homework.

There were cars backed up all the way down the street when we arrived. The reception, to be followed by a seated dinner, was at the house of an Iranian banker, an eligible bachelor with flair and perfect credentials. Thierry was the cohost. He couldn't have been more charming and attentive. I'd seen him melt stone, the exception being my husband. He towered with his brilliant blue eyes and immaculately cut suit, deferring to Houshang, who seemed to nurse a perpetual grudge against him. My husband doesn't like foreign competition.

The big director from Thierry's bank was in from Paris, graying at the temples, talking of Indochina and the Achaemenians and fresh litchis at Fauchon all in one breath. We chatted about museums and savory things, sounding conspicuously like glossy brochures from the National Tourist Organization. He said he was going to see the prime minister and spend a day in Ispahan, as he liked to pronounce it, instead of Esfahan.

Houshang steered me over to the rear admiral, who was there with his wife. He sits on the board of the Bandar Kangan project. Slim and trim, with pale skin, shiny medals, and bright eyes. His wife had come dressed for a jubilee, all pleats and flounces and gossamer print. She had tiny teeth and tiny feet. Houshang and the rear admiral stepped out of the room. I found myself casing her for diamonds the size of plums, like the general's wife's, but she had rubies. And we ordered government ministries to trim budgets and scrimp. The only thing she knew about gross inflation was her ballooning budget. Going on and on about their new house uptown, decorated of course by Jansen of Paris! And their brand-new villa on the island of Kish.

The rear admiral and Houshang were conferring in a corner of the hallway beyond the living room. I expected to see Houshang gratified; instead he seemed on pins and needles. The rear admiral's wife carefully placed a rubied pinkie to her blond coiffure, saying she'd had it done by Nahid, the most exclusive hairdresser in Tehran.

"I'd *never* entrust this hair and color to *anyone* else."

You'd think it was all about the upkeep of a national monument.

We were interrupted by a couple, and I slipped away. The rear admiral came in and whispered to his wife, then whisked her off. They left with the sort of muted spectacle associated with kaisers leaving drawing rooms, only shaking hands with Thierry's boss and Thierry and their Iranian host on the way out, the bevy escorting them to the door with unremitting panache.

They had left early.

"How's the rear admiral?" I asked Houshang as we went in to dinner.

"Things couldn't be better."

I find myself distrusting much of what my husband tells me.

At dinner I was seated next to the French journalist.

He whispered to me conspiratorially, *"Et cet etudiant en prison? . . ."* sipping wine and reeking of anticipation. He wanted the full scoop on Mr. Bashirian's son, as though Peyman were a juicy scandal.

Mr. Mostaufi, our old family friend, embraced me and sat to my right, praising Father and Mother's Friday luncheons. The foreign diplomat at our table greeted him. "Ah! Your Excellency," he said warmly. Posted back in Tehran, he said he'd traveled the world and found nothing again quite like Iran in the sixties. Dreamy halcyon days!

"Well, now the atmosphere's downright tense!" scolded a Polish writer across from him.

Someone had whispered to us that he was famous and was researching his next book. He kept referring to the perfection of his own objectivity. He liked irony, except regarding himself. He said he had talked to the people — he made it sound as if they were his, his people — on the streets. Breezed down his list, just short of an insulting caricature: our heady upper class, the disaffection and in fact virulent hatred permeating the lower classes and intellectuals — he meant for the Shah but didn't say it — the shadow world of dissidents and leftists, the regime's breach of human rights while it imported international hustlers and casino operators and Hong Kong sharks and Indian doctors and Asian nurses and Korean truck drivers, and of course, those brain-dead hicks, hordes of American army personnel.

Mr. Mostaufi turned to him, red-faced. "Why, His Majesty has done everything — I repeat, everything — to elevate and educate and industrialize this nation in the shortest time possible. That, sir, is no crime! If we must arrest militants and provocateurs, it's the price we have to pay for progress. But this regime isn't criminal! It is being maligned. It has brought Iran for the first time ever to the very brink of Western civilization. With proud and distinguished and loyal armed forces. These are our glory days. Who will record that?"

The Pole turned away, sulking, thereafter only talking to the foreign diplomat. The French journalist was relating his global exploits, brandishing his curriculum vitae. I couldn't tell what sort he was. He said he was staying at the Intercontinental.

"You could find a room?" I said, impressed.

"No cot in the hallways for me. I'm too important!"

During dinner he pontificated about reckless and ill-conceived economic growth. He was a heavy drinker. Later he came up to me with his glass of cognac, looking sheepish.

"You were quiet in there. Something I said offended you?"

"Let me warn you. I dislike preachy causes. This boy is a friend."

"I'd like very much to meet his father. Let me talk to him. His name and position will be protected." He smiled at my silence. "Don't tell me you're reluctant? Then how will anything ever change?"

It was the tone that got me, executed with indifference but definitely solemn. I told him I'd call the hotel the next morning.

BEFORE DECIDING to call the Intercontinental, Mr. Bashirian asked me to take a walk with him during lunch break. We spent half an hour outside the office, going around the block. He equivocated so dreadfully I was ready to abandon him myself. He said he couldn't bring himself to confide in a foreigner. He wasn't articulate and experienced. He didn't like their games. "What games?" I said, annoyed. He didn't speak a foreign language. He didn't want to discuss his son with a perfect stranger. He didn't want to make waves. He just wanted them to send back Peyman.

"I want the doorbell to ring. I want to go to the door one evening and see him standing there and hear him call out, 'Father.' So I can put my arms around him. I don't want anything else."

"Did you call the lawyer?"

He said they'd met. The lawyer had been loquacious, but legally he was without recourse. There were no laws to protect Peyman from being arrested and held by SAVAK. He could be kept without a hearing or sentence, tried by a secret military tribunal. SAVAK decided on and defined subversion — any deed, any word. He said the lawyer had asked him if Peyman was a Communist, Mojahed, Marxist Fedayee, follower of Shariati, or member of the National Front.

"Anytime anything happens, out comes the list!" said Mr. Bashirian indignantly. "He follows no one! I told him. So he ended with a sermon on civil rights. Hinting at some soon-to-be association of jurists to protest cases like Peyman's."

I knew nothing about this. Besides, no one could lecture the regime nor confront it openly anymore. An airtight regime, smothered by its own commendations of itself.

"Here's your chance."

"With a foreigner?" he said, starting all over again.

"He's a journalist. An uncensored one."

"That's true. Why don't you speak with him?"

"But you're the father," I said.

"You speak French."

I looked at my watch. "You've got to decide."

"What do you think?" he asked.

"Nearly anything's better than nothing."

"But what do you recommend?"

He wanted the decision to be mine. I remembered our director's baseless insinuations about his being unprincipled. Here was a man who couldn't even decide to meet with a journalist when his own son's fate was hanging in the balance.

"You should do what's good for Peyman."

"I'm not sure what that is anymore."

We made our way along the sidewalk thick with pedestrians and street vendors, the sun bright and high.

"I don't care what happens to me," he said. "I'm just terrified I'll jeopardize his situation in . . . there."

"You'll be protected. This will be your testimonial."

"I've got no cause or political agenda of interest."

"Who says you do?"

"I'm not a — an agitator."

"I know."

"Why should they care? These journalists want important people. I mean, why suddenly take an interest in my son? To use him for their own purpose?"

"Exactly which purpose?" I said curtly.

"How do we know this man's reliable?"

"We don't. Except for his reputation."

"I'm not so sure this is right."

He hung his head. He agonized. Maybe there were other considerations he wouldn't tell me.

"Will you be there?" he said. "Please, I'll do it only if you're there."

THIRTEEN

THURSDAY AFTERNOON I was there tutoring the two boys in the dining room when I heard Mahastee come in. I'd given the boys a quiz, and while they figured out the math problems, I heard her around the house and the phone kept ringing. The boys chewed the end of their pencils, eyes flitting about.

"Concentrate!" I thundered.

They pumped their legs, squirmed in their seats, shot out the room after the lesson. I was in the hall when Mahastee came out onto the upstairs landing, wearing a navy blue suit and high heels. She said she wanted to discuss my fee, her slender body exerting a strange hold over me as she swept down the stairs.

"What fee?" I protested.

We argued. I couldn't possibly accept payment from her. There was no question of charging her by the hour; besides, I was an interim tutor. We got all tied up standing on ceremony, and she insisted so much that I made to leave.

"I'd like your advice," she said.

She directed me into a smaller room with a television and large sofa and low table; she was steady, only her eyes troubled. I dropped my satchel, which held our group's commentaries on Latin American revolutionaries, by the sofa, staring at the painting on the wall above it. A large canvas in sepia colors by Hajizadeh of a father and son, inspired by an old turn-of-the-century photograph, it was a portrait at once decorous, tense, intimate, enigmatic, unyielding. To my astonishment, Mahastee said what I was thinking.

"It reminds me of you and your father."

There she sat, below it, and told me about a colleague whose son, a student at Aryamehr University, had been taken. I said I'd asked her father to intervene on behalf of Jalal Hojjati. So it seemed we both knew some young man who was a political prisoner.

"I'm just surprised you do," I said.

"Why, is that your specialty?"

I smiled. "Let's say my political views are different from yours."

"But I don't have any!"

"Exactly."

She waited for an explanation I would not give. I could never divulge anything about my underground politics. I told her something vague instead, which only confirmed there was a lot more I couldn't say.

She gave me a knowing stare, changed the subject. "When I told Father about the boy in prison, he was appalled. In fact he was disappointed — I mean with me. He may be a wise and weathered old hand, but he's — out of touch. He used to be forceful and obdurate. But they set him aside years ago. They like burning their bridges behind them. Of course, they hate old-timers, and Father despises playing the sort of toady they need. He's aged."

"I found him barely changed," I said.

She held my gaze. I couldn't lie to her.

"My friend doesn't eat," she said. "He's on Valium. He's about to have a nervous breakdown. If something happens to his son, he'll never forgive himself. I — I haven't consulted Houshang about this."

She leaned forward, close, bringing traces of her perfume.

"As I watch him fall apart," she murmured, "my own sense of equanimity is falling apart too."

I stared at the table.

"In a way," she said, "I've made a decision for him. It could go wrong. It's treacherous deciding for someone else, isn't it?"

"He must be grateful to have you."

"He's grateful to have his son."

She got up, went to a cabinet, pulled out an album, and, flipping through the pages, pointed. There we were, scrawny adolescents with younger parents. Her brothers, my sister, boys from the village and gardeners' children in Morshedabad. A photograph of the house there fell from her lap — the slanted roof, the front steps, the sunlit grove up against the house. The shadows underneath, where life had once passed. We had left it all suddenly, and with it the Mosharrafs. After the incident in Morshedabad that summer, we left — I'm the only one still alive who knows the story, an insidious secret that ate away at us. Father, humiliated and embittered, packed us all off to Tehran, and then, once there, he fell into quiet days hollowed out by gloom until he went back to farm his own villages in Azarbaijan. And despite a heart attack, for years he worked his land. But then he lost it with land reform and went bankrupt and finally lost all he had. He died a broken man. They don't know that either, the Mosharrafs, how Father ended up.

"Most of the garden's gone," she said. "Now Father wants to sell the house."

She wanted me to have the photograph, but I said it was for her to keep. She didn't know what I meant, and I wasn't about to tell her about that miserable incident and why we had left Morshedabad. I say let that too stay buried. Erupting suddenly that summer, it had poisoned our life, then receded, dying off with each passing year bit by bit. After that, in Tehran, Father paid the formal and customary visit once a year only to Mahastee's father. But I refused to go and so had given up seeing Mahastee. Except once, when Father, insisting, had taken me with him, and she had led me through the summer garden that evening, her dress fluttering against the green underbrush and her eyes incandescent, and I'd been seized with a wild and brutal remorse and kissed her there and then. Then, steely and remote as if to punish her — though it was nothing she had done but my emotion at seeing her again and my remorse — I'd left, never to return, and she'd left for school abroad.

She pointed to a picture of Father — erect, calm, long before he withered, long before his ultimate defeat — with high forehead, austere eyes, dark mustache, the Adam's apple. A sensible man standing in a field with Nasrollah *mirza* and village elders.

"Your father was the most wonderful man. Grandmother adored him."

"Father always said you look like her."

"Did you get my letter of condolence?"

She'd written a moving testament, simple, heartfelt, when Father died.

The phone rang again for her, and I wrote down my number at work before leaving. Winding down the garden path, I wondered about her equilibrium, and mine with her, by the immaculately pruned rose bushes and inert fountain.

HER FATHER CALLED ME at the office in the morning. He said he'd just returned from a short visit to the Caspian.

"We had splendid weather!"

He got talking about orange trees and mimosas and rice paddies just long enough to make polite conversation. Otherwise what he was calling about could have been summed up in an indelicately short amount of time.

He cleared his throat. "About that friend of yours. Before leaving, I spoke to Kavoos, who has his ways. Dear boy, I'm afraid the news is — is that for the time being, nothing can be done. But I was assured there would be the utmost . . . care and deliberation in handling the case. If you see what I mean."

"Yes, of course," I said, wondering if he believed this himself.

"Needless to say, your friend should've known better. Now, I'm passing no judgments here —"

"Of course —"

"But you know these things can be quite difficult. The atmosphere is . . . charged. Perhaps with a bit of forbearance everyone will see the light."

He'd lost me now. Did he mean SAVAK would see the light, or the regime, or nasty leftists like Jalal? I imagined us all dazzled by clarity.

"I'll let you know — that is, if anything new crops up. There isn't much that can be done for the time being. But —"

I interrupted to spare him the inconvenience of offering other excuses. He meant well and had called himself instead of passing on the message. A gentleman from the old school. I thanked him, saying I hoped it hadn't been a terrible inconvenience.

"Come by and see us," he said. "Don't stay away now."

I HAD FORTY-TWO STUDENTS in my class of trigonometry at the Rahnema High School on Moniriyeh. The first month of the academic year, and already several were behind, and this time I was angry. "You expect to pass the final exams like this?" I called out. Most of them were between twenty and twenty-six. All of them had day jobs and took night courses to prepare to sit for the national examinations to get their twelfth-grade diploma.

Hossein Farahani had lost his father at fifteen and ever since had been obliged to support a family. He was the one I had recruited who worked in the auto repair shop. For two years I had watched and listened to his arguments. He was hard on everyone but hardest on himself. His most interesting instinct was to disagree. I never recruited the ones who didn't contradict me. He sat insolent and unrepentant in the back.

After class I kept Hossein and Massoud. They sat, my youngest students, hunched in their seats, and I asked what they had to say for themselves, and Hossein said he had family trouble. I asked if it was his mother again, little sisters, two brothers. He wouldn't say. Massoud, who was a typesetter for a small publishing firm, said he had no family but had problems. Hossein wasn't really listening, for usually he argued. After my last course I saw him in the hall downstairs and we walked out together.

"Something wrong?" I asked.

"Nothing." He shrugged.

"Where were you last night?"

"I dined out at Shekoufeh-Nau with my mistress, and after the show I whistled for my chauffeur, who took us back to my white villa."

His jaw was clenched he was so angry. We walked on. At the corner of Simetri, he turned to me.

"I drag along this family my father left me. Mouths to feed, clothes to buy, doctors' bills. What do I own in this world? We're miserable, and uptown they're fattening up. If I get hit by a car tomorrow, my sisters and brothers will beg or sell themselves, and mother will die and make them orphans."

"The auto repair shop you work for," I said, "— I want to see it."

"Zaffar's Garage."

"You said they've got empty rooms in the back."

"Filthy rooms," he said.

"Tell them you know someone who needs a workshop behind a garage."

He had a purity and intensity that reminded me of myself way back. He believed the things he said honestly and with feeling and with the kind of simplicity and forthrightness that the rest of us had lost.

He followed me to our appointment. Our *Night Letter,* ready for distribution, was on the week-old hunger strike of eight political prisoners in Qasr Prison and the execution of a member of the Tudeh. Some on the Left were insisting this Tudehi was no political prisoner but a spy for socialist imperialism and the Soviet Union. The dispute was whether those of us against the Tudeh but for human rights should protest this execution. Six hundred copies to distribute that night on political commitment.

I left Hossein at the street corner and went up to the third-floor apartment to collect the copies from Dr. Hadi. In the dim light of his back room, among his books and papers, he pointed to the stack. "Only students care about such things," he said, shrugging. Essayist and translator, he said he'd heard from his publisher that they and others were banding together — big publishers like Amir Kabir — to formally protest censorship and demand a meeting with the prime minister and SAVAK censors. The only ones immune from censorship were the Islamic publishers. "More than thirty new ones in the last decade!" he said. "Their journals sell forty thousand copies a month, and the finest literary journal sells two thousand. Qom is a factory! Islam, an ideology like Marx. Yet the clergy get slush funds from the state, and all the rest of us are forced underground." "They're more afraid of us!" I said. "They fund them to keep them irrelevant. We must work harder, write faster!" "But it's spreading uptown," said Dr. Hadi. "Vacuous society ladies are frequenting the houses of dervishes and celebrating religious feasts, all decked in the latest fashions and lace and high heels. Even pop singers are crooning about the call for prayer and the second coming. Disco-Islam!"

We divided the stack into bunches, and I ran them down to the street to give to Hossein and three other students he'd recruited, who were waiting by the curb on motorcycles.

Then I slipped off into the side streets to give a lecture at ten in a basement. My favorite topic — the young Marx and extreme voluntarism.

Late that night in my room, while correcting papers, I stared at the framed incantations Father had penned years before. That steady hand, drawing letters like rivers. The words swooping down, then soaring, waves, gathering like a mighty ocean. Arrangements of faith in ordered syllables, stroke by stroke, root by root. The very web that sustained him, splendid, impermeable.

Our time is tormented by a hunger for convictions.

FOURTEEN

WE'D ARRANGED TO MEET the French journalist at the Intercontinental early in the evening. He was waiting in the grand lobby to take us up to his room. We shook hands, and he pointed us to the bank of elevators.

Mr. Bashirian was visibly nervous. I knew he understood French, but he refused to acknowledge this before the journalist. He kept looking to me or down at his shoes. Leaving the elevator on the seventh floor, he hesitated long enough for me to think he'd decided against going through with it. He looked riddled with guilt. Out in the corridor he took a white handkerchief from his pocket and patted his forehead.

The room was crammed with two beds covered with stacks of books and papers, a typewriter on the desk. Several chairs were around a table at the far end by the window, which had a view to the back, overlooking the flat tarred roofs of midtown, spawning television aerials.

"Ugly roofs!" the journalist said.

Then, as if to make up for this slight and immediately ingratiate himself, he offered us tea or drinks. We declined. Mr. Bashirian stood, wooden. When I'd made arrangements for the meeting, he'd indicated to me he wanted no one else present and no tape recorder. He feared reprisals, reports to SAVAK. He feared the interview would have grave repercussions despite all assurances of anonymity. He didn't trust anyone. Still, he'd come with a sort of morbid fascination, like a man testing his wings by running off a cliff.

We sat round the small table. Mr. Bashirian sat erect in the armchair by the gray-blue drapes, looking ashen. The journalist kept smiling at him as if this would help, making little quips and asking me to translate. Mr. Bashirian rejects gratuitous affability, and any such attempt brings out the worst in him.

"Mr. Bashirian's favorite novel is Victor Hugo's *Les Misérables,*" I volunteered.

The journalist beamed and was about to respond when Mr. Bashirian said under his breath, "Why tell him I like some French book without mentioning Hafez and Sa'adi?"

"It's just a book."

"Ask if he's familiar with Enayat or Al-Ahmad."

"We're not here to be confrontational."

"Ask him."

"Maybe if you said something in French?"

"You said you'd translate."

The journalist watched this exchange warily, probably longing for his own translator to capture nuance, the full scoop.

"My friend wants to know if you're familiar with any of our authors, such as Enayat or Al-Ahmad?" I said.

"No, no. Are they available in French? I'd be most interested."

When I translated this, Mr. Bashirian said, "See! I told you. He knows nothing about our intellectual life. Yet he expects me to know about his. Otherwise he'd think me ignorant. An idiot."

"How do you know?"

"It's obvious."

"Shall I translate what you said?"

He shook his head. All three of us were already getting on one another's nerves. Mr. Bashirian was a hostile participant; I'd arranged the interview and was apprehensive about the entire event.

The journalist leaned forward, holding his notepad, like a doctor with an unwell patient. He said, a shade too earnestly, "Tell me about your son."

"He's in Komiteh Prison," said Mr. Bashirian tersely.

"Has SAVAK admitted this?"

"Of course not officially. Not yet."

"How did he get there?"

"He was arrested!"

"Is he a political activist?"

"He's a student."

"Why was he arrested?"

"You think I know? Every day I ask myself from the moment I wake up, What did he ever do to deserve this?"

"How did they take him?"

"The army trucks were called into Aryamehr University. They herded in rioting students at gunpoint. I think Peyman got swept up with the rest."

Mr. Bashirian stopped suddenly.

"So then?"

"That was one-thirty in the afternoon. He was late getting home that night. I'd left dinner on the table. I started worrying. He always called. A little after eleven the doorbell rang. Peyman had a key. No one rings our doorbell so late. His friend Kazem was at the door. He said he'd seen Peyman being pushed into a truck. Then he left."

"Is he a leftist?"

"Who — the friend?"

"Your son."

"He's studying to be an engineer."

"What happened next?"

"I stayed up all night, pacing. Certain it was some terrible mistake."

"When had you last seen him?"

"That morning at breakfast. He had tea and rinsed his glass and left it by the sink. He was going to buy bread in the evening. He needed a haircut. That's the last thing I remember about him."

"Is he a guerrilla? Like the men at Siahkal?"

"What, Siahkal?" said Mr. Bashirian indignantly. "They were a handful of terrorists in the jungle four years ago! What does that have to do with my son?"

"Is he a Marxist or a Maoist?"

"Why should he be?"

"Couldn't he be part of something you're not aware of?"

"Like what? I live for him. He's all I've got. I cook and sew and clean and shop and I've watched him grow up."

The journalist turned to me. "Your friend feels insulted whenever I insinuate the term *leftist* about his son."

I shrugged.

"No, no! He resents the question. He finds it offensive."

"Of course, he's a civil servant!" I said. "Leftists are considered treasonous. They're not part of the mainstream of our culture as they are in France. But — well, I should let him respond."

"My son's no Communist, if that's what you mean!" said Mr. Bashirian. "He loves his country. He wouldn't betray it."

"No political affiliations?" asked the journalist.

"He's never been trouble to me in any way. He wouldn't make trouble. It's not like him to cause grief or indignity."

"Holding a political belief is no indignity," said the journalist.

That struck me in a big way, as it did Mr. Bashirian.

"He's in prison for nothing," repeated Kamal Bashirian.

"He's a prisoner of conscience, yes?"

"You ask again if he's political. How many times shall I tell you? He studied so hard he barely had time for anything else."

The journalist threw a sidelong glance at me. "What did he do for fun?"

"Fun?" said Mr. Bashirian. "What fun? He studied."

"Did his friends tell you anything?" the journalist asked.

"The one who came by that night, he calls regularly. But there's nothing left to say. Several of them used to come to the house to study for exams. They stayed until all hours, and I fed them. That's a tough university. My son passed all his exams with flying colors. The others looked up to him."

"Who's the friend who calls?"

"Kazem — he's a nice boy, religious, very composed. He belongs to an association of Islamic students. He came to see me with a girl. She was nervous. In fact, high-strung. Several of their friends were taken that day. They've disappeared."

"Did the girl say anything?"

"She had tears in her eyes when she spoke of Peyman. She was angry."

"What about?"

"She detests the regime."

The journalist's eyes sparkled. "Really?"

"She said a lot of things in anger. She's young. She thinks she has all the answers. Thinks she can save the world. What do you expect?"

"She's his girlfriend?"

"My son's not the lovesick type!"

"What was she angry about?"

"Censorship. The meaningless propaganda of the system, so remote from the people. The mindless westernization of our society. The fascist overtones of the Rastakhiz Party. The hyped nonsense of the White Revolution. I don't know. The student arrests. She went on and on. Very indignant, very angry."

"Did your son ever speak that way?"

"He's quiet. Nearly withdrawn. He likes to take pictures. I showed Ms. Mosharraf some of them. He's much better with a camera than with words. SAVAK took his albums when they came to the house. And some letters."

"What was in the albums?"

"Photos of his travels. I think there's something there they want to use against him."

"Like what?"

"Something. Otherwise why would they take them?"

"Is there something in the letters?"

"He wrote me wherever he went about the color of the sky, the fishermen of the Gulf, the plants of the desert. He took pride in such things. I treasure them. I've devoted my life to him."

"If he's as withdrawn as you say, he might have been withholding information from you."

Mr. Bashirian turned to me. "There he goes again. And they accuse us of believing in conspiracies. They're no different!"

I did not translate this.

The journalist smiled blankly, shrugged. "Tell me about your son's friend — the one who calls you."

"He's a scholarship boy from Kerman. Quiet but intense. His father's nearly illiterate and owns a grocery store back there. The boy used to come often for dinner. So shy at first that he always hung his head. Completely lost when he came to Tehran. Recently he looks like he's found a new sense of purpose."

"What does he think?"

"How should I know?"

"You've never spoken to him?"

"Of course I have."

"Anything political?"

"Well, once. He was at the house, waiting for Peyman. There were just the two of us. He told me we've gone from feudalism to a society enslaved by Western capitalism. He spoke politely. He said there's only one great enemy: imperialism and its local collaborators, who rule through propaganda and terror. Like SAVAK — a secret police trained by the CIA and Israeli Mossad against its own people. He said we've lost our self-respect and identity, and that only Islam can restore that to us. Because Islam inspires a sense of duty and struggle and self-sacrifice."

"An Islamic Marxist?"

"There was no talk of Marxism."

"Perhaps he was being tactful," the journalist said, not without irony. "What about the girl who visited you?"

"She seemed quite fond of my son. I don't know. She was nice to come. No one else did. She stayed late. She kept talking. She wouldn't stop. In the end I got tired. She was very excitable. Quite outspoken about the regime. Fearless, actually, to say such things."

"Like what?"

"Well, she called them —" Mr. Bashirian paused, reconsidering. "She said they're monsters and rapists and bloodsuckers and . . . torturers."

The journalist leaned forward, taut with attention. "Interesting . . ."

Mr. Bashirian sat back, stony.

The journalist jotted things down. Then he mentioned one of our writers in exile, released from prison after sixty-four days, thanks to international pressure. The journalist smiled at Mr. Bashirian as if to say this interview could do the same for Peyman. "It's damning stuff he's written abroad about the regime and its torture chambers."

Mr. Bashirian and I hadn't heard about the articles.

"I met him in Europe," the journalist said. "He's consumed with rage and loathing. He speaks ferociously."

Mr. Bashirian said, "That's what they want to hear about us abroad?"

"He's a cultured man, an intellectual. With a scathing commentary about the evils of your history and kingship all the way from Cyrus the Great" — the journalist referred to some notes — "through Anoushiravan and Yaghoub-e-Leis and Shah Abbas and Agha Mohammad Khan and Reza Shah to the present. In fact, he calls them murderers and monsters! Each and every one."

"Really?" said Mr. Bashirian, red-faced. "We can't do anything right!"

The journalist threw up his hands, as if to say it wasn't his fault all our illustrious kings had turned out monstrous. He quoted incriminating excerpts from his notes, edifying us in an aggressive fashion. Mr. Bashirian looked more and more uncomfortable by the second.

"Your compatriot." The journalist shrugged. "I'm just quoting."

"Has he got anything to recommend?" said Mr. Bashirian. "Anything constructive? Criticizing is a religion for us."

"Tell me, then," the journalist asked him. "What do you think?"

Mr. Bashirian went blank. "It's not what I think that's important."

An awkward pause followed, then moments of silence beyond decency. His answer hovered like a pathetic affliction. The journalist was stretching time for effect, toying with Mr. Bashirian to make a point.

"To be perfectly objective," the journalist said finally, "his facts check out. I think he makes a good case for this terrible despotic trend in your history —"

"You should talk, as a European!" Mr. Bashirian snapped back. "Your history's pillaging and murdering and colonizing others over whom you've built your cities and museums and mighty industrial world. You lecture us with your two-faced humanism. Your exploitations have ravaged the world!"

I'd never seen Mr. Bashirian like this.

"Of course, anything disparaging about *us* is always convincing!" he continued, breathless. "Every time we slander and disgrace and slash ourselves to pieces, it's interesting to you. It's what you want to believe. It confirms all your darkest suspicions about us in the first place —"

Mr. Bashirian's voice broke off. His hands were trembling.

The journalist shook his head. "Look here, SAVAK has taken your son. He's in prison. You say they've —"

"You think I don't know what you want?"

"I don't understand."

"Please! You want me to make a fool of myself by spilling out my guts or to watch me dig my way out of this great big historical hole of ours by confirming what some writer told you in Europe!"

"I only mentioned him because —"

Mr. Bashirian was seething. "He's the perfect example of the treachery of our intelligentsia. I'm dumbfounded you find him a remarkable source. That you have such bad judgment! You mean you're all that gullible? It's the worst kind of indignity I've ever heard — damning the entire history of a country. It's self-serving and cowardly and pathetic. You think that's daring? You think that's intellectual? It's downright vindictive. A detestable way to make a point. If this man was imprisoned, so is my son! I love my son. You don't understand. I worship the very dust he walks on. But I'm not going to tear down my whole way of life, my entire heritage, to make cheap and repulsive points. Not now or ever. *Qu'est-ce que vous pensez? Qu'on est des sauvages et des idiots?*" Mr. Bashirian was suddenly speaking in broken French. *"C'est ça! C'est ça que vous cherchez?"* He got up abruptly, jolting the table.

"Time for me to go," he said to me in Persian. "I'm leaving."

I rose. "Wait, I'm leaving with you."

The journalist stared in bewilderment. Mr. Bashirian looked out of the window at the tarred flat roofs of the city.

"My friend feels he can't continue this interview," I said.

"Why? Look — there's been a misunderstanding. Please ask him to —"

Mr. Bashirian was making his way to the door. He grabbed the handle, yanked it open, stepped out, disappeared down the hall.

The journalist turned to me. "You stay at least. We can talk more reasonably, you and I. He's being irrational. He's too emotional. At least you and I speak the same language —"

"And what language is that?"

Abandoning inconsequential words of etiquette, I rushed down the hall. Mr. Bashirian was waiting by the bank of elevators, impatiently pressing the Down button. Neither of us said a word.

Going down in the elevator, he kept shaking his head bitterly. I was waiting for him to say something, but instead I felt him pull away, a hostile, disquieting estrangement.

Before we parted outside the hotel, he said curtly, "Forgive me if I caused you embarrassment in any way."

For the first time ever I felt he didn't mean it, that he didn't care anymore one way or the other, so much was his disappointment. I walked to my car with an astonishing sense of regret.

FIFTEEN

SHIRIN CALLED, all breathy on the phone, to say her boss had just left on Swissair for Zurich and she could leave the office early. Couldn't we go dancing? Couldn't we go uptown and dine on steak with pepper sauce at Chattanooga and watch people? I said I had a busy night.

"I've got something for you," she said, unrelenting but sheepish.

It wasn't like her to be sheepish or insistent. I asked what she had, but she wouldn't say, so I said I only had one hour.

Her white car was at the corner as usual. We drove up Pahlavi past the Hotel Miami and parked by the towering plane trees opposite Sa'yee Park. She slid out of the car in her tight skirt and heels, and I followed, watching her strut across the sidewalk, swinging her purse and blond mane, straight for a café marked Nice Teria. The place was overheated and smoky, swarming with lovesick couples, mostly students, crammed into narrow booths, with textbooks stacked on the tables under dim low-hanging lights.

We got seated by a window of smoked glass. Shirin asked for

tea and creamy roulette, then pulled out a cigarette. As I extended the flame of the match, she cupped my hand, lips puckered, eyes sultry. I found the artful gesture comic. She had oodles of eyeliner and green eye shadow and mascara. In the other booths they had heads together, all snug and whispering. The waiter brought tea and cake, Shirin joking around with him. We ate creamy roulette.

"I love these new *terias!*" she said. "Nancy Teria and Pretty Teria and Fancy Teria and two opening in Vanak."

I couldn't have cared less.

"You know, my English teacher at the Iran-America Society? He says *teria* is a word in Tehran, not in English. We laughed when he explained!"

"You let another foreigner patronize you again? Don't be a sheep. You love everything foreign. Careful, or you'll turn into a cheap imitation."

"I'm already one to you."

She slid a parcel wrapped in brown paper across the table. "Jalal gave it to me. He said if he ever disappeared to give it to you."

The brown paper was unmarked and sealed with tape.

"You opened it?" I said.

"You don't trust anyone."

"I know you slept with him," I said.

She flinched, slid off the bench. "I have a headache," she said imperiously.

She sauntered off, swinging her hips, waiters eyeing her appreciatively.

I TORE OPEN the brown paper of the parcel. It was a book, *The Selected Poems of Forough Farrokhzad.* I leafed through, and a white unmarked envelope fell out by my cup and saucer, a letter.

I tore open the envelope. A single sheet of white, unlined paper with five lines in blue ink. I recognized his lousy handwriting: "If something happens, call the number written in the book I gave you. Call at night after eleven. Tell whoever picks up: 'I bring news from Varamin.' He'll tell you where to meet him. When you see him, give him this message: The group has been infiltrated by two SAVAK agents. Tell him one of them is Omeed, and the other is Shaheen. It happened after the assassination of Colonel Fotouhi. I'm Omeed. I'm under surveillance. Trust me — I trust you."

There was no signature. A letter to no one from no one, only the bearer imperiled. I was stunned. Omeed — that was Jalal's code name? He was a member of the secret police? A Savaki? Impossible! I looked around, reread the letter. I couldn't believe what I was reading, couldn't believe I'd been misled. It came up against all my intuition and years of experience. I could have sworn he couldn't be a Savaki, not in a hundred years, not Jalal — he could never sell out, he was no squealer. The very idea was absurd. Since when did they hire agents who quoted poets like Nima and Shamlu? A new breed. I couldn't accept that I'd been betrayed. Ice in my veins instead of blood. He wanted me to trust him. He had some nerve! If he was a Savaki, then where had he drawn the line? Had he reported me, our underground group? Set us up, then lied about the SAVAK raid against us this summer? Already late for my class, I flagged a cab on the street.

THAT NIGHT we appraised the progress of the New Left — the Trotskyists, the Golehsorkhi group, and others. The new round of mass arrests at Aryamehr and Tehran Universities, where students had rioted and been hauled away, though we'd been told none were our recruits. Dr. Hadi sat pale and shaken. He said they had arrested his niece, an assistant lecturer at a technical university. She had called him from a police station, told him hurriedly that she'd be away at the Caspian all week — which he knew was nonsense — then managed to give the number of the station before getting cut off. Immediately he'd run out and called another number from the street. An influential lawyer had accompanied him to the police station, where they were told she'd been sent home. Two hours later they'd finally found her at her downstairs neighbor's, severely bruised and beaten. Dr. Hadi had examined her contusions and given her sedatives. She'd refused to go to the hospital. They had arrested her during a lecture by an activist writer that night. She and the other detainees had been taken to the police station, questioned; then several of them had been told to report to SAVAK headquarters the next day. She'd been put in an unmarked car with several men in plain clothes to drive her home, but ended up on a deserted road, where they'd clubbed her in the dark and abandoned her. What mattered most to her was this — they called her a fucking whore. "You fucking whore!" they said, beating her. "We know you're whoring around with faculty and students. Corrupting them. Fucking whores, all of you!" She wept with rage telling Dr. Hadi. "You see? If I speak up, I'm a whore in this country."

Our playwright said, "I must write a play about this! Why a woman is mother or whore in our country. I'll write it like a Greek tragedy."

We got down to business. The clique of three from the provinces, who had feuded, then split from us, had now appropriated the name of our paper. They had just come out with a very second-rate issue. Our reputation was at stake, so for the first time we decided to officially denounce them. We discussed details on coordinating the upcoming strike at Tehran and Aryamehr Universities, for the eight political prisoners on hunger strike, as well as at the Pars Technical School, where our feelers had formed two new cells. For the next three nights, and in different safe houses each time, I was scheduled to lecture preselected groups. Lenin, Kautsky, Debray, the politics of insurrection.

I reported on my friend from the confederation, Majid, and

how I'd settled with him about renting the garden by the Karaj River belonging to his uncle. We needed a covered truck to move our printing press out of town and needed to keep two volunteers there. We considered suitable candidates, tallied how much money was in our account at Melli Bank under Dr. Hadi's name. Again I told them about Majid's ambitions for the Left. Again they accused the Left in exile of being factional while supposedly promoting a coalition. Of snooping and fraternizing just to case their competition. Of being infiltrated and funded by foreign hands like the CIA and SAVAK. Of championing guerrilla warfare instead of political process. We agreed to stay focused and refuse to be swayed. These guys who come back from abroad are always patronizing and theoretical.

TWENTY-FOUR HOURS LATER I still had the letter in my possession. It lay in the inside pocket of my jacket — I couldn't leave it anywhere else.

The handwriting was his without a doubt. He'd used the blue felt pen. His penmanship was awful and I always ridiculed him.

I looked for the book in my room and found the phone number scrawled on the very last page. His plan was already in place when he'd given me the book. I considered my options until nightfall. Jalal had disappeared. It was a lie that he was in prison if he was working for the secret police. So where was he, and what was he up to? The only way to get to him was to do what he'd asked and call the number and give his message. I had to find him to find out if he'd double-crossed me.

At eleven-fifteen I sprinted down to the corner, went into the public booth, and dialed. The phone rang four times, and a man picked up.

"Yes?" he said, decisive and abrupt.

"I bring news from Varamin," I said.

He hesitated, for too many seconds. I didn't like it. I could hear the murmur of a radio and paper rustling.

"I've got news from Varamin," I repeated.

This wasn't working, and I decided to hang up.

"Wednesday," he said. "Let's go to the movies. Radio City. How about the seven o'clock showing? You buy the tickets and wait by the door."

"All right," I said.

"Don't forget to bring the book this time."

The phone went dead. I had forty-eight hours.

SIXTEEN

THE NEXT MORNING I called Mr. Bashirian. I felt guilty about the interview and how everything had gone wrong. I valued his friendship, but I was also angry. He had roped me in, ever more dependent on me, and now he was sulking.

I told him I needed to discuss the new directive with him. He said he had other pressing matters and I'd be better off discussing it with Mr. Makhmalchi. Especially since I was seeing so much of him already. Someone had let him know that Mr. Makhmalchi, his rival, was constantly in my office, perhaps Makhmalchi himself. I humored Mr. Bashirian, but he was curt, brooding. I'd known him so long that I was familiar with the intricacies of his temperament. It mattered a great deal to me what he believed. In the end, he made polite excuses. I felt offended; still, I kept up a warm and tactful end to the conversation. I wouldn't have done it for anyone else.

At the tail end of the day, there was a note on my desk. The director wanted to see me. Going past Mr. Bashirian's closed door down the hall, I wanted to barge in and shake him and tell him I was on his side. I wasn't sure how he saw things anymore.

The director was standing behind his desk talking on the phone when I went in. He waved me over to a chair, got off the phone, rubbed his temples.

"It's been a bad week," he said. "I know our economic realities have no bearing on the way things are run."

I nodded politely.

"In other words" — he cleared his throat — "it's not as simple as writing papers and sending memos. Our advice doesn't really count. I mean, it should — but if we argue our side too forcefully, they accuse us of harboring leftists. The truth is, whenever there's a big conference and everyone gathers, the only real players are way at the top. Everything — everything comes from the top." He sat down. "Edicts, endless monologues, lectures. We're ordered, like servants. And that's that."

He stared, solitary, dubious.

"There are too many political interventions from the top," he said. "Too many things. One option is to resign in protest. Of course, it's hard to let go of power. So if one knows what goes on and stays, that means one accepts."

I thought he'd lost his mind to speak that way. If word got out, he'd lose his position and kill his entire career.

"I — I've spoken frankly, but, well, we go back many years and after all I know your father, though he and I are different generations. Please give him my best."

Thierry called just as I was about to leave my office, his voice full of mischief. He'd already heard about the interview at the Intercontinental.

"This is the sort of thanks I get?" he said.

"You only want gratitude."

"All that nonsense about the poor little wretched father. I hear he quotes Fanon and gets downright nasty."

"Will it get printed?"

"Who knows," he said. "Anyway, I'm in excellent humor, since I've made another conquest."

"Tell me," I insisted.

He dodged, but it was a game — he wanted me to know. He was having an affair and finally admitted it was Pouran.

"You call that a conquest?"

He laughed again, entertained and gratified I had ridiculed a mutual friend.

MY BROTHER KAVOOS DROPPED BY early in the evening. The children were doing homework upstairs. They came running down to greet their uncle, then went running back up again. Houshang had called to say he'd be late because of a meeting followed by a reception. I handed Kavoos a Scotch and soda in the living room, and he took off his tie and jacket.

"Everything all right?" he asked.

"Why?" Kavoos can be cagey.

"What happened to that boy who was arrested?"

"Nothing. His father saw the lawyer."

"Then it's out of our hands."

"It's in nobody else's."

"There's something you should know," he said.

I looked up.

"I heard something from a friend this morning. Someone high up."

"Bad news?"

"It concerns Houshang. It's very confidential."

I reached for the pack of cigarettes.

"It doesn't look good. They're about to indict two rear admirals and several naval officers and, so far, two civilians. Several of the officers are on the Bandar Kangan project. The charges are embezzlement — payoffs in the millions. So far your husband is not on the list."

"Thank God."

"I don't know how . . . involved Houshang is," he said. "Let's hope he's clean as a whistle. Father will have a heart attack if he gets indicted."

My palms turned clammy at the word *indicted.*

"I'm not sure when the story's going to break. Right now they're meeting behind closed doors. One of the naval officers has decided to come clean and name names. He's been promised a more lenient sentence for betraying the others. I don't know if Houshang knows, but this is very confidential information. Very sensitive."

I nodded.

"I'm not one of your husband's closest friends, and he's never confided in me. I mean, I don't know what he does. Right? But what if — anyway, even if he isn't directly involved, it can get nasty. They could investigate his company. You know how it is — they blame others for their own corruption. They want scarecrows to leave twisting in the wind."

He sipped his Scotch, the ice clinking. He'd just put distance between the corrupt system and Houshang and himself quite nicely.

I smoked, my gaze fixed on the miniatures nailed to the wall. The studied poses of the robed women, turbaned men, uniform gardens, the gold, astonishing colors. The figures shimmered. Their roles were cast for them, like their fate. Arrested. I saw myself up there with them. Stylized. Paralyzed. Ornate and immured.

I felt I was suffocating. I went to open a French window, stepped out onto the terrace for air. Kavoos came out and stood with me.

"What if he's implicated?" he demanded. "Anything you suspect?"

"Nothing," I said, lying so he would leave.

Kavoos was terrified for our good name and reputation, terrified for himself. Father had accumulated a lifetime of unimpeachable deeds large and small, already shelved and forgotten, his ambition muffled with decorum and self-effacement. Today they laugh at such modesty.

"What's your gut feeling?" Kavoos asked me.

"Don't worry," I said.

"Don't let on I've said anything. Wait until Houshang tells you."

Kavoos stuck around, but I wanted him to go. He wanted more reassurance than I could give, and I wanted to be alone. I let the help go home early and cooked and fed the children while they told me about their fistfight in school and detention at the principal's office. Then they watched *Morad Barghi* on television. I tucked them in. I briefly called Mother, who talked about her bulbs and bedding her plants.

In the dark stillness of the house, I turned on a light downstairs, sat opposite the Persian miniatures. I saw their beauty, minutely executed, constrained. The faces expressionless, one indistinguishable from the other. The tyranny of form. I'd never seen them that way before. I heard the wind, the creaking of the shutters. I stared, trancelike. Then I saw them — the robed men and women — rising out of their pages, propelling themselves. Casting off their mantles, their eternal strictures, millennial and crippling. Tearing off their configurations — the ceremonial robes, the eternal words, the props. Flinging themselves out of the impossible geometry of their pavilions and courts and gardens. Into an unpredictable future.

I MUST HAVE BEEN DOZING when a door slammed. Then I heard another door and flushing in the downstairs powder room. Two-thirty. Houshang had stopped off somewhere after the official reception. I heard him come up the steps, taking the treads slowly — he'd had too much to drink again. I imagined my sons taunted in school because their father's name was denounced in the papers. Big headlines, a picture.

I lifted my head from the pillow and listened. Houshang knew better than to get caught. He knew better than to get himself implicated; he didn't want anyone's advice or opinion. He needed to come out on top, for himself, for the money, the sheer pleasure. Testing that fine line between big success and corruption — a populated line, judging by prevailing standards. I had no idea about the intricacies of his dealings.

He came down the hall, turned off the light, going into our bathroom through the hallway. He flicked the switch, light seeping from under the adjoining door into the bedroom, an incandescent strip adhering to the dark. I could hear him move in there. He picked off his shoes, let them fall with a thud. His belt buckle struck the tiled floor, then dragged. He turned on the faucet, brushed his teeth, rinsed, hitting the toothbrush against the sink four successive times. I heard the vanity mirror slide back and forth, then the faucet again, water rushing into a glass. He was drinking. He needed pills for a headache, pills for his stomach, pills to go to sleep. I turned toward the window, my back to the door through which he'd come.

When had I started disliking him? The first time I'd seen him. But I hadn't noticed then.

Long ago suddenly. Fourteen years. I had just returned from London with a fine degree and the finest prospects, Mother said. I had wanted to choose my fate, whereas Mother believed one could not escape it. She thought deliberating endlessly about marriage vulgar and lacking in imagination; I thought it pride equivocating with emotion and logic. So I had started life by getting married. Houshang had stalked me. He wanted me all for himself. I had evaded him, knowing he would finally have me and I couldn't escape him. He was nine years older, charming, persistent. Whispering, "You're my paragon of goodness." He brought his family to ask for my hand. His mother, hair-sprayed to perfection, fingered her jewels, adoring him. Mother mimicking her later. His father, a noted surgeon and sometime politician, was more discerning. His mother was a member of a royal charity and changed the color of her gems and expensive suits with the days of the month. Our families started seeing a great deal more of each other. His father soliciting Father's advice in the corners of living rooms and on evening walks, which pleased Father no end. The mother cogitating about high society in her high trill, which amused and exasperated Mother. Mother's ironic quips way above her head. We had a short engagement. Forty-five people at his parents' in Mahmoudieh, then eighty-five people at the Hotel Darband for dinner and dancing. Well-attended luncheons, elegant afternoon teas, dinner at La Résidence, Friday lunches of *chelo-kabob* at their country house by the Karaj River, followed by interminable games of rummy and poker.

Father and Mother had considered others but agreed to Houshang. He looked promising, he had luster, zeal, drive. "That's fine!" Mother said. Father had smiled, but that had had more to do with the vision of his one and only daughter in a white lace dress. Summer. A wedding in the garden of the old house. The fragrant rose bowers in full bloom and the night dark velvet. The massive trees lit like phantoms, the pool shimmering from the light of paper lanterns. The largest rugs cast over fine-graveled paths, with the music of the orchestra rising and children running across the lawns like fireflies. Mother's friend the portly Mrs. Vahaab singing that night like a large-bosomed nightingale. Pots of white jasmine and red geranium set all around the front porch and down the steps. Old Tourandokht — old even then — in a brand-new blue satin dress and diaphanous voile chador, crying under the Russian crystal chandelier. Watching me turn in the downstairs hallway, lifting up my white veil with one hand. The bride. *"Aroos khanom, aroos khanom!"* she kept repeating, snapping her fingers in a lop-sided dance with her funny bowed legs. Murmuring prayers and blowing on me to ward off the evil eye. In the upstairs rooms, she had burned wild rue, carrying it in a small brazier on a silver tray, circling through the rooms to ward off evil spirits, and we had inhaled the mesmerizing scent in our frenzied state while applying French makeup and perfumes. And she had come close and whispered to me, "May you grow old with your husband. May you have capable sons and beautiful daughters. May you live together for a hundred years." And I'd known then as the gates were closing that revenge would come. I'd seen myself pass before the bedroom mirror, shimmering in white, and knew even as I prepared to descend the stairs that I was relinquishing a certain instinct, that deeper rhythm of life, for certainty and logic. Doing what was expected. Drawn deep into a system, easing into it as though slipping on gloves for a formal and inevitable occasion. Already waiting for the end. Houshang and I virtual strangers, despite our all-consuming social calendar. Always with others, barely knowing each other. "What's to know? What's to know?" Mother kept repeating as we descended the jasmine-lined steps of the front terrace before all the wedding guests. "You'll never know until you live with him three dozen years. Even then."

I heard the bathroom door open and his footsteps on the carpet. He sat on the edge of the bed, then slumped back. I stiffened without moving, my back to him. I closed my eyes. The boys were still young; I had obligations. Houshang possessed. He liked being in that position. Anything else was losing.

THE NEXT MORNING Houshang was gone by the time I went in to shower. He was avoiding me. As usual his clothes from the night before were in a heap by the chair. As I lifted his blue shirt to put it in the hamper, I caught a whiff of perfume. The shirt I'd given him that summer. He liked blue, the finest shirts from Paris, but that wasn't my perfume on his favorite shirt. He'd been out drinking and picking up women. He went, always accompanied.

I called Pouran and woke her up. She said it was just as well, since her masseuse would be there any minute to wrap her flesh in her eternal fight against cellulite. I told her I was dropping in on my way to work.

She lived four minutes away. The new Filipino maid opened the front door. She'd been over at our house with Pouran's two brats and knew Houshang and the children. I asked if there had been a party the night before, and she mumbled about a group of friends and card games.

"Like other nights, madame," she said.

Across the hallway, two Bangladeshi servants — new arrivals — were in the living room dusting and vacuuming. Pouran had sacked all the local house help, as she'd pledged, and imported. "Our masses stink!" she always says, grimacing.

"When my husband was here last night, did he leave his jacket?" I asked.

"No, no jacket, madame."

That settled it. I went upstairs. Pouran was in the bedroom, seated at her gilt rococo dressing table, a half-dozen pairs of expensive shoes strewed by her feet. Her yellow hair was disheveled, the black roots out. She looked wasted first thing in the morning, her vulgar sexuality in remission. She was in an apricot peignoir, applying greasy cream to her yellowish skin and yawning nonstop.

"I was going to call you," she said.

"About last night's party?"

She registered surprise but recovered admirably.

"Houshang was here," I said.

"We missed you!"

"Of course you did. Did he take off with Iraj at any point?"

"Iraj had guests!"

"That's nice. So you supply the liquor and women."

"What?" said Pouran, indignant. "We played poker until late."

"My husband never whores around alone. Neither does yours, of course. They go together. Don't bother — I know."

"I don't know what you mean. Men must be men. You understand that! Houshang was tired and just had a couple of drinks an —"

"Did any of your guests need a ride?"

"What do you mean?"

"You" — I pointed — "know perfectly well what I mean. I know what's going on behind my back. I'm warning you. Don't you dare pimp for my husband. You understand?"

"How dare you insult me like that!" she said, all haggard and slovenly.

She went on about how she was shocked at my odd behavior, how I'd come barging in, how much I had changed. I had always been such a perfect lady! I left her as the masseuse came in, a stocky Maronite from Beirut with bulges and porcelain skin and bedroom eyes.

"Bonjour, mesdames!" she chirped, lugging her bag of potions.

It took forever to drive to work, traffic gnarled, downtown a hundred times worse.

Iraj and Pouran's first and only allegiance is to Houshang. They will always lie for him. Iraj and Pouran keep a permanent state of open house. They live off others, seemingly living for them. Their friends congratulate them for this. It's a perfect arrangement. Theirs, the grand central station, the clearinghouse, the private boudoir and drawing room for all seasons, where Iraj can play host and Pouran can fritter away her life publicly. My husband and Iraj and Pouran were three of a kind, tight like a fist. I had always been the odd one out. Every time we'd done anything, from the very beginning of our marriage, Iraj and Pouran had tagged along. To Cannes, Florence, the Greek isles. Houshang needed them, and whenever I objected he called me a snob. Iraj was the invaluable old friend and ally; they did business together. Pouran was scrupulous at leaving a very good impression on her husband and mine, her affair with Thierry another one of her backroom forays. She doesn't know I know. She'll never understand foreigners have big mouths and short attention spans. Iraj is so full of himself that he doesn't notice her carnal incursions, or perhaps it helps business. He's a developer on a grand scale, speculating in land and building high-rises and hotels and offices in Tehran and around the country. With homes in London and the south of France and New York. Pouran impersonates the role of dutiful wife, plopping herself forever center stage as hostess. Admittedly she's perfected the role — the dulcet voice, the gushing warmth, the fortitude of an all-terrain tank for pushy hospitality. All the while catering to her husband's hubris as though it were some hothouse flower guaranteed to stand her in good stead, which it does. She lives like a queen, but she's restless. The last time she was in a frenzy was over the cultural attaché of a certain embassy — diplomats, not bankers, the ultimate conquest to her. I was acquainted with the attaché. Who wasn't? He was slim and tall, and he had a bit of a stoop and silky hair collapsing into impish eyes, with a degree from Oxford and aristocratic bloodlines and all the markings of the European degenerate. An incurable collector — ancient glazed pottery and rugs and kilims and tribal silver and Eastern knickknacks — he shopped along Manuchehri Street every week like a fox. A friend said he was a spy. I was there the evening of that swank cocktail party in a garden in Niavaran — Iraj roving with his tycoon comportment and come-get-me look, Pouran all dolled up and on the lookout, stepping out of their chauffeured gold Mercedes-Benz with the starry-eyed look of some of our new mercantile imperialists. She'd caught the cultural attaché bored out of his mind, slumped in the armchair of the deserted living room. He'd attached himself to her on the spot. The local girls were too girlish for his tastes, too prudish for his pornographic requirements. He told me himself, taking great pride in his indiscretion. Pouran took pride in their lecherous afternoons knocking about the antique wares in his apartment off Ghavam Saltaneh, delighted with his great breeding, the cultural part completely wasted on her. He told me, with considerable condescension. "God, you've got *such* great breeding!" he'd say, mimicking her. "It's *such* an honor!" Laughing his head off. Not that she ever knew. The last time I saw him, he said with amusement, "She likes giving juicy tidbits to the right customer. She'll do anything! The husband gets foreign concessions. Both of them awful people."

Early last summer, by the pool at our house, Pouran came right out with an astonishing admission. A rare moment of disillusionment. We were on the deck chairs on the sunny side. She said, "Iraj is hairy and stocky and dull. He's got no real class. You want to know something? He's got a dinky instrument and is one lousy lover. And he thinks he's a stud!"

Her laughter hammered, all caustic and tinny.

I took one good look at her that day and suddenly saw her as an old tart with nothing left to peddle, sunning herself by some swank pool in the south of France. Decomposing in her favorite Eden.

SEVENTEEN

AFTER TEACHING my last trigonometry class at night school, I gathered up the quizzes and rushed off to see Mother. There was a chill in the air.

The bus came late and we all squeezed in like cattle. The ticket boy was rude and pushy, the driver amusing himself by braking and accelerating erratically. Two irritable mothers with overstuffed plastic baskets pulled at the whining and sniffling children tugging about their skirts. We stood rocking to and fro, the bus lurching and pushing through evening traffic, the city streets a jumble of bright neon lights over the heads of pedestrians. Two bullies in the front picked an argument with the driver and the ticket boy, pushing and shoving the rest of us. I was about to lose my temper when they muscled their way out at a stop, firing back four-letter words like bullets.

Zari opened the door, wiping wet hands on her skirt, brushing off a strand of hair from her pale face with her wrist.

"You've been neglecting Mother!" she said, in a temper.

She holds me responsible for everything. Not that she, the apple of Father's eye, Zarrindokht, would ever admit it. I'm the one she blames for letting her get married to Morteza. She told me after Father's death, since which Morteza's outbursts and cruelties have grown. Now he dares get into fights with Mother, who lies in bed the next day, disconsolate. Zari blames me for letting Morteza drink and carouse and avoid coming home until all hours of the morning. She figures I should keep threatening him. I could beat him up, but he'll get even by beating Zari. She nags at me that he's still a lowly underling at the Ministry of Post and Telegraph, as if I were withholding the magic word to get him promoted. She nags at me that her life is being washed down the toilet and holds me responsible for not lecturing Morteza every chance I get. He doesn't need a lecture. He needs a lobotomy.

Zari's children came running. I took out little brown paper bags of dried mulberries and sour cherries from my pockets. They hopped higher, stretching up their hands.

"Me, me, me!" they shouted.

"Don't shout!" Zari screamed at them.

She struck her firstborn, Ali, on the head. He backed into the wall, staring up at her from behind his dark lashes as she loomed over him.

I followed her into the kitchen. She had lentil rice with dates and raisins steaming in the pot with chicken. The children went by, each on a plastic stick with the head of a horse, whinnying and bucking through the small rooms as they clutched their bags.

"I'm hungry," I said.

"You're selfish!" said Zari.

Mother looked tired. She'd just finished saying her prayers. I carried in the Aladdin portable stove and fetched her a glass of tea.

"Zari doesn't belong in this marriage," I said.

"She's got three kids. I'm the one who doesn't belong," Mother said.

We ate and I helped clear the plates and went back to sit with Mother, who was knitting, her eyes enlarged like saucers behind thick glasses. She had a big operation last year and she's still weak. She has arthritis and bad circulation, and when she exerts herself she gets heart palpitations and shortness of breath. She may live in her daughter's house, but she still lives with Father.

"You're quiet," she said to me.

Her hands are comforting. When they hover, a lifetime appears a sheltering place, an illusion worth every moment.

"What're you waiting for?" she demanded. "Get married. Before your teeth fall out and you lose all your hair and I die like your father."

"It's not so simple."

"You're involved in something political. That's it, isn't it?"

"It isn't that."

"Yes, it is. Politics means misfortune and prison. You want me to wear black? What sort of life is this? You'll grow old, you'll be lonely, you'll be miserable," she said on that first chilly night of autumn.

The children were crying and making a racket in the next room. They ran in and jumped into Mother's lap and threw their arms around her.

"We don't want to go to bed!" they pleaded, sobbing.

She told them a fable and they squealed in delight, repeating the refrains to the end with her. They wanted one from me and I told them about Rostam and Zal. Zari leaned in the doorway, arms crossed, scowling.

"I'm tired of the same old heroes," she said.

She yanked the kids by their arms off to bed, pulling them and cussing. They were her burden. They went, throwing desolate glances back in our direction.

"Zari's high-strung this year," Mother said.

I lit a cigarette and she put down her knitting.

"I have a vow. I'm going to Shah Abdul-Azeem to light candles. Will you go with me?" I said I would. She asked about Jalal, and I said I'd been to see Nasrollah *mirza* and was temporarily tutoring Mahastee's children.

"When you were just a boy you . . . admired her."

In those days Mother would whisper, "Never be beholden to anyone. Never accept a handout, no matter what they promise you. Never overstep your place in the world." In Morshedabad there was only a grove between our house and the Mosharrafs'. They always kept the customary distance with impeccable courtesy on both sides in the same garden. But Mother and Father had first lived in Tehran, where their first child, a daughter, was born. In her second year the child fell ill with a mysterious fever that came suddenly and took her within ten days. Mother fell into a wild and inconsolable grief, until finally Father took her away from the city and brought her to Morshedabad to rest and convalesce. She had liked the village, the shrine, the open fields and country life, and in time, when Mahastee's father started a school there and then a clinic, she helped and then managed the clinic, and she and Father had stayed on. The village had grown, and two of her relatives had also bought property there and started families, and then Mother started sewing and knitting classes for the village women and finally one year became pregnant again and went back to Tehran to give birth to me. After several months she took me back to Morshedabad, going back to Tehran another time to stay with her relatives to have Zari, and then back always several times a year to the capital for us to visit family there.

Morshedabad was home. When the Mosharrafs arrived, she paid them a formal visit each time Mahastee's mother was there, during which they would say how much they esteemed each other, how much each husband respected the other, and going on from there about how to make jam and pickles and about Sobhi's radio program and the marvelous voice of Banu Delkash and the latest fashions in Tehran and news of the school and clinic in the village and Mother's classes for the women, but more than anything, about how to bring up their children. Mother never said anything about how Mahastee was at our house all the time, but Mother's eyes would light up when Mahastee came and plopped down against our bolsters, and they'd talk about the village, and Mother would take her to the classes, and Mahastee would chatter with the children and come home late with Mother and often curl up against the bolsters and fall asleep until she was called home for dinner and she would yawn and stretch and run back through the trees. She watched Mother sew and cook and make sweetmeats, especially quince-blossom paste in spring, which was her favorite, listening to the quiet stream of Mother's unassuming comments, listening even when she withdrew to say her prayers in the next room. Father, she listened to in a different way, demanding stories from him, questioning him, and it unfailingly surprised me how much he liked it. Mother took her mother fruit preserves and pickles and votive bowls of *sholeh-zard* for the proper occasions, and then gifts of satin pillowcases she'd embroidered herself, and bedspreads by the village women, and Najibeh *khanom* brought her cotton fabrics from Tehran for the sewing classes and fine imported ones for the New Year, which Mother sewed up on her Singer sewing machine for Zari and herself for visits to the capital, and whenever the Mosharrafs came back from Europe, Mother got perfumes and creams from Paris and London, which she left sitting unopened on the shelf but Zari would tear open with delight and use extravagantly, though the sight of them sent her daydreaming and lurching between envy and regret until Mother had to give her a lecture about the world. And that was how they had lived the years out, Mother and the Mosharrafs, circumscribing the limits of their relationship.

Mother glared. "Admire all you want. But not the illusions."

She knew — she was related to them.

In the street I pulled on my jacket.

SUNRISE CAME with the birds chirping in clusters in the plane trees. The trees were losing leaves, browning steadily. Masht-Ahmad was out, sweeping them away. Coming up from behind, I saw his stoop and his bowed legs and aimless broom and apathetic effort. A picture of futility. I decided I'd tell him he looked like Charlie Chaplin to cheer him up.

"How're you doing?" I said.

"My mother passed away."

I stopped in my tracks and offered my condolences. He looked down at his shoes, worn shoes, and dark, faded trousers billowing against bony legs. When he looked up, tears were streaming down his face.

"I was born stupid and will leave this world stupid," he said. "Poor Mother. What did she know?"

He turned away, wiping his eyes on his sleeve. I left him to his work, and at the corner I looked back. He hadn't made much progress, though he'd been out since the crack of dawn.

I got to work so early that only the janitor was there. He brought tea and office gossip. At three-thirty I saw our director in the hall, smiling with superfluous charisma. He's back with a master's degree from America, which has inflated his ego. He came over and pumped my hand.

"I've heard nothing but praise about you," he said.

He needed a dependable workhorse to complete the big report for the department on schedule, so he could take all credit and glory.

"Why don't you join us at Casbah tonight?" he said.

They were a select group. The guys in the office longed to be asked even once. I hesitated and he insisted one more time, and I agreed to join them later after my appointment. He took off all pleased, smoothing back his hair and tie, admiring his reflection, newly perfected abroad, in the mirror by the elevators.

The copy of Forough's poetry was on my desk, the one Jalal had sent me. I'd already told Rahnema High School to find a substitute for the evening.

I went out to deliver a message to a stranger at seven in the street.

RADIO CITY CINEMA — like Niagara, Diana, Moulin Rouge, Odeon, Paramount. In their halls, packs of voracious boys dream of becoming men. Spitting out sunflower seeds and leering at the girls and letting out wolf whistles and keeping up a running commentary in the dark. Dreaming of Technicolor liberation, the bourgeois Dream Machine. The kind with easy girls and easy sex and fast cars. Envisioning themselves towering and swank and freewheeling.

I turned down from Valiahd Square. If there had been a betrayal against our group, and the betrayer was Jalal, then I was the offender. I'd given us away because I was the link. They could point the finger at me, and I was as good as dead.

I had half an hour. I knew the drill — I trained others for this sort of thing. Approaching Radio City Cinema from the north, one block up I crossed the street, checking behind me as if about to flag a taxi or catch the bus, making sure I wasn't being followed. I walked on purposefully, right past the cinema but on the opposite side of the street, on the lookout for any telltale signs — slow-moving cars, loiterers, extra policemen, parked cars with idle passengers. Nothing was out of place. Across the street under the big movie marquee a crowd gathered for the seven o'clock showing. I stepped out to the very edge of traffic as if to cross over. Instead I looked out, taking in the crowd, then continued on the same side briskly, turning west at the traffic light. I went right one block and, across the street from Golden City Cinema, turned up Sabba. Then up one block, and turning right on Dameshq and back into Pahlavi, full circle, I crossed over, heading down, this time on the same side as the cinema, eyes peeled but sauntering. Up against the towering facade of Radio City, I felt the rush of adrenaline. I cut through the loosely gathered crowd under the marquee — mostly young men — a passerby in the flow of evening pedestrians. I didn't go for the small window of the ticket office. Instead I took a quick look around and immediately crossed at the intersection. No one had been waiting alone at the entrance. The contact wasn't there yet. I looked back over my shoulder, into the crowd and the street. That's when I saw the two men in dark suits, higher up, crossing with me. I stiffened, walked faster, right through the intersection on Takhte Jamshid. They followed. I cut into a side street, a dead end with a hotel marquee, and walked straight into the lobby of the Commodore Hotel, all glass and brass and lit up, two bellboys in silly blue uniforms with gold braid, smiling in a corner.

They stared and I walked back out. The two men in dark suits were not there. I went up to the corner of Takhte Jamshid, checked up and down Pahlavi. Eight minutes to seven. There was no time left. I had to get there right away.

Cars honked at me as I skipped through speeding traffic, walking fast, then slowing down suddenly right before Radio City. I went straight for the ticket window, eyes fixed on the woman inside, who looked bored. I asked for two tickets, whipped out bills from my trouser pocket, grabbed the tickets, and turned away.

"Your change," the woman called after me.

I grabbed the change, dumped it in my pocket, then pulled out the book of poetry from the outside pocket of my jacket, making sure the cover with the title was facing out: *The Selected Poems of Forough Farrokhzad.* In my other hand I held up the two tickets like

Popsicles. I backed into a rowdy group of boys standing together, and one of them threw back his head with an idiotic smile.

"Wow," he said, "an intellectual just bumped into me!"

They laughed. He was pointing at me. *"Porfessor,"* he said mockingly. *"Porfessor,* is this a good movie for morons like us?"

They doubled over laughing. People turned to watch — we were attracting attention. I was between the rowdy bunch and the entrance to the cinema. I looked past the succession of glass doors, my eyes sweeping past pedestrians and the magazine stand by the curb. I saw a man at the far end turn around and look straight at me. He wore glasses, was young, unshaven, nondescript, with a medium build and wavy black hair, and was wearing a pea green jacket. I saw him look at the two tickets and the book against my chest. His eyes widened but he didn't budge.

Just then the tickets fell from my grip. I swore and bent down to sweep them up, seeing trouser legs and car tires on my way up facing traffic. Then I froze. I'd seen a maroon car parked across the street past the group of boys, who were partially blocking it. I straightened up behind the group. There were three men in the car, a driver in front with a dark jacket, and two men in the back, whose faces I couldn't see. SAVAK? I turned quickly, locating the young man with glasses. He was walking toward me. I looked across the street. Had they come for him, for us? The two men in the back of the maroon car were now talking; the closer one had his face turned away from the window. Then suddenly he turned his head. I first saw the other one pointing to the cinema. What I couldn't believe was the one who'd just turned his head. It was Jalal. Whose side was he on? Why had he told me to call a stranger and bring a message, then come to Radio City himself? In a flash I understood what was about to happen. I whipped around to warn the young man with glasses, now just a few feet away from me. This was a trap. They'd used me and drawn him out to arrest him. Jalal was about to give him away, the snitch. The young man was nearly within my reach. He couldn't see the car because he had his back to it. I went to grab the sleeve of his jacket to tell him, all the while calculating how to make a run for it myself. Then I saw Jalal lean forward and look straight at me. He saw us, my eyes locking with his, not a single emotion on his face, not even acknowledgment. He stared as if looking through me. He could have betrayed his own mother, the son of a bitch. Then something strange happened. Jalal shook his head slowly, and the man next to him said something insistent, and Jalal shook his head again twice. Then he leaned back into the seat. The man beside him tapped the driver, and the car pulled out, merging with traffic.

If Omeed was his code name and he was with the secret police, why watch from across the street, then leave? I turned suddenly. The young man with glasses was behind me. We came face-to-face.

"What are you waiting for?" he said under his breath.

"I've got a message for you."

"Give it right here."

I whispered, "The message is, the group has been infiltrated. Two Savakis got in after the assassination of Colonel Fotouhi."

"Which two?" he demanded.

"Omeed —"

"Omeed?" he said, confounded. "Who's the other?"

"Shaheen."

He looked like he'd bitten into a capsule of poison.

I lunged to grab his arm. This was my only chance to wheedle information out of him, but he pivoted quickly and turned on his heels. I saw the back of the pea green jacket disappearing quickly in the crowd, and I started running.

"Wait —" I called out. "Hold on —"

He rounded the corner into Takhte Jamshid, nimble and quick, zigzagging between pedestrians. I saw him turn left again and look back over his shoulder, eyes nasty and dead-set. I ran into the side street after him, but he ran faster, the flaps of his jacket billowing. Nightfall, the streetlamps on, the side streets shadowy. I'd lost him.

THE TAXI DRIVER TALKED nonstop all the way up Pahlavi. I sat in the front. If the secret police had brought Jalal to Radio City to point the finger, he hadn't. He'd come with another set of plans. I couldn't decide what had just happened.

The taxi driver had the radio on and was shouting over it. Another self-proclaimed philosopher. The inside of the cab, from the front windshield all the way to the back, was adorned with green velvet trim dripping with little green pompons. A picture of the disciple Ali in the front with halo and sword under winged angels, and verses from Hafez and the Qur'an plastered all around, with postcards of mermaids and seamen and strange islands at sunset and virginal girls with doleful eyes, big tears plunging down their cheeks. Hanging from the rearview mirror, a cluster of amulets to ward off the evil eye, an enormous set of dice in red velour, and two pale blue fluorescent plastic swans. "They're unrequited lovers!" he said, fingering them lecherously. The last leg of the trip, he took no other ride and flipped open the dashboard to reveal nude pictures of big blonds with big tits and high heels and black lace stockings and big behinds. He chuckled, going through the register of low-class brothels in the red-light district, District Ten. He kept telling dirty jokes and elbowing me in the ribs like a jackass and swearing at every politician he could cut down, berating the lot of them.

"They're all servants!" he said.

He screeched to a halt by the curb. "Your car's in the repair shop?"

I nodded and paid.

"Women only like flashy cars! What's yours?"

"Me? A red Camaro," I said, smiling.

I could see the group from where I was standing, up by the short end of the restaurant facing the side street. The director from our department was there with my other colleagues, eyeing the competition at other tables, drinking.

I watched them as I crossed. The director held forth with some story while they all listened and laughed, slapping the table when he finished. One hell of a story, judging by their reaction.

I crossed the side street and came up alongside Casbah. Traffic whizzed by along Pahlavi. I walked on along the panes of smoked glass, stopping to light a cigarette under a tree. I didn't feel like making small talk with the director, another vain, rootless, just-returned-from-abroad braggart. The new breed.

I pushed through the glass doors. I gave the maître d' a brief message, pointing at the far table, and left; then I got into the phone booth on the street to dial Abbas. I watched with anticipation, already laughing. Within seconds the director came running out of the restaurant, very agitated, flailing arms about, his buddies on his heels. He looked up and down the street frantically; then they all ran to the corner. The message was, "The owner of a brand-new red Camaro that is on fire and burning in the street is that man."

Abbas was working late as usual at the National Television, just up and across the street on the hill. He said he'd be able to leave shortly and told me where to go.

I walked up Pahlavi, past the Hilton, turning right on Fereshteh, past new mansions faced in white travertine and marble for the new rich. At the end where the street turned left at the bottom, I turned by the summer compound of the Soviet embassy, its old walls running along the road, the immense plane trees towering behind them. Father had told me stories on cold winter nights about Colonel Liakhoff plotting around old Tehran, and Colonel Starosselsky, White Russian commander of our own Cossack Brigade. In Father's days the big scare was the Red Terror and

Pishehvari and the Communist movement. He disdained all foreign interferences and schemes and handouts.

Down past the embassy the road was dark, the rocky riverbed under the bridge bearing a trickle of water from a summer with no rain. I went over and up, turning down into the residential backstreets behind the Old Shemiran Road. I found the small restaurant at the bottom of a dead end, stuck between trees, with a string of bare lightbulbs on the porch and Formica chairs and tables in white vinyl. I took a corner table overlooking the phantom river. The owner was a quick and efficient man, sweating from the charcoal grills going in the back. I said I was Abbas's friend, and he brought out a bottle of Ettehadieh vodka and a glass with ice.

I poured the chilled vodka. The sky was a dome of black rock with stars; the moon, at its prime.

The owner came back out with a saucer of dill pickles and bread and cheese, calling out to his sons, who were serving other tables.

I heard laughter inside through the open window, shrill and flirtatious, more suited to jammed cabarets. From the porch I looked back over my shoulder. I could see them through the window, the table of four, two men, and two women tossing yellow hair, with tight and revealing tops. One of the men had blond hair, and I could see his patrician profile. Some foreigner. The other, with ebony hair, had his back to me, his expensive blazer slung over the chair, a gold ring with a seal on his right finger. When he put out his other arm with the sleeve rolled back, I saw the expensive gold watch and wedding band. They were the only such customers, slumming, far from the haunts of the upper class. The other tables were dowdy family types; and on the porch, tables of only men, workers, and students.

Several patrons left, going for their cars in a dirt lot by the restaurant. A Peykan came down the road and swerved sharply into the lot. Abbas, ever the careless driver, emerged, his shrewd eyes even more pronounced above his beard. The owner came to greet him, taking our order with affability and rushing off.

"The boys were at the British embassy in Gholhak," said Abbas. "This English group was scheduled to go on camera to explain some dig. Our director says: 'I'm not going in!' Now, they're already inside the gates, clustered by the door, the archeologist and special guests waiting inside. The director says to the boys, 'Fuck the English! The sons of bitches screwed us for years.' The film crew agreed, so they turned around and left."

I poured him vodka, and we touched glasses.

He leaned in. "We've become all theater! All make-believe. Like that ridiculous paean to the royal family in the Marble Palace. A monumentally garish sound-and-light show by that charlatan Czech. Like this festival with English brass bands in our parks, their ambassador arriving in his Rolls-Royce to cut ribbons." He shook his head. "Who're they kidding? Scratch the surface and there's rage."

One of the owner's sons brought the chicken kebab. We tore into the pieces, stuffing ourselves with raw onion and pickles and spoonfuls of buttery rice.

Abbas wanted to know if I had anything more on Jalal.

He said, "You can't be too careful. There's proof SAVAK was running a Communist cell a few years back. Imagine! Like shooting fish in a barrel. Even Radmanesh in Moscow had endorsed the cell. What do those guys know in exile? They're out of touch."

We downed vodka, the restaurant emptying around us. We ordered tea, picked our teeth with toothpicks from a glass. An emaciated dog came out of the dark, sniffing around the tables on the porch, and I threw it bread. One of the workers two tables over kicked the dog, and the animal went off howling and the workers burst out laughing. They got up to leave, still laughing. The boy brought our tea and was clearing our table when the blond foreigner appeared in the doorway, the one from the table of four inside. Tall, with dazzling blue eyes, nearly silvery. The worker who had kicked the dog turned around and blocked his path, saying something obscene to his face, which the foreigner didn't get. But I saw the flicker of tension in the blond man's eyes. Not on his face. He was still smiling, like some surefire movie star on screen. Way too good for the worker, way too good to acknowledge an obscenity in any foreign language. He made a small sweeping motion with his hand. A conceited gesture — a "Get out of my way, boy" — saying something in what I thought was French as he moved forward. The girl behind him had her arm snug around his waist, her face against his back as though he were her protector. The worker stepped back, ogling them. The girl gave him a triumphant look, then called back to her friend inside to grab the pack of cigarettes from their table. I saw the girl inside, framed by the window, snap up the pack. She had heavy makeup and dyed strawberry-blond hair and the tightest jeans riding up her buttocks. She was running her fingers through the ebony hair of the man paying the bill. He stood with his back to the window, peeling off bills and tossing them on the table. She smiled, sliding her arm into his, kissing him on the neck. He laid a hand on her buttock and squeezed, leaving a large enough tip for the owner to be bowing and scraping while he turned to whisk his blazer off the chair. I saw his face as he turned, recognizing him, to my surprise. Mahastee's husband. I looked away. I didn't want him to see me.

"Thierry," he called to the Frenchman, as he came out on the porch. Then something quick in English about a house. "See you at your house." I've been teaching myself English.

Abbas slurped tea, and I watched the foursome. The workers had disappeared. Mahastee's husband had his arm around the girl, whispering in her ear until she broke out into a titter.

They stepped out toward the parking lot, paired off. A few seconds later we heard cries and the sound of running. Abbas rose, but the owner came out and stood on the porch, facing the lot. I heard Houshang Behroudi shouting about two bricks hurtling out of the dark straight at them. The workers had aimed and missed. The owner called to his sons to chase after them. "Go! Quickly!" he said. They quickly obeyed, running up the street, their father cursing the workers loudly for effect. Behroudi was cursing in the parking lot with authority. He wasn't about to go after them himself, demeaning his social standing by chasing laborers, jeopardizing his pretty face. I didn't think he had the balls. The two sons came back within minutes. The owner apologized profusely to Mahastee's husband and the foreigner on behalf of the runaway workers and everyone. Such a wimp! Waving dutifully as the two Range Rovers pulled out of the lot.

"They're all pimps now with foreign advisers!" he said, coming back on the porch.

Too bad the brick had missed Houshang Behroudi; now he'd be at the foreigner's drinking and fornicating. Did Mahastee know? How could she stand him?

Before midnight, Abbas dropped me off.

"We're an American puppet regime," he said. "Only puppet regimes buy so many arms and keep drawing-room generals and a rubber-stamp prime minister and parliament. And fortunes stashed abroad. How long can this last?"

EIGHTEEN

TWENTY-FOUR HOURS AFTER HEARING about the charges accumulating behind closed doors against naval officers, I sat doing house accounts, worrying. A photograph of the port town of Kangan was on my desk: palm fronds up against an old house with traditional wind towers and reticular windows, in the distance the deep dazzling blue of the Gulf. The naval project outside the town had broken ground. Houshang was building their new port, hobnobbing with the top brass. To get that far, he had given kickbacks. I knew; it was no use pretending.

The summer of the year before, Houshang and I had been arguing on our way back from a dinner party. That very evening, after dinner, he'd been taken aside and promised a lucrative contract by the man we referred to as his contact. A man very high up. I knew this man. The big contract was Bandar Kangan. In return, Houshang's company was going to build this man's vast summer home in Ramsar on the Caspian as a gift. Houshang told me in the car, perhaps imprudently, for he never told me much anymore. But he wanted to break open a bottle of champagne — he was jubilant. I accused him of unscrupulous dealings. He became incensed. He parked the car at one o'clock in the morning on a side street in Darband to lecture me. What did I think? he demanded. Most of the really big jobs were awarded way at the top. You bid, but the bids were rigged. Nothing happened without a powerful contact and payoffs. It was political, very sensitive. When you got the job, you inflated all your prices up 200 percent. You overcharged, they expected it, it was part of the deal. Suddenly you needed five times more concrete. The kickbacks were given up front — right into a drawer or the Swiss bank account. There was no real accounting; there was so much cash floating around, nobody checked. He asked why I was playing the naïf and goody-goody. "But I thought you liked me good," I said. "This is business!" he cried. His company had taken on projects where they had let themselves lose good money, just to get into the big league. Exactly six months before, on a housing bid for the navy on the Gulf, they were finally told their prices were too low and dismissed. The man in charge claimed Kaviyan General Contractors could not get the job finished at such prices and would end up not only unprofitable but in the red. "Write a letter saying you can't do it!" the man said. Houshang had subsequently discovered that the prices on a similar housing bid for the navy up by the Caspian had come in so high the man in charge was afraid to be seen taking anything lower. He said he'd learned his lesson. He was a capitalist, he wanted to make money, the economy was booming, they were building the country. What was he supposed to do, sit on his hands? He wasn't blind. He saw opportunity, he saw how to make it. If he didn't, someone else would! He had turned to me in the dark. "What's the matter?" he said. "Our company's on the A list. You begrudge my success? You begrudge my finally getting a project like the port in Kangan?"

I called Kavoos. My voice must have been clipped, because he pulled the older brother routine and I changed my tone. I felt a headache coming.

"Anything new?" I asked.

He told me to call Father and go there for dinner with the children.

"What's wrong there?" I asked.

"Stop asking what's wrong all the time. Just go. It'll do you good."

I called and told Mother I was coming for dinner.

"Anything wrong?" she asked.

Indictment was not a word for our family, nor *embezzlement*. Our good name and reputation meant everything. So it should, Father always said. He liked to think the old adage had been honored. Old family, old bones, old values, old gardens. Instructing all my brothers like a drill sergeant. Kavoos, his eldest, never contradicted him openly but thought Father naive, old-fashioned. Bahram, the youngest, didn't really care. Ardeshir argued everything. Mother had taken to instructing me about being a lady, in between her bridge games and orchids and interminable parties and high teas and ceremonial lunches and charitable works. Being a lady was an imperative, as though it were a profession, like being a doctor or an engineer. As if you could draw a salary from it, with pension. One time I told her. She said, "That's what I get for sending my children abroad."

I checked my face in the mirror. I looked haggard and tense. I despised this collusion Houshang had going behind my back with Iraj and Pouran, his needing only those who submit to him, and finding there his kind of freedom, like his well-chosen infidelities. But I've come to think he wants me to know, to teach me a lesson — put me in place now that he's acquired me, arrived completely. When we were first married, I'd admired his aggressive drive for success. He'd admired and misunderstood the very qualities in our family for which he wanted me most: that sluggish procession of obligation and depth of thought and gravity of purpose, minutely considered and hard-won and timeworn. In time, he had found them time-consuming and tiresome. He had envisioned something and found us altogether different. And he had taken my system of existence as a nuisance to his. An oppression. As he is to me.

I told Goli to leave dinner for Houshang. She hesitated by the door as if she wanted something, yet another raise. She wasn't going to get one. She'd been gossiping up and down the street, idling at front doors with cooks and gardeners and chauffeurs, comparing notes. Disapproving of the in-flowing house help from Bangladesh and the Philippines.

The children fought in the car all the way. I interrupted to ask if they liked their tutor, Mr. Nirvani.

"He's strict. But he plays great soccer! He's in a league!"

They played soccer sometimes for a break. I hadn't even paid Reza — he refused to take money. I would call and insist, now that he'd given me his office number. Something he had not said still bothered me about why his father had retired abruptly that year, leaving suddenly that summer when we were fourteen. They had vanished between one month and the next. Father had never given me a proper explanation, considering how Reza's family had been a part of our lives and how Hajj-Alimardan had had Father's complete trust and run his estates to his complete satisfaction. In time, though it seemed impossible, I was certain Father didn't even have a proper explanation for himself.

Evening. The properties by the mountains enveloped in darkness, fenced in by walls. The air bracing, cool. I felt the strangest tranquillity, driving through the gates of the old garden. Father was standing on the front porch waiting, hands clasped behind his back. He waved as we came out of the car.

When I went up to kiss him, I lingered and he said, "You're sad tonight."

He sent the children in and took me for a walk. Past Mother's pond of water lilies with goldfish, past the vanishing petunias and snapdragons of summer. He pointed here and there, linking his arm into mine. Beyond the cypresses, the pine trunks were draped with ivy.

"You know, those days," he said, "they're forgotten. This is a city with no memory. Everyone and everything is forgotten here."

Father liked to tell stories while walking. The warring factions during the 1906 Constitutional Revolution and Mohammad Ali Shah's rebellion. The bombing of the new parliament. The old aristocracy, appointed, dismissed, exiled, bribed by the Russian and British legations. The terror of invasion from the Bolsheviks, with Khiabani in Azarbaijan and Kuchek Khan in Gilan. Famine and typhoid and cholera in Tehran. The government bankrupt and humiliated. The British imposing the disgraceful 1919 Agreement, contemplating how to break Persia into pieces to safeguard their empire. The old regime. A new one. And always, an uncertain future.

By the fruit trees at the end of the garden, there was no light. We turned back, the black facade of the house looming.

"Change comes as surely as the seasons," he said. "We must fight for a place in this world. It's no use losing heart. We must hold our heads high."

On the porch we stood facing the garden, the dark slab of sky over us. The night breeze bore the faint scent of perishing roses. A lone bird trilled high in a tree. Father's wizened face was intent on some purpose long abandoned.

When we went in, Mother glared at him disapprovingly.

"You'll catch cold without a cardigan," she said to him, kissing me.

Father ignored her.

Mrs. Vahaab and the colonel arrived for dinner. She had her domed coiffure and penciled mole and another frilly dress on. The colonel was ramrod and solicitous. Mrs. Vahaab was telling us about the rabbits and chickens and hens they kept in their garden. And her parrot, Ghamar.

"Such a ridiculous name!" said Mother.

"Please, madame, try keeping some of your opinions to yourself," said Mrs. Vahaab, puckering her lips.

A manservant brought around a tray of freshly squeezed pomegranate juice in old bohemian glasses. Mrs. Vahaab clutched a glass with her pudgy pinkie in the air and drank from it as if from the fountain of youth.

For dinner we had borscht and cabbage rice and fat Tabrizi meatballs. The children amused themselves by peeking at each other from across the table between the fruit epergnes and giggling. For dessert we had ripe persimmons and apples and pears from the garden. Mother loves persimmons and she loves autumn. We took tea in the living room, bolstered by a succession of her antique Russian chintz cushions presenting the first motorcars, czarist steam engines, and steamships, all backed in claret velvet. Mrs. Vahaab said she had a cough, patting her plump bosom. The colonel, fingering his walrus mustache, issued a directive that she take mint tea with rock candy to assuage it. Mother was about to call for the house help, but I went into the kitchen. The colonel gets pushy only when it comes to his wife, his military career docile and dull and cut short. She was his only compensation. He was discussing the war when I got back with mint tea.

"Which war is it this time?" Mother said.

"Why, the Second World War, of course, madame. When the Allies overran our country. We were called, and I bade my sweet young bride farewell early that morning and went off to fight."

Mother smiled angelically. "But Colonel, you got back home for lunch!"

The colonel, blushing to his ears, coughed politely into his starched and monogrammed white handkerchief.

Mrs. Vahaab, sipping mint tea blithely, turned to me. "Remember when I sang at your wedding?"

"How could I forget?"

"I was inspired that night, you know. I was communing with the universe. I felt a mystical light within me, a majestic surge."

Mother rolled her eyes, as indiscreetly as possible. We all ignored her.

So she spoke. "Mystical surges must be like electrical ones. You're a veritable generator, dear madame. The colonel should plug you in to iron his shirts!"

Father suppressed his laugh, and the colonel immediately quoted a verse from Hafez to dispel this affront. A fitting but ineffectual cure for Mother's unremitting sarcasm at the universe.

Father took me into his library after they left. First he shelved a bound volume of Montaigne's essays that was lying open on his desk. Then he looked through his books, pulled one out, and gave it to me. It was a new and scandalous tome written by a journalist against the so-called thousand families, the landowning oligarchy.

"They're trashing us again," he said. He settled into his armchair. "You know, I feel bad. We haven't seen Reza's family since Hajj-Alimardan's death. May he rest in peace, he'd be proud of this son. I think for years Reza wanted to stay away. That day he came, he came back to us. I can't tell you what it meant to me. How happy I was! But later, I thought about it and realized he was already lost to us. Perhaps forever."

"Lost to us?" I said, startled.

"He was aloof, judgmental. You know, like a stranger."

"He's no stranger."

I asked him about Hajj-Alimardan's retirement. Had there been some incident? Father wanted to know why I thought that.

"Reza's got that stubborn streak of his father," Father said, shaking his head. "I didn't help. When I called him about the problem he came to see me for, I suppose I sounded oblivious. I meant well."

He sank into the armchair by the faded sepia photographs.

"If I'd left it to Kavoos to call him, or any of the boys, it would've been worse. They don't care."

He hadn't thought of asking me.

"Talk to him," Father said. "If he respects us, it's by choice, not instinct. You know, he may be in trouble. These things happen."

Father had suddenly turned clairvoyant. I promised to call Reza.

I STAYED UP past midnight, the bedroom a bunker where I'd retreated to wait. Houshang came late, all flushed, his jacket slung over one shoulder. He loosened the knot of his already loosened tie with guile, as if to brag he was exhausted, overworked, meriting peace and quiet. He looked well. I watched out of the corners of my eyes, pretending to read the book Father had given me. I was unable to muster up a single emotion in Houshang's favor. He poured out a glass of water from the carafe on the table and drank, big avaricious gulps. Especially his last "Ahhh!" as he wiped his mouth, cocky and unrepentant.

"What's the matter?" he demanded.

"Father's given me this book," I snapped.

"He's a bookworm all right."

"What's that supposed to mean?"

He went into the bathroom, slamming the door. When he came out I was sitting up in bed, stiff as a board.

"Your meetings go past midnight?"

"I'm in no mood to fight!"

"Answer me," I said, teeth clenched.

"I want to sleep," he said, yawning, as if he were the only one deserving rest. The only one who wanted.

"I want an answer," I said louder.

He held my ugly stare with bloodshot eyes, then turned off the light on his side. I wanted to pounce across the bed and smash the lamp over his head and shoulders. A raving shrew with a liar and cheat for a husband.

"You were at Iraj and Pouran's last night! Where were you tonight?"

"Is this an interrogation?"

"No, this is married life!"

He laughed with that slow hyena-like sound he emits — the one he's perfected for gilded drawing rooms and gambling partners and titillating call girls and boardrooms where the stakes are piled high in his favor. The laugh that says, Look at me and how far I've come. Nothing can stop me now!

"What is it?" he demanded. "Is it that time of month?"

"You prefer Iraj and Pouran. Right? Right?"

"Cut it out," he said.

"You prefer their house, their booze, their jokes, their friends, their entire nauseating lifestyle."

"You're jealous."

"Of them? Don't be ridiculous!"

"You're *such* a snob. You and your whole family!"

He lay down and pulled up the sheet. I slammed my book shut on the bedside table and turned off the light, still sitting upright in the dark.

"Move in with them if they're so great!" I said.

"I might, if this goes on every night."

"Go ahead! Don't think I don't know what goes on behind my back."

He got out of bed, stood facing me in the dark. "Tell me, like what?"

"Like how you whore around with Iraj and have Pouran pimp for you and how we don't have much of a marriage!"

"So we don't have much of a marriage! Since when?"

"Since forever." The words jumped out of my mouth.

"Since forever, huh?" he snapped back. "Whose fault is that?"

"Seems you already know."

"You," he said, pointing, "you're the one who violated our trust."

"What trust?"

"Aha!" he said, now incensed. He switched on the light. "You think I like some French charlatan telling me my wife — my wife! — has gone pleading to him about some fucking bastard she wants out of prison?"

He stared, face flushed.

"You never told me you saw Thierry for some rotten rebel who should be shot. You'd rather confide in a foreigner than in your own husband! And you talk about trust? I'm a contractor for the navy! Don't you get it?"

"Not everything's about your business," I said.

He paused, incredulous, fire in his eyes. "What? I hope they shoot this guy, whoever he is! Right through the heart."

I got out of bed, grabbed my dressing gown from the armchair, shot my arms through the sleeves, wrapping it around me with newfound fury and drive.

"That boy deserves justice before the law, you hear? Since when do you listen to Thierry so much?"

"He's a good friend."

"Since when?"

"Since forever!" Houshang said with cunning eyes.

"You're a fine, shining example to lecture me about trust!"

"You" — Houshang was apoplectic — "are hiding things from me. You go to the houses of other men. You went to his alone. Didn't you? Didn't you?"

"You need a report on everything I do?"

"He told me! You must like him a lot. Just the two of you alone together, huh? All cozy to discuss SAVAK! Our marriage is sacred!"

He swung out an arm, smashing his fist into the wall.

"What do I care about some bastard in prison?" he shouted. "You're crazy running around town with this. I've got millions at stake. You want to jeopardize my business? Our whole way of life? You're doing it on purpose! Tell me, what else is going on?"

"You care?" I said, incensed. "You've got no eyes or heart or conscience left anymore."

"Don't lecture me! I've given you the best life!"

"Given! Given?"

"I've given you whatever you want."

"You only know what you want."

"You want what? Rights for some ingrate low-class leftist with an inferiority complex! Some bullshit freedom for a traitor in the shithouse with SAVAK? What's it to us, huh? Why tell Thierry, huh? Why hide it from me?"

"Traitor to what? Your money, your morals, your country? You decide?"

"Damn right I decide! And I don't want my wife —"

"I'm beginning not to give a damn what you want," I said, walking out.

I SLEPT in the guest room. Early in the morning I heard Houshang slam doors and bark orders and bawl out everyone before leaving the house.

At ten-thirty Mr. Bashirian walked into my office. I hadn't seen him for days. The secretary said he was very upset with me for taking Mr. Makhmalchi into my confidence and having him in my office all the time. He felt I'd taken sides. That was how much confidence he had in me and my judgment and himself. We stared at each other with the wary restraint of old friends who have had a breach of trust.

"You look unwell," he said.

I rearranged folders on my desk, waiting for him to say what he'd come for. To finally have it out about his rivalry with Makhmalchi.

"Mr. Bashirian —" I began testily.

"I — I thought I'd come tell you. But if you're too busy —"

"Oh, please!" I said, exasperated.

"They called," he murmured.

"What did they say?"

"They said I could see Peyman. This week," he said, voice quavering.

"Thank God," I said, overcome.

"Yes, thank God," Mr. Bashirian said sternly.

"When do you go?"

"Thursday. I owe this to you."

He knew I had appealed to yet another person the week before who had only been vague and pessimistic. Maybe something had come of it after all.

Mr. Bashirian hemmed and hawed as if there were nothing left to say, which made what he said even more shocking. "Will you come?"

"Where?" I asked.

"With me."

"To see him?"

He shook his head. I was relieved I'd misunderstood.

Then he said, "I know it's asking too much. But if you'd just come to Komiteh with me. I've waited for this moment for weeks. Frankly I — now I'm afraid, I'm terrified. I want to be strong. To hold up beautifully for Peyman. I'm afraid I'll break down. I've said you're his aunt. That is — I've already asked if I could bring my sister, since the boy's mother is dead."

"Your sister's in town?"

He shook his head.

"What did they say?"

"They just repeated the time and place." He sat waiting.

I was dumbfounded. But how could I refuse? By saying no immediately.

"Let me think about it," I said.

He left, sensing he'd sabotage his case by lingering.

I called that afternoon. He picked up on the third ring.

"Mr. Bashirian?" I said.

"Yes?" he said, with painstaking indifference.

"About Thursday. I'll go with you."

"Thank you, thank you," he said. "I'm forever in your debt."

I HADN'T BEEN HOME five minutes when Goli came upstairs to announce a foreign gentleman was waiting downstairs.

"A *Moosio* —" She giggled, covering her mouth. "A *Moosio Tolonbeh!*"

Tolonbeh! A Mr. Pump? No wonder Goli couldn't stop giggling.

"Dalembert?" I suggested.

The boys were with Reza in the dining room, the door shut. I found Thierry in the downstairs study, urbane but crestfallen.

Immediately he said, "I've come to make amends."

"You should've called before coming."

"You wouldn't have seen me then. All for an unfortunate mistake."

"Everything you do is deliberate."

"You flatter me," he said, downcast to appear virtuous. "But Houshang already knew."

"You told him. Knowing full well I hadn't."

"Pouran told him."

"Pouran? How did she —" I stared incredulously. "You told her?"

He stared back, not chastened, just aware his standing had shifted irredeemably.

"Why — why would you do that?" I said.

"To defend you!" He shrugged artfully. "I was enumerating your virtues in my bedroom. She's there occasionally these days. I don't know exactly what was irritating me most at that moment — her presence, I suppose — but we got into an argument about you. I said you had a backbone. She laughed at you! So I told her why, to teach her a lesson. She's such a bitch. She told your husband about the boy. All this cloak-and-dagger's so disagreeable. Of course I tried to make light of it, but Houshang took it badly."

"I know he did."

"I thought I'd appeal to him man-to-man. But he didn't see it that way. He's so touchy!"

"He's my husband," I said defensively. "What did you expect?"

He smiled, spreading his arms. "Will you forgive me, *ma chère?*"

He repulsed me at that instant. His gallantry was frivolous and willful, like his endearments, well timed but chilling.

"Come on," he said. "Let's embrace and make up, and how about —"

"Did you also tell Houshang about your affair with Pouran?"

"No! And I wouldn't."

"How honorable."

He shrugged sheepishly. I asked when he'd seen my husband.

"We talked on the phone yesterday."

"You discussed Peyman Bashirian on the phone?"

"Actually, he dropped in to discuss some business matter. Yes, last night." Thierry smiled. "I see you still haven't forgiven me."

I looked at my watch. "He'll be home any minute and we've got a dinner —"

"The Spanish embassy? Their ambassador's a poet, you know."

I accompanied him to the door, anxious to be rid of him, my utmost civility and inscrutability the rudest affront.

Just then the dining room doors flew open and my sons rushed out, Reza behind them. The boys circled, charging with plastic rulers and shouting all the way up the stairs. I noticed Reza staring at this foreigner at home with me. A frank scrutiny. Thierry, reproducing niceties to me on his way out, didn't even acknowledge his presence or greet him, ignoring him completely.

I shut the door and turned to Reza. "He's a banker friend of ours."

He nodded politely. But I sensed disapproval.

"You disapprove of foreigners?" I said casually.

"Considering our history, they hold a dismal record of involvement."

"We were the ones giving away concessions and monopolies."

"We?" he said. "No, not the people." He smiled. "Discussing foreigners is a treacherous business."

"You know, the last time I saw your father — when we were sixteen and you came back for a visit? What was in that large sealed envelope my father gave him that night?"

"After all these years!" Reza said, surprised. "They were old letters a servant had found in a trunk in your grandmother's house. Copies of the letters she'd written my grandfather over the years, and he'd written her from Tabriz. They corresponded after she took Father away and he was growing up in her household. And long after."

"You read the letters?"

"Yes. Much later. Father left them to me when he died."

"Had my father read them?"

"No. That night he was returning them to their rightful owner, he said."

I wanted to read them but felt it was better to ask for them some other time.

"They're not just about a boy far from home," said Reza. "But the personal correspondence of an outspoken woman and a learned cleric — who shared not only an affection for the same boy but an insightful and deep concern for their country. Father was overcome when he read them. He was old and ill by then. He said they were the most unusual and affecting documents he'd ever read."

"Did something happen that made your father leave us suddenly?"

"No. He just retired."

He would never tell me. "And after that?"

"He went back to being a farmer. He was a landowner in Nirvan. He had villages and fields. But then he fell into debt. With land reform he lost everything. In the end he was . . . defeated. He died a disillusioned man."

I was shocked at Hajj-Ali's defeat, at hearing about it so many years later. For the man I remembered, defeat would have seemed as far away as the ends of the earth. He had had that kind of vitality.

"He could make you see things about yourself better than anyone else," I said. "I remember the way he admonished my brothers, which often left them dumbfounded. I remember the stories he told me. Once, he told me about the Constitutional Revolution on the porch in Morshedabad. His voice still trembled over what had happened so many years before — and what hadn't since then. I think he carried such emotion — such a tremendous burden with him. That's what I loved about him most."

Reza stood rooted to the spot. A hush fell into the hallway like the inside of a well, except for the ticking of the antique clock on the console. Overcome by the memory of Hajj-Alimardan, I felt immense distress at his passing. More than when he had died that winter and I had attended the services with Mother. The past was rising, resurgent, bringing back that deepest rhythm and relinquished instinct, and emotion for Reza. He looked stricken.

The creaking of the front door startled us. From the doorway, Houshang stared at us as if at two conspirators.

"What's wrong?" he demanded impudently. "Someone's died?"

Reza walked out, even while I was carrying on with a hasty introduction. Houshang stared after him without so much as a word.

The door was still open when Houshang said, loud enough to be overheard, "I don't like that fellow."

"You're rude," I said.

"I am what I am. Are we out tonight?"

NINETEEN

NIGHT FELL, the specter of the mountains to the north looming like a bad omen.

She had an imperious and deceitful husband, imperious and deceitful foreign friends. Didn't she know better?

I walked all the way from Darrous to Gholhak, winding down the ever-changing neighborhoods, rich and tranquil to crammed and run-down. In the backstreets by a small mosque with a white minaret and a string of bare lightbulbs, a handful of boys played soccer. I stood watching, then showed them how to kick and pass. In the meagerly tiled doorway, under the light, a mullah in turban and robes listened to a man cry, consoling him. The man, in billowy trousers and overshirt and a buttoned-up, threadbare brown jacket, kept pointing to the sky, then hitting his chest. A woman stood a little bit away from him in a black chador, clutching the hand of a little girl with a flowered scarf and runny nose, dark trousers poking out from under her short flowered skirt. The little girl turned and smiled at the boys. She had dimples, a rosy chin and cheeks.

Her mother slapped her head, telling her to look down. She did as she was told, then turned her head just enough to stare at us sideways, fixing us with an inquisitive look. The peasant kissed the hand of the mullah with gratitude, then bowed, motioning salutations to God.

I greeted them, crossing the street, thinking how for a thousand years and more that scene had repeated itself. One man with one woman behind him with child, beseeching. We would never break the mold.

If Mahastee knew about her husband and foreign friend, she wouldn't be so quick to defend them. But she would always be loyal to her own class. She'd given me the photograph of the house in Morshedabad, trees in shadow and light, and asked me about Father, why he retired. Her father doesn't know. If he did, he wouldn't be so quick to defend his own kind. And they don't know what happened to him at the end, the last few years of his life, when he was ruined.

After that last spring in Morshedabad, we packed up and left. Father sent Mother and Zari and me ahead to Tehran to rent a house and find schools. He told Nasrollah *mirza* that he was unwell. He went to him and made excuses, and Mahastee's father believed him. "I'm getting old, sir, I want to retire and go home. Find someone young and able." They were excuses with which to save face for everyone — not only for himself and his family, but for Nasrollah *mirza* Mosharraf and his. We packed up and left like hired help. Mother and Zari never knew why. Father just told Mother, "It's time," and she believed him.

After Father left the Mosharrafs, they held on to most of their estates in Azarbaijan until they were confiscated and divided up with land reform. In the complicated subdivisions of pastures and villages and entanglements with the government, everyone lost cash crops and harvests and orchards, and though the sharecroppers and peasants were given the land in time, they couldn't maintain and farm it as they had before, and many finally gave up and migrated away to the cities.

In Morshedabad, the gardens grew neglected and the house fell into disrepair.

THAT YEAR I turned fourteen, spring came early. Mahastee's father came to Morshedabad in late March for the holidays with his entire family and stayed ten days. I didn't know it would be the last time I'd see her in the garden. "Our garden!" she said, as children only do. "You live here too."

It had been a bad year for Father. His long-ailing and aged father, a respected and enlightened mullah, had passed away in Tabriz while still embroiled in a controversial and bitter dispute on obscure religious texts. The year before, Mahastee's grandmother had had a stroke and died in her sleep. Father stood ashen in the room when they came to tell him. It's the only time I've ever seen him weep. He left immediately for Tehran and then for Tabriz, where he delivered a moving eulogy for her on her estate and the crowds had wept. It was as if he'd lost his own mother. Three months later, two of her nephews started on him, questioning him on the handling of two of her large estates, which he had only advised her on. Bypassing Mahastee's father, they demanded to see all Father's accounts — questioning him on the division of property, and how and why certain estates had been sold, and their share of earnings for wheat and barley and fruit from the orchards tallied against the generous share given to cultivators of those lands, besides what they called other immoderate expenses. They tormented him — especially one of them — and for several months kept him running back and forth to Tehran and the estates in Azarbaijan, and Father came home to Morshedabad at the end of winter, white with fury, and cried, "Now they say I'm a swindler! Now that she's gone. They're dumping everything on me to cover up. But I know what they're up to! If Mahbanou *khanom* were alive this would never have happened."

So it was that, after her death and then his father's, he said one day that with their passing an entire world had passed away for him.

It was a bad year until early spring. Mahastee came and left, the car receding down the road; she turned around in the back as usual, waving to me, crammed between her brothers until she lurched toward the window suddenly and popped her head out, shouting, "Reza, Reza! See you in two months."

The first week of that spring vacation, she'd thrown a big party and I had refused to go, and she'd come looking for me. I knew her family and cousins and some of her friends — as she did mine — but still I didn't go. That year she'd filled out, all flesh and curves. I had to readjust to her all over again every time I saw her. I watched her walk and swagger, the light in her eyes, the rise of her breasts above the dip of her waist and commotion of flounced skirts. I could see the other boys staring at her. I didn't ask Father about attending her party, knowing full well he would have disapproved, nor Mother, forbidding as she was, who never said a word, though with her it was her silence that was especially effective. I had stayed outside to avoid them both that evening when I heard Mahastee calling under the trees. In the garden, with the music and their party, and thinking about her and my parents and hers, I'd come to realize for the first time that year the distance between us, she and I — all of us — and how it was greater than I had ever imagined and understood. Her grandmother and my father had been close, and her father and mine in their own way, each with a different arrangement, but it was ours — that progressive world — that closed us off to each other, she and I, and even for the others I felt that with the passing of years the distance had increased between them too. Then I heard her call through the trees and I stepped out so she could see me, and she came up and said something, but I was angry already and grabbed her arm and pulled. Our faces rushed up so close I saw her lashes up before my nose, and her astonished look, the sudden flutter of her warm breath on my mouth. One tug of possession and for the entire vacation I felt as though we belonged to each other.

Two nights later, while they played cards at her house, she brought the phonograph out to the clearing by the pool and plugged it into the socket by the left tree and put on a record. There, with the two of us alone, she said, "I'm going to teach you to dance tonight." I laughed first, then refused, although I wanted to. I said I didn't need to learn. She insisted and I stood rock-still and obstinate.

"Reza! Stop it," she said. "You're being stubborn like a mule. Everybody learns to dance!"

"No, they don't," I said. "My parents didn't."

"It's no crime to dance! My parents dance. My uncles, cousins, everyone I know."

"Mine don't. Even if they do at weddings, it's different from yours."

"I mean two together, like they dance abroad."

"It's unthinkable for them."

"Then you're going to be the first."

She stepped right up and put my hand to her waist, slipped my other hand gently into hers, and turned. I thought it was the most wonderful thing to hold her in my arms and call it a dance and have music. I liked this, what they did abroad. I liked the dance, the night, the music. Then I stepped on her toes and she laughed, and I tried looking off into the trees instead of at her hair and radiant face and skin emitting the sweet scent of perfume there in my arms. And she laughed and said this was only the first lesson and I needed to practice more. And I said, "Who with? Who is there except you?" And she gave me the strangest look and I knew we were young and thought nothing else existed nor mattered. When I arrived two years later in her garden and heard the music rise between the trees, she evoked the night we'd danced together.

That spring she taught me to dance in the clearing by the pool, and the next thing I knew, she was waving to me, speeding away to Tehran, shouting, "See you in two months."

Her father came back again soon after, this time for a weekend alone. The orchards were in full bloom. He told Father they'd all be back in early summer. "See you in Khordad or early Tir, Hajj-Ali," Nasrollah *mirza* said. He patted my head. "You have a good son," he said. Father and I waved by the poplars as the car disappeared down the road, the fender glinting crimson in the last rays of the setting sun. The fields were washed down from the rains earlier in the day. A perfect evening, the stars out before the night was on.

"By the way," Nasrollah *mirza* had said to Father before getting into the car, "my cousin will be coming to visit." I saw a frown cloud Father's eyes. As the car drove away, Father muttered under his breath, "God keep us from trouble, as if we haven't already had enough this year."

Ten days later, late in the afternoon, a car appeared, raising dust on the horizon. I saw it in the distance, then approaching down the road. I ran in between the trees, following it all the way to the main house. An elegant car from Tehran. I read the license plate as I stood in the grove by the driveway. Instead of a driver, a gentleman emerged from behind the wheel. He had pressed trousers and an ivory shirt and a vest and jacket, and elegant shoes like Nasrollah *mirza*'s and a cane that he didn't really need but with which he pointed things out to his rakish friend, who got out of the car after him. Pointing — to the house, stables, other lodgings, the orchards and fields. I could hear them, high-handed. Out of the back door two women emerged the likes of whom I'd never seen. A redhead and a fake blond, they had low-cut blouses and tight pants over curvaceous hips and high heels and puffy hairdos and painted faces. They wiggled out, pecked the men on the cheek, laughing. The gentleman-driver smacked the redhead on her bottom.

"Boy!" he called out to me. "Get Hajj-Alimardan!" He spoke, landlord of the world.

I ran to get Father and watched as they exchanged greetings. The women had a mesmerizing way of moving their bodies. Father turned and caught me gaping, and I backed into the bushes. He conducted them to the main house and called for the gardener's wife and fourteen-year-old daughter. The gardener — a gruff and grumpy man who had been there forever, a Turk from one of the Mosharraf villages in Azarbaijan — brought in the suitcases and several cartons and two rifles. He brought yogurt and butter and heavy cream and sour cherry jam made by his wife. From outside the screen door of the kitchen, I saw the daughter unpacking bottles of liquor from a carton. She was pretty but had one roving eye, and the parents worried about finding her a suitor. The two guests from Tehran, accompanied by Father, went off to inspect orchards and fields.

At night by the trees I watched the house, all lit up. The visitors were drinking; I heard their laughter, the shrill giggle of the women. I decided they had a different idea of fun than we did. Our bungalow was behind the thicket of trees behind the main house. Mother and Zari were in Reyy visiting relatives. Zari had been sick with a fever, and Mother had taken her to stay closer to Tehran, worried about her health. Mother always worried, ever since losing her first child to a mysterious fever. Father said Mother had wept for a year. It had taken her years after that to get pregnant.

Father and I went to bed, and I heard him muttering under his breath. I asked who the visitors were. He said they were the cousin of Nasrollah *mirza* and his friend from Tehran. I decided he didn't like them. I asked if those were their wives. "Mind your own business," he said. Whenever he was angry or scolded me, he always spoke in Turkish. Then he read to me under the hissing gas lamp, admonishing me to listen, his gray mustache turned down, his hands large and still. His voice rose with the names of mountains and feats, descending low into the valleys of betrayal and destruction.

Lying back listening, I thought how old he was getting. That year he'd complained about chest pains to Dr. Atabak, family friend and physician to Mahastee's father and her grandmother, whom he'd attended to her dying day. Dr. Atabak had given Father an appointment to be examined in Tehran. Each time there was a sickness or burial in the family, I watched Father. But he was larger than life, inimitable, though I could never explain exactly how.

The next morning Nasrollah *mirza*'s cousin ordered the horses saddled and rode out with his friend and the stable boy. After breakfast I saw the gardener's daughter leave through the kitchen door. She stood in the clearing, chewing the end of her sleeve, a clump of her light brown hair catching the sunlight. She kept tugging at her head scarf, jittery. I came up and asked if they needed anything at the house, but she rushed off. Her name was Amineh. We'd grown up in the same garden. She was fair-skinned and moony and sweet. When we'd all played hide-and-seek, the rest of us had been impatient and excitable and braggarts, but she was always the most difficult to find, she hid so well, patient and quiet and still.

The men came back and went around the garden with the two women, who had slept in. I followed, careful not to be seen or discovered by Father. They touched one another a lot. The two women had to be funny, the men laughed so much.

After lunch, Amineh was in tears, her mother reproaching her in the kitchen for breaking two plates. "You're all thumbs and irresponsible!" she shouted. "You clumsy idiot!" The mother was young herself and not very bright. I heard them from my usual spot under the trees, by the clearing behind the kitchen. I heard the two painted women come into the kitchen and scold and ridicule the gardener's wife and Amineh.

Early in the afternoon the main house grew still. I was doing schoolwork. That year, Father and I kept arguing about everything, especially about school in Tehran, because he wanted to send me to relatives in Tabriz. Behind our bungalow he was talking to the gardener and the window was open. I heard Father mention Tehran and Tabriz and the Mosharrafs, and I got up to listen. "They're staying longer," Father said. "Those educated blockheads just returned from abroad!" The gardener said Nasrollah *mirza*'s cousin was angry. Father said it was because he hadn't succeeded yet, though he'd bribed and plotted and created the situation, trying to appropriate the two estates in Azarbaijan for himself and swindle Nasrollah *mirza*'s family and muddle the accounts behind their backs and blame Father. "All last year he kept me going back and forth and blamed me for everything! Now he's hounding me," said Father. The gardener said, "Hajj-Ali, good thing you stood up to him." Father said now the man was trying to take his land. Father's. Mardanabad, which Mahbanou *khanom* had given him. "It's hard to believe she and he are from the same family!" he said.

The afternoon was hazy and hot and the visitors took a nap. After tea the men went shooting in the fields, insisting that Father accompany them, along with laborers from the garden. I rode out on my bicycle to buy bread from the baker in Morshedabad. When I got back, Father was home doing the accounts, jaw tensed. I delivered the bread to the main house. The women were cooking in the kitchen. The gardener's wife had her sleeves up, chopping herbs, frying meat, boiling rice. Amineh washed vegetables and peeled. She looked distraught and wouldn't go in to set the table for dinner. The mother was about to scold her when I insisted and set the table myself. The guests were taking showers and had the phonograph on loud with foreign music, their rifles propped up by the door in the hallway. I saw packets of cigarettes and bottles of liquor piled on the living room table. In the alcove at the far end, arranged with bolsters and cushions, they had a tray set with a brazier. Provisions for opium. I leafed quickly through the foreign books on the cushions. They had no pictures, except in one book, which had drawings of stark-naked men and women in odd positions and even in groups, all tangled up, and with animals. I shut the book, left the house. Father would have killed me.

By dark I came back to my spot by the trees. They'd started drinking as they had the night before but were getting louder. "Girl, come here!" Nasrollah *mirza*'s cousin called out. He meant Amineh. They knew she had a name! But they had no use for it. They laughed. Maybe they were making fun of her one roving eye. I saw their shadows up on the white walls, framed by the window. They had put on music and were dancing, the women wriggling up to the men, rubbing themselves up against them. In the kitchen the gardener's wife dished out the food, and they were served by Amineh. Soon enough the back screen door to the kitchen slammed open and Amineh ran out and stood in the clearing. I could hear her gasping in the dark, but her mother called and she went back in. "Don't be useless and lazy!" the mother said. "They want tea." They washed up in the kitchen, making a clatter. In between I heard Nasrollah *mirza*'s cousin. "Girl!" he thundered. He wanted her again. Then something crashed or fell over and the men howled with laughter. I hated how they laughed. They were laughing at the world. No, at us. Amineh ran out of the kitchen, and this time she was crying. The mother came out and stood talking to her in the clearing. "What's wrong?" she said. Amineh said she didn't like those men. "What's it to you?" her mother said. "It's how they look at me," said her daughter. "Don't look at them!" the mother said. "Even when they try to grab me?" said Amineh. "Or say those things?" "What things?" said the mother. "Tell me." Amineh stood mute in the dark. "May God humble you, tell me or I'll slap you!" the mother said. Amineh whispered, and the mother gasped, "God kill me!"

They were calling for them from the living room. Mother and daughter stood in the clearing, rooted to the spot. The mother whispered to Amineh, "We can't go in — we have to tell your father." They went off through the trees.

The guests called out again, and Nasrollah *mirza*'s cousin came into the kitchen, swearing at the women. "Where are those morons?" he shouted. The girlfriends were sent in to get tea and fruit. I waited by the trees and within minutes saw the gardener coming through the trees. He wasn't a big man but had broad shoulders and big hands, and he was wielding a big stick and swearing. I jumped out into the clearing. "Where to?" I said. "I'm going to defend my family and reputation!" he said, pushing past me up the kitchen steps.

I ran to our house, shouting, "Father, Father, run, run!" Father came out onto our porch, still tucking in his white shirt. He disliked it when people shouted. I said, "Father — quick, run! The gardener's going to beat up Nasrollah *mirza*'s cousin!" We ran through the thicket; we could hear them shouting. Father burst into the living room, proud and upstanding man that he was, and stopped dead. The two women were plastered against the wall in short, transparent nightgowns and high heels. Nasrollah *mirza*'s cousin and the gardener were in a shouting match. The gardener, holding on to his big stick, was yelling about their indecency before God and the chastity of his only daughter, until he choked on his words and lunged at Nasrollah *mirza*'s cousin. Father pounced to keep them apart, but the rakish friend picked up the bellows from the fireplace like lightning and hit the gardener. Blood oozed from the side of his head and he stumbled back, then lunged again and struck Nasrollah *mirza*'s cousin on the leg. The man let out a yelp. The painted women had disappeared.

The gardener was bucking to get at the two men, Father between them, admonishing the visitors about shame and scandal. "You should know better! What did you expect?" He ordered the gardener to leave. The man glowered, blood over his shirt, and didn't budge. Father shouted, "I tell you, go, now!" He backed out, holding his stick, blood trickling from his head.

"You impertinent ass," Nasrollah *mirza*'s cousin called Father. He turned, grabbed the riding crop on the table, raised it. "You deserve to be whipped for speaking to me that way." He flailed the riding crop around once, glaring at Father. "Everything you have, you owe to us! I should've had you sacked the last time you interfered in my business. If you go whimpering to your master again, it's my word against yours, you dog! I can buy and sell a hundred like you anytime I want."

I lunged to attack him. Father pinned me back with both arms, ashen. Then the man told Father what I can hardly bear to remember. He said, "You must beg for my forgiveness." He pointed with his riding crop. "Beg! Remember, you only exist by our grace and benefaction."

Father turned, looked me straight in the eyes, and said, "Get out." I didn't budge. Suddenly Nasrollah *mirza*'s cousin lashed out with the whip. The leather straps ripped at Father's back, and just as they were about to fall on him again, he caught them flying through the air. He grabbed, jolting the man who wielded the whip with a sudden jerk. Then he let go, grabbed my hand, walked out of the house.

Past the clearing, he walked faster, nearly dragging me through the trees. I ached to go back and hit them; I wanted them to come after us. I didn't know what kind of men they were. I overestimated them. On the front porch of our bungalow, the gardener's wife and Amineh sat crouched against the wall. Father went into the house. When he turned his back, I saw the slender trickle of blood spreading on his shirt. I heard the visitors' car rev up by the driveway of the main house, and then car wheels skidded on the gravel and the engine grew loud. Father came out on the porch, wearing his old black jacket. I could hear the car driving away as he went through the trees. They had fled.

He came back with the gardener, and the two of them went in. The women sat out by the flower bed, and I sat on the porch staring at the black grove. I heard the men arguing inside. Father was bandaging the gardener's head. The gardener was angrily insisting on justice and going after the men to Tehran and complaining to the mullah and elder in the village. Father reasoned with him, and the gardener said then that he was obliged to leave. This was no place for his family! The door opened and they came out on the porch. The women got up by the flower bed, and they left, the gardener, bandaged, walking ahead of the women, still swearing under his breath. Father only told me this: "You will forget about tonight. You will tell no one. I won't either, but not because they threatened me. You don't understand the world yet. Understand?" He told me to sleep, but I didn't sleep and didn't understand, though I wanted to. In the other room the light stayed on. At dawn the cocks crowed, the moon a white sliver high over the fields.

The gardener, his wife and two sons, and Amineh left within the week. Those last days I would run through the gardens and watch Amineh. I knew her father had beaten her twice that week with a stick. He blamed her for being obliged to leave the garden. I saw her cry at dusk, sitting behind the dovecote all alone. I could hear the doves cooing. On the morning of their departure I went to find her before the open van from the village took them away. I ran down through the orchards, sunlight speckling the ground. For a moment I nearly called out, "Amineh! Amineh!" the way I did when we gathered the children to play in the gardens. She was sitting in her favorite place, staring out, neglected, forgotten, a nobody. I said good-bye to her under the mulberries. She looked down at the ground. "You're leaving?" I said. She nodded, still hanging her head.

Years later I heard — from a laborer from Varamin whom I saw in town — that she had drowned a year after leaving us and that the mother had taken ill after her daughter's death and died too. The husband hadn't minded and remarried soon after.

We moved out of the garden of Morshedabad. Of course Nasrollah *mirza* was upset, and Najibeh *khanom* spoke to Father in her soothing way that week we were packing, but Father wouldn't budge. Whenever he made a decision, it was final. Several times Nasrollah *mirza* asked after the gardener. "Why did he leave?" he said. "I thought he was happy here. And you, Hajj-Ali," he said to Father in front of me, "you don't want to work for me anymore? I can't do without you." Father said, "Sir, it's not that. I've spent years in your service and now it's time to go."

Years later Nasrollah *mirza*'s cousin died in Europe in an automobile accident. They found his body mangled behind the wheel, high above Monte Carlo. One day I recognized a photo of his friend in the papers. He still had the face of a rake and coward, but he was an important man. A pillar of society.

That year when I was still an adolescent, it was the one thing I saw and remembered. The man who had held the whip against Father, now needed him more, needed his obedience, needed his obedience to exist. In time I came to understand it as my first lesson in politics. I may have left the garden of Morshedabad like a boy leaving Eden, but instead in Tehran I found politics, rebellion.

The way I saw it, Father had retreated from the world, all because of someone who was half the man he was. I couldn't stand to see him that way. I wanted him to fight, to go back and demand his right and place in the world. Why couldn't he go back to being what he was?

He went back to Azarbaijan, to his lands and villages in Nirvan, jointly owned with other relatives and landowners. At first this revived him. They drew up plans for granaries and new pastures and improvements. He borrowed money so they could buy an electric pump and machinery and repair the underground water channels. But the second winter he had his first heart attack, and the doctor kept him in Tehran through the spring. He hated hospitals; he hated a prolonged convalescence. He said there was work to do and he owed money. He wasn't going to live like an invalid! They had several good years, but then there were two years of drought, and Father ran into serious debt and mortgaged his land, and then the rumble started about land reform. The government was preparing to confiscate land, especially from the big landlords, and transfer it to cultivators and peasants. Father said, since when was it a crime to own private property? Hadn't the Crown for years appropriated the best lands for itself and overtaken the Caspian region? They were making decisions without a proper rural census. Chopping up the country meant chopping up the livelihood of people who had worked the land for generations. No good would come of it. Big landlords? What about all the small-land owners all over the place?

This was my second lesson in politics. I was in university by then. I saw how the regime was ignorant. Ignorant in its haste, in how little it knew about landholdings and the complicated web of owners and tenants and peasants and water and crop divisions. Ignorant in its great distance and estrangement from the people it proclaimed to serve, in the shallowness of its posturing. The bill for land reform passed. Several ayatollahs issued fatwas against it. Some people said the Americans had interfered and pressured the regime. Father belonged to an agricultural group of landowners, and they protested and petitioned the government, but to no avail. They charged that for the purposes of transferring their lands the government had undervalued their properties, and the long-term bonds issued to them would be no restitution. They appealed to the provincial court, but their case was rejected. In the muddled execution of land reform and mounting rhetoric pitting all sides against one another, Father not only lost land — gaining nothing from the stipulations of the decree — but he lost his entire income from the land and so lost everything in one clean sweep when he couldn't pay his heavy debts and his creditors took what remained. He was ruined.

We lost our house in Tehran and took rooms in the house of my mother's brother. Father remained there like a caged bird, this man who had loved the open fields and open skies and lived to oversee the land. A man whose entire language was about working the land. He had always taken measure of its divisions and crops and seeds and water and roots. *Daimi* and *saifi* and *abi* and *maalek* and *ra'iyat* and *mosha* and *jareeb*. A lifetime he had repeated the words into the night. A lifetime I had heard them, like the chanting of birds. When it stopped, the silence was terrible, as if someone had cut off his tongue and hands. He didn't say much, not even to me, and never talked much after that. Once, he'd taken on the world, taken on peasants and tenants and government agents and landlords, a lion in the desert of God. I felt my blood boil every time I saw him in a corner reading. I'd see him as I came and went from university, when I returned nights from arguing politics with friends, and there he sat under the light with his book and the ghost of his dignity, a broken man. Mother was heartbroken. Zari felt nothing but shame. Then Morteza's family came to ask for her hand, and they were married under a dark cloud, though I think our family always kept up an admirable front. In time, through my fury and humiliation and guilt for the things I could not change, I learned to have the strangest tenderness for Father — and outright defiance for that edifice that had brought about his ruin.

One evening we found him lying in the street, where he'd collapsed from a massive heart attack on his way home from buying bread.

Then only death came to honor his old age, his life's work commemorated by a simple slab, a grave.

Looking to take on the world, to change a destiny I would never again leave to others, I learned to rise up against a system that maintained that everything had to be the way it said, had to be obeyed and submitted to without question, unbroken for all eternity.

TWENTY

I CIRCLED FOREVER, looking for parking. Mr. Bashirian had said nine o'clock, the Central Department of Police adjoining Komiteh Prison.

"You won't forget?" he'd said self-deprecatingly the day before. As if I could. "I hope he's all right," he'd repeated all day. He was afraid they'd harmed him, afraid they'd bring out a different son. "I hope it's no trouble to you," he said finally. "No trouble," I said. "Just something between friends."

That night I worried — not just about going into Komiteh or what could happen, but about reaching out to somewhere unfamiliar, hostile, where I would be forced to reassess everything I stood for and took for granted.

The sun shone; the sky was enduringly blue.

My wool overcoat caught in the door of the car. I tripped as I crossed at the traffic light. I never thought of turning back. From that distance I could see Mr. Bashirian pacing with a small black duffel bag. He'd never seen the inside of a prison, never thought he'd deserve to.

Past the front gate and main office, where we checked in, we were directed to a waiting room. We waited, other visitors inhabiting steel chairs against the wall. Two families, one with two small children. I watched the children jump around. The duffel bag, which they had inspected, was on the floor next to Mr. Bashirian. He got up several times and went to the window, the only one, giving on to the courtyard, and the children jumped up and down in his way. You could still hear the noises of the city, buses, honking, the hum of traffic — reassuring sounds, from in there. It was reassuring to see children, though there was nothing reassuring for them there.

Mr. Bashirian didn't want to talk, he was so nervous. I had nothing to say. He'd taken off his raincoat and carefully draped it over a chair. He wore gray trousers and a white shirt with a striped green tie under a navy blue sweater. And he had his eternal handkerchief, which he kept taking out to wipe his eyes and forehead. Nerves: he couldn't bear waiting. I couldn't wait for the whole thing to be over.

We ground out our cigarettes nervously into the glass ashtray on the steel table by the wall. For once the walls were blank. There was nothing identifiable, no official portraits. No one wanted to own up to this room. He stuffed the handkerchief in his pocket. The door opened and a man in a black suit in the doorway motioned to the family with children. The mother started to cry. Mr. Bashirian turned his face away; he'd gone pale.

"What did you bring him?" I whispered.

"His favorite sweets. One book."

"Which one?"

"Les Misérables," he said.

I nodded, recrossed my arms next to him, twitching my foot.

He turned to me. "That day at the Intercontinental, I reproached you for mentioning the book. Forgive me."

"No, you were right."

"No, but I want to tell you I'm ashamed. Ashamed of what I had to say to the reporter. Instead of telling him all about our great progress and fine universities and wonderful medical centers and modern institutions, I had to —"

"I know. I know what you mean."

It was miserable. He saw the world not for its flaws, nor for what it owed him, but for what he gave in service. He'd made the pact long ago. It would be tested.

The door opened again. Mr. Bashirian looked up, panic in his eyes.

"Bashirian," the man said impassively.

We were going through the door, Mr. Bashirian walking ahead with the duffel bag. I followed, the impostor. A guard had checked our identities at the main office as I'd held my breath. I'd deferred to Mr. Bashirian, standing demurely behind him while he'd handed over identification cards and the duffel bag for inspection. He'd shown his sister's identity card with an airbrushed picture of her, which strangely enough resembled me — the high forehead, the slightly beaked nose, the heart-shaped face, even the squint in the eyes. We were roughly the same age. I'd memorized her date of birth and particulars, just in case, but they had not asked.

What would his son think of seeing a stranger, an intruder? Too late now.

We were led halfway down a narrow corridor into a small room to the right. No one there. No windows, but two feeble strips of neon lights above, casting an anemic hue. A rectangular table was in the middle with chairs around it. The man left, slamming the door behind him, the glass pane in the door rattling. Mr. Bashirian paced, intent on sounds from the corridor. I stood away from the door.

Within minutes we heard the distant clanking of a metal door, the reverberating echo. Then footsteps, not one set, but a cluster. I tensed up, casting quick glances from the door to Mr. Bashirian. He stood frozen in the middle of the room. I kept to the side.

When they brought in Peyman Bashirian, time stopped. Even for me. He hung for a moment in the doorway, a guard behind him. The dark hair, ashen face, dark eyes. He looked as if they'd forced him to come. I could only see the back of his father's head and how his arms hung loosely, then twitched up, to fall back, resigned. Such yearning. I was mortified. I looked down.

"Fifteen minutes," the guard said.

It sounded like a lifetime.

The door slammed shut, the guard remaining outside. Behind the pane of glass a jowly man appeared, about to open the door. The man who'd conducted us to the room interrupted him, and they conferred behind the glass pane.

Freedom, the most indefinite possession.

Inside, neither spoke, Father nor son. Peyman had no handcuffs, no visible signs of being a prisoner. He wore dark blue jeans and a brown sweater and sneakers. Tall, thin, clean-shaven, he seemed haggard for his age. He'd already been in Komiteh too long. Still, the handsome son of an ugly man. Why wasn't he embracing his father? There was no vestige of anticipation in his eyes, no relinquishment in his posture. I panicked for Mr. Bashirian.

He spoke up. "How are you, my son?"

Peyman nodded several times, then looked through me with stony eyes. I stood rigid like a stake in the ground. He hadn't asked who I was. He knew I was no lawyer; they didn't get lawyers in there.

"Sit, sit here, my son," said Mr. Bashirian.

Backing into chairs, they sat down. Peyman sat at the head of the table at a right angle to his father. I took a chair at the other end. Both of them had their hands on the table. Mr. Bashirian's were clenched together; Peyman's at the edge as if he were about to rise, knuckles white, hunched over.

"Tell me, how are you, are you all right?" he asked his son again.

"How are you?"

He'd used the formal "you." Hadn't said "Father."

"I'm — I'm so grateful to see you," said Mr. Bashirian. "I haven't had day or night without you. From the moment you were arrested."

Peyman looked down, the buzz from the neon lights above permeating the room. Mr. Bashirian wrung his hands.

Then he said softly, "This is Ms. Mosharraf. Remember? I always talked to you about her. She's been so — so helpful, trying to help. Doing all she can. She's —"

"Don't mind me," I said quickly. "Your father has done everything possible for you. Maybe it's best I leave you alone together."

They stared back, Peyman impassive, Mr. Bashirian alarmed, verging on panic, taking out his handkerchief to wipe his forehead. I didn't budge.

"What happened, my son? What are they telling you? What's the accusation?"

Peyman began to speak, strained, inaudible. Mr. Bashirian leaned in to him. I couldn't hear from the other end. Mr. Bashirian was wiping his forehead again, but this time when his hand went down I saw it tremble.

"How can it be?" he said. "What do they mean?"

Peyman shook his head. He looked up, our eyes meeting for the second time. His were more pliant, as if he'd relinquished some terrible bit of deception, just a trace, indisposed to telling everything.

"Look," Mr. Bashirian said, pointing. "I've brought you a few things." He bent down to the duffel bag.

"I'll look later," said Peyman.

The father sat up lamely. "You're . . . thin, my son. Do you eat?"

Peyman nodded.

"You appear tired. Don't you sleep?"

His son shrugged.

"Give your father your hand. Let me hold your hand for a moment."

Peyman remained rigid, eyes averted, his hand resting on the table. Mr. Bashirian looked to me, bewildered, strangely humbled. I was about to intercede when the door opened and the jowly man in the business suit walked in. He was smiling, a green folder under his left arm. Peyman instantly tensed up. Mr. Bashirian, his back to the door, turned and, when he saw the man's outstretched arm, rose and shook hands with him.

"This is my sister, who's come from Sari," he said, introducing me.

"Please be seated," the man said ceremoniously. "Carry on, carry on. I got detained outside with an urgent problem. Do carry on."

He hadn't introduced himself. But Peyman knew him: a chilling look had overtaken Peyman's face. The man came around and sat at my end, his balding pate and flaccid cheeks lending him an agreeable patina despite the intrusive eyes.

"Why are you seated at this end?" he asked me.

His smile was glassy. He stared at Mr. Bashirian and Peyman.

"You do well not to live in Tehran!" he said to me with congeniality. "Your air up north is so much cleaner, the coast lush and green. I wouldn't mind moving there myself."

He turned to Mr. Bashirian. "You said your sister-in-law or your —"

"My sister," Mr. Bashirian cut in.

"Your wife is deceased, yes?" the man inquired.

"Long ago," said Mr. Bashirian.

No one spoke, as if we had forgotten how in front of the newcomer wielding authority. Mr. Bashirian was defenseless, unlike his son, who was seated with the anger of a thousand years. Like a memorial. Eyes sunk above cheekbones into dark circles below heavy brows. The most beautiful mouth, full, elevated with pride.

"If I may inquire, with respect —" Mr. Bashirian said, addressing the official, "what now? I mean, how long will you be . . . holding my son?"

"Don't worry, don't worry," the official said.

"How much longer?" I asked.

Mr. Bashirian was on the edge of his seat. The official stared at me.

"Please, tell us," I implored. He would pity an imploring woman.

"I most certainly will not!"

"But what's he being kept for?" I asked.

"I repeat! A family visit is a rare privilege few prisoners are granted here. I think you're aware of that."

"I — I've traveled all this way to see my nephew," I went on, agitated. "My brother's sick with worry. Can't you tell us something?"

He looked at his watch. "Time's up," he said to no one in particular.

He rose, folder up against his chest. He'd never opened it once.

Mr. Bashirian was overwrought, eyes flitting left and right as if he couldn't focus. He looked ill. Peyman kept his eyes on the table, jaw tensed. I was conscience-stricken our time had been cut short because of me.

A man poked his head in the door and motioned to the official.

The official exited, assuring us he'd be right back. Who was he? We hadn't asked. He had every right in that room, including the right to question. Not us.

"Peyman," said Mr. Bashirian hurriedly, "what shall I do? Tell me! What do you need, my son? Say something!"

"What's in the bag?"

"Sweets and a book, but next time —"

"You saw the man who just left?" his son interrupted.

"The gentleman who was just here?"

"He's no gentleman!" said Peyman. "He's one of my interrogators."

"Interrogator?" said Mr. Bashirian. "Him?"

The door opened. The official stood poised in the doorway, smile solicitous, the guards at attention behind him.

Mr. Bashirian had fear in his eyes. He picked up the duffel bag, handed it to his son. He hugged Peyman, kissed him, pressing him in with both arms. He clung to him, tears rolling down his cheeks.

"My beloved son. May God keep you, my son," he murmured.

Peyman removed himself from his father's arms.

The official was watching from the corridor. As was expected of an aunt, I went over to Peyman and embraced him. I whispered to him, "He loves you more than life itself. You'll be out soon . . ."

A few steps away, Mr. Bashirian was shaking, wiping tears off his face.

"Father —" Peyman said, and Mr. Bashirian looked up. "Don't grieve. Don't think about me. Stop thinking about me."

They were gone. Only the quiet sobbing of Mr. Bashirian. The convoy of receding footsteps. The distant thunder of a metal door, echoing. Final.

NIGHT CAME, OBSIDIAN, PREMATURELY. Autumn was deepening.

The children had eaten and I tucked them in early. I sat with them reading for half an hour, proclaiming legends and pointing at pictures. They stuck their faces under mine. They squirmed, they yawned, they stretched. I hugged and kissed them, immeasurably thankful at that moment.

Goli brought our dinner trays into the upstairs study.

Houshang and I ate together so seldom that we were out of

practice. We liked to be invited out as often as possible, to know, be assured, that we were mainstays of the society we upheld.

I had the television on. Houshang came in with a Scotch on ice and occupied the sofa, jiggling his glass, his gold ring with the seal tapping cut crystal. It annoyed me when he tapped. He turned up the volume on the news, a deliberate snub, since he never watched local television.

We ate without a word, knives and forks clinking against our plates, water glasses going up and down like elevators. Both of us entrenched, intractable, in the same house with the same life.

Goli came back with tea and a bowl of dates and took away the trays. Houshang said he had something for me. I thought he had bad news. From the top drawer of the cabinet, he took out a small black velvet box and left it on the table. I pried it open; it was a sapphire ring encircled by hideous prongs set with diamonds from a jeweler I neither trusted nor liked.

"What's the occasion?" I asked.

"I give you a present, and you ask why! Put it on."

A pudgy hillock of stones, several sizes too large. True to himself, Houshang always gave the expendable.

"Don't you like it?" he said, for a moment distressed, nearly attentive.

"No, I — Thierry was here yesterday afternoon," I said suddenly.

To my surprise, he grinned equably. "The fox! Did he grovel?"

I balked. Thierry had been forced to come. Houshang had required it to force his hand, as penance, a measure of his control and manipulation. It was his sort of revenge, transmuted into an apology. He had Thierry exactly where he wanted him.

"You have to pull all the strings all the time?" I said.

He blew up. "Don't you like the ring? You want to throw it back in my face? You and your family are all the same. I'm sick and tired of your remoteness. Who the hell understands you anymore?"

He stood up, about to storm out, but changed his mind. "You know —" he said, pointing his finger, "let me tell you. It's sad. Really sad."

"I know," I said.

"No, you don't! The truth is you're cold with me. You have no devotion left for me anymore. There's no sweetness or gentleness in you. You're not the woman I fell in love with. The one I married."

HE LEFT RIGHT AFTER dinner. The phone rang. Eleven-twenty: I knew it wasn't him.

Mother called late, often on a whim, to chat before going to bed. "In case I die in my sleep," she'd say. Late at night she was at her most creative. And awake. She would wander through the large house, baking cakes, making quince and sour cherry and carrot jam, checking her pickles, reading Hafez, playing solitaire and listening to old records, painting, complaining how all her friends were getting old and tiresome.

I'd been rummaging through photo albums in the downstairs study. I went into the kitchen to make tea, carried the glass back to the study. The ringing telephone startled me. I picked up on the second ring, immediately recognizing Mr. Bashirian's voice. I'd given him my home number, advising him not to hesitate to call. This was the first time.

"It's me . . ." he said tentatively.

I asked how he was. Desperate, he insisted, and unwell.

"What kind of unwell?" I said.

"I have chest pains."

"A cough? You must have a cold."

"No, it's a sharp pain — all over."

I asked what kind of pain, where, what he'd eaten, which pills. His voice tremulous, he apologized for disturbing me, for calling so late.

"You should see a doctor."

"What doctor? It was terrible to see him today. Terrible."

I heard a click on the phone. Someone was listening in. The door of the study was ajar; beyond, the dark hallway, the curving silhouette of the staircase. On the table next to me in the study, a single light, a wheel of light in a darkened room.

"Hold on," I said.

I went through dark rooms to the kitchen. The lights were out, but there was a nip in the air — the back door to the kitchen had been open. Goli and her husband each had a key and locked up when they left at night. Whoever had been eavesdropping on my phone call had left in a hurry and hadn't had time to lock the door. The key was still in the outside lock. Down the garden path I thought I heard footsteps. I locked the door and returned to the study.

"Are you still there?" I said when I picked up the receiver.

Mr. Bashirian was coughing. When he recovered, he said, "I must give you the extra key to my house."

"You're going on a trip?"

"If — if I die, I want you to give him this letter. I'm leaving it on —"

"Why talk about death? When we can talk about living."

"I'll die alone in this house, and I will never see him again."

This filled me with a terrible foreboding. "You mustn't say that!"

"I've been pacing for hours, thinking awful thoughts. I — I can't breathe. I'm being swallowed up by darkness. I'm drowning, you know. Drowning with every hour, the darker it gets. I'm thrashing for air."

I cradled the receiver by my neck, whispering. "Think of him. How you finally saw him. How you love him. Nothing else matters. Didn't you hear what they said? Any day now —"

"I don't believe anything anymore."

"Please, listen. So far things are improving. Right?"

I heard the labored breathing broken off by his agitation for keeping me up so late.

"Don't worry," I whispered. "Sleep. Take a sedative and go to sleep."

"When I sleep I have nightmares. I lie down waiting for them."

"I know, I know. But they will not come tonight. If you take the sedative now, you'll sleep, and by morning you'll feel better. Believe me."

He disavowed equilibrium, endurance, and I repeated, whispering into the phone until he acceded to notions of trust and sleep.

In the bedroom I drew the curtains, their skirts rustling, like the wind outside hunting fallen leaves. "Believe," I had told him. We lie to others with the same words we use to lie to ourselves.

TWENTY-ONE

FRIDAY AFTER MY MORNING HIKE, I decided to stop by to see Mother.

The hike up in Tochal — a meeting of one of the university cells under my supervision — had been disrupted by a third-year physics student. Once a hothead in high school in Qom, he still argued like the mule-headed son of a minor cleric. "Kill or get killed!" he threatened, lecturing us on the immediate need for an armed struggle. He bickered with the others about the ideal revolutionary condition, quoting Jazani and Puyan and the independent Marxist, Sho'ayian. Then suddenly they lunged at one another, thrashing around on the mountain ledge, threatening to bash one another's brains out. I wanted to bash their brains out myself. Despite the training, they still had no discipline. For a political front to have breadth and depth it had to exist separately from an armed struggle.

Early in the afternoon, still angry, I arrived with a big box of sweetmeats for Zari's children.

"There's a message for you," Zari said at the door. "Why can't you get your own phone? I'm not your secretary!"

She could be so touchy and tiresome. I made for Mother's room.

"Why's her door shut?" I said. "She's sleeping?"

"Morteza blew up again. He wants to know why you can't take her."

Mother had elected to live with Zari, for which Zari received something from me every month. I also gave something to Mother. Morteza wanted it all.

"He wants money," said Zari, tears welling up in her eyes, her hand still covering her cheek. "He still thinks we're hiding it from him."

"What does that mean? Why's your hand stuck to your face?"

"He thinks we were loaded, since Father worked for Nasrollah *mirza* all those years. He screams all the time, 'You think I'm gullible and stupid? You think I don't know you're hiding things from me?' He says we're sneaky liars and misers. Or else, Father really was an incompetent, bankrupt idiot."

"He said that about Father?"

"Mother came out of her room and I saw her turn white, and she went back in and shut the door."

"He said that in front of her?"

"You think that's all? He says our family went broke and pawned me off on him. He says he was tricked! He wouldn't have married me and only did not to dishonor the family. And after Father died . . ."

She stared at me, grief and shame in her eyes.

"When he shouts, even the neighbors can hear him! He screamed so much today he scared the children and they started wailing. So he hit them. Mother locked herself in her room. The children went to get her, but she wouldn't come out. They begged and cried and stamped their feet and pounded on her door until I started crying. Morteza said he'd hit me so my teeth would jump out. Then he slapped me around."

Zari wept. I yanked her hand off her face and saw the bloodred welt on her cheek. The son of a bitch was slapping my sister. Now I would find him and kill him so that she'd cry only as his widow.

"Where is he?"

"How should I know? He's gone to hell!"

"When did he leave?"

"Right after he beat me and my children and kicked the doors and broke plates and threw around our belongings! He's an animal!"

"He must be taught a lesson once and for all," I said.

"What's the use?" Zari burst out sobbing. "He's got some goddamn slut. He goes on and on about her — about some whore to my face. That's what he wants the money for. For her! Imagine adoring a slut! What am I — his goddamn maid? You should see how he torments me. He says I'm dirt-poor, I'm a shrew, I'm getting old, I'm useless and cranky. He calls me a nobody!" Zari said, wailing. "He does what he wants since Father died."

I didn't want to hear another word. "Stop crying, I said!"

"But he's the father of my children!" she said, sobbing.

That was his worst defect. I went out in the courtyard and lit a cigarette and smoked. Zari hid away inside the house. She had insisted on marrying Morteza, abandoning her studies, making three children with him. I came back in and knocked on Mother's bedroom door. I heard her murmur something and barged in. She lay on the bedding, invested with dignity and helplessness. I was so angry I wanted to beat the walls.

"So, you've come?" Mother said to me.

"Haven't you had lunch?" I said.

Zari leaned against the door, red-faced, with red eyes, arms folded.

"Shall I bring you lunch?" she asked Mother.

"Bring me poison."

A copy of *Tehran Mossavar* lay by her hand. She motioned for me to sit.

"See what sort of brute he is? If only your father were alive . . ."

Tears rolled down her cheeks. She hid her face in her hand, momentarily overcome, then wiped the tears off efficiently.

"Did she give you the message?" Mother asked.

"What message?"

"Jalal called."

"Jalal? That's impossible."

"It was him," said Zari. "I talked to him."

He'd called at one-thirty, asked after Mother, the children, and me as if he'd been away on vacation. He'd left a number for me to call immediately.

"What's going on?" said Zari.

"How should I know?" I snapped back.

We got into a bitter argument overflowing with recriminations until Mother had to intercede. The children came in from the neighbor's all quiet, then all happy to see us together, and I fetched the box of *zoulbiah* and *bamieh* that I'd bought at the confectioner's, and we sat by Mother, eating golden treacly sweets with sticky fingers and glasses of tea, and made Mother retell stories about the days in the old house in Darvazeh Daulat until she took out the black-and-white and old sepia photographs from the small, battered suitcase behind the curtain, and we spread them on the bed — Father like a general with pensive eyes standing behind Mother, seated demurely and airbrushed; Grandfather in clerical robes and turban at the entrance of a mosque in Tabriz; Zari at five with a bow in her hair like a bumblebee; Zari radiant at sixteen before marrying the jackass; me with a crew cut, buttressed by Father and my bicycle; graduation from the Teacher's College; a family picnic with the samovar under trees. Mother pointed here and there, looking astonishingly young all at once, then surprisingly tired, and trying, always trying, to tell us something else.

"Things were different then" is what she always said.

THE PHONE NUMBER WAS for a crowded café. The man who answered had an Armenian accent. His name was Khachik and he told me to call back. I did, three times in two hours, until he put me through.

"Jalal!" I said.

"Reza?" He gave directions, said to get there immediately, and hung up.

When I got there, the neon sign was blinking blue and green. They had tongue sandwiches and bologna with fat pickles and tripe on Thursdays. Inside they'd laid out the vodka at a corner table for a bunch of men. Khachik was the blond Armenian at the corner table telling jokes, his arm around a whore, his customers hollering with laughter. He shoved back his chair, took me through a door to the small kitchen in the back. He had dimples and blue eyes and two gold teeth.

"He's not here," he said to me.

"Don't jerk me around! I just talked to him."

"Call tomorrow night at nine," he said, going back out to the front.

I exited through the back alley, imagining Morteza and how I was going to beat him until he'd cry and beg like a woman. My knuckles ached to sink into his face, finally breaking it open.

I STOOD SMOKING in a dark side street off Jaleh Square. I'd called Morteza from the café where I ended up having dinner. I was waiting for him. I saw the liver-red Peykan come down the street. He slammed on his brakes, screeched to a stop, jammed the car into a space with his lousy parking. He was still behind the wheel when I went over and tapped his half-open window. A brother-in-law with a nose like an eggplant and shiny black hair like a wig and lecherous lips, once handsome in his youth for half an hour.

"Get out," I said.

He hesitated, leaned over to grab his jacket from the front seat, and got out of the car. He slung his jacket over one shoulder, barrel-chested and fleshy. He'd put on weight; he looked bloated.

"What's the problem?"

"You're the problem," I said.

"Ha, ha," he laughed, braying. He asked for a cigarette.

"Tell me something," I said. "You pamper my sister? Care and protect her and her children as is your sacred duty?"

"Of course I do! But you know her, she bitches constantly."

"You mean it's her fault?" I said. "And Mother? You respect her as you should? How about Father's memory?"

"What d'you mean your father — of course — he's, he was — what a man!"

I took out my keys and said to him, "See this?" Then I drew a line, scraping paint off the side of his car.

"You crazy?" he said, lunging for the key.

I threw a punch to his face so fast he looked stupefied. He put his hand to his mouth, and his fingers got bloody.

"I'm here to give you a lesson you won't forget," I said.

"What've I done to you?" he protested loudly.

I pushed him back against his car. "Me, them — what's the difference?"

"What did she say?" he yelled. "What lies did she make up this time?"

I punched him again, to the left side of his face. He swung right back out, but missed me.

"Wait, let me explain — you don't know —"

I grabbed him by the collar and dragged him over to the side-walk. He kept taking wild swings and kicking, blood dripping from his mouth.

"Listen, motherfucker," I said, "lay a hand on my sister and you're dead. Tonight the emergency ward. Next time the morgue. I'll dance on your grave."

He reeled back, hurling insults at me, swearing his innocence by saints and prophets and members of his family. He was pathetic. I left him propped up in his car with a black eye and cut lip and enough gashes and bruises to keep him in pain for a week.

I walked to Jaleh Square to catch a taxi.

THE NEXT DAY, MOTHER CALLED my office very agitated about Morteza. He'd come home after ten the night before, received a call, and gone out, then come back an hour later all bloodied and bruised.

"They nearly broke all his bones! Maybe he owes money and he's in trouble with some lowlifes."

"He's a lowlife himself, Mother."

"He's bruised and limping," she said. "He's your brother-in-law, for God's sake! What if they'd killed him? What would become of Zari and the children?"

Morteza should have received the beating of his life sooner. From the first day, the first brick had been laid crooked. Men like Morteza never repent. It's a complete waste of time. They just respond to punishment.

I left the office late in the evening. In the street I dialed the café from a public phone but could barely hear over the din of traffic. The man said something like, "Wait for the message," then dropped the receiver with a thud, came back, and said, "Dinner is waiting for you."

There and then I flagged a cab. I had to squeeze in the back with a man and woman. When I got off, the scent of her perfume still clung to my sleeve.

This time Khachik came out from behind the counter to greet me and we embraced like old friends, and he whispered. I went back through the kitchen. There was no one there. The door to the back alley was open, facing the back wall of a brick building, and I stepped into the dark. I saw a man's shadow against the wall, the pinpoint glow of a cigarette. The shadow moved out.

"They said you were in Komiteh," I said.

He nodded. I lit a cigarette, stood against the wall.

"For years our group received instructions from Europe," Jalal said. "Two years ago, several of them came home. I was told to form a cell. The coffee shop was doing well. We had money. A while ago I had a hunch we had a traitor in our group. Shaheen was a new member. He was clever, but he was the traitor. I made sure. We had a serious problem, so I volunteered. I went over. It was the only way."

"You let them recruit you?"

"I exposed a couple of student groups. You know, gave in some names. I made myself useful."

"What about Shaheen?"

"SAVAK should've used someone more intelligent. You met him. He's the one you talked to at Radio City."

"You reckless bastard! You had me give a message to a fucking snitch?"

He put up both hands. "You did us a favor. My comrades were in the car with me. You helped expose an informer. A true revolutionary act!"

"Go to hell," I said, incensed.

He stood against the wall, staring at me.

"Come on," he said. "Nothing's changed. We trust each other."

"Tell me exactly what happened."

"Omeed was my code name to Shaheen. I was in charge of our intelligence. At first he checked out. But I tailed him after he joined us. I knew everything about him — what he did, where he went. The license plate on every car he got into, the address of every house he used and the time and date of each visit, every place he ate, every office building he walked into."

"He never suspected you?"

"He never saw my face. That's how I work. Until I walked in at our last meeting. I had a file of incriminating evidence against him. I handed it to SAVAK. My best work! Proof he ran a cell and had plans to attack a gendarmerie and rob a Melli Bank. It was all in the file — the codes, his contacts, how he was double-crossing them. Recruiting, buying arms! He was a rat, a double agent. They're so jittery. The slightest hint and they jump! They're a knee-jerk establishment. They took him out."

"He's dead?"

"He's in prison. He's going to have to confess. My word against his. They kept us on the same floor. Twice he saw me when they took him down the hall. They had me there to unnerve him. I wasn't afraid. I'm not afraid of them! They let me out and told me to lie low."

But he looked worried. He asked for a cigarette.

"When he got your message, he figured we'd drawn him out to kill him, then and there. In the street. The son of a bitch! We didn't touch him. We let him sweat. He got arrested and roughed up by his own people. He's going to be paranoid forever! From now on he'll be no good to anyone. Not even to himself."

"I met your parents," I said.

"My sister gave the address, huh? When did you see her? She's always enjoyed humiliating me. Did she flirt with you?"

"She looked everywhere for you. Your parents are worried."

"Didn't they disgust you? Weren't you relieved to get away from them like I was years ago? He's another tyrant, my father. Bigoted and stupid. My mother is pathetic and haggard. In that dark, oily, suffocating house. He's a brute, you know, with all his moral gibberish on dogma and piety and alms and the Absent One and doomsday. I hate him. I'm ashamed of her. She's a servant in every conceivable way. I detest servitude!"

"The poor woman —"

"Reza, you and I are the only honest people I know! Look at us — stuck in some back alley in this phony and meaningless city. Sitting on top of a volcano. It's been a bad week."

He said there was trouble. His group was splitting up — there was a great deal of hostility on ideological differences. He was in the radical wing. He had set up a network to deliver information, give refuge, get medical help in time of combat. They were a bunch of theoreticians and dialecticians. Sometimes he wanted to strangle them. They were accusing him of playing anarchist.

"That's what you say about me," he said. "But they're always bickering with mind-numbing ideological debates. They're being stubborn and petty. Endangering the rest of us."

"You should leave for a while," I said.

TWENTY-TWO

I HAD INSISTED my brother check back with his special contact about corruption charges on Bandar Kangan. How did he know? "He knows," my brother said ominously. He's ominous these days.

"They're after blood," he said over breakfast.

Houshang had already left. Kavoos was buttering toast.

"I think they won't be able to trace anything to Houshang. He's clever."

"You mean corrupt?" I said.

"It's the only way to get contracts like Kangan. Houshang's always been shrewd. They drink and play cards and shovel into each other's pockets."

Kavoos shrugged and sipped tea, lit a cigarette, stared out to the garden.

"I feel . . ." He hesitated. "I don't know, underneath all this reckless abandon there's something — something's changed, but I can't tell what it is."

Then suddenly he said, "You know, I married the wrong woman."

Their wedding had been the most elaborate and well-attended wedding of the decade. Politicians, ambassadors, the prime minister — she had insisted.

"You fell in love with her, remember?"

"No, I don't."

When he left, I went up to find the gaudy sapphire ring Houshang had given me to return it. I ended up rummaging through the upstairs rooms. Goli, a mediocre housekeeper, moody and sloppy, was no thief. Ramazan, although an uninspired cook, had kept exemplary house accounts for years and once found the diamond ring of a dinner guest in the powder room. I left a message for Houshang, headed downtown. He called back, cut me off to say he had the ring.

"But you gave it to me," I said.

"You just want to return it!"

He said he'd taken it because he planned to return the ring immediately. Ultimately his gifts were his. He was so busy he never had time to do anything with the children, no matter when. Now he was going to sit in traffic to return a ring.

At midday I had an appointment for a haircut at Balenciaga and stopped off at the jeweler's. The owner, Mr. Tala'afshan, made a big show of welcoming me — how I was honoring him with my presence, how he'd feared I'd withdrawn the kind and eminent patronage of my family. He inquired after Mother. Such a lady, the most distinguished he'd ever seen! The crowning flower of society. She never visited anymore. I pretended to survey the glitter he kept under polished glass. He wanted me to try on a parure of diamonds and rubies.

"I hate parures," I said. "I hate rubies."

He looked baffled. Fashionably overdressed women circumambulated the cases like predators, and the phones kept ringing. When he took a call on his faux antique-gold telephone, I saw my chance. I called over an assistant I'd never seen before, who smoothed down his tie, smiling with deference. I introduced myself.

"Aren't you the one who helped my husband?"

"Of course —" he said enthusiastically, "that is, Mr. Behroudi spoke to Mr. Tala'afshan and sent Mrs. — I forget the lady's name —" He stopped.

"Oh, he sent his sister?"

"Mrs. Mazaher! She's Mr. Behroudi's sister? I'm sorry, I didn't know."

I flinched. Pouran Mazaher's degree of intimacy with my husband was astonishing. She picked out women for him behind my back; now she was picking up jewelry for him. I asked the price of the ring.

"Mrs. Mazaher charged everything to your husband's account."

"Everything? She selected the ring —"

"And the gold-and-diamond bracelet! She has excellent taste."

The owner rushed over, whispered to the assistant, and sent him packing.

"Forgive me, Mrs. Behroudi. He's new here. How can I be of assistance?"

I told him I wouldn't be keeping the sapphire ring. Did I wish to select something else? he offered gallantly. I wanted to see the bill.

"There is no bill if you're returning the ring!"

His assistant could have misinformed me; still, I had to be sure.

"What about the gold-and-diamond bracelet?" I said.

He looked startled but quickly pretended to deliberate about this.

"It must be on the bill," I said.

"The money isn't at all important! You're a valued customer."

"Please check now," I said.

He cleared his throat politely, offered tea, Turkish coffee. He went to the back, summoning the errant assistant, then dismissing him and summoning another. They whispered. Evident complications, as I'd suspected. They would try to reach Houshang. Tala'afshan, impersonating the very model of tact and discretion, could not admit to the gold-and-diamond bracelet. He had received instructions not to. He came back, earnest and now amiably perplexed.

"Forgive me. We can't seem to find the bill. There's been a misunderstanding. I checked, and nobody knows anything about a gold-and-diamond bracelet. It was a bracelet, you said?"

He was lying. What made it worse was that I disliked him. Houshang had purchased the gift, and Pouran had picked it up. The bracelet was for someone else.

LATE THAT AFTERNOON Mr. Bashirian kept me after a meeting in the conference room, and while other colleagues filed out of the room, he fidgeted, realigning his pens and papers, and I thought, Here we go again. Only the day before, the last person I'd consulted had told me his son could be kept in Komiteh indefinitely and there was nothing he could do at all.

Then the door slammed behind the last person, and Mr. Bashirian quickly whispered, "They called. They're going to release him!"

"What? That's incredible news," I said, astonished.

"I know. I can hardly believe it."

I felt overcome, overjoyed for him. "When are they releasing him?"

"The next two days. They said they'd call again."

It was over. Peyman was coming home. But then Mr. Bashirian shifted in his seat, suddenly anxious again, and I thought, He'll never break the habit, never stop, even when given good news.

"Something they said worries me. They asked if Peyman was on medication."

"Is he?"

"No, that's just it. I — I wonder if something's gone wrong.

Why else would they ask? Why ask about medication? I think something's happened to him."

"It's nothing — you'll see. Just go home and wait for their call."

When I got home, I was short with Goli, who had given the children dinner a whole hour later than usual. The upstairs was a mess, clothes and plastic guns and toy soldiers strewed about and dinner trays with untouched food still in the study.

The phone kept ringing, and Ehsan and Kamran followed me around, complaining how Mr. Nirvani was their tormentor. They didn't want a tutor. They didn't want so much work. Their fingers hurt from writing! "Look, they're deformed!" they said, curling their fingers before their faces, making horrible grimaces. They hated Ramazan's dinner. Couldn't they pop popcorn and gobble candy? Couldn't they have friends over Thursday and Friday and go to the Ice Palace? Why had I come home so late, and why hadn't I gone out with their father for dinner? Why did they have to go to bed? They wanted to stay up and watch television like all their friends.

"Enough!" I said.

"You sound just like Mr. Nirvani," they complained.

I tucked them in. They'd be pulling out flashlights in no time, enacting war games. I went down and called in Golchehreh, addressing her by her full name, as I did whenever I was angry. I explained again about housework and schedules and meals. She complained my sons never listened.

"They're demons, madame. How did you make them? They were guerrillas again with black shoe polish on their faces, running through pretend jungles. I haven't enough work? My feet puff up at night and kill me, my back hurts. Ramazan's worried to death for me. You're never pleased. I can't keep up."

I told her I wanted her to keep to her schedule. She listened, sulking, said that if I was so dissatisfied with her, then she should leave. She threatened every few weeks. I showed her the key to the back door of the kitchen and asked if it was hers or Ramazan's.

"I don't know," she said.

She knew. I had two and they had two. I asked her to go check with Ramazan and waited, leafing through the evening papers until she returned.

"Ramazan must have lost his," she said sullenly.

"It isn't lost if it was in the door."

"Whatever you say," she said, looking past me.

"One of you came in around eleven-thirty."

"Who says we did? Swear to God, we didn't!"

"So who did?"

"I don't sleep behind the door! How should I know? Don't you trust us?"

"What's the matter? Maybe Tourandokht can talk sense to you."

Goli turned beet red, chewing her lip. I made for the door.

"What does she know?" Goli said about her great-grandmother. "Like she's got a doctorate or something. Her ideas date from the time of *shah-vezvezeh!* What does she know about our problems today?"

"What problems?" I said.

Goli shook her head bitterly. "Until when must we swallow our words?"

FRIDAY I TOOK the children to my parents for lunch. I hadn't seen Houshang in two days.

Mother announced she was worried for her youngest brother, Khodayar, who was finally seeing a specialist after weeks of severe migraines. Of course, she had had to hear this from someone else. "All because of that birdbrained, spiteful wife of his!" she warned us. Father had a cold. He was wearing his gray argyle cardigan from Harrods. Mother was babying him with an iron fist and sarcastic harangues. We lunched at two, listening to Mr. Malekshah, eminent scholar and Platonist. He droned on at the dining table, dividing white rice and eggplant stew on his plate into neat fractions, then spooning them into his mouth. He chewed like a camel. It took forever for him to eat and forever for him to get through Plato's *Republic,* enamored as he was with the ideal, with words, with perfection. Father listened intently, always fascinated by his friend, always a gracious listener. Mother tapped the table, making remarkable grimaces at the chandelier.

"Eat, Malekshah, so we can get to dessert!" Mother said.

Mr. Malekshah looked extremely miffed.

"Najibeh, dear," Father said to her, "these are great thoughts."

"They disrupt the flow of lunch," said Mother.

"But they're Plato's!"

"Who says?"

Mother was being particularly contrary, and Father unusually admiring of Plato that day, just to get even. Later in the living room Father confessed he wasn't about to contradict Mr. Malekshah or Mother or Plato anymore.

"You've never liked criticizing anyone to his face," I said.

Mother came along to give him dagger looks, and whispered, "Can't you ever do anything, for God's sake, when that old bore rambles on like that?"

Father watched her formidable back vanish into the kitchen. "She gets tougher to live with every year," he said.

He pulled me aside to ask if Reza Nirvani was an effective tutor. When I said, "Of course," he said he had no doubt. He wanted to know if I'd spoken to him about other things. Was he troubled? Was anything the matter?

"He didn't give me his life story, if that's what you mean."

Father sank into the couch, disappointed.

I went to see Tourandokht in her room, down the hall behind the back staircase, taking a tray of tea and Mother's almond *sohan* and two slices of pound cake. She lives on dark tea and sweets. We had a rundown of her aches, the kitchen gossip. The gardener's sons were rude and uppity and sullen; the new eighteen-year-old maid was infatuated with one of them; the cook, Masht-Ghanbar, who attended the mosque all the time now, was threatening to leave after the scandal about cooking oil. "Of course, we all know your mother tests the patience of a saint!" Tourandokht interjected. I complained about Goli.

"Oh, she's just impulsive, my dear."

I said Goli was hostile, lied to my face, listened in on my phone calls, snuck into the house late at night. No, I wasn't imagining things. Tourandokht shook her head, her white hair and white head scarf a celestial aura. When I left I kissed her, and she stroked my cheek with the abstracted and restful expression of someone anticipating her own vanishing.

In the living room I kissed Father, who was plopped beside a large potted palm listening to Mr. Malekshah. Malekshah was discussing the Neoplatonists, one by one. Father looked drowsy and was blowing his nose.

Mother gritted her teeth by the door. "When is that warthog going to leave your father alone?" she demanded.

She elaborately hugged the children, who ran away, kicking up dead leaves. Then she instructed me to take a nap.

"You look terrible. It's that pretentious brat you live with!"

This I ignored.

When we got home, the boys went off to play soccer with the neighbor's children. Thierry called just as I came into the front hall. He wanted to know if I'd forgiven him, if I had it in my heart. It was important to him.

He had a hangover, he had gossip. The night before he'd gone from a cocktail party to the Italian embassy dinner to the Key Club to a late nightcap at someone's house. Someone high up! The husband was in the Far East on business. Thierry was ascending through Tehran society, cheek to cheek, bed to bed. He yawned. It was so inconvenient — this one was in love with him.

"You love convenience," I said.

"I prefer you," he whispered.

He asked to talk to Houshang. I said he wasn't in, but I felt he already knew that. He asked when Houshang would be home. I had no idea.

"You're unhappy," he said.

"You're impertinent."

"Don't be so touchy. I've got good news!" he said blithely.

He wanted me to know he'd spoken to the journalist from Paris. The journalist didn't mention Mr. Bashirian or his son, nor our hostile and ill-fated interview at the Intercontinental. He just said the article was going to be out. It was going to be big, important. Splashed around Europe.

"See how nice we are! Even though your friend threw a tantrum with the *typical* Eastern touchiness of a porcupine."

"Stop your *typical* this and *typical* that."

"You're not typically Iranian," he said. This, the ultimate compliment from a foreigner.

"I consider that an insult."

"How typical!" he said, laughing. Then he whispered over the phone, "You know, I could make you happy."

HOUSHANG CAME IN furious. He was running late, he hadn't eaten all day, he had a splitting headache. He wanted a drink. He wanted to know why I wasn't ready. I said I wasn't going, but he said, *"Yes you are,"* jaw tensed.

"Don't make a scene," he cautioned. "Just *get* ready!"

He disappeared to shower and dress. I longed to have it out with him about the diamond bracelet. For which floozy and mistress was it this time? But hectoring wasn't punishment. I held my tongue, organized my thoughts.

I wanted him punished.

In the bedroom he carefully combed back his hair, regarding himself in the mirror. I slung on my black satin heels, sitting on the bed, ran fingers up my stockings. Envisioned turning my back on him. Neither of us was sure why we were in the same bedroom that night. We were unacquainted in some immeasurable way. Unlatched. Long before going our separate ways, we had already come unfastened, biding time by going to dinner parties and kissing our children.

He doused on more cologne, more than usual, puckering his full mouth. He slipped on his gold watch, his gold ring with the seal. He was worried. He was aging this autumn. Lines even he couldn't erase. I sprayed myself with Joy, the perfume I wore by habit. I was becoming like the house I inhabited, by an uninspired and copycat architect — like our life, fixed and entrenched, all the while the underside was decaying.

"I'm tired of Joy," he said, pulling on his dark jacket.

He had an urgent phone call to make before leaving and went into the study. I sat waiting downstairs in the dark living room.

The orchestra had played by the mountain the night we first met under the trees of the Hotel Darband. We were a party of twenty-four. A long table. Houshang had walked around the table past young women with expectant smiles and asked me to dance. He pulled out my chair, radiant, eyes steady. He handled the chair deftly, turned, put a hand to the small of my back. Rising, going forth, Houshang a step behind me winding through the tables, I looked out to the mountain, the dark trees, the old hotel, the sea of people, and felt the overwhelming reassurance that I was part of this whole, which I belonged to and which belonged to me. A moment of near mystical certainty, moving, eyes to the distance. I took it as a good omen. We stepped up to the dance floor and he took me into his arms and smiled the knowing smile of a man who has eyes for no one else and is at his most potent. Because he sees what he wants. He brushed his lips against my hair and said, "Joy, you wear Joy." I said I did. He held me closer. Swaying under the enormous canopy of trees, slivered moon, far-flung stars. "You wear it like no other woman," he said.

I hadn't wanted to go out that night. My oldest brother, Kavoos, a bachelor then, had taken me by coercion. I'd worn a white sleeveless dress, turquoise earrings, silver sandals. "And such breeding!" Houshang later said, well before he felt the full burden of its effect. At first I hadn't even noticed him. Later, I realized he'd been staring, already informed, wily, alert, attuned to what he needed, what it took. The summer nights of Darband were always intoxicating. We danced, returned to the table, and chatted about London. He'd been educated in New York, he was easy to talk to. Until the host asked me to dance. From the dance floor I saw Houshang in the distance, moving around the table — inordinately popular with his short attention span — talking to others. When I got back to my seat, he kept his distance but watched over me, watching the men who sat next to me, who hovered, how long they lingered, maybe for their mistakes. He smoked, mixed pleasure with business, smiled at me from across the table. Took other women away to dance, returned smiling at them as though he'd divined things in them he tolerated but disliked. For a moment I found myself alone at the end of the table. That's when he looked down the long white table, past the competition and pink and white carnations and procession of wineglasses and water glasses and crumpled white napkins and abandoned dinner plates. He asked me to dance one more time and escorted me to the dance floor, already possessive. He danced closer, murmuring, laying out his plans. A big house, children, devotion, travel. He had deftness of movement and expression and the well-sedimented contentment of a well-pampered childhood, as well as the peevish edge — the sudden flicker in his eyes, the urgency to domineer coiled like a spring. He asked me about the things I liked, trotting them out like toy soldiers to be inspected. He wanted. Me, success, trinkets. I thought then I wanted what he wanted. "Can I see you again?" he murmured. "Next week, maybe forever?" He handed me to my brother and stood talking to him. I said it was late. In the car my brother said, "He certainly doesn't waste time."

There's something tragic in our age of innocence. And pitiful, how it deserts us suddenly.

A door slammed upstairs. Houshang descended, stood in the front hall adjusting his tie in the mirror. This was the man I would grow old with. This man. I didn't want to go out to dinner. I wanted to burn a hole in our marriage, pull in the roof.

In the car, neither of us spoke. Houshang slipped in a cassette of Italian music, like the summer evenings of the Hotel Darband. In the backstreets of Zafaranieh, he condemned the divorce of two of our closest friends. She had asked for it, and for the children.

"I believe in marriage," he said. "For me, there's no question of divorce. Ever. No question of taking children. It's barbaric."

I defended her.

"You defend her because she's a woman. She should have the mettle to stick it out. She's selfish."

He smiled, his gold ring glinting in the dark on the wheel. "When a woman leaves her husband, it's only because she's being unfaithful. Because there's another man." He looked over at me.

I looked out the window at the walled gardens we were passing. The moon was out, a sliver between huddled clouds. The street a straight and dark incision. The trees phantoms. He wanted to pick an argument with me that I wouldn't have. He wanted to draw me out. I saw the inky sky, incomparably distant.

"I like my life," he said. "I wouldn't change it for anything."

"Would you fight to keep it?"

He laughed. "Fight? Fight for what?"

TWENTY-THREE

MAHASTEE HAD CALLED ME at the office earlier in the week and made an appointment for midday at a café on Naderi.

She was already sitting at a far table when I got there. She looked unusually pale, abandoned with a guarded grandeur in the far corner, and was smoking, with a cup of coffee before her. The radiant eagerness of her adolescence had faded and instead she carried a convalescing patience.

I knew why she wanted to see me. But I wasn't sure how she could argue about the effrontery of her husband that night in their front hall without being disloyal to him or insulting my intelligence. I'd already decided not to set foot in that house again. But I kept the purpose of our meeting separate from her husband's rudeness, which had brought us together, and waited for the moment to tell her.

We ordered more coffee; I insisted she was my guest. She insisted back, finally calling me obstinate.

"I could say the same about you," I said.

"I remember you were always more obstinate!"

"How's that?"

"Under that fierce — even savage — reserve was a mulish temperament."

I had to laugh. "Fire away. What else?"

"Well, that and your aloofness, defiance."

She meant the years I had stayed away. We fell into an awkward moment of silence, the clatter of plates and cups and other people's conversation falling between us.

"Did your father leave us because of some incident?" she asked.

"Did I say 'incident'? No, it was nothing."

"But everything changed suddenly —"

"Life changed. Like it will for us."

"But he lost everything at the end."

I regretted how I'd slipped and told her. I felt that Father's pride and memory would remain intact if I never talked about it. He would want it that way.

She looked past me, aware I wouldn't slip again.

Then suddenly she said, "Reza, for the longest time I . . . held it against you — how you left suddenly that summer."

It shook me to hear her say that. To have her invoke our entire history together. I saw it all at once, shaken loose, revealing itself, as I saw her.

"Please continue tutoring my sons. Just a bit longer."

She said "my sons" as though the husband didn't exist. She knew we wouldn't have any success mentioning him.

"Even better," she said, "come to my parents' for lunch. You'd make Father very happy! Just like the day you came back."

I digressed. If I went to lunch, I would be a serpent returning to their nest. She returned to make her point, inviting my mother and sister and her children. The next day, Friday, was perfect. I lied and said I'd call them and let her know.

"Call now," she insisted.

I went in the back to find a public phone, called, and came back, reciting.

"Mother thanks you for the invitation, but she's under the weather. She wanted to make a trip to Shah Abdul-Azeem tomorrow. But now she'll be home — and Zari says the children have colds and coughs."

They didn't want to come. How could I tell her? Why hadn't any of them insisted they come before? Finally I too gave excuses by the door, but before leaving I said I'd continue with her sons a bit longer. "This afternoon, then?" she asked. And I conceded, to prevail in her world awhile longer, though I'd already found her a tutor who could start at the end of the month.

TWO DAYS LATER, on my way to the dry cleaners past Sheesheh Mosque to pick up my jacket, I went by Jalal's apartment on Jami. At the corner, teenage schoolgirls in dark uniforms flirted with a group of boys. I went past the dead end but went back and rang the bell. I could hear the shuffle of the landlady's plastic slippers on her tiled floor, and her whiny voice inquiring who I was. Esmat *khanom* opened the door a crack. When she saw me, her eyes narrowed as if I held an ax.

"Did you see them smoking at the corner?" she said. "Did you hear their brazen laughter? They should be ashamed. My dearly departed father would have killed me for that sort of behavior. He believed in virtue."

"What's happened to the apartment?" I said.

"I've got a new lodger! A graduate with impeccable manners."

"What about Jalal's stuff?"

"One morning I went in and the apartment was cleaned out!"

"You know, he's been released."

"Good riddance. He's nothing but trouble."

"Did anyone come asking about him?"

"God forbid."

I asked about the new lodger, and she said he was a Tehrani who liked the neighborhood. A believer who carried a rosary.

"He brought me a bag of pomegranates the day he signed his lease. What good are they to me with my teeth?"

She was still scowling at her door as I waved good-bye. For all I knew they'd planted someone else in the apartment — SAVAK.

"Wait," she said, shuffling out. "His sister came by once and wanted to go upstairs and asked questions and also about you. She's a nurse. She told me if you came by to tell you to call her."

I called Najmieh Hospital the next morning and asked for Soghra Hojjati and left my office number. She called during lunchtime; from the background clatter it had to be from the hospital. She seemed to bear a grudge against me. We agreed to meet after her shift was over.

That night I waited outside the pharmacy just below the intersection of Naderi and Hafez. She was late. I stood leafing through the evening paper. We have two countries; the one they've designed for us, and the one we've got. They have movers and shakers and social engineers with policies and blueprints and facades, but without that flash of revelation at what we are from the inside out. They don't see it, that great force of a man's private history. The springboard of ideology is the intimate clockwork of blood and upbringing and personal rituals and daily existence ticking away. They leak out and subvert all the great forces of history. Nothing lasts from the outside, finally, unless it's willed from the inside out.

I went into the pharmacy and bought aspirin and came back out and saw her come up the street before she saw me. I prided myself in my perfect eyesight. She obviously prided herself in her short temper.

"Some friend you are," she said right off the bat.

She liked being pushy. She had cheap pink lipstick smeared

over thin lips, and eyes like pellets, ringed in black kohl, and dark hair snaking about her shoulders. We crossed the street. Right in front of the Park Hotel she stopped.

"I've always wanted to eat dinner there," she said.

She didn't like being denied. We stood by the open gate and she eyed the green lawns and luxury hotel beyond. I didn't have much cash in my pocket and suggested we get meat piroshkis on Naderi. Round the corner, the street vendors hawked plastic wares spread out on the pavement, and she eyed them disdainfully, bumping into two men and bad-mouthing them as they stepped aside. She cussed like a hooker. Jalal — educated and self-reliant — had left them years ago. Soghra had his arrogance without the intelligence; his determination, without the ability to break free. It made her bitter.

The café was overheated; the piroshkis were hot. She made no bones about being hungry and devoured two in no time flat and let me pay as though I owed her and would eternally. She downed Pepsi, asked if I had an apartment, what kind of job I had. I didn't want to talk. She wore cheap gold dangling earrings like a maid.

"Some friend you are," she said. "You never look back."

"What's that supposed to mean?"

"Why didn't you come back to see us?"

"Your father dislikes visitors."

"So you've seen Jalal?"

I shrugged.

"The bastard," she said. "Keeping his own mother in hell."

She had tears in her eyes. She was upset for herself. She hated Jalal.

"First I had to run around like a maniac looking for him, so we're finally told he's alive and in Komiteh, and they finally allow us a visit — he doesn't give a damn he's disgraced us by being in prison — and we go all that way, tense and nervous after I'd convinced Father, and Mother had prepared her pathetic little bundle of provisions for him, and he doesn't show up! He refused to see us, the bastard. Mother whimpered and cried until I couldn't stand it anymore. She only thinks of him. To hell with him. Father stood there like stone. When we got home, he said, 'I forbid you under pain of death to see him again or ever mention his filthy name in front of me.' Father scares me. Every man I know's a son of a bitch."

"Didn't he call you when he got out?"

"Mother waited by the phone night and day and jumped every time it rang. One night I got so mad that when the phone rang I pretended it was Komiteh. You should've seen her face. A goddamn suffering saint! I don't know what possessed me, but I said to her, 'They're going to shoot him tonight.' Before she let out her death wail, I took it back. Her one and only son. The shadow hanging over me. If we're never going to see him again, he might as well be dead. If you see him, tell him. Tell Jalal to put an announcement in the papers saying he's dead so I can show her."

"You're joking."

"Tell him. That's all I've got to say to him."

She shrugged, went on about the classy doctors at Najmieh, the smelly suitors she'd refused who were bazaar merchants her stupid father brought home. "That stupid peasant," she called her father. She said she had liked me from the first instant she'd laid eyes on me. She could tell I liked her. I was her type. How much could I possibly make working for the government and teaching night school? she demanded. Her father had money.

"Take me to your home," she said.

I delivered a sermon on how she was the sister of a friend and I respected her and could never abuse the sanctity of our relationship and how it was neither right nor ethical nor advisable, especially since she was so nice, and considering her parents, until her eyes glazed over.

At the bus stop she said, "Call me when you change your mind."

TWENTY-FOUR

Mr. Bashirian called me at home before breakfast.

"They haven't called," he said. "I'm worried."

He was expecting Komiteh Prison to call for him to go collect his son.

"I've already smoked half a pack. I've been up since five, sweeping and cleaning. You should see how much food there is in the refrigerator. I'm so restless I've been cooking and cleaning for two days. He's so thin! He needs to eat. You must come and have dinner with us. You'll get along wonderfully! I've got butterflies in my stomach. I can't wait."

He said he'd call me back when he had news.

That evening when I got home I dropped my coat by the bouquet of fragrant pink and yellow roses on the table in the front hall. I tore open several invitations, noting dates for an opening at the Seyhoun Gallery and a lecture at the Imperial Iranian Academy of Philosophy. I called out to the children, who were upstairs. The house was clean and tidy and serene, a sanctuary away from the city, all because Tourandokht had come for her visit.

She was in the kitchen with Goli, preparing dinner, winter stews bubbling on the gas range. I hugged her and she poured me a glass of tea from the teapot on the samovar. Goli seemed placated for the first time in weeks, but not exactly content. I wanted to keep Tourandokht forever. She dispensed serenity with a spiritual dimension and unremitting warmth.

"Who sent the flowers?" I asked.

The card was in the pantry. I ripped open the small white envelope. It read: "With exceptional affection, Thierry." I tore it up. He was incorrigible.

I went up to hug Ehsan and Kamran, who jumped up and down on my bed until they heard Tourandokht coming and then escaped before she could pile them with noisy kisses again. She huffed and puffed up the stairs, leaning on her cane. I drew a bath, and she sat in my bedroom as she had in the old days before I was married. She tried to explain about Goli.

"It's nothing," said Tourandokht.

The entire late-night incident could be blamed on a cassette tape left behind in the radio–tape deck in the kitchen. Goli and Ramazan hadn't meant to bring it into the house. After cleaning up for the night, they'd forgotten to take it with them. Goli had come back to remove it out of consideration! She'd panicked when she'd heard me, leaving her key in the back door.

"She panicked because she was eavesdropping on my phone conversation."

"No, she knocked over the receiver. She swears by the Twelve Imams —"

"I hate how she swears, then lies. She was listening in."

Tourandokht shook her head. It annoyed me that her authority had waned.

"So what's on this tape?"

"Some sort of sermon."

"What's so scary about that?"

"She was afraid you'd listen to it. Especially Mr. Behroudi."

"Why, what's on it?"

"Nothing much, she says."

I laughed. "Fire and brimstone and talk of doomsday?"

"Sermons from Najaf by an old ayatollah in exile."

"What's the big deal about that?"

"Exactly what I said, my dear. She got it from the mosque in Gholhak."

"She's changed, I tell you. Even Ramazan. He's tense, he broods."

"It'll all blow over."

I went in to take a bath and left the adjoining door open while Tourandokht inspected old framed photos in the bedroom, recollecting the days of the horse and carriage and summer migrations uptown to the big garden and back downtown to the old house in Ghavam Saltaneh for the winters. "What a production life was then!" she said. I could hear her dentures clicking and the interjecting rhythms of her uneven breath and the occasional tap of her cane. Then she came into the bathroom and, teetering, bent over, insisting on scrubbing me down with the mit as in the old days, just as in the public baths.

In the bedroom she stared at a photograph of Houshang with our sons.

"You're satisfied with him?" she asked as I dressed.

I didn't want to say anything. Once, she had wished me a lifetime with Houshang, a hundred years. A sentence.

"Marriage is our house of refuge," she said. "A woman builds it, and not just for herself."

"Maybe I built it so I could leave it," I said.

She murmured a prayer, blew it around the room the way she always did.

Mother called to say the driver was on his way for Tourandokht.

"She's staying with me."

"She belongs here," Mother said. "She's the light and soul of my house. Once, she went to Tabriz for a month, and everything went wrong. We had bad luck nonstop! When she's not here, I feel depressed. I think I'll die in my sleep and the house will buckle and our trees will wither and the garden will perish. She's the guardian spirit. Don't tell her! She'll get all uppity and take on airs. I have no patience for that."

"Really, Mother. Don't you think it's time you tell her?"

"Why should I? She already knows."

The car came at the appointed hour. Tourandokht, in white chador and white socks, slipped on her shoes by the door. I packed her into the car carefully, and when I kissed her she chuckled, and I handed over her cane and waved. She waved back ever so slowly, as if she were a head of state being driven away in a motorcade.

Houshang's secretary called to say his meeting was running late and from there he would be going straight to his social gathering. Their circle of close friends, fifteen men, gathered once a month.

He doesn't like coming home. I prefer it when he doesn't. In that way, we're compatible.

At ten I called Mr. Bashirian. I let it ring, but he never picked up. I wondered if anything had gone wrong. Maybe he was on a walk. Unless they had called for him to go to Komiteh to get Peyman. They were already together, he would call to tell me the next morning, put Peyman on the phone to talk to me. Releasing a prisoner took time; there was red tape and last-minute glitches. They'd stopped to get something to eat. But he had so much food in the house.

Midnight. Up in the bedroom I looked out to the mountains, then redrew the drapes.

IT WAS THREE DAYS LATER that I learned Peyman Bashirian was dead.

Mr. Bashirian had promised to call me, and I worried when I didn't hear from him. I invented reasons. He was busy running errands, pampering his son, talking until all hours. He never showed up at work. The next two days I was locked into a seminar all day. The last evening, I tried calling him, then went to a family party without Houshang. I tried him the next morning without success. I wondered if he'd asked again for a few days off to be with his son, but no one in the office had heard from him. That didn't sound like Bashirian. I called that night. I was nervous. A woman answered, much to my surprise.

I asked hesitantly, "Is this Mr. Bashirian's home?"

She said yes, her voice oddly hollow. I quickly introduced myself. She acknowledged knowing me, gave her name. Shahrnoush, his sister. I wanted to tell her how much I'd heard about her.

But she said, "Oh, Mrs. Behroudi. Something terrible has happened."

"Mr. Bashirian had an accident?" I said immediately.

"No, Peyman — Peyman passed away."

Her voice broke, and she wept.

I was home. It was evening. I fell back in the armchair, clutching at my head, at the convulsion brought on by what she had said. I repeated, "I'm so sorry, so sorry. How is that possible? He was supposed to be released. What happened? When?"

"Three days ago. He had a heart attack. Before Kamal got to him. Yesterday afternoon we buried him at Behesht Zahra."

She exhaled, breath quavering, words broken off and jagged. I asked for Mr. Bashirian. She said he had retired to his bedroom for a bit. But I could come anytime I wanted.

I tore through my closet and changed into black and rushed down. I left a message with Goli for Houshang not to wait for me for dinner, kissing my sons at the foot of the stairs as I slipped on my coat. They veered off, arms out, imitating jet fighters. Goli, sulking by the door, said Ramazan wanted the final number of guests for our upcoming dinner party.

The last thing I wanted, could imagine in that state, was to entertain the rear admiral and more than fifty guests for Houshang. I drove fast and furiously. The hills and mountains were blue-black at that hour. That poor father, waiting by the phone, never to see his son again.

I turned into their street and parked by the trees. Mr. Bashirian's front door was open. A woman in black stood in the doorway, arms crossed, the light from the hall behind her. She was short, heavy in the hips. As I locked the car and drew close, heavyhearted with dread and remorse, she raised her hand as if she'd left the door open for me. She was the sister. We shook hands, then our eyes met and we embraced as if we'd known each other a lifetime.

"He will not survive this," she whispered.

We walked in and she shut the door. I turned to several people standing in the hallway and she introduced us. Relatives from Mazandaran, two neighbors; one of the men took my coat. Her husband brought in chairs from the dark living room beyond. He spaced them slightly apart at the end of the hall, close to the kitchen, and offered me a seat I did not take. Instead I watched his wife in the kitchen. She moved about, opening cabinets, murmuring about teaspoons, sugar. I'd only seen her black-and-white picture, the one we had used to gain entry for me into Komiteh Prison. For one hour I had been her, his relative, the dead boy's. I could see how we resembled each other, though airbrushed photos were deceptive. She had a fuller face, wide-set eyes, and an aptitude to radiate happiness, from what I could tell in her picture. Now stricken, she emerged from the kitchen with a tray of tea and set it on the small, rickety table by the chairs in the hall. We all sat, except her husband.

"Mrs. Behroudi," she began softly, "Kamal is unwell. I called

despondent, and I wasn't prepared for him to be home. In the bathroom mirror I looked ashen. I prepared for sleep. When I emerged, he was in bed reading.

He looked up. "What is it? You won't talk to me?"

"I'm tired. I need sleep."

"So sleep. Don't I get an answer?"

"That boy died in prison. That should make you happy, no?"

He stared, speechless. I turned off the light, slipped under the covers, turned my back to him. We lay in the dark, still for a moment, listening for each other's breath. Then he stretched out his hand, laid it on my upper arm, pressing bare flesh, his fingertips barely touching my breasts, moved it down, grazing my silk nightgown, and slid his palm down to the curve of my waist. I stiffened. He hesitated, his hand still on me. Then quickly he withdrew it.

"You're made of stone," he said.

"And what are you made of?"

He turned away, both of us alert, ready to strike.

That night we didn't. He sensed the magnitude of what I hadn't said. There, the promise of complication, upheaval, undoing, frightening him away. We were like rival armies; Peyman, a battlefield. There was something narrow, selfish, in the way Houshang and I lived together, in the way we did not meet each other's requirements. But he had spoken with regret, caution. His voice had moved me for a moment — though I would no more admit to him — and I remembered how it had felt at the beginning, when the freshness of life had been ours and we had embarked, with the utter confidence of our place in the world — secure, whole, exuberant — prevailing, shielding us. That had changed, shifted — maybe forever — though we could not see it. And so, in that tenuous interlude before sleep, still lingering in Mr. Bashirian's tiled and half-lit hallway with his grieving sister, I groped along the contiguous and frayed borders of those attachments we chose, and those we were given. Kamal alone in his room, sedated, wanting nothing more than to live with this son now taken from him. I, in the dark, beside my husband. I shut my eyes. And in the weightless freedom before sleep, in those moments before drifting off, I felt something altogether past — irretrievable, distant, floating — for Houshang, some memory carried in me with which I sensed I could still forgive him, from which we could emerge, begin, erase, as if we could still be tender. I floated in this presentiment, this garden laid open, between night and day, sleep and waking — a promised land — mutating, strangely conscious it was not to be. And I saw there, between the pale flower beds and green box hedges and towering trees, Kamal Bashirian walking toward me, and though I wanted to cringe, as he approached down the path I saw his face, beatific, strangely radiant, and he put his hand out, and there through the trees — the green shadow of cypresses — his son emerged, his Peyman, tall, thin, self-assured, and they walked together toward me, Peyman speaking; he was speaking to me, his mouth moving but without voice or sound, and though I struggled I couldn't hear what he was saying, and then he pointed to the book in his hand — a white book — and let the pages fall open, and I looked but they were blank — white sheets — but he didn't know it, and I turned, distressed, to tell others, but they passed and I stood stricken, turned to the father and son and knew that he was dead, Peyman, dead, and the father, bent over on a stone bench, was weeping, and when I got close enough I heard him whisper; softly he was saying, "The world is made of stone, stone."

TWENTY-FIVE

EARLY IN THE MORNING the phone rang on my desk. I picked up on the third ring.

"Listen," Jalal said. "See you at the corner after work."

At the end of the day I assorted my papers and pulled on my jacket. The doorman cracked a smile from behind his steel desk. In the street I looked right and left beyond heavy traffic; then I turned right and kept going, twice looking over my shoulder. Pedestrians and more traffic. I got to the corner and scanned the street. No sign of Jalal. I kept on walking down Karim Khan Zand.

From behind, someone swept up beside me. I turned and our eyes met. He had a newspaper rolled under one arm, longer hair, a bomber jacket, scruffy jeans. He'd lost a bit of weight, all fit and wiry, always exuding vigor. This was his most distinctive trait. His shiny black eyes flitted, surveying the street.

"We've got ten minutes. Let's go."

We went down Kheradmand. He walked fast, alert and impatient.

"I need a big favor," he said.

"Another one?"

"If you don't want to hear me out, tell me now," he said.

"What is it?"

"Reza, you're my good friend. You're an honorable man. I trust you like a brother. More than I trust my comrades. Listen, I have to leave the country. I don't have a passport. I can't apply for one. I don't want to alert them. They've told me to lie low. You think I believe that? How much time do you think I've got? Any day they'll put it all together and arrest me. Maybe they've known all along. They've been waiting to see where I lead them. It's a brutal business. They shoot people like me in the street! Don't think I'm afraid. I want to stay alive. I want to leave."

"I told you to leave."

"Here's what I want," he said. "I know you don't own a passport. I want you to go to the passport office and apply for a brand-new imperial passport."

"For you?"

"I'll pay for it. An officer I know checked the list. You're not on the blacklist. You can leave the country. It's your passport I need to use."

"Let me think about it."

He shook his head. "Tell me now. There's no time. I'm asking you this once. If you can't, I won't hold it against you. Honest."

He was lying. We both judged a man only by the risks he took.

"What will you do?" I said.

"Change the picture. An old classmate in Esfahan specializes in that. I need two weeks. When I arrive where I'm going, your passport will be useless. Two weeks only, that's all I need."

"Where will you go?"

"I won't tell you."

"I saw your sister," I said. "She told me they came to Komiteh but you refused to see them."

"I'm glad that stupid peasant thinks his son is a godless Marxist! It'll poison his existence forever."

"Soghra said your father has forbidden them to mention your name ever again or see you. Think of your mother! She's heartbroken. Soghra thinks she can put your mother out of her misery once and for all. She must really hate you. She told me to give you this message: 'Tell Jalal to put an announcement in the papers saying he's dead.'"

He resented giving them a moment's thought. But he paused, his eyes flashing.

"If I'm dead, no one will ever bother me again. I take your passport, run a classy announcement about how I've passed on, then cross the border."

The only way left for him was to leave. If he did, he couldn't ask me another favor. I said I would do it.

He embraced me by the curb, slipping a white envelope from the inside of his jacket into my pocket. "Keep this money for me. Wait for my call."

He jumped into the street, one arm raised as if hailing a taxi, and a Vespa moped sped toward us, skidding to a stop. The driver, a young man with a helmet and orange goggles and longish hair, dragged his feet over the asphalt, revving up the engine. Jalal hopped on behind him and lurched as they veered off, shooting through the traffic.

TWENTY-SIX

THAT MORNING THE FLOWERS WERE arranged like peacocks in all the rooms, the round tables rolled into the dining room and set with heirloom starched hand-embroidered tablecloths and napkins and china and bohemian glassware and crystal and polished silver. The house smelled of tuberoses until the kitchen door opened and you could smell fried oil. The pantry was jammed with serving platters and bowls and slim-necked decanters and silver trays and boxes of sweetmeats. Goli had chosen, purposely of course, to be in her worst temper. She glowered. The day before, Ramazan, looking ashen enough to require a blood transfusion, had botched up several dishes and come in with his head hanging, muttering that he refused to cook anymore and was leaving my service. I'd showered him with compliments and consolations and given him enough Valium to drug a horse, so he'd withdrawn dutifully to take a nap and had remained comatose until the next morning. Then I'd called Mother and asked for Mashd-Ghanbar, her cook, who arrived in a taxi, charging in like Napoleon and setting about the kitchen making such a fuss and mess that he only tripled everyone's work. To make matters worse, he criticized Ramazan and Goli all day, withdrawing periodically for his prayers, then coming back to criticize them again, slamming down pots and pans and tossing utensils and behaving abominably.

The next morning he was still being a pain in the neck. So I called Mother.

"Can't you talk to him?" I said.

"I haven't spoken to him for two weeks," she declared. "Tell him to drop dead."

"I have a seated dinner party for fifty-six, Mother."

"He's vindictive and sulky and a general nuisance. The spoiled brat."

"He's your cook."

"As if yours is any better! Anemic and impotent, with a turd for a wife."

I went back into the kitchen. Mashd-Ghanbar was in the eye of a storm, barking orders to his flunkies — my house help and their small children, the gardener, who had been called in, and two young adolescents, who turned out to be Mashd-Ghanbar's nephews from Reyy. The telephone rang, and from somewhere in the house, one of my sons called out in the loudest possible shriek, *"Mother, it's for you!"* I went out into the hall and there were two pairs of muddied tracks all the way in and up the carpeted steps. Goli would throw a fit.

The electrician was calling to say he was running late, but he'd be there before the party to fix the outside lights. At six my sons clogged up the upstairs toilet and it overflowed and flooded the entire bathroom, and the pantry ceiling below started leaking, and Mashd-Ghanbar's nephews ran up with mops and pails and a plunger and tried their best, mustering all their technical knowledge until they felt heroic. Houshang arrived, so the jaunty chauffeur could join the already crowded kitchen, but instead of letting him lounge around drinking tea, Mashd-Ghanbar sent him off to buy ice and soft drinks, and freshly baked bread on his way back. The two waiters I had hired to serve arrived with sassy expressions and bathed in cheap cologne, and I heard Goli grumbling about how they were useless because all the important work had already been done by her, but obviously her mistress preferred outside help. She ordered them to watch the china and crystal because if anything, God forbid, got chipped or broken, she of course would be blamed as usual.

Upstairs, Houshang declared the house a zoo.

"Why can't you organize better? Don't you care?"

He locked himself in the bathroom for half an hour with the *Economist* and *Playboy* and soaked in the tub and shaved until the masseur arrived with his oils and folding table to tend to Houshang's body, that holiest of sanctuaries. The telephone rang and it was Mother. She said Father was depressed and unwell. There had been another death. She paused for effect. "Who?" I said, worried. Abbas Sobhi had finally died of cancer in the hospital. He was one of Father's oldest and dearest friends, and our families had known each other for several generations. I said I'd call on the Sobhis the next day. Mother started crying on the phone. I consoled her and said I'd come to see Father the next morning. "If we're still alive," she said, hanging up. Five minutes later my uncle Khodayar's wife called to see if I'd received the bad news about Abbas Sobhi. She said she had more bad news. Uncle Khodayar had a tumor. He was going in for surgery at Pars Hospital in two days. But she wasn't going to tell Mother. "Why not?" I said. "He's her brother." She started down her list of grievances, interjecting here and there melodramatically that Mother didn't care about anyone anyway. We got into an argument. Mother had never liked her and thought her a tedious and uneducated hypocrite given to hysterics, and she'd always found Mother meddlesome and overbearing and made sure she got back at her as often as she could. "I'm going to tell Mother," I said. She protested about onerous expectations in families like ours — "Of course, God forbid that you should ever lower your standards!" she said, all acerbic and overwrought — nagging on about a host of old and unrelated and miscellaneous affronts, and since nothing in the world could stop her, I kept an eye on my watch, until I finally had to cut her short and say we would all be at the hospital for the surgery. "You're just like your mother!" she retorted, and hung up on me. Mother called back two minutes later to tell me about the services for Mr. Sobhi and the phone calls she'd received about him since we'd last talked. "Why was your phone busy for the last twenty minutes?" she asked. "Mother," I said, "I have a party and I have to get ready, and I'll call you tomorrow morning." "You're very short with me tonight!" she said, all miffed, and hung up. The telephone continued ringing nonstop — with messages for Mashd-Ghanbar from his overattentive and hypochondriacal wife, and several calls for his nephews, who were buzzing around like horseflies, and four consecutive calls from friends of mine who wanted to discuss which jewel to wear with which shoes and which dress. I chose a navy blue silk chiffon dress, no jewelry. Dusted loose powder lightly over my face, sheer lipstick on my lips. Then I shut myself in the upstairs study to quickly check all the local papers, then the French papers I'd bought from Larousse downtown. Nothing from the French reporter in Tehran about Peyman Bashirian's case; nothing about a naval scandal involving charges of corruption. Suddenly the electricity went out.

Houshang bellowed from the bathroom, "What the hell's going on tonight?"

The telephone rang by my elbow and I picked up in the dark. Kamal Bashirian's sister was calling to thank me for my flowers and visit. She was very worried for him. They'd taken him to Alborz Hospital late that afternoon and the doctors were keeping him overnight. It was his heart.

"I hope this isn't serious," she said anxiously.

I was saying good-bye when Houshang barged in with a flashlight.

"We have no electricity and fifty-six for a sit-down dinner and you're still on the phone gossiping?"

"Fifty," I said.

He went out and shouted from the top of the landing, and the driver yelled back up from the foyer that the electrician was outside and not to worry — the lights would come back on in five minutes. "Are you all dead down there?" Houshang thundered from the top of the stairs. "Get some candles up here!" Then he came back in, pointing his flashlight. He saw the jumble of newspapers around me and asked how I could be reading instead of supervising the preparations for a dinner party that was so paramount to his career. Then he demanded to know who was not coming that night, for those who weren't had snubbed him and would pay for it.

"Iraj and Pouran," I teased, smiling in the dark.

"What? I just talked to them."

We heard a crash downstairs. They were breaking Grandmother's rose-medallion china. Houshang left, slamming the door, leaving me in the dark. I sat alone, serene, for the first time all day, all week.

The lights came back on finally, but only just before the guests arrived. Our sons cheered, running through the living room blowing out the candles and bumping into furniture. Houshang surveyed the rooms and tables and flowers, then threw me a critical look. He wanted to know why I wore no makeup and insisted on looking plain and severe and unadorned.

We argued, just as the first guests walked in the door. The house help was jittery from the high-strung griping of Mashd-

Ghanbar, anguished and angry without electricity just before his culinary masterpieces were to be presented.

Our sons crouched at the top of the stairs and gawked. Under the chandelier in the front hall, the guests removed their furs and coats, and Goli, grouchy and curt, grabbed and carried as if dispensing with an arsenal. Drinks were served. People mingled, breeding prevailed. I went back to make my rounds in the kitchen. From the open door to the pantry, I kept hearing snippets of Goli's conversation with the waiters, disparaging the guests and lecturing on alcohol and abstinence and the teachings of the Prophet. Then all of a sudden she said she'd heard the dead bodies of political prisoners were being dumped in a salt lake outside Tehran. I'd heard enough. I barged in and ordered her to go help the cook, warning the waiters they were there to tend to the guests. In the living room the guests effervesced and conversed. My brother Kavoos and his beauty-queen wife split up as soon as they arrived, moving in different circles. Pouran and Iraj worked the room like worker ants, Houshang laughing with delight whenever they spoke. Pouran had another low-cut dress on and crimson rubies that matched her sharp and glib tongue. She wasn't making eye contact with me, though she had kissed me on both cheeks and raved about everything.

"You have *such* taste!" she said. "Isn't Thierry coming tonight?"

Thierry arrived late, brushing his lips expertly over the hands of chosen women, speaking attentively in three languages to both genders and all ages in every circle. Pouran, he ignored. This she noticed too quickly, though she pretended not to, which forced her to become shrill and insincere and overwrought. She kissed Iraj, fiddled with the ties of several men, then patted their cheeks, dragged off Houshang and conferred with him theatrically. Thierry was asking about my Qajar pen boxes when I told him Peyman Bashirian was dead. "Who?" he asked, dashing and amiable. "The prisoner whose father met your reporter from Paris," I whispered.

"Where did he die?" Thierry asked. "In prison," I said. He leaned in, whispered to me, "I told you it was wiser to leave this alone." As I turned I caught Pouran giving us dagger looks. Five minutes later she cornered me.

"Iraj hates Thierry," she said. "Strange how your husband likes him."

"But I overheard Iraj and Thierry making plans to meet in Paris."

"Iraj is a dope. He can't read people like I can. Where's your ring?"

"Houshang didn't tell you? I sent it back. Just between us, it was hideous. Houshang can have gaudy taste."

She winced. She had chosen it, and had chosen always to side with Houshang.

I wanted to interrogate her about the diamond bracelet. I wanted her out of my house.

Our guests of honor, the rear admiral and his wife, arrived last of all. They swept in and around the room and settled on the French sofa, with Houshang and Iraj and Pouran in attendance, and asked for fruit juice. The rear admiral stared into the room, ill at ease. His wife kept poking her hairdo and puckering her lips and recrossing her stubby legs with tiny feet in spiked heels.

For all I knew, this was the man they were about to indict any day now on charges of embezzlement. Maybe he'd already been told of the proceedings against him. He definitely looked tense.

My back was killing me and I was about to sit down when I saw Goli out in the front hall motioning frantically to me. I went out and she grabbed my arm and said the boys were fighting upstairs and Kamran had a broken nose. We rushed up and barged into the study. The armchairs were upended, and there was blood on the sofa and broken glass on the floor. My youngest, Kamran, had blood trickling down his face and chin and over his shirt. His nose wasn't broken, just bloodied. The boys sulked, glowering, then lunged at each other to have another go at it. I ordered them to cut it out and wash up. The glass on the floor was a Baccarat crystal vase, a wedding gift. Goli picked up the pieces, muttering about how my sons could terrorize the world. I thought of finally having that talk with Houshang about sending them off to boarding school in England.

I went back down, and from the living room Houshang saw me in the front hall and came out to lecture about how I was ignoring our guests, especially the rear admiral and his wife.

"What's the matter with you?" he said. "Pouran has to play hostess now?"

"If you mention her one more time —" I began.

"Serve dinner," he snapped.

He went straight to the rear admiral and picked up where he'd left off, telling some joke, but not before throwing me an angry look.

In the kitchen the nephews of Mashd-Ghanbar were scooping out steaming white rice from enormous pots. The gardener washed dishes. Ramazan had already arranged the stuffed fish with pomegranate sauce and was slicing roast beef and braised lamb, which his daughter decorated with bunches of parsley. Goli was spooning out the sour cherry rice while griping at the chauffeur, who was spooning out the almond-orange rice onto a silver tray while smoking and slurping tea. Mashd-Ghanbar, his back to everyone, was spooning out three different stews into serving bowls and arguing with Goli, his most recently sworn enemy.

"Enough!" I said. "You've been cranky all the time here."

"Me?" Mashd-Ghanbar said, indignant. "That's the sort of thanks I get, when I come to save you from them!"

As I passed through the pantry, I startled a waiter guzzling down whiskey with his back to the door. I announced dinner. I wanted to go to bed.

We were all seated and served. Under the candlelight, the room hummed with the pleasures of conversation and delectable food. I had the rear admiral seated to my right; Houshang had his wife at the next table. As we were being served and I turned to instruct one of the waiters, I caught sight of Setareh, the daughter of my mother-in-law's best friend, seated at a table to my left. She was a seductive and eligible girl in her mid-twenties, and we were forever trying to fix her up, but she spurned the attention of admirers. I saw her smile and nod to someone at another table. So I followed her gaze, thinking rather smugly that she'd finally decided to approve of one of my bachelor guests. To my surprise, it turned out to be Pouran. I looked back to Setareh, saw her ever so slowly raise her hand, languorously stroke back her blond hair. That's when I saw it. The gold-and-diamond bracelet on her arm. A bare and milky-white arm. I stared. She was mouthing something to Pouran, and then she winked. It was not my imagination. She had pointed ever so discreetly, with red lacquered nails, to the bracelet. Sharing a moment, a pleasurable secret. Of course she looked radiant. She'd been given a gift; she was wearing it to my dinner party, acknowledging this to Pouran. Houshang had splurged for her! She was having an affair with my husband. No wonder she was so finicky about other men. Why hadn't I seen it before? Setareh was at most parties we attended. I always invited her myself. Sweet, educated, sociable. Apparently shameless.

At our table, the rear admiral talked about his latest shopping list of hardware for the Persian Gulf. Then a technocrat with ebony hair and manicured nails and a well-stocked repertory bragged about the lofty Club of Rome, its dire projections for the future, and the RIO Project, Reshaping the International Order, meeting that month in Algiers. "But wait a minute," said a guest across from him, "if a think tank is proved wrong, doesn't it become a sink tank?" There was laughter, effulgence, chitchat about trips abroad. The weather in Rome, the cafés in Paris, the pleasures of Bond Street. I imagined Reza watching this. I stared at my husband charming his guests at the next table. I wanted to go over and slap him, then go upstairs, pack, and catch the first plane out. He was bedding a girl half his age, and certainly taking good care of her.

I turned to the rear admiral. "How do you think we should deal with our record on human rights?"

Nothing could have killed the conversation so fast. The question was unforgivable. Everyone stared. I was being a tactless hostess, a most tactless wife. In the split second that passed, I saw in their eyes how we were unprepared, disapproving, thin-skinned.

Someone quickly covered for him. "That's the sort of wicked question foreign journalists ask!"

"That's true," I said. "One of them asked me a few weeks ago."

"And what did you say?" said the rear admiral.

"I dodged the issue."

"Well you did, bravo. They have no business snooping around here."

"Then something happened," I said.

I saw Houshang staring at me. He had an uncanny ability to sense trouble.

At our table, a high-ranking civil servant said, "Human rights? What bunk and distortion! A direct affront to the visionary leadership of our country. A naive and unrealistic point of view. Look what it proposes! To indulge a bunch of Marxists and religious fanatics who want nothing less than to destroy us. What are we supposed to do, accommodate them? They're ready to slaughter us! Show me one country in the world that tolerates that. They get to hunt down their own terrorists. We can't progress without law and order. The foreign press is crucifying us abroad! We have the right to decide who threatens our government and how to deal with it. Self-preservation is a basic right! Who are they to lecture us?"

Houshang quickly rose with his glass of wine and toasted good friends and good food and fine wines and beautiful women. Setareh was watching him with a sweet and timid smile, her tapered fingers caressing the bracelet he'd given her. He had some nerve. We raised our glasses, drank a toast. The waiters brought dessert: crystal goblets of homemade ice cream with ribbons of caramelized sugar and fresh raspberries, and Mashd-Ghanbar's specialty, an assortment of Viennese chocolate tortes and fresh fruit tarts that he'd perfected during his stints at the Austrian embassy whenever he'd got into his typical funks and abandoned Mother.

My dinner partner asked me what I meant by "something happened." I said the son of a friend had died in prison.

"Anyone I should know?" he said.

I hesitated and he turned away, amusing himself with someone's joke.

Dinner broke up. On our way back to the living room, while the rear admiral praised the splendor of our dinner, I asked, "Don't you think that despite our naval bases and Sherman tanks and Phantom jets we're vulnerable?"

He smiled, patted my arm. "Don't worry, my dear. A beautiful woman doesn't worry!"

"So when do you worry?"

"When my wife goes shopping! When I see how much hair I've lost!"

He'd patronized me, I'd played ingenue, and neither of us was the wiser. People came over to talk to him. He joked and laughed, quite recovered from his earlier unease, presiding with the aplomb of an emperor. Coffee and tea and after-dinner liqueurs were served. I tended to our guests, all the while watching Houshang and Setareh. She was whispering with Pouran across the room.

The high-ranking civil servant who had spoken up at my table cornered me before slipping away. "Who can expose the opposition? We can't; the foreign press doesn't want to. Today they own the truth. This we can't face. The question is — do we possess the words, the heart, the guts? Even to convince ourselves? I don't know."

Half an hour later the rear admiral and his wife prepared to leave. Houshang beckoned me over, and we were exchanging niceties when out of the blue the rear admiral mentioned mistrusting foreign journalists. He said they were on a rampage to undermine the regime, dredging up every cause they could find. He said it was advisable not to speak with them. Houshang agreed wholeheartedly. I took this as a warning. Then he went too far.

"In fact it's downright unpatriotic," said the rear admiral.

"Unpatriotic?" I said. "I know a father whose son died in prison this week. That's unpatriotic."

"Mahastee," my husband said, "it's late and the —"

"Don't you think that's unpatriotic?" I asked the rear admiral. "Laws that don't safeguard the life of a university student, of anyone?"

"Not in this case." Houshang smiled. "He must've deserved it." He turned to the rear admiral. "You must excuse Mahastee. I can't imagine why she's bringing this up."

Houshang glared at me, disapproving, humiliated.

So I said, "He was about to be released from Komiteh. But he was dead when his father went to collect him. He was twenty. He died in their custody. I should think they'd *want* to prove they didn't kill him. He was interrogated four times. They say he died of a heart attack, but there was no autopsy."

"Who is this boy, a Marxist?" the rear admiral demanded.

I told him.

"Plotting against the government is sedition," said the rear admiral. "You understand that."

"But he was innocent if they were going to release him," I said.

"Then what's there to investigate?"

The argument had erupted suddenly. We were speaking softly, huddled in a corner. The rear admiral's wife kept a bored and frozen smile on her face. A pink and white and blond marionette. I sensed Houshang's blood pressure rising and avoided eye contact with him. The rear admiral stared at me, dismayed.

"So you see," I said, "here's the perfect case of how we're at the mercy of our own sense of justice. Injustice, actually. Injustice is unpatriotic."

"What are you — a judge now?" Houshang said.

I turned to the rear admiral. "I want to ask you to please help us find out what exactly happened. It's for the father. He's an old friend of mine."

"Who is this chap?" Houshang said. "I don't know him!"

"It's not so simple," the rear admiral said to me, suddenly very formal. "I'm sure you know very little, and the father was told certain things, but the boy must have done — well, let's put it this way, we know he was arrested. But little else."

"We know he's dead. What kind of terrible retribution is that?"

"Now, let's not be naive," said the rear admiral.

"But that's exactly what I'm trying not to be."

"There are many cases like this," he said irritably. "Don't believe what you hear. I'm sure it was handled properly."

"You mean the sensible thing is to arrest and imprison without due legal process and in secret, then send home the corpse and claim —"

"What's wrong with you?" Houshang demanded.

I looked into his eyes, saw how he wanted to throttle me. It gave me pleasure, that look, causing him anguish.

"If someone you loved died in prison," I told the admiral, "wouldn't you want justice then?"

"This is a ridiculous and theoretical conversation!" said Houshang.

"Will you help the poor father?" I asked the rear admiral pointblank.

"It's out of my hands —"

Houshang took his arm, and they moved away into the foyer. His wife stared at me with haughty astonishment.

"Thank you for dinner," she said vacantly.

Long past midnight, the last to leave, as usual, were Iraj and Pouran. I left the threesome drinking in the downstairs study and went up. Houshang was so angry he wouldn't even look at me, and I was sure he was going to leave with them for a nightclub. But I was wrong. Thirty minutes later he came up and threw open the door to our bedroom. It was dark; I was in bed.

"Tell me, what was tonight all about?"

He slammed the door shut, turned on his bedside light.

"I want an apology!" he said. "Now."

He threw his jacket on the chair.

"I warned you, but no, you went against me, embarrassed me — embarrassed yourself! Your behavior was —"

"Don't yell, you lecher. I know who she is."

He stopped and stared, eyes bloodshot. He'd had too much to drink. I kept my composure. Slowly and rigidly I told him. I knew about Setareh, the diamond bracelet he'd given her, how Pouran did all his dirty work.

"That's ridiculous. Me and Setareh?"

"I know, so stop lying."

"This was your revenge? Your calculation? How pathetic!"

"Don't you get it? That poor boy is dead. Dead! Go amuse your —"

"You're so blind. So — high and mighty with your truth. Do you know whose mistress she is?"

He asked right up in my face, the veins popping out on his neck, the smell of alcohol on his breath.

"The rear admiral's. You hear? He adores her! They're happy together! He doesn't want a scandal. But he loves to spoil her, so he asks me. I sent Pouran and charged the bracelet to my account. You understand?"

I flinched. To my eternal surprise I still wanted to believe him.

Then he said, "You're turning into some liberal leftist, whatever the hell you want to call it."

"Right, I'm a Marxist!"

"You're starting to behave like one."

"Then you won't mind if I rant about reckless capitalist pigs?"

"What the hell's the matter with you?"

An indicted rear admiral didn't exactly qualify as a model patriot.

"He lectured me," I said, outraged, "about how to be patriotic."

"You shouldn't have talked to a foreign journalist. He's right."

"It's none of his business."

"You shouldn't have embarrassed him like that."

"What is he, God? Your only source of income? With whose money is he buying extravagant diamond bracelets? Look at him and his wife! We have to kowtow to them nonstop to get ahead? Oh, I hurt his feelings? God forbid. As if there's no one else in this country with feelings worth considering!"

"I've got a radical wife. You want to dishonor me and yourself?"

He spoke of honor and let disgrace hang over our heads. His naval projects were being investigated behind closed doors.

"I'm going to find out what happened to Peyman Bashirian," I said.

"You know what people will think. You want to ruin our reputation?"

"I want to petition with his father."

"You will do no such thing. This is none of your business. You will stay away. I don't want us mixed up with SAVAK. I've got contracts with the government. I'm not going to permit this. Your duties are to your family."

"Don't you talk about duty. You're a negligent father, a mostly absent and vacuous husband who whores around and drinks an —"

"That's right. That's me! You should've married one of those highbrows your parents preferred. I bet they're disappointed."

"No, I'm disappointed," I said.

He stared, offended, repelled, eyes calculating.

"Well then, I better go out and find myself a whore and a drink and, if I get real lucky, a girl like Setareh!"

He picked his jacket off the chair and walked out. I heard the garage door, his car speeding away.

I SWEPT AROUND the bedroom, drawing back the drapes. Sat back in an empty room staring at far ridges in darkness. Perhaps I had precipitated a drama at my own dinner party to take my freedom, erase the false clockwork of an entire life.

Perhaps Setareh had been my blunder — a blunder set in motion by a husband I now considered second-rate. Houshang had assured me I was making a fool of myself. There was in fact a time when it mattered to believe him. He had grabbed the high moral ground, feeding me small doses of humility like poison. A chastened wife makes a virtuous husband. But I am sick of goodness. Of being that paragon, a lady. The very reason for which Houshang married me.

He's always counted on my loyalty. Tonight he'd been forced to take its measure. Facing the rear admiral, I had become a disloyal woman.

He had seethed about dishonor. But the only thing he really cared about was our reputation — that public and eye-catching display, infinitely malleable, a chameleon — for what did honor really matter to him when it was something solitary and modest and absolute, an inner life?

At three in the morning I felt certain he was not only keeper of Setareh's secret, but indulged as her protector. He was her refuge from the predatory tide of society's ambitions. I'd seen the look they had exchanged after dinner, that devoted smile of acknowledgment. There was too much there to have given her away untouched. He'd had her himself before giving her to the rear admiral. There would always be others. Always another to come between us.

I WAIT FOR THE DAY Reza teaches the children. I make sure I'm home. I listen for the front door, his eyes on me as I sweep down the staircase. Those vigilant eyes, seeing through me, seeing beyond. A man among men. And I think now, What was life before he walked in? I wonder what he's hiding from me. What he's done all these years he's stayed away. I want him to tell me. I hear him in the other room and remember the boy in the garden of Morshedabad. Even then, what distinguished him was character. When we had guests, the house brimming with people, children running through the gardens, I was always looking for him. "Reza, Reza!" He would stand grinning by the trees and say, "Calling me again?" I would ask him to come play, come swim, come learn to dance instead of being so defiant, come ride through the fields with us. Then between one month and the next he was gone. That summer I had gone back to Morshedabad expecting to see him. Morshedabad and Reza were one and the same for me. One couldn't be without the other. I had run to the bungalow, calling out to him, yanked open their front door, and faced an empty house. My first thought was they'd gone for another visit to Tabriz. But they wouldn't have emptied the entire house for a trip. Gone were the rugs, the first sura of the Qur'an penned in black and gold ink by the door, his mother's sewing machine and the large peacock she'd embroidered on magenta satin and hung up on the wall, the old brass samovar and huge bolsters and paisley shawls, the candleholders with dripping crystals that Zari and I liked to run our fingers up against, the canary green pair of opaline hand vases — the hand of the beloved — sitting on the mantel, and above them all, crowning the room, the family photo taken by Sako on Naderi, which I'd compared to ours, where we'd been all airbrushed into perfection. The rooms were bare, white, stark. They had packed up and left. I'd run through the trees, shouting, "Father, Father, they've gone. How did this happen? Can't you do something?"

I'd never forgiven him for leaving, for disappearing one day, never to look back. I had considered it a personal insult and form of contempt, realizing that day that our lives were two things apart. Until then they had seemed as one to me.

I PUT ON a black suit the next morning and drove to Niavaran to pick up Father and Mother and pay our condolences to Mrs. Sobhi. Mother, stately in black, sat in the back of the car brooding, reciting an elegiac poem by Maulana. Father recollected forty years with Sobhi. The house was only a few streets away. It was grueling to sit with the grieving widow and listen to her and watch Father, who had lost one of his closest friends, look as devastated as she did. Mother and Father stayed on and other visitors streamed in, but I left for work.

That evening I left the office late, knowing Houshang would stay out all night. He was waiting for me to show regret, waiting for me to reform myself. My home was no refuge. My children were at a sleepover. I had nothing to say to my friends that night. I couldn't sit in a restaurant and eat out alone. I wasn't about to wander into the lounge at the club — I wasn't the type, even if I did know everyone there. And I didn't want to see that crowd. I'd go home. I realized that what I meant — perhaps would always mean by that — was that I'd go home to my parents' house. I would console Father about Abbas Sobhi's death and play gin rummy with Mother and have dinner in the upstairs hallway, where the picture frames were crooked and the tiles several rows in from the top of the stairs had come unstuck ages ago and wobbled when you stepped on them but were covered by the large Esfahan rug, and where one of

Mother's large and chaotic bouquets from her garden always covered the dreadful and anemic portrait of Father, which had been painted by his well-meaning friend who had studied forever at the Fine Arts Academy and which Father insisted on keeping there as a matter of principle, and so, facing it — just to annoy Father — Mother had placed an oil painting he detested of an Edenic though lugubrious garden, which she had bought from an antique dealer on a lark and which we strongly suspected annoyed even her, day and night, but she kept it there because she would rather grow horns and a tail than back down, and there in the upstairs hallway they would sit, my parents, taking their meals when there were just the two of them, listening to the old radio, defending their life. I wanted that.

I drove eastward. We were in the midst of a few days of Indian summer. I rolled down the window, slid out of my wool jacket at the red light.

From the street I called Reza's number on impulse. He was still at the office, working late on some report. I could barely hear him with all the traffic by Cinema Diana. It took half an hour to get across town and find parking near the place where he'd said to meet. He had an appointment around the corner and had suggested the first place that popped into his head. I waited at the corner table in the Hotel Semiramis. He was late and apologized when he appeared suddenly. There we were, the two of us, for a rendezvous in the evening in a hotel downtown. He removed his jacket, slung it on his chair. "So unusually warm," he said. We ordered coffee with milk and I told him about Peyman. He listened, quiet, absorbed. The phone call, the heart attack, the photos he'd taken on his travels, his diary, the guidebook to Khorassan. I told Reza that day at the Intercontinental the French reporter had insisted that the son had to be involved in some clandestine activity. "You know, the father told me he was afraid to go to Komiteh," I said. "I went with him. But I think he was afraid of Peyman. He couldn't understand him. Maybe he couldn't look into the eyes of this stranger who had lived with him. That's why." Reza asked about the petition. What kind of answer did we expect? Now that the boy was buried in Behesht Zahra. Now that his body was rotting and his files swept away. Would they exhume the body? Never. What could the authorities investigate? Hearsay, wardens, the prison doctor and coroner, their own interrogators. Tainted versions. Fiction. That was all that was left. I said, "Then the difference between the necessary and the sinister just depends on which side you're on finally?" Reza asked point-blank, "How about this case?" I leaned in. "The dead can't defend themselves," I said. "Who decides the kind of evil considered necessary? Makes the rules, logical consistencies, the exceptions? Should we trust them?" There was a clock on the wall. Sometime later he offered me dinner. I wanted fresh air, so we walked. The hotel was opposite Saint Paul's Church. Walking with him, I felt like an outsider in the city. We crossed streets here and there as if by mutual consent but apparently at random. The longer we walked, the better I felt. He asked what I wanted to eat. I didn't mind, I didn't want to stop walking.

The evening was warm. Somewhere along the way there were colored lanterns strung between trees in a garden. There were plastic chairs and tables and the sounds of laughter and the smell of grilled chicken. We asked for a table on the last night you could eat outside that autumn. He ordered, and we realized we were hungry when the food came. He was no longer diffident and talked about the time when he had taught in far-off villages. "Four years," he said. "Each year a different village. I was young, idealistic, impatient to change the world." We talked of our fathers, and then, insisting, I said something about Hajj-Ali's bankruptcy, how I felt, that we should have known, should have helped, my words turbulent. I said, "I know it's too late. But your parents were like a second family for me." I said it long after its passing, though it would always remain true. He stared at me, his eyes like a dark tide coming in, the strangest emotion breaking on his face. The moment scorched us, like a season of mourning. We looked to the night, now murky like brackish water, shutting us off from the world. At the periphery of our vision, people were moving about us. He asked about my university days abroad, my three brothers, and we talked of his sister's children, Morshedabad, the daughter of the gardener whose family had suddenly disappeared. What was her name? I couldn't remember. "Amineh," he said. "Ah, Amineh," I said, looking up into the trees, with their garlands of lanterns. "I liked that garden," I said. "I liked the trees."

He said he liked riding his bicycle to the nearby village, Morshedabad. Liked the village children. Eighty years before a *morshed* had passed there and stayed for two years. A spiritual guide from Mashhad. A geomancer with white hair. He had healed their children, bidden beads to make good auguries, interpreted their dreams, and divined the future. Spoken of the Guarded Tablet written by God to transfigure fate. They had venerated him. There was a shrine in the village, a place of pilgrimage. Mud brick, with a dark interior. The large plane tree outside, where the village children played, had shreds of cloth tied to its branches for the vows they made. I remembered the glazed blue tile he'd once given me from the shrine. "But whose shrine is it?" I asked. "That's what I mean," said Reza. "There is no name on the tombstone. People in the village claim it's his, the *morshed*'s. They say he left but came back later to die there. But there's another story." Reza said he believed this one. An old man had told him when he'd gone back years later to visit. The old man had remembered him. Son of Hajji Alimardan. He had offered him tea, talked of their dry wells, the heat. They had walked in together, stared at the bare slab sunk into dry earth. "Dust of time," the old man had said, pointing. They'd come out and sat in a corner. And the old man had said, "I want to tell you something. All those years ago, when he tried to leave, the *morshed,* they stopped him, the villagers. They were incensed. They wanted him to stay. He refused. So they plotted to keep him. Late one night they fell on him. They killed the old man and buried him there." "They wanted him that badly?" I said. "They wanted something sacred to remain among them," said Reza. "Something to believe in."

Under the trees, time vanished. I wanted him. His patient voice, his steady hands, the intensity of his gaze. "That's it," he said. "History, superstition, in so many layers." "It has power," I said, "undertow. A fierce memory. It's intimate. Don't you have any?" He smiled. I liked his smile, so much about him. "No, really," I said, "tell me." He said, "I keep Father's prayer stone at night by my bed." "Always?" I said. "Always," he said.

The plane trees shed dry leaves. I felt impossibly alive at that moment. The colored lanterns swayed. Even the breeze was warm. "I have something to tell you," he said. I smiled. "What, another superstition?"

"Remember that afternoon concert at Bagh Ferdaus? I was there."

"The one when it hailed?"

He nodded. So he had been there. The day the sky had turned gray, then black, and hail had pounded the gardens. He hadn't talked to me. He'd seen me come up the lawns with my friends, the two men. He had watched and waited. Had been several feet away under the porch when it hailed.

Long past midnight, alone in bed, I imagined being in his arms. For even one night. Without the future.

TWENTY-SEVEN

I NEVER EXPECTED this night with Mahastee, from her phone call, to my ridiculous proposal to meet in a hotel like lovers, to our long dinner under colored lanterns. But I had also been dishonest ever since that day I'd walked back into her father's house. I had taken his tea, and every night I plotted against their world. I hadn't told her about my politics. The more I saw her, the more I was determined to tell her. This passion for the truth, served up for her, intruded at first during our dinner together, until it vanished.

Of course, I was not obliged to explain anything. There under the paper lanterns we had mesmerized each other. She was oblivious to everything I did — oblivious to this city of smoke and mirrors, though she spoke of Peyman Bashirian, another dead boy who had played with sedition. There is no such thing as a cushy life being a partisan! There is no such thing as the absence of politics! To be apolitical is equivalent to assuming a political posture, but one that appeases nobody. When the haze lifts, she will know.

We know. We count on it. Living dangerously has its own rewards.

I had imagined her in that high society, anesthetized with the moral indifference of those with nothing at stake, surrounded by insolent men like her husband. They condescend if you're from humbler birth, anticipating your slightest blunder so they can shake their heads. So they can say, Well, what can we expect from these types! They overlook class warfare, getting chauffeured around, perched high where they rest with their foreign education. Her father and mine were a different generation. They had had each other's respect and affection, the same vision for the longest time. I don't think it's possible anymore.

I ran down to meet her from Amjadieh on an unusually warm evening, darting down from the American embassy and across the intersection to the Hotel Semiramis. I was really late and figured she'd already left, but she was there. There were several tables of foreign men, mostly Americans, drinking. Businessmen, I thought, or embassy people churning over the latest tidbits from their informants. Still plotting to overrun our country? I wanted to say, walking by. Who have you bought out recently? Then she looked up with those hazel eyes, and the shadow lifted, and I removed my jacket and apologized for being late and ordered coffee. She talked of Peyman Bashirian, who was dead. I could see the hairline cracks forming on that smooth surface of glass that was her life. "Dead," she whispered, shaken. In her world, people only died of old age and disease. Not torture and execution. I didn't like talking about the dead boy. Talking about him made me angry and preachy and dredged up politics. At some point I suggested dinner, and we left and started walking through the streets. We found a restaurant with paper lanterns and ordered dinner as though we ordered every night and would forever, so severed were we by then from the worlds from which we came. She asked questions, listened, the expressions on her face shifting but familiar to me, inscribed on the template of my memory. Then she talked about my father and his ruin with such emotion and resolution I felt a great wall crumble inside me. And I thought, The past never lets you be. This is what it wants — to direct and consume you. All the time pretending it's the present, the future, the better to outwit you. Jalal, always evading it, always moving, has only the future in his sights. It's a feral instinct for him, like an animal's. He told me once I would finally make the ideal revolutionary the day I left everything behind. Everything.

The waiter brought dinner, and Mahastee laughed at how much food we'd ordered, then ate ravenously. I told her a story, and Jalal withered with the pity I felt for him suddenly, living as he did only half a life. Then I told her something else, and she leaned back in her seat and threw back her head and looked up at the colored lanterns with the warm breeze disheveling her heavy hair, and I felt elated, so deep and moving and mysterious was the moment.

We sat under the trees, she and I, seduced, whiling the hour away. The dark was stealing in. She had passion, and if she'd lost it in her world, she wanted it back now. I wondered about passion, hers and mine, how it lived or died, and what would rise from the ashes. To possess it was to swear by its long life. And its price. I watched her against the night, gauging the price of her resolve, her loyalty, to me, to anything. I wanted to reach over, draw her in, this woman I had loved as a child and now wanted as a woman. Every man has the right to an imprudence. I sat there thinking, She is my transgression.

As the night wore on, I came close to saying, Let's take a hotel room. Let's go back to Semiramis. I nearly let the burn of that desire liquefy my coldhearted life for once. To hold her. I held back. I was trained to renounce, discard, a perfected instinct for a revolutionary. Renunciation as well honed as passion.

THE NEXT MORNING I went to the passport office. I had the black-and-white photographs I'd taken on Zarghami in the tiny photo shop whose owner coached soccer with me in the same league. I went upstairs and turned left into the section marked for last names beginning with *N* and stood in line. People were pushing. A young man with an obnoxious smile cut in, then had the gall to lie to our faces with a typical story that went on forever and made no sense. Another donkey like my brother-in-law! Two men reached over and tapped his chest and sent him packing to the end of the line. "Another sissy boy from the upper class!" they grunted. The man behind me asked where I'd had my photos taken, just so he could strike up a conversation about his family back in Azarbaijan. Finally it was my turn. A vacation, I said. No spouse. The officer looked fed up. "I can't read this," he said about Mother's name. "Shaukat ol-Zamon Eftekhar," I said, "born in Tehran." "And this, your father?" "Hajji Alimardan Nirvani," I said. "Born in Nirvan, in eastern Azarbaijan." "You have lousy handwriting," he said, just to stress his authority. The man behind me started poking me and repeating, "I knew you were a Turk!" The officer ordered him to step back. "Wait your turn and stop interfering," he snapped.

In the evening the three of us went to the movies, me and my friend who works at Amjadieh Stadium and the owner of the photo shop. Bright lights, shops chockablock with knickknacks, meandering mobs, young boys roaming like hyenas eyeing monster-size posters of busty actresses with deep cleavage and brawny movie stars like Behrouz Vossouqi towering over the rest of us.

A little past eleven, I was undressing when something struck the window, the one looking onto the back alley. Then again, thirty seconds later. I poked my head out, and there was a man standing in the alley. It was dark and I couldn't see him properly. He motioned, calling, "Come down, come down." He said it irritably. I slipped back into my trousers, my shirt hanging out. I picked up my keys and walked out wearing slippers — I was only going down to the back alley. I went around the building. He was waiting a few feet into the alley.

Immediately he said, "Did you do it?"

"Do what?" I said.

"What you were told," he snapped back. "Don't play games with me."

He was insolent. The worst thing I could do was admit to anything. I didn't know him, and I never forget a face. He wasn't the guy who had shot off with Jalal on the Vespa, nor any of the ones in the car that day in front of Radio City. He wasn't more than twenty-two or twenty-three. For all I knew he'd been sent to entrap me. I said I didn't know what he was talking about.

"Don't shit me! Did you do it for Jalal? Or did you chicken out?"

He had some nerve. "Who the hell are you?" I said. "I don't know you."

"And you never will. Now answer me!"

I was angry with Jalal for sending some jerk to harass me. So I told him.

"Watch your mouth, motherfucker," he said. "You want to end up in a ditch?"

He was a nasty piece of work. I didn't care who he worked for. I poked him straight in the chest.

I said, "Don't think I'm afraid of you. You hear? That's my answer."

I turned and walked back into the building.

TWENTY-EIGHT

The service for Peyman Bashirian was at their home the next evening. The house was overheated. Cold weather had come suddenly. People in overcoats were backed up all the way to the sidewalk. Coming up to the house, I encountered Mr. Bashirian's elderly next-door neighbor and we walked in together. The house was lit up and filled with flowers. White carnations and roses and gladioli in baskets sat in the hallway.

The crowd was swelling inside and they had run out of chairs, and people were leaning against the walls talking, many of them students. They glowered, huddled in corners, whispered. Some of the girls stood out because they were wearing the emerging political uniform — head scarves and overcoats over matching trousers. The brother-in-law saw me from the kitchen and came out and shook my hand. He said Kamal was in the living room. I saw him from the doorway. A crumpled man among men, slumped in a chair at the end against the wall. He wore his suit loosely, his tie black and rigid under a face impossibly sallow and drawn. His eyes were red, his cheeks flaccid as he leaned in, listening to an elderly man speaking next to him. I thought Kamal could not possibly hear him, so bewildered and remote was Kamal's gaze. Then his gaze lifted and he saw me. He rose, lifted out his arms, and shook his head, as if to say, You see, you see what happened? Someone next to him tactfully vacated his seat and I sat down. We tried to say something to each other but choked up. Finally he managed to say, "I know you were here last night." Together we wept quietly, heads bent, neither of us able to speak.

On the table beside him there was a large framed photograph of Peyman. A black-and-white portrait, a handsome boy.

"He's gone," he said, "forever."

A manservant came around with a tray of tea. There was fruit on the side table, small dishes of sweetmeats, the traditional bowl of halva. In the rooms people rose and sat in waves, gathering, coming forward, murmuring to Kamal, retracing their steps, the house hot, stifling. He insisted I remain next to him.

The phone kept ringing. Colleagues and friends and neighbors came with words of sympathy. His sister came and whispered to him. When he rose and left the room, I went into the kitchen and asked a maid who was washing up for a glass of water, then found a chair in the hallway. By the front door, Mr. Bashirian and his male relatives greeted a mullah in flowing robes. The mullah preceded them into the living room. Through the archway between the hall and the living room I saw him being shown to his seat, Mr. Bashirian and his relatives taking seats to his right and left. The mullah, gathering his robes about him, conducted the service with solemn decorum, uttering suras from the Qur'an and eulogizing the deceased. The rooms grew still, resonating with the echo of the lilting prayers and eulogy for the dead young man accompanied by the intermittent sobbing of the living.

After the mullah left, Mr. Bashirian came out into the front hall. The group of students quickly flocked to him. I couldn't hear what they were saying. They closed in on him, heads bobbing as they talked. Like autumn crows — dark, intense, pecking at him, their shriveling and brittle morsel. I wanted to shoo them away. They lingered, heads drawn together, then suddenly parted, Mr. Bashirian emerging from their fold. He looked contrite. Going by me to the kitchen, he whispered, "Please, God, kill me and deliver me from this grief." He carried a glass of water to a room and shut the door behind him.

One of the students, slim and tense, raised his hand, cleared his throat, asked curtly to make an announcement.

"There's a lecture Wednesday. We've left the address by the door. Come in Peyman's memory. They snatched him from us, kidnapped him. He disappeared. It happens every week. What happened to him could've happened to any of us. Your sons and daughters! They prey on us! We are their carrion."

A girl in a black scarf and black overcoat let out a wail: "We must rip off their mask! Expose the evils they hide so cunningly. What they —"

Like a clap of thunder, from the other room Mr. Bashirian's brother-in-law called out, "This is no place for politics. Please, you're among the deceased's family and friends."

He came through from the other room, motioning with one hand to say it was enough. People turned and stared.

The girl, disturbingly high-strung, started protesting again in her shrill voice, but the boy interrupted her quickly, this time more strident.

"They murdered Peyman. We mourn him. But we're defenders of the innocent. Why remain silent? Because we're afraid? See what they've done to us!" He motioned quickly, including all those assembled in the rooms. "Peyman is our hero. He died a heroic death! We want everyone to know. Is that a crime?"

"What do you want here?" the brother-in-law said, up against him.

"Justice, reckoning! Don't you? You want to let them get away with it?"

Next to me in the kitchen doorway, Shahrnoush, red-faced, chewed her lip, flicked tears off her face. Her husband was ashen.

"This is state-run terrorism," the boy said. "They're killing our generation! A heart attack? You expect us to believe that? There's a list. Every name a story of brutality and terror and abduction. You want to see the list? Beware of their propaganda. They buy our hearts and souls with scholarships and casinos and factories and F-14s. They're selling us out to foreigners. The bloodsuckers! Ask their prisoners. It's inside their prisons you see their real faces."

The brother-in-law grabbed the boy's shirt, shoved him into the kitchen. "I don't know who you are or what you do. And I don't want to know! You're causing us shame and grief. You want to make more trouble so they come back for us? Take your friends and get out. You hear? Don't make me repeat it, or I'll throw out every one of you personally."

"You're not angry with me," the boy taunted him. "You're angry at your own impotence."

Dark with indignation, he went over to the students, consulted them momentarily, then turned to the brother-in-law, enraged. Those of us close enough heard what he said next.

"You're cowards. We're ready to give blood! Fight in the streets. We believe in an armed revolution. And we'll never give up!"

They exited in a flurry. When they left, I noticed the two young men sitting by the far wall, hanging their heads.

THE ROOMS WERE QUIET. The manservant collected the empty glasses and plates, and the maid finished washing up in the kitchen. Shahrnoush came in from the kitchen and insisted I take dinner with them. "Please," she said, "this is your home."

Then she whispered, "I'm staying for a while. I don't want Kamal alone. He's in a terrible state of mind. I'm afraid he'll take an overdose and slip away."

The front door was open. A van pulled up and parked, and two men came in and took away the chairs along the walls. The brother-in-law paid them, peeling off bills. He was solid, efficient, but it was impossible to read his thoughts. Mr. Bashirian was still locked up in the bedroom. The two neighbors were there — the elderly man and the engineer — and the relatives from Mazandaran, and the two friends I'd seen seated against the far wall. Kazem and Ali. They stood in the hallway talking, the women preparing dinner in the kitchen.

There was a palpable sense of relief once the crowd left. The evening had been a strain, especially the disruption by radical students. The brother-in-law, still in a rage, smashed two plates in the kitchen. Then he came out, pointing at Kazem and Ali, and said, "What stupidity! I should never have called them. Their visit was a shrewd calculation. If they loved Peyman they wouldn't behave like that. The nerve to say he died for them! Those bastards talk like they own him!"

No sooner had the students left than people started talking behind them. To the family, they said they were stunned. How brazen! How reckless! How downright dangerous for those kids to have barged in and mouthed off like that! But to one another they murmured other things, judging by the looks on their faces — tactful, circumspect — those who had previously been in the dark about Peyman's arrest. They'd heard the words: *prison, disappearance, murder by the state.* Their unease became even more conspicuous as they gathered to leave. I overheard one of them say by the door, "So it turns out he was arrested! God knows what he did."

A bedroom door opened, and Mr. Bashirian came out and said he wanted to talk to me alone in the living room. He drifted in, moved about the furniture, a ghost in his own house, then lowered himself into an armchair.

"You know," he murmured, "he took pictures."

I nodded. Outside, a siren wailed.

"That was his crime. The accusation."

"What crime?" I said, startled.

"You remember that morning we saw him in there?" He choked up but kept going. "He told me something. You couldn't hear, he was whispering. He said they had asked about the photos. Interrogated him four times, he said. They wanted to know which group he belonged to. They said he'd followed orders and taken pictures of military installations."

"What? Which installations?"

"It was in the photos, they claimed. They wanted him to confess. They said he was a traitor. He said it was all lies."

"Traitor?" I was shocked Peyman would have any crime to confess. That he could ever be a traitor. "I remember you said to him, 'How can it be?' You meant the photos. The accusation."

"Maybe he didn't have a heart attack," he whispered. "Maybe they tried to — to punish him. It's a terrible thought. What if they knew — knew all along they were never going to release him?"

It was an awful thought.

"When they gave back his belongings, the photo albums weren't there. They gave back his clothes, his sneakers. I asked for the photos. They told me they couldn't find them."

His hands shook. He wanted a cigarette. I got my pack and lighter and we lit up under the dark oil paintings I'd examined the first day I'd visited him there, which he'd painted over the years with such somber effect.

"What do you think?" he whispered.

"I don't know," I said.

"What if they lied about how things happened?"

I shook my head. I didn't want him to believe it.

"I agonize about it," he whispered. "Please. Don't tell my family."

I stared at the stony river he'd painted, the silvery moonlight over spectral hills. They had accused Peyman of taking pictures of military installations. That was what he'd told his father that morning, at the other end of the table under feeble neon lights. His father had leaned in, shocked, but he hadn't told me. Until tonight.

"Last night I imagined terrible things. I imagined him screaming out for me. Father, Father! he was screaming, strapped to a table. Helpless while they tortured him —"

"You mustn't torture yourself," I said.

"That night when they took me in, I — I saw him laid out on the table," he said numbly. "I remember looking. Before I passed out. To see if they had harmed him. He looked so peaceful."

He slumped back.

"I wanted to keep on looking. To divine his last thoughts. I wanted to throw myself on him. To embrace him for the last time. I'm weak, so weak. He was my rock, my reason for existing. Why didn't I die instead?"

He sat, nearly lifeless himself.

We were called in to dinner. A dozen people were around the table. Kamal refused food, leaned over, and said to his sister, "Tell me it's a bad dream." She laid a hand on his, told him to try eating some white rice at least. She had such milky-white skin and dark hair. She gave him a glass of water and watched him down pills. Then she fetched him a glass of tea from the samovar. More than gentle, she was mothering. I was introduced to Peyman's two friends, Kazem and Ali. Kazem kept to himself. He was the boy from Kerman on scholarship, with the face of a stoic, maybe angelic if you didn't notice the discreet tenacity in his eyes, the austerity of the jawline. After dinner, Ali, who had traveled with

Peyman all over, spread his photos on the table before us. He had the chiseled looks of an athlete, sinewy and distraught, and his right leg never stopped pumping. He talked, lectured us, considering the tone of his voice. Once in a while he'd repeat: "So what military installations are they talking about? You see any signposts, barbed wire? You see anything here?"

We had looked. We didn't.

He showed us the groupings: towns, portraits, vistas. Under this last heading we peered at everything he passed around, which didn't look like much and wasn't of anything in particular. Dusty spaces, lone trees, scrub brush, amber and purple horizons dawn to dusk.

"The charge was an obscene lie," Ali concluded.

"They don't worry about such details," Kazem said modestly.

Ali leaned in. "Think about it. They already had a trumped-up charge against him. It carried a sentence. They claimed they had evidence, not that they're obliged to prove anything! Then suddenly — they want him out. I keep asking myself why."

"Maybe because they realized he was innocent," I said.

He eyed me suspiciously, went on. "They call his father to prepare to come get him. But they ask about medication. What for? The next day they call in the evening and say Peyman is ill, and Mr. Bashirian panics. He was right to panic. I think Peyman was already dead then. Perhaps he'd died the night before under torture. His heart had stopped suddenly. It was a sentence carried out following a secret verdict. Even if it was an accident, what's the difference? They'd managed to get rid of him quietly. So until when was he still alive? When they made the first call, or the second call, thirty-six hours later? Was he actually alive when they said, Something's wrong, come right away? If he was, that's good — at least they weren't lying. Which means he had to die within the hour. By the time Mr. Bashirian got there. But what if he was already dead — and they called? That would prove there was a scheme. Pretty sinister. They had a corpse lying around and they call the father and pretend, saying, Come get your child! The coldhearted, shameless, lawless sons of bitches!"

"What's your point?" Kazem said calmly.

"We must find out if Peyman was still alive the first and second time they called."

"What are you talking about?" said Mr. Bashirian's brother-in-law. "How can we? You kids are all the same. So idealistic."

"Idealistic?" Ali said, incensed. "You're his family. The only thing he left behind in this world. Go back to Komiteh. Pretend you believe the heart attack. Cry, plead! Whatever it takes. Ask to speak to the doctor. Ask for his photo albums, the diary. Say they're precious mementos — all you have left of him. Can't you do that?"

"For God's sake," Shahrnoush said, "you're all so pushy!"

Ali looked to Kazem, then looked down.

"Who saw him alive?" Ali repeated. "Did they see him right up to the last day? Maybe another prisoner saw him. A guard. Forgive me for asking again, Mr. Bashirian, but what did you see?"

"I told you," Kamal said flatly.

"I know."

"When I got there, they kept talking about Military Hospital Number Two. I thought they'd already transferred him. They rushed me down a corridor. My legs felt wobbly. A man in a white coat came out of a room. He was a doctor and talked about a heart attack. How they'd called for an ambulance but it was too late — too late. We went in. He pointed to the steel table; the body was there on the table. He pulled back the sheet. Peyman was dead."

There was silence. We shifted, uneasy in our seats. Ali nodded, tender and grave, disguising his considerable edginess. He wasn't satisfied with the answer but let it go. Shahrnoush asked Kamal, "You're ready to go back to Komiteh? Ready to face them again?"

"You go," he said. "I can't."

She looked to her husband. "I don't know how to talk to them. I mean —"

"Do what I said," said Ali. "I told you."

"It's not so simple," snapped the brother-in-law.

"You must begin somewhere."

The brother-in-law looked away in stony anger.

The only way left was to see the lawyer the next morning. There was to be no more procrastination. They would have him write up the petition demanding an official inquiry into Peyman's death. The sooner the better. None of us really held much hope.

"But you need prominent names," Ali said. "Lawyers, judges, writers, anyone with balls left these days."

Quickly he apologized, regretting the slip. Mr. Bashirian told him to gather up his photos and take them with him. "This house is no refuge from anything," he said.

I WAS SPENDING more time at Mr. Bashirian's house than at my own.

When I got back, the house was dark. On the console in the front hall by the antique French clock there was a list of phone messages scribbled in Goli's crablike handwriting. Friends had called to thank us for our dinner party. As though I didn't know all they wanted was to drag information out of me. We were the subject of the latest gossip in town. My in-laws had already called to tell me at work. My two best friends. And of course Pouran, from her grand central office — the hairdresser — early in the afternoon. I heard hair dryers whirring in the background, and the noisy chitchat of other women, bejeweled and fashionable arbiters of the city. Pouran repeated to me how the wife of the rear admiral was bad-mouthing me all over town, commiserating with Houshang for putting up with me. Who did I think I was? I'd insulted her husband, I was uncontrollable. Whose side was I on — the leftists' and radicals'? Think of it, considering my family. What was I — playing pushy intellectual? Pouran quoted, suddenly prissy, sanctimonious. Taking advantage of the occasion. The very woman charged with maintaining the rear admiral's mistress, now outdoing herself for the wife. From my mother-in-law and sister-in-law I got lectures on propriety and wagging tongues and the sheer stupidity of any political opinion. They were worried. Terrified of being out of favor, cut off from their only source of heavy income and oxygen — the right people.

Mother called with the uncanny prescience of a fortune-teller just as I stepped into my bedroom.

"What's going on?" she demanded. "You're never home."

I sank into a chair, kicked off my shoes. Houshang wasn't home again.

"Is your husband home?" she asked.

"He's sleeping," I whispered. "It's late."

"Why are you whispering suddenly? You're hiding things from me."

"Who could do that, Mother?"

"The phone hasn't stopped ringing here. Your father is extremely upset! He doesn't need this right after Sobhi's death. What happened the other night at your party?"

"Nothing."

"Who's this prisoner?"

"He's dead."

"What's going on with your marriage? I hear you and Houshang aren't talking. I hear he doesn't come home at night."

I felt a rush of indignation. How did she know?

"Who says, Mother?"

"Goli reports."

"She spies for you now? Since when?"

"Since I caught her in your bedroom in one of your evening gowns with your high heels and jewelry. I told her I wouldn't tell."

"Under what condition?"

"No condition. She's been very forthcoming since that day."

"I should throw her out."

"It wouldn't solve a thing. Anyway, she looked ridiculous. So what's going on? Your father wants to know, the worrywart!"

"I'll tell you tomorrow. I want to sleep."

"Sleep — while we lie awake worrying ourselves sick! Just the sort of selfishness that runs in your father's family."

I heard Houshang come up after two in the morning. He slept in the guest room. Early in the morning he barged in for a change of clothes, his face and eyes puffy. He'd been drinking, maybe smoking opium with Iraj. On my dressing table he saw the list of people who had called.

"What a dinner party!" he said. "Everyone's talking about it."

"Thanks to that pompous upstart woman — who should be calling to thank us instead of gossiping all over town."

"She's waiting for you to call her and apologize."

"What? Over my dead body."

"I tell you," he said. "You must apologize."

He grabbed his clothes and walked out, slamming the door. War. Every step corrupting, distancing us from what it was we truly fought for.

TWENTY-NINE

THAT WEEK I GOT my passport. Jalal's contact had been right: I wasn't on the blacklist, not yet. So I had a passport for the first time, and now that I had it, I wasn't sure I wanted to give it to Jalal. He'd asked me for it, but it wasn't a request, it was barter. Ever since he'd informed me about the SAVAK raid against us, he wanted favors, each one more treacherous. I could see how they'd never end unless he left.

Early one evening his sister called me at work and said her shift was ending at Najmieh Hospital. She wanted to paint the town red. Dinner, the movies, one of those new cabarets. I got rid of her by saying I was leaving town. Mahastee called and said she had tickets to a lecture. Would I attend with her? She wouldn't say where nor what it was about.

I had been scouring the papers, half expecting to see Jalal's name any day. Ten days before in the evening papers: "Two Women Killed in Armed Struggle in Tehran — Simin Taj Hariri and Akram

Sadeghpour." Last week: "Bahram Aram Killed in Ambush on Shiva Street." This week: "Mohammad Hassan Ebrari, Political Prisoner, Executed." Then the long article stating officially: We have only thirty-three hundred political prisoners, and they're all Marxists. In the next paragraph: Yes, we have torture. But we don't need physical torture anymore, when we have psychological torture at our disposal.

What an admission! Obviously they don't feel the need to win anyone over.

I took the bus to visit Mother. I sat with her and we smoked and sipped tea and listened to the radio. Zari kept to herself in the corner, sighing and brooding and blatantly ignoring me. When she left the room, Mother said, "Your sister's turned mute ever since that husband of hers got beaten up that night in the street. She doesn't even scream at the children anymore. If you ask me, it was better when she screamed. She's told me it's all your fault! Now he's threatening to divorce her. You want to ruin her life?"

"Now it's my fault?"

"She thinks I always side with you because you're my favorite, even though I live with her. You beat him up! Didn't you? Now go see what's wrong with her."

I was sick of the whole business, so I went out to talk to Zari. She was folding clothes in the other room and I asked if something had happened.

"He hasn't hit you or the kids again, has he?"

She turned, red-faced. "Leave us alone. You don't respect us."

I asked if Morteza had shaped up. I felt sorry for her. Did she need money?

"My husband provides for me! I don't need your handouts. What happened to our two bits of land in Varamin? It's all I've got left in the world. Why can't you do something? Why can't you get that illiterate peasant Doost-Ali to cough up our money?"

"He's always got excuses. The crop was diseased this year. He spent all the loan from the Agricultural Bank on a family pilgrimage to Mashhad. He swears he'll pay us next year."

"It's already been three years! I hope he drops dead. Aren't you ever going to sell the other land? The six hectares? I want my share! I want my money."

"No one's buying. I told you I'm going there this week."

"Morteza claims you hide things from me and you're going to sell the land and keep the money."

"And you believe that?"

"He says you're jealous of him. Because he's bought a car and he does business and has a household with a wife and children!"

She wanted an upheaval again, to calm down. I turned to leave.

She turned shrill. "Don't tell me he's right?"

"How could I possibly be jealous of him?"

"Of course, Mr. Intellectual, who reads books and thinks big thoughts and prefers educated women. Morteza swears you're a leftist!"

I wanted to see the children and sit with Mother, but I was tired of Zari's harangue. So I told Mother I had to go see a friend in the hospital. "Which hospital?" she asked quickly. I said, "Alborz," thinking of Mr. Bashirian. She asked why I'd bothered to come if I only intended on staying a measly half hour. Zari kept the children in the other room, away from me. From the doorway they stood and watched me leave, moping, their baby faces pressed against the door frame. Who knew whom they'd turn against once they grew up.

On the bus, lurching past the shop fronts along Baharestan Square, I thought about Jalal and Peyman Bashirian. It's brutal how a man loses his innocence. One day he wakes up and looks around and it's gone. Not only is it gone, but instead he has self-loathing for having ever possessed such innocence.

I called Mahastee from the repair shop in Shahabad. I'd left my radio there and it was ready. I was curious about this lecture she'd told me about the day before. She gave the name of an intersection that wasn't near any concert or lecture hall. "That's where it is!" she said. "See you at six."

THIRTY

I CAME BY ORANGE TAXI to avoid parking. It was already getting dark. Reza was at the traffic light. I paid the cab, showed Reza the address I'd copied from the sheet at Mr. Bashirian's house. "What is it?" he asked. I said it was the lecture the radical students had talked about that night at the Bashirian house. I'd decided to take the risk. I wanted to find whatever it was that I kept thinking I couldn't find. I couldn't have said to him on the phone that I felt compelled. I said if he didn't want to attend I'd understand. I was sorry to have dragged him all the way there for nothing.

"No, you're not," he said.

I stared into the street. I was annoyed at myself for talking in circles. I knew attending the lecture would be considered a betrayal. I was incensed that it would. I'd called Reza because there was no one else to call.

I pointed to the address. He knew how to get there. He said it couldn't be a school or institute but was probably a private home.

They'd let people trickle in without attracting attention. He warned me about showing my face in such places, about informers in the audience. How such meetings and so-called lectures got raided. Sometimes they sent thugs. He was testing me.

"We're not far from Qasr Prison," he added.

We were in the backstreets.

"See," he said, "you haven't noticed anything. Those students, strolling at corners, like that one there. They're on watch. They call ahead if there's a raid. They see them coming."

He told me that all those years ago after they left Morshedabad, it was in this neighborhood that his father had rented an old house for them. His mother had loved the house — the porches, the interior courtyard, the persimmon tree — until she'd had to give it up. I started counting the number of students we passed. One of them, holding a book, stared back when Reza greeted him. Then he pointed down the street, walked back to the corner. The address turned out to be a large brick two-story private house. At the front door a young man told us to go through the corridor, turn right, cross the courtyard, and turn right again to the back. I felt that fluttering sense of panic. Inside, the house seemed vacant. We went down a half-lit and empty corridor, across the tiled courtyard, where people stood talking — they stared, and I stared past them — then right again into the next house in the back, going through two empty front rooms, following others.

We were ushered in from a small side door. The long room was already packed, and people were wandering down the aisles on either side to find seats. Rows of folding chairs were set tightly squeezed together on the bare concrete floor. They'd done a pretty crude job of knocking down a wall in the middle to make a larger room. A metal roll-up garage door took up part of the far wall. Two impatient young men were directing people to get them seated as quickly as possible. A woman in a navy scarf and overcoat and trousers handed out leaflets, murmuring, "Please photocopy this and help circulate it." There were hardly any seats left. Reza spotted two way in the back. We grabbed our leaflets and made our way. The audience was all under forty and the majority looked like students. Reza joked about attending a lecture in a garage.

A young man in the front, in his early twenties, scrutinized the gathering, the commotion and the incessant reports coming from the sentries outside, the unanticipated number of people who had turned up. People were now cramming in, sitting on the floor along the aisles and in the front.

The speaker raised a hand to indicate they would start. He said if everything went as planned, there would be two lectures. He would give the introduction. He said they had a surprise lecturer, looked around the room and at two men standing in the doorway, then informed us that this guest hadn't arrived yet. "He will!" he assured us. Then he turned to the young man beside him, who was unshaven like himself and had been attracting a great deal of attention, and, referring to him as one of their most inspiring speakers, introduced him as the first lecturer.

The young man looked back out to us stonily. He said that since the internal coup and split-up of their organization, the rival Marxist group had betrayed comrades to SAVAK. They'd shed the blood of their own brothers! They now called Islam a petit-bourgeois ideology! Tonight the two main speakers would directly address the rift, the ideological divide, the treachery.

The young man hadn't introduced himself or given the names of the other speakers.

He began, a slight tremor in his voice. "The living expression of our nation isn't found in the ostentatious decrees and edicts of the regime, but in the enlightened commitment and action of our men and women. In us. But they don't know us. They don't see us. We exist!" He raised his arms. "Look at us."

Reza wasn't listening. He was surveying the room.

"Shariati said we must create social awareness. The elevation and progress of our consciousness. Otherwise we hold the empty title of citizen. He said this in his writings for years, in his lectures five years ago at Hosseiniyeh Ershad before they closed it down. They were afraid of him. He inspired! He possessed that exceptional gift — fire! He set our generation's mind on fire! With his remarkable vision. They imprisoned him. This year they made him write those revisionist lies in *Kayhan*. We don't believe them! Islam is as revolutionary an ideology as Marxism! The real battle in our hearts today is between Muhammad and Marx. But first let's look at our intellectuals! Miming what they've learned abroad. Cardboard words learned in foreign tongues in other continents. Our rich are no more trustworthy than vultures. Their fortunes are the fruit not of their labor but of exploitation. They think they own this country — it's their personal money press! Look how much they amass, how they rush it out! Look at them — all educated abroad! Not even completely literate in their mother tongue! Let's throw them out! Our traditional clergy is another elite. Old puppets of colonial powers. Perpetuating centuries of a passive religion of mimicry, submission, dogmatic ignorance. All blood and martyrdom of Hossein at Karbala and eternal tears. Time has come for change. Radical action!"

He paused, looked out, his audience rapt. He could sense the audacity, the thrill of his words. Lecturing on about alienation and economics and Islamic ideology and a return to our roots, growing increasingly fervent.

"Break it up!" someone suddenly shouted from the front. "Get out!"

The speaker was being hurtled out by his watchmen, along with the other prominent revolutionary lecturer. People shot up from their seats and lunged forward, shoving chairs, pushing in the aisles, crushing people seated on the floor. There were bottlenecks by the far doors. Reza shoved back chairs and went for the garage door. He bent down and, grabbing the handle, tried to yank it up.

It wouldn't budge. I looked back to the room. Two students were shouting from the front, "Get out! Turn right, not left. Not through the courtyard! Don't jam the doors." I imagined the side streets blocked off. The army trucks outside. Their impassive faces as we came running out, the transgressors. How long did we have? I felt light-headed, as much from anticipation as from fear. Reza said the garage door was locked from the outside. We were trapped. He pounded on the metal. I had walked into a trap, and I had come willingly. "These idiots must open the garage door," Reza said, angry. He shouted, his voice booming. "Get the garage door open!" He pounded on the metal, the echo reverberating over the panicky audience. Several men joined in and we tried the door again. Suddenly someone yelled from the other side, "Wait! Don't pull." The garage door rolled up. Dark skies, cold air. Night had fallen. A young man holding the metal rod he'd removed ordered us, "Go this way! They're coming in the front." People spilled out the back, running past us into the alley. Reza grabbed my arm. "I know the backstreets," he said. We rushed down the alley and into another, which was darker, and then another, turning in the warren of narrow backstreets away from the direction we had come earlier. We heard police sirens in the dark, screeching brakes, people shouting in the distance. Every time we rounded a corner, I thought I'd come face-to-face with them. Name, father, address, marital status, occupation? Why is he with you? What were you doing at the meeting? Why? Who do you know? Tell us. Reza said, "We're near the shops — don't rush." In the main avenue the streetlights were bright, traffic moving briskly. Calmly we took in the street. We went past the bicycle repair shop, a grocer, then a bakery where there was a line. He turned to get me a cab.

"Wait," I said suddenly. Then I told him. I was closing the house in Morshedabad that weekend. Did he want to go back one last time to the garden?

He looked straight into my eyes, leaned in. Whispered, "If you stay the night with me."

He looked back at the approaching traffic. Hailed an orange taxi for me, pushed me in.

It was a dare. He had dared ask; it was that or nothing. Spend the night. This was no ordinary transgression and betrayal for me, but the desire for another life. I'd already shifted into its quicksand, its consuming ambitions looming with consequence. The question left was what to tell Houshang. My husband doesn't understand that I've always known the art of finer deceptions but have waited for the day I would truly need such fineries to conceal a deep-seated and devastating emotion. And perhaps find a way out.

THURSDAY I DROVE TO Varamin early in the afternoon. I outdid buses and trucks and vans, going eighty-five miles an hour dead south.

From the distance I saw the trees of the village of Morshedabad. A clump on the horizon in the tranquil undulations of the plain. The sun was high, beating everything white. There was neither a sign nor an arrow to caution the accidental traveler. I turned off the main road to an unpaved one, raising dust behind me, approaching the village. Past the old trees with gnarled limbs like cripples, their strong branches flexed like the arms of peasants. Dusty leaves on a dusty street. Alongside the road, the water channel was without even a trickle. The old mud-brick walls running along the road were crumbling here and there to reveal gardens behind them. I went over the humped bridge of packed earth and wood, right by the clearing, where children playing soccer turned and came running up along the car. Beyond — the square, the baker's, the grocer's, the shrine of the *morshed,* the school building and clinic our family had built for the village.

I parked and the children gathered around the car. I got out and greeted them and they surrounded me. I saw the black mulberry tree against which we had once parked our bicycles long ago.

I walked around the village, the children in tow. The sun was sliding down, hovering orange. I stopped by the shrine of the *morshed.* A monument to dust and fate and superstition. I walked around greeting old men and young boys and mothers clutching babies, and the village elder, and the grocer, who gave me an orange Fanta, and the baker, who introduced his son and grandchildren and offered me fresh loaves. They murmured salutations to Father. They asked after Mother and my brothers. They'd heard we were about to sell off the garden and house. The garden of Morshedabad. Who was going to buy it, then?

Early in the evening the birds came out for an hour and chattered. The air cooled down. The plain glistened gold with the setting sun. I drove along the fields and the irrigation channels and embankments until the gates and walls of the garden rose up before me, a vision after years.

The gardener helped bring the bags into the main house. We went out to survey the garden. He said, "This place isn't what it used to be! What orchards? The cherry trees are diseased, but the grapevines are still solid. What stables? Only a donkey there." We walked. The pool was cracked and overridden with green moss. The flower beds overgrown with weeds, no new flowers were planted anymore. Only the rose vines bloomed regardless of who came and went. He said his wife had died and he lived alone. His children were gone. "What shall I bring you to eat and drink?" I thanked him, saying I had brought food with me. He said he'd called Zobeydeh from the village to clean the house. "How's Tehran?" he said. "I didn't think I'd see you back here anymore."

He walked me back to the main house. Through the trees I saw their bungalow back in the far end of the clearing. The house of Hajj-Alimardan and Reza. The wooden door, the front porch. I told him someone was coming from the Nirvani family to look over their land in the village. Maybe they'd drop in to see me. "The daughter or the son?" he asked. "What a man he was, that father!"

He left for the night. I went back into our house to get ready. Rummaging through old records abandoned there, I put one on and music from a long-lost song filled the rooms. I'm still young, I thought, I can choose, transform the future. I shed my clothes and stepped into a hot shower, emerging to stare at my reflection appearing slowly in the bathroom mirror as the steam vanished. "Twenty years!" I whispered. I felt young again, freed, as if I had come back to the garden that night to cut loose from everything, so certain was I of this, so resolute in embracing its dangers, so serene and invulnerable, knowing it had always been destined to be. Wading in this haze of strange calm, I dressed and dabbed on a scent redolent with jasmine. I made tea. I dragged out a chair and sat out on the porch. Waiting for Reza. Looking out at the garden, I knew I had been waiting for years.

He had said he could be delayed. I waited. At dusk the generator kicked in. Then quiet. The moon came up above the grove, silvery. The gardener, watchman by the gate. But he did not come.

I went back in to put out the food I'd brought from town for the two of us. I tore into one of the fresh loaves from the village I'd carefully laid out for him. I flitted through the rooms, slammed shut a door. Worried, pacing to and fro. Something bad had happened to him, no, something terrible. My equanimity was caving in to apprehension, then anger, anguish. Where was he?

I felt ice running through my veins. He wasn't late. He hadn't been delayed. He was never going to come.

I was there to claim my freedom, to say I wanted him. Didn't he know? It was astonishing how the two went together in my imagination. My freedom and Reza. I imagined him changing his mind, imagined him going home and grabbing a duffel bag and running down the stairs. I'd never seen his home. No, two rooms, he'd said, a functional place, not a home. I imagined him finding the last diesel Benz out of Tehran and speeding in the dark down the road, even while knowing he wouldn't. I felt a brutal remorse. He was gone. I had waited twenty years for this. Twenty years, only to come back and bury us here, in this garden. He and I. This was the place. There would be no shrine to cover it, no slab of stone to say, Here lies not one man or woman but a whole way of life, buried here — in this garden — for here too was buried the memory of his father and the life he had lived with us, Hajj-Alimardan, taken from his parents in Tabriz as a child by my grandmother because she had loved him, as had my father, though finally my father had never understood him enough to know why he had left and how to breach the distance, nor how Hajj-Ali had ended his life ruined, and even if Reza and I understood or tried to, it was still the end — for us, for them — too late, and we would sell the garden, and someone would buy it and make and unmake another life here for a time, and children would play under its shade and wade in its waters and run through the orchards blithe and blind as we had been, carrying our fate for each other until tonight, when I had come to bury it here, and here it would be forgotten.

I felt we had been broken. I could feel the breaking, like a great tree falling dead in the forest. I threw on my coat and went out, down through the trees where life had already passed. The garden was silhouetted, moon-washed. The wind picked up and I looked up to the night sky opening vast and fired with stars beyond the trees.

Wasn't he certain of my will? Had he held back because he did not believe in it? But he didn't need my will anymore. He had outgrown it, like a man crossing a river who sees the bridge over which he's running crumbling behind him. I knew. It was too late and he could never come back now.

I had watched him at the lecture by the radicals. He had watched them like a professional. With a cool head and heart.

They weren't slashing away at his world; they were slashing away at mine. Attacking everything I lived with, turning it on its head. Warping, redirecting, this world I thought I knew well. Reza had watched them as if he were assessing the competition. How and what they said, their polemics. Then he'd looked away like a man with an ulterior motive. A superior intellect disdaining them, competitive. He'd leaned in, whispered about them, disparaging. There only to protect me.

He was forced to carry his politics like a thief carrying loot. He lived with this and hid it well because it was so much a part of him. I could see why now. He was not concealing anything — he wore it all over. Like a badge of honor. It kept him passionate, alive, rooted. It kept him from me.

Our fate could not be rewritten; it was not ours anymore. We were on either side of a divide, he and I. I represented the status quo, what he fought against, what accorded him dishonor and betrayal for thinking and doing as he did. Each of our lives negating the other's existence, the divide between us an eternal form of contempt. So many things between us. I considered them, my life and his. It was painful, this inevitable tallying up. It comes one day, as if everything we've ever done is working against us, so trapped are we in what we make of ourselves.

Dark night. The lone bird trilled. There in that garden, I thought, if anywhere, all ideology, all else, would have ended, breathing life into the present so it could live.

When sleep came, I dreamed he was writing me a poem. Ancient verses, about an eternal garden. I writhed in sleep, wept, as if told a harrowing secret.

THIRTY-ONE

I HAD TOLD MAHASTEE I'd get to Morshedabad around six-thirty. But I was already running late. The afternoon meeting had taken forever, the guys on edge over polemics. I had to pack a bag and rent a diesel Benz taxi to get to her. The streets were crowded, the bus crawling eastward through rush-hour traffic. I got off before my stop and starting running, zigzagging past pedestrians.

I rushed up the stairs, unlocked my front door, and pushed it open. I heard rustling and stopped. Someone was in the room. I didn't switch on the light.

"Shut the door," he murmured.

I closed the door, locked it, turned back in the dark. There was light coming in from the street. Jalal was by the window.

"What's wrong?" I said.

"You have food in the house?"

"What happened?"

"They ambushed and killed our guys yesterday. There's an informer way at the top. He's going to take down every last one of us."

He was looking out at the back alley.

"I'd just left Shahr-Ara. They were waiting for instructions clear across town. For two weeks I was the messenger. I was told to stop at the pharmacy to buy medicine. I was running late. Three blocks before Vossuq, I told the cab driver to let me off. I saw the commotion. I ran up Bastami. looking for a phone to warn the others. The line was busy. I redialed. I wanted to save them! I ran to Behfar Hospital to grab a taxi back to Shahr-Ara. But they'd hit both places at the same time. I think I know who it is. Don't touch the light."

I set down my keys, but I didn't take off my jacket. I felt a rush of adrenaline. They were looking for him, and I was giving him refuge. I had no way out.

"Go get dinner, and candles. And the papers. I need cigarettes. I'll sleep here tonight."

I left my cigarettes on the table. I rushed down, thinking of a way out. Mahastee was waiting for me. I kicked out the door in an incredible rush of anger. For an instant I saw my famished dreams carved out of rock, suddenly garish ambitions. I felt no contrition, just loathing. Everywhere we plotted lay our own ruin. I saw her in the garden waiting.

I had chosen this fate. Mine was another world. I would never reach her now. My obligations came first, my revolutionary politics. I had to protect myself and our underground group from any outsider like Jalal. His eyes had been cold and hard, staring at me in the dark. He expected my help, and I was either with him or against him. If I didn't help him disappear, he'd hunt me down and hunt down our group. He wasn't useful to me anymore, but a grenade now with its pin pulled, waiting to explode. I had to get him out that night.

I rushed down the street and got kabob rolled in fresh bread, and from Habib *agha*'s, three packs of Zarrin cigarettes and candles and matches and feta cheese and sweet *halvardeh*, and down at the corner I grabbed the evening papers. I dropped the ten-rial coin I gave the boy. He bent down and I scanned the front page. "Pakistani Prime Minister Bhutto Due in Tehran." "Eight People Killed, Eleven Arrested, in Armed Clashes with Security Forces in Shahr-Ara and Vossuq." From my window, Jalal was watching the city close in on him.

I slipped in and locked the door. He was still by the window.

"I couldn't find matches," he said.

"It's all over the papers," I said.

I laid out the food, lit two candles, and stuck them on saucers. He lit a cigarette, dragged on it, grabbed the papers, reading by candlelight the list of the dead, cursing under his breath, pointing to their pictures. He said only one name was missing. The wife of one of their leaders, a doctor who had studied in Rome. He'd been shot in the throat; maybe she'd escaped.

"You have the passport, the money?"

I said they were under my shirts in the cupboard.

"Last night I walked all over Vahidieh. I slept in the park. I need to wash up. I need a change of clothing."

He washed up and I gave him clothes and turned on the radio. "Keep it down," he said, buttoning the shirt. The clothes were slightly baggy on him. I found my passport and the envelope of cash he'd given me where I'd left them. He flipped through the passport and counted the money. He said he needed the name of a contact on the Gulf coast to help him cross the border. I wrote down a name and number in the port of Bandar Abbas.

"You've got vodka?"

I got the bottle and glasses from above the sink. We sat on the floor to eat. He wolfed down his food, chugged the vodka, tore into more bread with *halvardeh* as he sat under the photo of Father.

"For years our leadership quibbled. Castroist versus Maoist tactics, socioeconomic doctrines based on their seven-year research in villages, the necessity for a mass uprising versus guerrilla warfare. They're all dead now! This summer I was taken to meet one of them. He picked me to go abroad for training. Yesterday they killed him. They wiped out our entire revolutionary wing. We were betrayed by one of our own. Someone high up who knew everything."

He poured more vodka.

"Reza," he said. "You're the only one left."

It was a chilling verdict. We lit up, and I made tea in the white teapot with roses that Mother had given me.

He pointed to the pile of handwritten papers. "What are you writing?"

"An article on why we oppose an armed struggle."

"What for? Who'll believe you? SAVAK, your interrogators? Never. The students won't — they'll think you've all turned into apologists and revisionists and distrust you even more. The Left will accuse you of being liberal. The establishment wants your heads no matter what you say. They're digging your graves. There's no honor here. It's each man for himself. You're shouting in the wind."

He stared at me; I stared at the wall. At the future.

He said, "The only truth in the world is chaos and change. There's nothing out there for our beliefs to correspond to! I believe in drive, instinct, power. There is nothing else. Except the will to power."

"What about ideology?"

"Ideology bolsters the weak. The mediocre — the people. It empowers them enough to submit to the few who will inevitably dominate them."

"I thought you pitied the masses."

"Pity who — like that religious brute, my father?" he said, eyes fiery. "That detestable peasant who raves about the denigration of the flesh and this world? He's a fucking nihilist himself! If that's the will of his God — it's the will to nothing. A religion that disguises nihilism so it can preach it."

"Don't you want to liberate the masses?"

"The weak, oppressed? Those shameless hypocrites! They want it for themselves — the power. You might as well shoot them."

I picked up the dirty dishes. He sat against the wall, took out a piece of paper from his jacket, and studied it. Then he asked if I could spare a map, a sweater, a book — "You pick," he said — a pen and notebook. And a small duffel bag to pack. I was ready to give anything to get rid of him. I gave him the black plastic zippered bag that I kept in the back of the cupboard, from my soccer league. I rinsed the dishes, turned up the radio a notch for *Golha*. The veil of music, the soulful voice of Golpayegani, tremulous incantations — the drug that was the world.

Jalal rolled up his pea green jacket under his head and stretched out, all dressed, with his boots on.

"You can have the bedroll."

"I don't need it," he said.

I poured tea, went over to the bookcase, grabbed a book. He snatched it and turned it over without looking at the cover.

"Early tomorrow morning I'll hitch a ride south. Call my parents. Tell them I'm dead. Tell them I got killed in the raid."

I SLEPT BADLY, in fits, waking up repeatedly to watch the night behind the window. I dreamed, though it seemed to me I was between sleep and consciousness, between being and nothing, between the world as it was and as I imagined it dreaming. I saw my entire life all at once. Felt the razor's edge of my own death and undoing. I woke up before Jalal, but when I sat up, he asked the time.

"Five-twenty," I said.

"Time to leave."

The wail of an ambulance went down Sepah. I left water on to boil and washed my face. He made rolls of bread with feta cheese, wrapped them in newspaper, tucked them in the duffel bag. I told him to take the rest of the *halvardeh,* but he left it on the table.

"You must come with me," he said. "You carry the passport and money. It's safer."

I didn't know where he was going. He said he hadn't decided yet which square to leave from. I got dressed. We stood and each downed a glass of tea without a word. In the half-light he looked more impatient than ever.

He flung on his pea green jacket, grabbed the duffel bag.

"We go down Nasser Khosrau. I walk ahead of you. If something happens, don't wait. Reza, no matter who gets me — and they won't — I don't know you."

A man will say anything and even mean it when he's escaping. I locked the door. I had the passport and money in my jacket. We trudged down the stairwell. It was one thing to be hidden up in my room, but now we were out on the street. The sidewalk was practically deserted. He walked fast, arms loose, torso slightly swiveled so he could look back and flag down a taxi. Several cars whizzed by at full speed. There were mostly open vans and buses on the road, the storefronts shuttered. The dark was changing. Contused skies, bruised purples and charcoal instead of light.

He threw out his arm again. A cab screeched to a stop and he darted over and threw the door open.

"Maidan Shoush," he told the driver.

They sped away, and I watched and continued down the street. It was my turn to flag a cab. I had an appointment with Jalal in the traffic circle. Fifteen minutes later I was in a taxi watching the streets change through South Tehran.

At the corner of Shahin I paid the driver. I hadn't needed Jalal to warn me about disaster striking anytime up to the last second. Crowds of laborers and factory workers and vans and buses and diesel trucks were coming and going. The start of a new day. I was rubbernecking, but I couldn't see him. I felt nearly heroic. Felt nothing could happen now. I saw him in the distance at the intersection with my black duffel bag. From that distance he was another face in a million. I took the longer way around in his direction. Traffic came between us. I knew he would stop at the point where the traffic was heading south to Reyy. He crossed, now over at the corner across from me. I walked faster and beyond the oncoming traffic caught glimpses of him with his arm out. I picked up my pace and waded through traffic, looking left, then right. A bus stopped in front of us and I couldn't see him anymore. I rushed across the road. Down from the corner, a truck had stopped where Jalal stood by the curb. He looked up, and from the way he looked at me I turned quickly to see what was behind me. I groped for the passport in my pocket, felt the sharp rim of plastic, the wad of money. As I passed slowly behind him I whipped them out, and he turned and grabbed the passport and envelope and they disappeared inside his pocket. The truck was waiting. He had the duffel bag in his left hand. He jumped out into the street, and as I moved on, I looked back and saw him leap up on the running board and get into the truck. Honking at traffic, the truck pulled out. It was a beat-up old thing for lugging soil and gravel, the exhaust spouting black smoke above the fender, which was set with the verse "If you don't have the heart of a lion, don't undertake the voyage of love," bracketed by the eternal invocation: *"Ya Ali."*

The truck rumbled down, merging with traffic.

I crossed at the intersection and headed back up. I saw the first sweep of light. Tehran was lumbering awake.

THIRTY-TWO

ABBAS SOBHI'S FUNERAL HAD BEEN the week before. That evening we were at their home again for a memorial service. Mother and Father looked ill by evening. At such times they aged within hours. We stayed on with Mrs. Sobhi, who was ever gracious and gentle even in grief, and after dinner I took them home.

In the car Mother said to me, "Goodness is a state of grace. Like art. Like faith. When we die, you must remember."

In their upstairs hallway she fidgeted with her possessions, and Father fiddled with the evening papers and stared at the wall. I knew he wanted to have his talk, but neither of us could dredge up what it took. We dropped into the dark velvet armchairs. Above Father's left shoulder was the photograph of Mlle. Hulot, decorous and looming with a high collar and parasol. She was the French governess summoned more than half a century ago by Grandfather for his only son and many daughters. She had arrived thin and choleric from Paris, and the household and gardeners had called her Houlou — the only way they could pronounce her name — and so in Persia she had finally been transformed into something sweet and delicious. Mlle. Peach. Father kept rustling the papers and coughing and clearing his throat until Mother threatened him.

"What is it now?" she demanded. "Bronchitis, pneumonia? You never listen to the doctor, you never listen to common sense, you never listen to anyone!"

"Look who's talking," he said.

"All my life I've spent listening — to all of you — and now I'm tired."

"You're not tired, I'm tired," he said.

"Tired of what?" Mother countered.

"I don't want to say."

"No, I think you better tell me!"

"Oh, for God's sake, Sobhi is dead, I — I don't know. Forget what I said."

Mother glowered and rolled her eyes, and just as she was about to launch one of her invasions, I said, "Uncle Khodayar is having an operation tomorrow."

"What?" she said. "How come you know and I don't?"

By the time I got through telling her that his wife had called and when and that it was a brain tumor, she was pacing, raking fingers through her hair. Mother was a world-class orator. She gave a fiery speech denouncing her sister-in-law. How she was nothing but trouble. That social-climbing cow from the provinces! That poor, irrational, perpetually resentful midget! That piglet with the eternally stunned expression! Father started flipping through the papers again. She wanted to call her brother immediately, but I said they were already at Pars Hospital, and she jumped up to call, poking her lit cigarette menacingly at the receiver.

"Najibeh, dear," Father said gently, now that the storm had passed over his head, "any of that delicious pound cake left?"

"He's got a brain tumor and you want pound cake?" she wailed.

I volunteered to get cake. Father said he'd forgotten his book in the library. I said I'd get it, but he insisted. We went down together, leaving Mother arguing on the phone with the nurse's station at the hospital.

"Put him on," Mother commanded. "We may lose him any moment!"

Father said she should have been a general. She would have had four stars by now and left everyone alone.

"So tell me," he said, "what happened that night with the rear admiral?"

We were in the front hallway under the Russian chandelier. I told him and he sat on the banquette against the wall, listening. Oddly rigid. The grandfather clock chimed a quarter to the hour. I told him my marriage was going through bad straits. I told him Peyman Bashirian was dead, and the suspicion was infecting everyone. I said maybe I'd been wrong to take on the rear admiral. But I was angry. My voice shook. I said I felt I resented just about everything these days. I couldn't understand what was wrong with me. I said I'd heard young students with more heart and conviction — and worse, putting far more at stake — than anyone I knew anywhere. They staked all! Of course I was angry. I told Father, if we had been raised to respect the status quo, well, then, where was it? How did we support it? It didn't seem to have any shape or roots or definition anymore. We had grown up in a political vacuum — maybe not just political, but some sort of vacuum nonetheless. We hadn't questioned the status quo. Instead we had taken our dreams and ambitions, and our equivocations, in fact our entire way of life, our inheritance and therefore our children's, and settled into what only appeared to be the established order — because it was and wasn't established — and the awful truth was we were ill prepared to fight, or even face the consequences.

"What are you two doing down there?" Mother called out.

Father rose. "You get the cake, I'll get my book," he said.

When I got back upstairs with the tray of tea glasses and pound cake and pot of mint tea, Mother was sifting through a shoe box of old photographs. The box — marked "Magenta satin evening shoes" — was from her favorite shoemaker, old Mr. Mehran, who created custom shoes for a select clientele. Mother said she'd worn the shoes only twice with the magenta evening gown Ninon and Pierre had made her. Father said she'd looked regal with her blond hair swept up and her ample bosom and slim waist and magnificent hips. "Ah! The slim waist," Mother said, her perspective on the world mending as she pulled out photos she particularly cherished. "Look!" she said. "My angelic baby brother, the cutest toddler! Before the witch." Somewhere in those black-and-white and sepia photos, time had vanished. Mother announced she was going to bed. She hugged me, warning Father about staying up late and not to forget his pills.

Father hadn't had a bite of cake. He told me he hated the paintings Mother collected. He hated owning endless things. He couldn't sleep. More than anything he wanted to retire to the Caspian and enjoy the garden.

Then he said, "At one time we had a sort of loyal opposition, with many lessons for both sides to learn from the encounter. These days they only get to look in the mirror. This is a city paved with technocrats. They've brought in the young and educated-abroad and swept out the old. And why not? Except the old-timers were experienced and well schooled and well prepared and understood their people and their country. I think today people feel their problems, their privations and concerns, aren't understood anymore. They think of this crowd as usurpers. The last time they contacted me, a few years ago, they wanted me to be senator. Of course, they'd forgotten how they tried to sabotage my reelection when I was a member of parliament long ago. I was against land reform. At least the way it was executed. I said it would ruin agriculture in this country. It gives me no pleasure to say I was right. I was a landowner. My ancestors had cultivated and fought for and defended their land and this country. We used to be the backbone of this country . . . This time round, they asked me to be senator. But I felt I wouldn't be representing anyone. I don't understand the people running this show. I've lost touch. Most of our land is gone except for bits and pieces. I don't know the peasants and farmers anymore, especially since Hajj-Alimardan's death. Anyway, he always knew them better. I tell you, the more I think about it, the more I think he should have been a member of parliament. I think about him often. Now the farmers are disillusioned. They're unhappy with the agricultural cooperatives the government's set up for them. One of them came by again with a crate of fruit from his orchard, his family waiting outside in a van, and he told the gardener they long for the old days and want me back. Of course, that's impossible. And I don't really believe it. Anyhow, it wouldn't work without Hajj-Ali anyway. My dear, I don't want cake — I'm not hungry. Sobhi died, and I think about death. Old age is tiring after a while. But I don't want to be young again. Don't worry, nothing lasts forever. And that young boy's death — that too shall pass. Why don't you take a few days at the Caspian?"

THE NEXT DAY I was at Kamal Bashirian's again late in the afternoon. He was in the hallway on the phone. I'd come to sign the petition. They were going to deliver it personally the next morning to the Ministry of Justice. His sister and brother-in-law weren't home yet. Ali and Kazem were talking to me in the living room. I was waiting for Ali to answer my question.

"When I asked Mr. Bashirian what he saw that night?" Ali repeated. "You heard — I didn't insist. I couldn't ask him. But when he was in the infirmary, Peyman was on the table. I wanted to ask if — if the body was still warm. If he could tell how long it had been. Since he'd died. I know, that's brutal. But how else can we get to the truth?"

Mr. Bashirian had been telling me how he was getting calls from students he didn't know and who didn't even know Peyman but wanted to come by and see him. He refused them all. They argued on the phone with him; they said they had theories. One of them had come by the house anyway and told the brother-in-law he knew for a fact that Peyman had been tortured. "They're trying to torture me!" Mr. Bashirian protested. "They want me to listen, to come speak at meetings, they want his picture, they want me to discuss Peyman's convictions. He has become their torch! It makes me ill," he said. "Their obsession. Their cause. Their need. Don't they have anything else to think about?"

Kazem said the students had given their verdict: Peyman had been kept in solitary confinement, interrogated repeatedly, beaten, tortured, and then killed.

"Is there proof?" I said.

"Come on, how naive can you get?" Ali said.

Out in the hall, we heard Mr. Bashirian greeting Shahrnoush and her husband. Mr. Bashirian walked in and said they had news from Komiteh. The brother-in-law came in, greeted us, perched on the chair by the doorway, and smoked and complained about traffic. He said he'd talked to his children in Sari that morning, and he missed them terribly. He rubbed his temples; he looked ill. Shahrnoush came and sat by her brother. She was pale and rigid and edgy.

"What happened?" Ali asked them.

The brother-in-law said they'd gone to Komiteh that morning and repeated their story at least four different times. At first the officers had listened with a grudging ear, until they'd heard enough; then he and Shahrnoush had been passed over and patronized instead and lectured point-blank and finally ordered to go home.

One of the officers had been angry and threatening. "Didn't you see the medical report? Didn't you see it was a heart attack? What do you want? How many times must we explain things to you people?" Suddenly Shahrnoush had pounced, shaking from a bad case of nerves and stress, and she'd attacked them like nothing he'd ever seen before.

"Like a wounded lioness," her husband said.

He couldn't have stopped her even if he'd tried, he said, and she had shrieked and sobbed, denouncing the officials and everyone and everything, beating herself on the head and chest, and screaming, "Go ahead, do what you want! I don't care anymore." She'd ended up sitting on the floor, wailing, "I won't leave, never! Not until you tell us what you did with that poor young boy, not until you give us an answer and stop treating us like goddamn dirt."

Suddenly overcome, he stopped, covered his face in his hands, and wept.

"What sort of life is this?" he said.

It was shocking to see him break down.

He excused himself and walked out, Shahrnoush following him into the bedroom across the hallway and shutting the door. Peyman's room.

"What?" said Ali. "They got nothing?"

Mr. Bashirian stared at the wall. "What's left?" he said.

"Nothing, we have nothing!" Ali said, raising his voice, pumping his leg, eyes jittery. "There's got to be something to help us!"

"I think we better leave," Kazem said to him.

They said they would call the next day or maybe the day after that. Mr. Bashirian nodded. When I left, the typewritten petition from the lawyer was lying on the table. With all our signatures.

I HAD BEEN CALLED a few days earlier at the office. It was a polite and brief conversation asking me to come in on a routine official and bureaucratic matter. An address on Iranshahr, with no mention of the name of the organization, which was peculiar. Just a street number. After I put the phone down, I sat staring out the window. What administrative matter was it? What did they want from me? The official had asked — very courteously — for me to come in. At my convenience, ten-thirty.

I didn't mention the call to anyone.

The night before, Thierry had sent over his chauffeur with a large sealed envelope before dinner. I tore it open in the upstairs study. There it was — the article by the French reporter and our interview at the Intercontinental. I skimmed through and recognized Peyman Bashirian's story, his father's statements. The names had been changed, but the facts were all there, with a footnote about how the young student was now dead. There they were, father and son, in one of the most famous newspapers in the world. I sat back, slowly reading the long article, which described other cases of political arrest. Though it was perhaps accurate in detail, its overall effect was somehow warped. I felt overwhelmed by a sense of disorientation, even dread. Mr. Bashirian and I had in time regretted the interview. Here all our vitality and progress and national purpose appeared somehow distorted. In the article I could not recognize my own country.

At midmorning I drove up Iranshahr past the building and parked on a side street two blocks away. The building was nondescript yellow brick with small black metal windows. More like an apartment building, with no name above the entrance, which didn't make sense for a government office. Stranger yet, the door was locked. I rang the doorbell. A man in plain clothes opened the door and asked my name and conducted me along a narrow and dimly lit corridor. The place looked deserted as I trudged behind him to room 106, at the end. I was in a SAVAK building for an interview. What did they know? That I'd attended the lecture? I'd gotten on a list. Maybe they knew I'd lied about being the relative that day in Komiteh, when I'd gone with Mr. Bashirian to visit Peyman. I would be told any moment.

He left me at the entrance to 106. I knocked, although the door was slightly open. There were two men in the room, in dark suits and white shirts and dark ties. One sat behind a steel desk with nothing on it except a blue folder and a black telephone; the other was in an armchair in the corner. They rose when I entered. The one in the corner shut the door. The one behind the desk extended his hand to me, very cordial. The walls were gray-white, blinds drawn across the one window behind the man at the desk. The room was poorly lit on purpose. I sat in an upright chair with metal arms, facing the man behind the desk. He coughed ceremoniously, then got done with his cursory and bureaucratic introduction efficiently.

"We just have a few questions," he said.

I nodded, the pounding in my heart quickening. He went through some general personal information about me. I verified what he already knew. He confirmed that my husband was Houshang Behroudi, co-owner and managing director of Kaviyan General Contractors.

"Contractors for the Bandar Kangan Gulf project?" he asked.

I nodded.

"The port for the navy," he confirmed.

"Yes," I said, my heart sinking.

He cleared his throat politely, paused. Long enough to leave me uneasy once he'd made his point, and to impress upon me where this could lead, which made me even uneasier.

Then very tactfully he said, "Do you have a special interest in university students?"

"No," I said, taken by surprise. "I don't know what you mean."

"Students from Aryamehr. You know them?"

"No. I mean, well, I know a few."

"So you know them well?"

"No. I've met them briefly."

"Their names?"

I wasn't about to name names. "Who exactly do you mean?"

The specter of a smile hovered on his lips, as if to tell me he didn't blame me. "Be careful," he said. "You never know who you're dealing with."

I nodded. The man in the corner had been only listening. Suddenly he said, "Do any of these names mean anything to you? Peyman Bashirian, Hamid Haratabadi, Kazem Abbasi, Soheila Badri, Akhtar Nemati?"

"I only know — knew Peyman Bashirian. I don't know the others."

"But you were at the Bashirian house when some of the others were there. Try to remember."

"Maybe. A lot of people were there for the memorial service."

The man behind the desk again took over the questioning. "You have a special interest in the Bashirian family?"

"He's a colleague and friend of mine. I know the family."

"Of course you do. You've signed a petition for an investigation into their son's death."

I nodded, startled at the extent of his information. Perhaps we'd finally got around to the reason I'd been called in. He set his hands neatly across the blue folder.

"You've asked several people to intervene in this case," he said respectfully, "before and now on behalf of the petition."

"Well, of course I wanted to — to help the family."

"Didn't you know they were told their son died of a heart attack?"

"Yes. Yes, I did."

"Then did someone suggest to you that something else had happened?"

"No, no one did."

"You're sure?"

"Yes."

"So why would anyone want an investigation?"

It was impossible to give him an answer to his question. His colleague in the corner stared past me, very formal, serious.

I cleared my throat. "Komiteh was about to release Peyman Bashirian, so it was shocking how he died so suddenly. His family wants to know if he was ill while . . . in prison, before his heart attack."

He nodded. Then he waited for me to say more, and when I didn't, again he repeated, "I would advise you to be careful."

The man in the corner said, "These students have subversive political agendas. We know all about them. You don't want to be associated with such things."

The man behind the desk straightened the blue folder before him. "Did any of the students — anyone — ever tell you anything?"

"No. What do you mean?"

"Just what I said."

I shook my head.

"Who suggested this investigation into the boy's death?"

"Well, actually I — I did."

He nodded. "No one encouraged you?"

"No."

"What did the other students think?"

"We never discussed it."

"You've criticized the way this case has been handled. We know this. Don't you believe what the authorities said happened?"

"I never said I didn't."

"There are those who're prepared to use you for their own benefit. You realize this?"

He nudged the folder, brought his hands together.

He leaned forward. "Your, uh, interest in this case is of course understandable. You're close to the family. But please, refrain from any involvement in the politics surrounding it. We thank you for taking the time to come in. We hope it wasn't inconvenient."

Out in the street I pulled on my sunglasses, looked up at the building, sunlight glinting off the small windows. I walked up Iranshahr, faced for the first time with another miserable fact. There was an informer among the students.

TWO DAYS LATER in the evening paper the headline blazed: "Embezzlement Racket — Two Rear Admirals, Four Officers, Three Civilians, Indicted in Naval Scandal." There in print — the investigation, the millions taken, one of the rear admirals from the Bandar Kangan project.

Houshang had called me all day the day before. Four times, and two messages. Quite a record, considering he hadn't wanted to talk to me — and hadn't — for days. Even before that, we hadn't had any success talking to each other for weeks, if not months.

He wanted to see me immediately. Ten o'clock that morning I met him at his office in midtown, where he shut the door and sat me down and told me about an extensive investigation and the imminent arrest of several officers in the navy. "The rear admiral!" he said. "Don't worry, they're not going to touch us. It won't affect us." He talked as though his real business was suddenly protecting me. He said he hadn't wanted to tell me, though he'd known for days. He didn't want me to worry.

He ushered me out, whispering, "I trust you," as if I were the only one in the world. He was dashing off to a meeting at the Ports and Shipping Organization. He called again two hours later, curt, nervous. "What was the meeting?" I asked, anxious something unforeseen was again coming down the pipeline. "I told you not to worry!" he snapped. But this time he hung up with a small endearment. My stock was going up in the world. Early that afternoon he called and apologized for having been so terse and rushed. He said everything was completely under control. He was locked up with the accountant in his office. This went on throughout the next day. He called; he was in and out of meetings. He was waiting for two important calls. They came late in the afternoon. He called me right after. He sounded exhausted, defeated.

"It's been a strain," he said. "I'm tired. I'll be home early."

He called again just before heading home.

I had the newspaper on my lap in the downstairs study when Houshang came home, early for the first time that year. He left his briefcase in the front hall. I'd left the door wide open, and he saw me and walked in. He saw the paper. He rang for Ramazan, asked for a Scotch with ice. I waited. He dropped into the armchair, loosened his tie. He looked drained, but also sincere. Nearly fresh faced without the overindulged markings of success and high stakes and oodles of gratification. Nearly like the days when we'd first met and he'd first got started. I didn't say a word.

Ramazan brought the Scotch and left. Houshang took a gulp.

"For a while there, I thought they'd make me their whipping boy. Take me down to exonerate themselves. I saw it in their eyes. How they'd abandon me. Me! One of their most loyal attendants. I'd done everything they've asked for twenty years. You know, it shook my faith."

"Your ace in the hole just got indicted," I said.

"I have others."

"He's such a — patriot. Isn't he?"

"You're always sarcastic."

"I'm like Mother."

He stared at me seated across from him, jiggling his glass with ice. I set the paper on the coffee table. He was still staring at me.

"Can I take you to dinner? Just you and me for a change?"

"So after all these years we can discuss kickbacks and rigged bids and payoffs?"

"You're exciting when you're outraged," he said.

"That's not what you thought the other night. Level with me."

"You have nothing to worry about."

"Did you pay off the rear admiral?"

"No, I didn't."

"You mean he got paid off for Kangan, but some other way."

He shrugged. I sat back. There was no climax, no lesson, no punishment here. Just business.

"They're investigating your company?"

"They're investigating our joint venture for the port. And they will find nothing. My British partners aren't worried. I've been on the phone all day with London."

"So you're in the clear?"

"I don't make the rules around here, I play by them. I've earned my way." He smiled. "The port at Kangan will get built. I have no doubt. If not this year, then maybe next year. And we'll be here — here forever — willing and able!"

He smiled again, still working his way back.

"Let's forget the other night," he said. "The dead boy and rear admiral and his wife. The whole damn thing."

"You mean I don't need to apologize to those two anymore?"

He laughed, his spirits nearly restored, and then drained his glass of Scotch.

"Tell me something," he said. "You knew, you knew he was going to be indicted, didn't you?"

"No. No, I didn't," I said.

"I like the way you lie. Even when you lie, you're virtuous."

He looked at me with emotion. Leaned over, grabbed the paper, turned it around so he could read it.

"See!" He slapped the paper. "Nothing in the whole damn article. No, they're never going to say exactly. Now, if they did, that would be news!"

The phone rang at his elbow. He picked up but was short. When he put it down, he said it was Iraj. I said it was time for him to run over.

"The hell with Iraj — forget everyone."

"The rear admiral is going to prison?"

"With his clout I don't know about going to prison for kick-backs. But he'll get tried by a military tribunal."

"Imagine! His wife going to visit him in jail."

"You're getting vindictive," Houshang said.

I thought of Peyman Bashirian, how nothing would bring him back. In the end it was impossible to determine what exactly had happened, the circumstances surrounding his death, whether in fact he had even taken photographs of military installations. No one — no matter on which side — could actually prove anything anymore.

That evening Houshang and I didn't go out. We ended up at home all night for once, quiet, withdrawn, edging toward each other. Washed up as if after a thunderstorm. It had been months, longer, a year. Late that night we took a drive; he wanted to get out and just drive. It was a wintery night. We drove through the streets, both of us shaken. The indictments were a big jolt for him, a turning point, now that he'd seen how they could betray and forsake him. Now even he couldn't be indifferent anymore. He'd gone to the edge, but not over; I had too. My meeting with SAVAK had been a time-honored ritual. In that anonymous building and half-lit room, I'd seen precariousness awarded and withdrawn. That's how it was, living on borrowed time. I knew the edge was blurred now. Where you stepped, what you did and said, whom you met. How everything got perverted. The undefinable betrayals — and without exception we are all betrayers — connected and accruing like capillaries.

We drove around, then up toward the mountains. The lights of the city shimmered below us. There, the seat of our desires. The place where we'd been born and grown up and loved. That night Houshang made love to me. I had been refusing him for months. I'd floated out. He was seducing me, and I let him. We were biding our time, but it was already too late. On the bed he slipped off my clothes and whispered, whispering into the ear of night and fate. The moon a luminous dome behind the windows, drifting in a huge sky. Braced by minarets of stars. Rising toward winter. I thought of Reza, reached out as if to touch him. Imagined him, flesh and soul, pressing against me in the garden. Houshang was kissing my lips and flesh, murmuring about the sanctity of marriage and the honor of things. All at once afraid of his downfall. Afraid of losing me, of other things, at least for a while.

"Let's forget," he whispered in my hair. "Forget everything."

But I'm not the type who can forget.

THIRTY-THREE

FREEDOM BEGINS WITH remorse. For a man like me at least, not a man like Jalal. Though Jalal was right about one thing: first you must leave everything behind.

Freedom begins when the truth you pick — knowing a singular one doesn't exist anyway — is the one you can live with. And every other choice you make is wrong. It begins when the charms of the past are revealed and known to you, and the charms of the future don't exist anymore. For me it was that night Jalal came to me for help and I left him at dawn, though if things had gone differently I should have been leaving Mahastee at that hour after spending the night with her.

A man's will — the very essence of his life — makes him conscious of being free. But the choice I made that night wasn't about a night with Mahastee or the possibility of other nights. It was drawing everything I had through the eye of a needle. Father and Mother and family and my entire career and reason for existence.

And Mahastee, for she was a separate world and would forever remain so. You know nothing in life until you have to make a choice, and even then it's each choice and each time that remakes you. You know nothing until the metal blade of your own undoing slides and cuts between your teeth.

When Father had lived, I'd measured my life against his. His, the measure of history and heritage; the past was alive as long as he was alive. With Mother I have a gentle proximity, the guilt of her life and mine in our eyes. The remorse. She prays and I'm forced to remain as she sees me because I want her prayers answered for her. Father said Ferdausi's epic was like a Qur'an in his heart. The men who judge me from the outside — who judge my life, my convictions, my politics — have no right to the measure of my heart. I know, already know I'll remember this one day facing my interrogators. Whatever I do and they do one day against me, there is this interior life, and no one can take it away. I will know this looking into their eyes.

I had prepared to go to her in Morshedabad, rushing through yet another turbulent meeting arguing about politics in a downtown basement, then running through the streets to get to her. How long I had prepared. Since the first time I'd gone back to see her at sixteen. Since the first day I'd seen her in the hailstorm. I'd come to test my strength against her will, her world. I'd left her waiting in the garden of Morshedabad, where we'd grown up together like two limbs on a tree. She waited there, where I had first loved her and first learned the endless lessons of leaving. I imagined her then — how often I had imagined that moment — imagined her sitting there on the veranda at dusk by the towering trees with the dovecote to her east, the water channels and orchards to the west. I imagined her sitting facing the darkening outline of garden and beyond it the long road to the village twisting through the open fields, her face up against the fading light growing dimmer to the traveler coming down the driveway, and then the generator kicking in, the faint cooing of doves, a distant truck leaving the distant village, and then dark, the hush of night coming, the pinpoints of lights in the house like stars in a distant firmament. I would never leave in time to get there.

That night Jalal turned up like an unpaid debt. The story he told was meant not to unburden himself but to burden me. He hadn't come for a confession or cautionary tale. It was a threat. Help me or else. I had been expecting it. They were hunting him, and if anything went wrong he'd make sure they'd be hunting me. With his back to the wall and all his colleagues dead, he was capable of anything. Once, when they'd been alive and provoked by him, I had been an insurance for him against their betrayals and conspiracies. Now they were dead and I was the only one left he could provoke and turn against. I wanted him to leave as desperately as he did. I wanted to be sure, so I'd be free of him once and for all. He'd barged into my apartment, robbing me of the hours with Mahastee, and left me sober and disillusioned at sunrise in the street. He'd come like ill fortune, like a hot and searing desert wind, and I had hated him that night. I sat facing him, contemplating how to throw him out. How to rid myself of him and get to her. All the while seeing my entire way of life — the legacy of my attachments — measured against his stony resolve and selfless politics. His colleagues had been slaughtered, and seeing their photos in the evening paper by flickering candlelight, I'd seen how we too would be destroyed one day ourselves. His words had been ruthless, ill-spoken, and I had seen how everything we did — no matter how much finer we were, and we were finer, no matter how literate and principled — our very purpose and reason for existence, could die too a miserable and ordinary death. And they would write whatever they wanted about us one day to bury us. This was the end, and when it came it felt like no glory had ever graced it. No honor could ever persist. It was in that state of mind that, walking back from South Tehran at daybreak, I thought, Freedom begins now. I'll free myself. I'll leave everything behind. Give the cause everything I've got. Everything.

It's now, I told myself, now or never.

Epilogue

WE HAD A REVOLUTION within two years. Eight months before the revolution, three of us were arrested coming out of our headquarters late at night and taken to Qasr, where we were interrogated and sentenced and imprisoned. I was given eight years. We were released at the outset of the revolution, in an amnesty for political prisoners, the first wave of concessions by the regime to a growing opposition.

After that, nothing turned out as expected. What does?

I saw Jalal again just after the revolution, in one of those weeks that winter. What weeks! Prisons and army barracks thrown open, newspapers that made you stand up and cheer, no bloodshed, no anarchy. What a feeling, what illusion! The exhilaration of unlimited possibilities. But the world isn't made that way.

The guerrillas were out on the streets. Guerrillas in the capital city, speeding around in open jeeps, waving their banners. It was midday, unusually warm for winter, with blue skies, the sun hot. I was at a traffic light at the intersection of Pahlavi and the parkway. That's when I saw him. There he was, in an open jeep, sitting way up in the back, dressed like the rest of them in camouflage fatigues. Toting an Uzi finally in an armed insurrection. He had longer hair, a mustache, but it was definitely him. The jeep accelerated suddenly, their white banner fluttering in the wind, proclaiming their name. Jalal was waving his gun like his comrades, hair flying, a red bandanna across his forehead. Just like Che. He had become Che Guevara, like all his comrades. I accelerated alongside the jeep, stuck my head out of the car, blew my horn. I shouted, "Aay, Jalal! Jalal! You're alive! You're back."

But he didn't hear me. I followed the jeep, weaving through traffic, but lost sight of it at the next light. I never saw him again after that.

While the mullahs swept into power, we in the revolutionary Left unraveled. A supposedly free Left, splintered, exhilarated, now flaunted itself and a free press. Then came our betrayals, one by one: Those who collaborated with the religious Right, and who didn't decry the death of democratic freedoms, especially for women. Those who boycotted the alliance of the Left, then ratted on their friends. Those who, like the Khmer Rouge, planned in cold blood for internment camps and ultraradical massacres of the general population. In short order we were proved rapacious, shortsighted, ill-experienced, divided against ourselves. Like every other party kept underground for years. This was the ultimate legacy of the old regime. Then a peasant class with religious obscurantism took over.

The new regime was ready to slaughter us and everyone else, making the old one they incriminated look like a bunch of dilettantes. They rounded up thousands of leftists and shot them. The group Jalal belonged to has come to be known in time as perhaps the most effective and competent in our revolutionary history. A legend. Jalal faced the firing squad in Evin.

I survived. I always had a better understanding of timing than he did. A better sense of my roots.

Majid fled across the border to Turkey and now lives in Paris in exile and has written his memoirs of the Left. And like all memoirs, they contain a good deal of bluster and revisionism. It's the same story, on the Right and the Left. We're all revisionists, so we can forget better.

Hossein Farahani remained an invaluable recruit, and during that year they hunted the Left, he stashed away several of us in the warrens of South Tehran. Three years later he got killed in the war against Iraq with his two younger brothers. An entire generation slaughtered there. Shirin, the perfect bourgeois, moved to New York and later sent me a postcard of the Statue of Liberty with her address and phone number on the back and an offer to buy me a ticket, and two lines: "Darling, I'm withering here. See you in JFK Airport." The director of our department watched from an upper-story window as an angry mob smashed the windows of his favorite red American car, then threw in a Molotov cocktail, which erupted into flames, during those early demonstrations that ignited the revolution. He took the next plane out to California. To America, where people go to forget. Mr. and Mrs. Mosharraf left that winter of the revolution and settled in Paris. He passed away there. They buried him in a foreign land, but I think he would have preferred being buried at home. None of his close family lives here anymore. If he were buried here, I'd visit his grave as I do Father's. I always had respect for him, but there was a good deal more to it than that. Often I feel an astonishing sense of regret at his passing. An estimable gentility and benevolent enlightenment passed away with him. If I had contempt, it was for others and other things.

The graves of his ancestors in the Mosharraf family mausoleum in Reyy have been desecrated and built over. Who does that in the world? This shame to our religion, our very own history. These things we do to ourselves, then invariably blame others.

One night last autumn I took out my reed pens and ink again, writing out the old verses. A verse for old dreams turned to dust, another in Father's memory. Mother turned her face to the wall and wept.

Mahastee and her husband left for Europe at the beginning of the revolution. They divorced within a year. I heard she lives in London and her sons have graduated from the best universities. I'll never see her again.

I forswore politics and went back to my roots. I finally did the traditional thing and married Mrs. Amanat's daughter. We have two sons. Mother is old and often stays in bed. She now lives with us in our ground-floor apartment in Kisha. My brother-in-law, Morteza, flaunting a beard and rosary, got in immediately with the new crowd and finally got promoted in the Ministry of Post and Telegraph. Zari is always beside herself with her family's problems, complaining how her children have married the wrong type, as she did long ago. I've gone back to teaching full-time.

This year my sons came back from university one evening and we sat down after dinner for a discussion long delayed. I began my story with that eternal refrain, "Before the revolution. . . ." Far into the night we sat discussing my old days with the Left, our national heritage, our passing hysterias. The anti–National Front hysteria. The hysterias of the Left itself. The anti-Shah hysteria. And today. We are all responsible for the system they have inherited. They, the new generation, are courageous, resolute, with conviction. They believe twenty years of silence have ended. They want sweeping reforms. They're fighting for their rights, their political freedom. We have always been told we are a people unprepared and unfit for democracy. As if 2,500 years isn't enough time to get fit and ready.

Now I sit up nights, waiting for my sons. Waiting, for any day they could get arrested or disappear.

WE ARE BETRAYED by destinations. I read that somewhere; now I know it's true.

I left my country for London with my two sons that winter, leaving all too quickly as Tehran fell into revolution. Temporarily, I said. We're still here.

Father passed away ten years ago in Paris. In his absence, they reviled his good name and reputation. The house, they confiscated and looted; then they left it to rot. They ripped out the surrounding old gardens — like ripping out our heart — cutting down the old trees and arbors. Jerry-building into oblivion.

Father took it, stoic to the end. Even when he fell in the street of an adopted land and broke his hip and no one stopped to help him. He was wasting away from Parkinson's. Late one afternoon toward the end he was in the wheelchair, the newspaper on his lap. His head fell back, and thinking he'd dozed off, I went to rearrange his blanket. He had tears in his eyes and I asked if he was in pain. He said he'd lived his life. His regrets were for his country.

I would have given anything to reassure him. I sat quietly holding his hand. And he murmured his favorite refrain, "Those who haven't lived in the years before the revolution, can't understand what the sweetness of living is." There we were, far from home, our past ebbing like a receding horizon. We'd left everything behind. As we sat side by side in separate chairs, he dozed, and I dreamed of reclaiming my heritage.

Living honorably is its own reward, to the bitter end. I come from a country that confirms that time and again.

Mother moved to London, but she's still living with Father. Whenever the family gathers, she ends up cooking for at least thirty. It perks her up, reminding her of the good old days. My brothers live in the States, working hard, visiting seldom. Growing tough around the edges. Hard at heart? asks Mother often. Everyone gossiped behind her and Father's back about the millions they'd taken off with and their vast holdings abroad, while their sons supported them. People have no shame. Especially in hard times.

Kavoos was the last to leave Tehran. His wife divorced him while he was in prison. She bad-mouthed him all over Europe while shopping, calling him an inconsiderate husband. He was imprisoned in Evin. They accused him of everything under the sun, a litany of treacheries they keep just for the likes of us. At one point we thought they'd just drop the small talk and shoot him. Like so many others we knew in prison. Father aged just listening to the accusations. There was no mercy for our kind anymore.

When Kavoos finally managed to get out, he seemed perpetually unsettled. One day in Regent's Park, he said to me, "You know, when I was in prison I thought about that friend of yours. Mr. Bashirian, and his son. I remembered how I'd been heartless about them. And I said to myself, So that's what the world feels about me now. Nothing."

Houshang and I went our separate ways in Europe. There was

nothing to hold our marriage together once we'd left. He lives in the States and travels, still chewing cigars with leftover friends. I can only take him ten minutes at a time. His business takes him around the world but never closer to anything.

My two sons both work in London, and my firstborn, Ehsan, is getting married this summer. My home is a third-floor apartment overlooking a leafy square. I live with a Moroccan musician I met through the firm I work in. He strums the oud at night, sonorous music, world-weary, noble. He also comes from places in the dust.

The verses Reza penned for me reside framed on the wall by the window.

For years I had no news of Mr. Bashirian. I had written him several times. I thought of him often. Then one day I received an envelope in the mail, a letter with his impeccable handwriting. I tore it open in the front hall, carrying it through the rooms. He wrote that he was retired, old and ailing, living with memories. In the same house with the grape arbor, a lonely house. He hoped I was healthy and successful, my children prospering away from their homeland. He was enclosing photos, the few remaining ones Peyman had once taken on his travels. He wanted me to have them. "You will be their keeper," he wrote. I cleared the coffee table, laid them out.

Windswept places. No people. Except in one, the one with a mountain on the horizon. A lone cypress leaning into the dust. Half a human shadow there, elongated, as if the picture had been taken late in the afternoon. Just a shadow cut off at the knees, stretching over empty spaces. Perhaps it was Peyman or a traveling companion. Any man's shadow falling across his land.

And the father wrote: "I lost my son, and you lost your country. I still don't understand why."

I put my face in my hands and wept.

Exile is its own country. With obscure borders, unwritten conventions. It can bring unusual clarity. And exact strange sufferings, discreet mutilations. At its outermost limits, there may even be an exceptional freedom. It is beyond heartbreak to reach that far.

That other life — that world as I remember it, that grace of living — lives in me like a parallel universe. Always will until the day I die. No one can find it anymore. Not even the names of the streets, now changed and erased to complete its vanishing.

Sometimes late at night, with the oud playing, I open the window facing the square. I recite from the poem, the verses breaking in my throat: "My hometown has been lost. . . . With feverish effort, I have built myself a house. On the far side of the night. . . ."